Jean Pierre cupped Brittany's head and gently coaxed her face up to his. It was a perfectly shaped face, immortal, like one would see in a museum. The girl not only looked like a saint, but she smelled like one as well. He inhaled the sweet scent of sage and the sharp smell of strong soap.

Her hair was loose and a little damp, and he liked having his hands in it. He touched the tiny wet curls that coiled against her skin and then moved his thumbs across her high cheekbones.

Jean Pierre could see himself reflected in her eyes and he was suddenly reminded of a childhood time when he had loved and thought he was loved in return. Her eyes were still and very deep, the sort that would pull a man inside if he weren't careful.

He held her gaze as he lowered his head to hers. Softly their lips met and her eyes drifted shut. He kissed her gently and very carefully, but with the expertise learned in a thousand kisses. With a surge of feeling he did not bother to analyze, he deepened the kiss. She leaned into him and kept leaning as she kissed him with the sweetest mouth in the universe.

BOOK YOUR PLACE ON OUR WEBSITE AND MAKE THE READING CONNECTION!

We've created a customized website just for our very special readers, where you can get the inside scoop on everything that's going on with Zebra, Pinnacle and Kensington books.

When you come online, you'll have the exciting opportunity to:

- View covers of upcoming books
- Read sample chapters
- Learn about our future publishing schedule (listed by publication month *and author*)
- Find out when your favorite authors will be visiting a city near you
- Search for and order backlist books from our online catalog
- Check out author bios and background information
- Send e-mail to your favorite authors
- Meet the Kensington staff online
- Join us in weekly chats with authors, readers and other guests
- Get writing guidelines
- AND MUCH MORE!

Visit our website at
http://www.pinnaclebooks.com

DARE TO DREAM

Wynema McGowan

Double Dare!
Twins Irish and Brit Dare find the
love of their destiny.

Pinnacle Books
Kensington Publishing Corp.
http://www.pinnaclebooks.com

PINNACLE BOOKS are published by

Kensington Publishing Corp.
850 Third Avenue
New York, NY 10022

First Printing: December, 1998
10 9 8 7 6 5 4 3 2 1

Printed in the United States of America

Dedication:

To Pat McGowan and Margaret Rhodes . . .
Cecille B. and The Commander.

Prologue

Parisian Jean Pierre McDuff was wealthy and urbane. And dissolute and profligate. A favorite of the *filles de joie* from Paris to Berlin. And a notorious bedder of the wedded and bored. He was never at a loss for words, never caught unaware, and never shocked by anything anyone said or did.

Until he regained consciousness on a certain autumn morning and saw inches from his face, dangling hugely and swinging freely to and fro a pair of purply, pimply-skinned . . . objects. He muttered a curse, shut his eyes tightly and then slowly allowed them to open again. Unfortunately, nothing had changed.

There had been a score of times that Jean McDuff had awakened in a regrettable situation, but this? Without question, this was the worst predicament he had ever experienced. His head hammered and his mouth was fur-lined. Apparently he had been so thoroughly devitalized that his limbs had been rendered incapable of willful movement of any sort. What in God's name had happened?

Now that he considered it, he realized with horror that the last (indeed the only) thing he could remember about the previous night was the sound of a woman screaming!

An arduous effort to remain conscious inspired a vow to place the muzzle of his musket between his teeth and fire . . . provided he could ever make use of his limbs again and provided he could survive that long. He felt like he stood at death's door. Did he?

Unfortunately, his query would go unanswered. He had entered a dark tunnel with a black cave at the end, and as he spiraled downward something had cloaked his mind like the moss on a tree. As a result, the rather pressing question of whether he would live or die was to be his last conscious thought.

One

Some sound woke her. She lay on her side and listened and half expected to hear her sister talking in her sleep. Instead she heard frogs croaking and crickets chirring and a branch slowly scratching against the roof. From far off she could make out the faint yap of a fox, and from beneath the cabin, the rustle of some small animal in search of food, but none of these sounds should have awakened her.

Careful not to disturb her sisters, she slid out of bed, padded to the window and pushed aside the shutter. Judging from how the moon sat like a big bead on the tree tops, it was at least an hour before the rooster would announce another day, yet she had been awakened as if someone had called her name. Then she heard it again—the sharp cry of a whippoorwill—and it made the hair prickle on the back of her neck.

That whippoorwill's cry might be an ordinary sound to most but not to a Dare. She waited for her mother to answer and then she echoed the call.

Her sisters sprang up in a flash, Irish to parcel out the carbines that were propped in the corner, and Markie to sling her knife belt on over her night dress. Brit helped

Markie tie the braided horsehair rope around her waist and then stood looking at her while she knuckled her eyes.

She always did that—clear her eyes of sleep—and it always struck Brit as odd, for her little sister had been born blind as a potato.

"It's probably nothing."

Markie shrugged off her hand. "I ain't scared a' no ol' Indians."

"Well, I am."

Irish handed Brit her carbine then leaned over the opening where the rawhide-tied wooden ladder descended into the big room below. "Maw?"

A voice floated up out of the dark void. "Ayeh."

"It's a funny time for Indians, ain't it? So close to dawn?"

"There ain't no figurin' those red devils. Y'all ready?"

"Yessum," said Irish and then she dropped to the floor, laid her carbine across her elbows and crawled under the crossbeam to the west-facing window.

From a whittled peg on the wall Markie took another shot pouch and a powder horn and slung these around her neck, then she followed her sister with the tamper and extra carbine, all of which she aligned beside her just so.

"All set, Markie?"

"Yep. Ready."

Brit looked at her baby sister who sat with her skinny legs poled and her feet forked. She was not only ready, she was able. Blind or not, from long practice Markie could load and prime a weapon faster than most men could think about it.

Irish laid her carbine on the narrow ledge and sighted, then gatorwalked a bit to the right. She sighted again and then slowly lowered the barrel. "All right," she whispered. "C'mon if you're acomin'."

After closing and latching the shutter, Brit checked her own carbine, then looked through the slit cut for that purpose. The sky was overcast but a gleam of tarnished moonlight breached the clouds here and there.

Her view was east, overlooking the garden, whose yield—except for pattypan squash and pumpkins—had by now either been cooked and eaten, or dried and put up, for it was coming on autumn in this, the northernmost province of Mexico.

When she saw nothing suspicious there, she slowly shifted her sights to the cornfield but there was no movement there either.

Northward was a field of winter-brown grass and beyond that was the field where the harvested bundles of oats had been gathered into tepee-like stacks. When they were weathered to a pale yellow they would be ready to beat on woven mats to rid them of their chaff.

She lowered the carbine and grimly thought: they had better not burn those oats, that's all I've got say.

That oatfield had already soaked up a bucket of their sweat and it would soak up a lot more before they were done. She hated oats. If it were up to her, she would plant corn in every blessed field. When you're done with corn, you're done.

By harvest time it seemed to her that the only way a person can get done with oats is by dying!

Between the creekside cottonwoods she could see the waning moon's wavy reflection in the water and the two-rut path that led into Sweet Home, four miles distant. Westward a like distance rolled miles of woodland. Dare land. She closed her eyes and tried to picture it in broad day when the sun threw gold through the trees . . . But what she saw was a pile of smoking gray rubble, which was all that had remained of the Clancy place after the Kiowas attacked them last year.

It had been still smoking when she saw it, a full two days after the raid, and those charred and speechless walls were a sight she knew she would remember for as long as she lived.

Her throat tightened in anger. You will not fire this farm, she thought. Not unless you kill every man-Jack of us!

The Dare farm had never come under attack before, but it had been built for that possibility. It sat on a slight rise, two cabins with steeply pitched shag bark roofs that were connected by a narrow covered passage.

Unsawed and weather-worn to the color of oatmeal, the log walls had been chinked with mud and grass and then slitted at eye height in all directions as well as here and there along the floor, which was to foil those who would try to belly crawl up on them.

Trap doors had been built beside the two smoke-scarred chimneys and beneath each sat pine-stave barrels that were kept brimful with water hauled up from the creek by the bucket.

The twins, Irish and Brit, slept with their younger sister in the crookback loft above the big cabin, their mother in a little alcove in the main room and their three brothers—when they were home—slept in the smaller, adjoining cabin.

Unfortunately, two of them were not at home on this night—because—crazy as it seemed—they were off looking for Indians! It was a job that Jack and Blue had been doing almost from the day the Dares had reached Tejas from Tennessee.

Newly arrived settlers would soon find that a vigilant eye and skill with a weapon would not be enough against the Indians of Tejas, when countless horses and cattle started disappearing, and scores of humans were being carried off and never heard from again. A group was formed with the idea of retaliating for any Indian forays into the area, and Jack and Blue, the eldest and youngest of her brothers, had been asked to join. They were supposed to recover the settlers' stock . . . (often times it was the settlers themselves they were after) . . . and punish the murdering raiders with death or, if they could, by stealing the Indians' stock in return.

In a half dozen years Jack and Blue had been in countless pitched battles with the Indians. Sometimes it would be the Kiowa and sometimes the Lipan Apaches but more often than not, their enemy would be the Comanche. The Terror of the Night and the Butchers of the Plains. That's what the people of Tejas called them.

The Comanches were clever, mean, and treacherous and it was only in sheer desperation that the settlers sent their best young men out against them. By 1828 the seasoned troop had become the settlers' most effective defense, and their only offense.

It was the worst of luck, but that was where two of her brothers were right now . . . out chasing down some Comanche raiders!

Her sister's voice startled her. "Wonder where Goldie is."

"Over by the woodshed I think."

"Can you see him?" Markie asked.

"Not really. It's just a guess."

Brit would love to tell her brother that she had been able to spot where he was hidden, but she couldn't see the lee side of the shed unless she stuck her head out of the window and that was something she knew better than to do because if she could see Goldie, then Goldie could see her, and she would really hear about it for "offerin' the Indians an easy target like that."

Jiminy, she would almost rather have Indians after her as her brother Goldie!

Suddenly there came the *pee-ik pee-ik* of the nighthawk, the signal that strangers were approaching but not Indians. There was a collective sigh of relief but no one relaxed their guard. Unfortunately, Indians were only one of the perils in Tejas.

Finally, Brit saw a lone rider leading a biscuit-colored pack horse with a head-down man tied on its back.

Killed? Or wounded? A cloud moved off the moon and she caught her breath. The head-down man had a wide back and black hair . . . just like their brothers. "Oh, God!"

"What?"

"It's Sheriff Goodman and he's . . . he's got a man with him."

"Hurt or dead?"

"I can't tell."

"Must be hurt. He wouldn't bring a dead man out here unless . . . unless . . . Oh, God!" Her sisters pressed against her back.

"It ain't Blue or Jack is it?"

"What does he look like?"

"Can you see his face?"

"I can't see for your talking!"

"Talkin's got nothin' to do with seein'!"

"Lord, I guess you oughta know that!"

"Well, I guess I do!"

"The both of you hush! I can just about . . ." It seemed to take forever for the travelers to reach the rectangle of light thrown by the open door. "He's . . . he's not one of ours!"

Markie must have been holding a long sigh in her because she let one go then and whispered, "Thank You, baby Jesus!"

Two

Through slitted eyes Jean saw hooves plodding through dry brown grass, then the fetterlocks and testes of some four-legged beast of burden, and relief washed over him.

And then came grief. He had come to Tejas to find his brother and he had found him . . . dead and buried in a pauper's grave. He had also killed the man who was his brother's murderer but then he himself had been shot in the back and gravely wounded, perhaps fatally.

A moment more and he groaned. Everything returned in a rush. Dawn the previous day he had been sitting on a rock-like board in a wide-wheeled wagon pulled by eight funnel-eared mules that had been galloping as if they were trying to haul hell out of its shell.

He rode like a cat striving to cling to a marble pillar . . . arms rigid and elbows locked, and his fingers curved talon-like around the seat. Inside his shoes, his toes were curled in preparation for the next rock that was big enough to lift the back wheels of the wagon—and his rear end—and then pound the latter onto the seat like a hammer-driven nail.

The blast-furnace air had scrolled his lips above his gum line and sucked all the moisture from his mouth while fine particles of dust had grouted his teeth, stoppered his nostrils and scoured a layer of skin from his face.

He was madder than hell. At himself, for being such a fool, and at the idiot beside him who apparently did not know the difference between a grimace and a smile. Why else would he keep glancing over at him and nodding encouragingly?

Back in Brasoria . . . back before he wished he had never laid eyes on him . . . Jean had looked on his slouch-hatted companion with a degree of interest. Here, he had thought, is a man from the pages of history. A mule skinner, the saloon owner said and Jean had thought: Imagine that! It appeared that his brother Duncan was going to be proved correct. Indeed there *were* interesting and curious things to behold in this land called Tejas.

Since there had not been an opportunity to ask the origin of the expression "mule skinner," its genesis had been left to Jean's imagination and after an hour of closer than desired observation he had been forced to conclude that a mule skinner must be a man who makes all his apparel from the skins of mules; clearly the man's insect-haunted apparel had not been made of any cloth that was recognizable to Jean.

By way of introduction the skinner had shouted "Hap Pettijohn here!"and then spat with enough force to startle a horse tethered across the road.

"Jean McDuff," he had replied with a slight bow that was appropriate to the situation. Then he had flicked dust off his sleeve and patiently prepared to wait until the mule skinner had looked him over like a never-seen bug.

It was something to which he had grown accustomed; it happened with regularity in this Godforsaken country.

When apparently satisfied, the skinner pointed to a long wood wagon. It sat low between its wheels and had high paneled sides that were badly pocked and burned.

Hitched and waiting was a mange-ridden team of mules.

Beset by clouds of flies, they stood twitching their ears or lifting and lowering their legs. Pettijohn swept his arm in that direction.

"After you, McNutt."

"McDuff. Jean Pierre McDuff."

"Ngh."

As they walked toward the wagon Jean recalled his brother's recent admonition concerning his tendency toward being too stiff and formal. Loosen up, he had said. Be more folksy . . . more colonial . . . more American.

"It appears that your wagon has met with some misfortune."

"Got the hell shot outa it, that's what. By 'bout twenty ban-did-tos."

"Even so, it has continued to perform." Jean kicked at one of the wheels and tested one of the side panels . . . which rocked so badly it almost came off in his hand. "It must be . . . more sturdy than it looks."

"I guess. Why?"

"Well, for it to have lasted all these years."

"Years?"

"Since the attack."

"Aw hell, the attack was Sunday a week."

"Sunday . . . a week?"

Crab-like the skinner scaled the side of the wagon and settled himself on the seat and then looked down at Jean. "You comin'?"

The few valises he would take had already been stowed on board but Jean was not yet prepared to consign his person to such a piece of dog excrement. "I have paid to do so," he said while running a dubious eye up and down the wagon.

"Well? You figure on ridin' up here with me? Or runnin' alongside?"

Pettijohn was a knife-thin man of indeterminate age. Set deep in his wind-whipped face were close eyes underscored by a beard so incredibly spittle-thickened that it stood straight out from his chin and flapped when he talked.

Sadly this phenomenon had vanished along with the border town of Brasoria. Now pressed bib-like to his chest, the beard might easily be mistaken for the pelt of an unhealthy animal newly pounded to death by a horde of charging Moguls.

Naturally, conversation was now impossible but ever so often Pettijohn would let loose with a particularly primitive, savage-sounding *EEEE-yahh!* which would have sent Jean off the side of the wagon if he had not known that it was supposed to spur the mules on.

After he had been afforded further opportunity for reflection, he concluded that it could also be beneficial in the removal of loose rocks from the nearby ridges . . . and ultimately lowering the number of dangerous rockslides in the future.

Apparently the enormous cud that stretched Pettijohn's cheek white required a frequent explosion of spit because with clock-like regularity he would fire off a long brown stream that no longer reached the ground but instead lashed backward to splat onto a red leather valise that rode in the back of the wagon . . . a rather costly red leather valise that was once the valued property of one Jean McDuff, resident of Paris and renowned raconteur . . . a deadly duelist and exceptional swordsman . . . a sought-after guest at the châteaux of the wealthy and titled.

A complete and utter idiot!

Jean looked at his surroundings and was tempted to revert to the childhood ploy of giving up something extremely important to him—like wine or women or both—in order to insure his safe return home.

As the interminable time crept by, a nightmarish thought started running through his mind; namely that some diabolic force had used the vortex of swirling dust to hold them in a dimension from which they would never

emerge. Somehow suspended in time and space, they had
been duped into believing that they were making progress
toward Sweet Home when in reality they had not moved
one inch. When the dust settled—*if* it ever settled—there
would stand the barkeep from Brasoria, leaning squint-
eyed beside his tattered leather door, sucking his tooth
and smirking: "Right thar's yer best bet," he would be
saying still. "Ridin' along with ol' Hap Pettijohn. Believe
me, it'll be a lot safer'n tryin' to git to Sweet Home on yer
own."

Safer?!

Jean made a promise to himself: He must be sure to
take the time to stop in Brasoria on his way back to civilization. But only long enough to knock that saloon keeper
on his ass.

At last Pettijohn hollered, "Thar it is!"

"There what is?"

"Sweet Home!"

"Bloody Hell! Is that it?"

"Yeah! Nice, ain't it?"

A more miserable spectacle was hard to imagine. There
was one two-rut road that curved alongside a murky-look-
ing creek and a dozen or so clapboard and adobe buildings
that radiated from a plaza centered by a crumbling rock
well.

Beyond there was an ancient church topped with a
burned and badly canted cross and to the south, a lightning-struck tree, twisted and macabre against the sky.

Nearby was a small brush-choked cemetery with weed-
skirted wood markers encircled by a log fence in extremely
ill repair.

"Pitiful! Simply pitiful!"

"Whut?"

"Beautiful, I said. Simply beautiful."

"Ayep."

Once the mules were stopped, and once Jean had regained the use of his legs, he made his way to a tiny patch of shade afforded by a thatch-roofed shed, and used a gallon of well water to wash down at least a pound of dust. As he returned to the wagon, he was using his wet pocket cloth to wipe his neck when he was seized by a coughing spell.

"Dust stuck in yer throat?"

"No, I believe my cods are."

Pettijohn ceased unhitching the mules and started slapping his sides and making strange snorting noises and kicking up dust, all of which Jean watched with great interest. It looked like the man was either experiencing an anaphylactic fit or dancing for rain. In any case, it had a primitive, other-world quality that Jean found most fascinating.

Pettijohn finally gathered himself and wiped his eyes with an incredibly filthy rag.

"By gawd, if there's one thing I like, it's a good-natured man!"

My disposition to a tee, thought Jean. Good-natured.

"You know . . ." Pettijohn opened the gate to an enclosure. "I don't generally stick my nose in another person's business but Sweet Home don't see many fancy dans like yourself . . ."

"Allow me to satisfy your curiosity." Jean made a little bow. "I am supposed to meet my brother here . . ."

And while he explained the reason for his trip, he looked around . . . at a bonneted woman who was pulling a girl child along behind her . . . at a man who was watching them from an open doorway across the road . . . at a brace of noisy crows sitting on a fence rail . . . and at a smith turning a sharpening wheel within the dark interior of a shed.

"My brother is a resident of Scotland and I am from France. We are on a tour of America."

Which was to have ended in New Orleans. Instead it was there that they parted company.

The root of the problem was innocent curiosity and innate ennui, both of which had always been intrinsic failings of his younger brother. Duncan craved excitement. Jean was older by nine harrowing years and had thought their stay in New Orleans had been exciting enough. In less than a month he had been caught up in two bare-knuckle brawls and had been goaded into a duel. Yet Duncan claimed to have been bored, and kept suggesting that they take a brief detour west, into the interior of Tejas.

Jean had not been especially excited about the prospect. He had heard that the land was wild and sparsely populated and that its native inhabitants' favorite trophy was the other person's topknot.

Unfortunately, this small detail did nothing to dissuade Duncan. He had come all the way from Scotland to see wild Indians and by God, he would see one or die trying!

Prophetic words and, as it would turn out, the last Jean would ever hear his brother speak.

Jean had agreed to accompany him but while he was spending a few days stoking up, as the locals would say, with two young but quite ingenious whores, Duncan was losing patience. When Jean returned to their rooms in the morning, the concierge handed him a note from Duncan which stated that he had gone on to Tejas. Further, his note suggested that Jean meet him in two weeks in a town about a hundred miles west of the Sabine River and the Louisiana border. Brasoria.

Jean recalled that he had smiled as he strode back to the elegant brothel. He had two more weeks! Damn if his brother wasn't growing more considerate with age!

Duncan's note had specified Brasoria but when Jean got there—well within the allotted time—Duncan had apparently already come and gone. According to the black-whiskered owner of the best—and only—whiskey place in town, Duncan had probably gone on to a town with the most unlikely and heart-rending name of Sweet Home.

"Good Lord!" he had said. "Sweet Home? You jest!"

Apparently not.

Jean had every intention of waiting in Brasoria for Duncan to return—surely he would—but a few days later the precipitous arrival of a mule train helped to change his mind.

The freighter's business was moving supplies from Brasoria to none other than the newest American settlement, named Sweet Home. Bored and more than a little concerned, Jean decided to accompany the freighter on his return trip.

It was not one of his most rational decisions.

As Pettijohn carried water to his mules, Jean described Duncan to him and asked if he had seen him. Pettijohn replied that he thought he had, and removed his hat to mop the sweat off the band. The head thus revealed was a hairless globe wearing a skirt of long gray fringe.

Pettijohn watched a spotted dog trot by and then squinted up at Jean. "Sounds like the fella who rode in with me 'bout three weeks back."

Three weeks! His brother had not tarried very long in Brasoria. Poor Duncan! thought Jean. Stuck here all that time! Then his next thought was: Serves the dirty bugger right! Dragging me all the way to this piss pot of a town!

"Do you know if he is still here?"

Normally Jean would have noted the slow sad way Pettijohn nodded, but he was hot, tired, and thirsty and had left his observational skills about twenty miles the other side of town.

"If we've got the same fella in mind, then he's still here."

Pettijohn slapped the last of the mules into a corral made of hairy-looking hide-tied logs and then he turned to face Jean.

Pettijohn had compelling eyes, sharp and of such a light blue that they appeared white in spots.

"You best go talk to Ernie Goodman. He's the law in town."

He was pointing toward a row of buildings down the road, but Jean was looking in the opposite direction, towards a run-down building that sat off by itself. He knew his brother. "What is that place over there?"

He was indicating a low-slung adobe building with a thatched roof and tall narrow openings for windows. It had drawn quite a crowd. There were three horses tied in front and a wagon pulled up alongside.

"That thar's li'l ol' Dulce's Cantina."

"Ah! The sort of place that sells fermented beverages?"

"Ayeh. If a fermented beverage is pulque or tequila . . ." Jean had heard of neither. "They also got an Apache beer called tis-win. Now that stuff'll put some whiz in your gizzard. Guaran-goddamn-teed."

"I think that may be exactly what my gizzard could use right now . . . a fresh infusion of whiz. May I stand you a drink?"

"I might take a pulque after I tend my mules but I'd druther ride a curly wolf'n drink that Apache piss." He picked up two buckets. "You go on ahead. I'll wander over in a bit."

"All right." Jean laid a disgusted eye on his tobacco-streaked valise. "Is there some place I can leave my things?"

"Right yonder's all right."

"Ah!" Pettijohn had indicated a three-sided shed that seemed to be sliding into the depot. An open mouth was its door and its frame was kept off the ground by a wedged log.

"And a place to stay?"

Pettijohn considered the question, a visible process. "Well . . . if a fella found hisself short of cash, there's usually a extry spot on Dirty Dave's floor."

Jean was about to ask if the man was so called for his

personal habits or his personality when Pettijohn added . . . "Or if a person's in real dire straits, there's always my floor . . ."

"Thank you." Jean was truly touched, but it was a sensation so alien to him that he did not immediately recognize it for what it was. However he then took another look at the mule skinner's person and pulled himself together. "I'd better get a room some place. I, um, have a bad snore."

"Ha!" said Hap. "You oughta hear me!"

Noting the size of Sweet Home, Jean thought he could probably hear a mouse fart on the other side of town, and the idea struck him funny. The idea, certainly not the reality.

Meanwhile Hap was squinting due to the sun bouncing off McDuff's teeth and he was thinking: Fella's got more ivory in his mouth than a damn pie-ano!

Hap had already decided they weren't real. It weren't natural for a human bein' to have all those teeth. A brown bear mebbe. Or a 'gator. But no human bein' that he had ever seen.

"Maude Stone lets rooms out to two or three people at a time. She's real reasonable and clean as a whistle."

As he spoke, Pettijohn pulled a linty plug from his pocket, drew a knife that was fifteen inches long by five inches wide and with little consideration to personal dismemberment, he whacked off a huge chunk and lipped it into his mouth.

This was in addition to the one that already reposed there . . . unless he had swallowed it. Which was a particularly repulsive thought.

Jean waited until he had worked the new cud into a manageable shape before he spoke. It took a while. "And Mrs. Stone's establishment is . . . ?"

"Right yonder." He used his knife to indicate a square sturdy structure with a narrow porch girding the front.

"Maudie sets a real fine table. I take the evening meal there myself most every night I'm in town."

Apparently Pettijohn was a man without family. Maybe that was the something that Jean had sensed about him. Oh, yes, there was something. A great sadness or perhaps a deep weariness of the soul.

"Well." Jean bowed. "Thank you again. The ride was . . . quite an experience."

"Think so? Well, hell, my critters did all the work." Pettijohn gazed affectionately at his mules. "You know, I'll take a mule over a horse any day."

"For what purpose?"

Jean was just being polite but Pettijohn addressed the subject with great passion.

"You name it! Hell, count off every quality that's supposed to make a good horse an' my worst mule'll top every one. Pure stamina for starters. Smarts an' heart." Conviction rang in his tone. "Why, even a mule's nature's better'n a horse. I know there's some who'll claim mules're naturally cantankerous but I personally have never found it to be true. Nossir. You cannot prove that by me."

"Interesting," Jean said. "Of course, my experience with the species is somewhat limited, but if today is any indication . . ." He tactfully let the rest of that hang.

"I'll tell 'em you said so." Hap was liking the man more all the time.

"Good. Well . . ." Jean looked away from the swimming brown teeth that Pettijohn was showing him. "I will see you later then. If not at the cantina, perhaps at the rooming house."

"Could be."

"Until then."

"Ayeh."

Walking briskly, McDuff crossed the road, skirting a dog enthusiastically licking itself, and a goat that wore a one-note clapper on a leather necklace.

His path also happened to cross that of a bonneted woman with a basket crooked on one arm. While he tipped his hat and went on, the woman turned and walked backward for several steps.

Outside the cantina he paused to slap the dust off himself with his hat and then he disappeared inside. Hap squinted up at the sun. It was nearing five o'clock and he had a en-tire dollar that said that it would not be half past before somebody put two and two together and told the man what had happened to his brother.

Hap slung a sack of grain onto his back but he continued to stand looking at the cantina. He spat then drew his sleeve across his lips and thought: Too bad. I kinda like that fella. I ain't sure why, but I kinda do.

Inside the cantina Jean was talking to a young whore named Lucetta and a rough-acting man named Blue Jack Dare. Unfortunately both people had just told him the same story: that a young stranger had been found behind the cantina one morning, stabbed in the back. Since the stranger's name remained unknown, he had been buried in the cemetery at the curve in the creek with a marker that was inscribed John Doe. His was the third grave with the same marker.

Though both people had been convincing . . . Blue Dare's description of the stranger might easily have been Duncan . . . Jean preferred to believe that the dead man was some other poor devil who'd had the miserable misfortune of dying in a town where no one knew his name.

There was, unfortunately, only one way to know for sure. Jean talked to the sheriff next and heard the same story almost verbatim and once the lawman learned that he intended to dig up the grave, he insisted on going along.

Jean had so wanted to be wrong that he convinced himself Duncan was simply too alive to die. And too damned lucky! He seemed to have been born with an uncanny ability to sidestep catastrophe. Why, Jean had seen him walk unscathed from a score of death dealing incidents.

As he dug he had kept an inner panic at bay by ticking off those incidents like a litany. Even when the shovel hit wood and even as he pried open the simple pine casket he continued to tell himself that it would not be Duncan. Yet undeniably, unmistakably, it was. The only human being Jean cared one whit about was dead.

When their gruesome task was over, the sheriff and Jean parted ways. Supposedly each was headed to their separate beds, but Jean was simply too sick at heart to sleep and so he wandered the town until, in time, he found himself back at the cantina. He decided he would talk to the girl again. She had spent a significant amount of time with Duncan . . . enough, apparently, for Duncan to charm her into selecting his company over all her regulars.

Earlier the girl had told him that one of her customers had been furious when she rejected him but she had also said that although Duncan and the man exchanged harsh words, nothing had come of it.

Perhaps not then. Perhaps the rejected customer had bided his time and waited until Duncan was leaving in the morning.

Jean paused outside the cantina. The streets were silent and empty, the night dark and starless. A lopped-looking moon hung low in the sky. Law abiding townspeople could look forward to a few more hours of sleep, but a killer might be out and about. Before he entered the cantina Jean touched the sleeve where he kept a narrow stiletto and he vowed that before he left Tejas he would find and kill his brother's murderer, whoever he might be.

A fleshy but shapely woman sat alone at a table in the back. Snoring loudly at another table was a drunk with his head on his arms. Lucetta, the young whore who had been Duncan's bedmate, was not in sight.

The proprietress gave him a professional smile and used her bare foot to push out a chair for him. A one-armed man came through some curtains but he looked from the new arrival to the woman and then he left.

They had a brief conversation about her services—which he tactfully declined—and then she offered what information she had for the same amount of money he had earlier offered her colleague, Lucetta. The proprietress claimed she knew more and had better recall than the younger girl. He accepted, and without further prelude she told him that the man who had argued with Duncan that night was Gil Daggert.

She said he had come in with his brother Earl and a man named Bittercreek Clarke at about midnight. They had been drinking hard for hours. They smelled bad and acted bad, hollering for drinks and talking dirty. The matter-of-fact way that she relayed this information told Jean that their actions had not been out of the ordinary.

She said Lucetta had pretended not to notice them. She had been sitting with the same stranger for over an hour, but Dulce had not chastened her because the man had not only been quiet and polite but he had been extremely free with his money.

That Lucetta ignored Clarke and the Daggerts had apparently surprised her employer because it usually excited Lucetta to play one man off the other and then give herself to the bloodied winner. Dulce shrugged here as if to say: a small thing. On that night, however, Lucetta had allowed the young stranger to buy her services for the entire evening . . . and he had not lifted a hand.

Jean asked if either of the three men had seemed especially angry but Dulce had not noticed that one had been more angry than another.

There had been no loss of business. The Daggerts and Clarke stayed most of that night and returned the next night and the night after. Dulce shrugged again and said that Lucetta was entertaining one of the Daggerts even as they spoke.

Jean would never know the source of his sudden conviction that it was that man who had murdered Duncan, but whatever it was, it was irrefutable. In his mind he was convinced beyond a shadow of a doubt.

The next thing he remembered was crashing into the back bedroom, which took both of the room's occupants by surprise. Daggert drunkenly pushed the girl off him and sat up in bed. He was weaponless; indeed, with the exception of the mud-encrusted boots that stuck out on each side of the bed, he appeared to be stark naked.

Having already armed himself with Daggert's own weapon, Jean forced the girl to collect Daggert's pants off the floor and to empty his pockets onto the bed, an act that produced his dead brother's watch.

He remembered standing over the bed with the bore of the gun pressed against the narrow ridge between Daggert's eyes and he remembered coolly deciding to kill him. But he had not yet pulled the trigger when he heard a gunshot simultaneous to a fiery fist-like blow to the base of his spine.

The whore's scream was the last—and only—thing he could remember after that.

Three

Goldie appeared below and helped get the injured man off the mule. Once Sheriff Goodman had taken hold of his arms and Goldie his pants legs, they moved toward the cabin. Evie Dare lit the way holding the candle with one hand and keeping her nightdress out of the dirt with the other.

"Looks like he could be a mixed breed to me," said Irish.

The twins were wedged into the narrow window opening and Markie had her arm stuck in between their bodies, trying to squeeze her head out. Not that she could see anything, but she always had to do everything everybody else was doing.

"You mean he's a Indian?" Her voice was muffled.

"No, I don't think so."

The man's head hung back like a dead deer and through a veil of shiny black hair Brit saw a face that was all hard bones and sharp angles. Down one cheek was a scar that looked like a streak of fresh paint. Blood had stuck his shirt to his body and was glistening in the candle light.

"But look at his coloring," Irish said.

"I am looking at his coloring. And now I'm looking at yours! His hair's not a bit darker'n ours."

Markie said, "Does that mean we look like Indians?"

She had always been told that the Dares had what is known back in the hills as Indian hair—that stiff shiny kind that is without a hint of curl—but she had never heard that they looked like Indians. It was the sort of thing one person ought to tell another person. Unless a person meant to let the other person go through her en-tire life without ever knowing she looked like a durn ol' Indian.

She was still waiting for someone to answer, when she heard the ladder creak. "Hot blast it!" she muttered and hurried after them. They had gone off and left her talking to herself again. Boy, she just hated when they did that!

Brit was halfway down the ladder when she heard Goldie say,"Where at, Maw?"

"Yonder's good." Evie Dare pointed to a pallet that she had pulled out from the wall.

The man's mouth was open and his breathing was loud and rattly. "What happened?"

"Shot in the back." The sheriff was puffing. "Surprised he made it this far . . . amount of blood he's lost."

The man was laid face down on a shredded-husk pallet in the center of the floor, and it was Markie who voiced the question they all were about to ask. "Who is he?"

"Tole me his name was John Pierre McDuff," replied the sheriff. "But when I looked on his papers his first name's written as J-e-a-n."

"His name is Jean but he says he's John?" Markie again.

"There's many a man that comes to Tejas an' leaves his true name behind." Evie looked up at the lawman. "Ain't that so, Sheriff?"

"It is, but if a person's gonna take another name, it's generally his last. Whew! I'm about done in!"

Sweet Home's first—and only—lawman was a large, hearty man with short-cropped gray hair and a skin color that made him look slightly undercooked. He had only been on the job a few months but everybody liked him, even their brother Blue, who generally made a point of doing what nobody wanted him to. Most particularly people in authority. Like sheriffs.

There was a ripping sound as Evie cut McDuff's bloody shirt off and another as she slit his pants seam with her knife. He muttered darkly but otherwise he lay as still as a man already dead. Evie dabbed at the wound in his back but the blood continued to well. Brit toed the bucket closer and her mother tossed one sopping rag in it and grabbed another. Pretty soon he stirred and started to come around. Loud cracks and pops attended the sheriff as he knelt beside him.

"Hey McDuff! Can yuh hear me?"

The injured man slowly turned his head but his eyes didn't act like they wanted to work together . . . unless it was to see the top of his head.

"Am I in Brasoria?"

Irish and Brit exchanged a look that said, Listen to him talk!

Goodman shook his head. "You'd a never made it."

"The wound . . . is it bad?"

"Real bad."

Jean's gaze wavered on the sheriff's rough hazy face. "I have no feeling in my left leg."

"You're lucky you got feeling, period. Say, McDuff, this here's Evie Dare." McDuff brought his eyes into focus and saw a tiny dark-eyed woman of indeterminable age. "I brought you here insteada Brasoria 'cause Miz Dare's had a lota experience with wounds. What with her boys rangerin' an' all."

"Madame . . . Dare."

"You can call me Evie. Everybody does."

He gave a little nod. "Evie. Where is the bullet?"

"My guess is that it's up ag'in your backbone. Probably explains your dead leg."

"Can you remove it?"

"Mebbe so. Mebbe no. An' mebbe you'd be better off

leavin' it where it is. I once tried to pull an arrow outa a fella. Went in right about where that hole in your back is. Anyway, I yanked it outa there. Shaft came out all right but the head of the arrow got stuck. Wedged in between the bones I guess."

In spite of terrible pain and fading consciousness, Jean had to ask. "Did the man survive?"

Evie shook her head. "Less'n three years."

Jean nodded. "The arrow should have been removed."

"It weren't the arrow that killed 'im. He cut a man in a swamp saloon an' was stomped by the dead fella's friends."

The sheriff sucked his tooth and shook his head. "Proves what I have always said . . ."

"An' what is that, Sheriff?"

"That some men jus' ain't meant to die old. Say, I think he's gone again."

He was, and Brit had heard him say something like "mondew" right before he showed them the whites of his eyes.

But when he came around again he took up right where he had left off—arguing about that bullet—and Brit thought: Determined as a Dare!

"Madame, will you . . . at least try?"

Evie held the lantern close and took a good look at the wound. She shook her head. "Mister, I dast dare do it. What you need is a doctor."

"I am a doctor."

"You are?" cried Markie and held her heart. This was big! This was really big! She had met only one doctor in her whole, entire life! And she was already almost ten years old!

Jean lifted his head to look Evie in the eye. "Are you willing to help me if I tell you everything to do?"

Brit and Irish exchanged another look. It sounded like

he had just said, "Aire you willeng to 'elp me eef ah tell you eviary t'ing to do?"

"I don't know. I ain't never done one close in like this." Evie looked at the sheriff who shrugged as if to say: leave me out of it. "Well, all right. But I'll make no promises."

He slumped back, obviously relieved. "I ask for none."

Evie nodded. "Well. I guess we best get at it."

"Is there time to send someone for my bag?"

"I suppose. Where's it at?"

"A boarding house in town but I can't remember . . ."

"That'd be Maude Stone's place. We only got the one."

Evie nodded to Goldie who went out, slung himself on a horse and took off for town at a gallop.

"Mister, you want us to wait 'til he gets back?"

The knife Pettijohn had used to cut his cud flashed through Jean's mind and he said, "Yes. I have the proper instruments . . ."

"All right. We'll wait."

After a moment's silence the old woman and the sheriff began to speak quietly together while Jean struggled to remain conscious. The room was lost in shadow but a wedge of white drew his eye. He concentrated on it and an image slowly formed . . . that of a well-built girl wearing a thin nightdress that ended several inches above her bare feet. The thick ebony braid that lay between her breasts delineated their lovely shape and generous size.

Brit was transfixed as the man's eyes moved slowly down her body. They stopped for a time at her chest then slowly rose again and their eyes met and she caught her breath. Something about the exchange of looks was more intimate than a touch but she could not look away. She didn't know what to do. Smile? Make a foot? In the end she did nothing but stand like a stick.

"Girls . . ." Her mother's voice made Brit jump like she had been caught doing something bad.

"These pants are gonna have to come off."

Jean closed one eye, opened it and then closed the other. Good Lord, now there were two of them!

Before his head met the pallet, they heard him say, "Dew! Ah mus' be sickaire t'en ah thought."

Her mother was speaking. "He's gone again. This is as good a time as any to get a tarp under him too. No sense gettin' this pallet ruint." She looked around. "Now where'd Goodman go?"

"To tend the horses, I think."

"Well, all right. You girls'll have to help me."

"Me too, Maw?"

"No, Markie, you bring in some more wood. There's a good girl."

The twins came up on either side of McDuff, unsure of what to do. Their mother had both her hands under him, fiddling with something.

"Buttons! Imagine that! Hah! Got 'em. All right, now you girls grab his legs an' lift while . . . I . . . pull. Higher, girls!"

"Gol! He's big as a horse!"

"I didn't say it'd be easy." More grunts and mutters followed. "Bloody pants're worse'n pullin' off a wet boot! All right, girls. Look off a minute."

They did as they were told but not before Brit caught a glimpse of a nest of hair that encircled something long and pale and shriveled-looking.

"There. Done!"

Now his hips were covered with a quilt but the rest of him was bare to the curve of his butt, and with their mother's attention elsewhere, the twins could stare at him with open interest. Which they did. Irish looked at a dusting of freckles across his shoulders while Brit tallied up his scars. One on his cheek. Another low on his right side. One high on his left arm and one at the base of his neck.

Heck, this man carried almost as many old scars as her brothers' bodies did!

"Brit, you best get out of your bed clothes so you can help me. Irish, come over here an' hold the candle steady so's I can get a good look."

The girls moved to comply but Brit fiddled around long enough to judge her mother's face when she examined the wound. He had a small triangle of fine black hair at the base of his spine. The bullet hole was above and to the left of it. Sheriff Goodman was right; it did not look good.

Halfway up the rawhide stairs she threw a quick look over her shoulder and was stopped cold by the glow of candlelight on muscled shoulders and sleek honeyed skin. She stood there with her heart flopping around like a fish and when she put her hand on it, a sensation stabbed through her stomach that scared her with its intensity.

She jerked her eyes away and raced up the rest of the stairs and flung off her night clothes. Her work dress hung on a whittled peg on the wall but she had just reached for it when a hunting panther cried its high woman's scream and froze her in her tracks. A full minute must have gone by before she could grab her dress, and when she did, she was shaking like a rattler!

She couldn't wait to get back downstairs but she still took the time to splash water on her face and to spit-wet a finger and lay it in a dish of salt. She grimaced as she scrubbed her teeth and then moved toward the window.

A doctor! Why, that man was the farthest thing from her idea of what a doctor should look like. She checked below and then spat. They had once traveled to St. Louie to take Markie to see a man who was supposed to be able to cure sightless people. She disremembered his name but she did remember his sparse gray hair and tired little shoulders and most particularly, she remembered the shiny spectacles that he wore low on his nose. They had really impressed her but she had been a lot younger back then and had never seen a set of spectacles before.

In the end the doctor had not been able to do a blamed thing for Markie, but at least that man in St. Louie had *looked* like he could. This man looked like . . . well, she wasn't sure what he looked like, but it sure was not a doctor.

By the time she returned to the main room, so had the sheriff, and her mother was asking him how McDuff came to be shot in the back in the first place.

Brit moved closer and made her face a mask. While she intended to hear every word the sheriff said she did not intend to stand slack-jawed like Markie or frog-eyed like Irish while she was doing it!

"Earl Daggert done it."

"Daggert!" cried Brit before she could close her mouth.

"Poor fella! How'd he have the misfortune to run into him?"

"He was tryin' to make Gil Daggert tell him what'd happened to his brother."

"What did happen to his brother?"

"Somebody killed 'im. 'Member that young fella found back behind the cantina about three weeks ago?"

"I heard somethin' about it."

"That man was this man's brother."

"Did the brother have a place here?"

"No, just passin' through I guess."

Evie looked at her patient. "Poor fella."

Goodman nodded. "This one only got in town yesterday. Rode in with Hap Pettijohn. Heard about his brother an' braced Daggert with it an' now there he lies . . . about to join his brother in the grave."

Markie gave a little sob, and without thinking, Brit reached over and patted her on the back.

Maw once told them that there are people who get paid to cry at buryings. Markie could be one of those.

Evie Dare was looking down at the man and shaking her head. This land was still too dangerous for the likes of dentists and doctors. Lord knows they needed them, but they just didn't last worth a damn. Oh, they came with the best of intentions all right, but it did not take long for most of them to realize they'd made a bad mistake. The lucky ones went back to wherever they had come from. The unlucky ones got killed, like the dentist who had been murdered last year. Shot dead and thrown into a gully. He had apparently been killed for his shoes because that was all that the killers took.

She considered the stranger. He appeared sturdy enough, with strong shoulders and a large frame, and at first glance she had thought his long-fingered hands were especially capable-looking for his trade. But after taking a longer look she decided they might be all right for his trade but they were all wrong for Tejas. Too pale and un-marked, with the nails too smooth and the palms too un-callused.

No, this land demanded hands like the ones her sons had. Suited for the burning rope of a runaway horse. Or for swinging an axe three days in a row. Or for wielding a knife in a Kiowa death fight.

She no sooner had those thoughts than another thought intruded. One that brought her up as short as a canyon wall.

There may be times when *no* man can be big enough or hard enough for this land. Three of her own sons had been killed in Tejas, three men raised to be the toughest customers in the area . . . any area . . . and yet her boys had died anyway. In spite of all they knew about the coun-try and its perils. In spite of the fact that none had ever missed what they aimed at. In spite of being born brave enough to hand fight the devil. One killed by the land and two killed by its natives. Lord, Lord! The hurt has never quit!

"Makes you wonder why people come here." She didn't realize she had spoken out loud until the sheriff answered.

"Same reason we did, I guess. McDuff said that he and his brother had come all the way from Scotland."

"That far!" Evie exclaimed, though she had never heard of the town before. "An' then one gets knifed an' the other gets shot."

"I suppose the kid got in over his head. Bein' alone an' all, he was obviously no match for the, um, sort that, ah, hangs around . . . over at, um, you know . . ." Evie supplied one word that filled the gap and the sheriff made a choked sound in his throat and was so thrown off that he misplaced his thoughts. Imagine that Evie Dare! Popping out with "Dulce's" like that!

Brit rolled her eyes at Irish who had to turn her head to hide her smile. Why, they had known about Dulce's for years. They ought to. Didn't their own brothers spend most all of their free time over there, rolling dice and playing cards and fighting?

However, what the girls wanted to know was what else their brothers did while they were there.

About three years ago Clebus Deeds had told them that there were girls at Dulce's who scarcely wore any clothes to speak of. Said those same girls would dance with any man who would give them some money, and if that weren't enough, Clebus said that if a fella wanted, he could pay a girl to sit on his lap and let him play with her parts!

They really laid into Clebus then. Took sticks to him and beat him senseless. The nerve of him! Saying "parts" in their presence!

Unfortunately they would later wish that they had not given him such a thorough drubbing. Or that they had at least allowed him to finish talking first. While it was true that Clebus Deeds was a known liar, at the time it had seemed that his words had had the ring of truth to them. Anyway, what he had said continued to prey on their minds. What if it was true, after all? They got to thinking about it and decided maybe they ought to ask their mother . . . just in case. Having grown up on a farm, both girls'd had a clear picture of how animals went about mating and had thought nothing of it, but precisely how two human beings would go about accomplishing the same thing had been sorta murky. Not after their maw got done with them.

What they got was a downright embarrassing talk about mens' and womens' privates and about how those parts operated together. (The lock and the key talk. That was what they would call it later.) And yes indeed. Some men would pay a woman to touch her parts. Yeah, you bet. Pay willingly and pay well.

But did their brothers? That was the question that neither girl'd had the nerve to ask.

Over time and among themselves they would later decide that if other men did it then it figured that their brothers did it too . . . only bigger, better and more often. Like with everything else they did.

"I never met the killed man myself but Hap said he was a real friendly fella . . ." The sheriff paused long enough to light his pipe. ". . . young though. A person sure hates to see a young person go that hard . . ."

Brit's thoughts drifted.

The death talk had saddened her. She didn't want anyone to die, but she especially did not want anyone else in her family to die. They had already lost their father and six of their brothers and sisters and all were deaths that had been unexpected to her. Oh, she knew people died but she used to think that they were all old people like . . . like her Maw.

Until just that moment she had never considered the likelihood of her mother's death and the thought of it made her feel weak and sick inside. She could not imagine a world without Evie Dare in it. She could not even think about it. Not yet.

Old folks' kin ought to have a long time to get used to their beloved one's death. Little by little . . . maybe as the old person got weaker and weaker . . . or maybe as more and more stuff started giving out on them . . .

It struck her now that, unfortunately, her notion would only work if the old person's kin noticed those changes as they occurred. She sure had not.

Brit looked at her mother, who sat with one hand under her chin and the other pressing a padded rag to McDuff's wound, entirely engrossed in what the sheriff had to say, and for the first time Brit saw how old and little she looked! When looked at as a whole, her mother had seemed to look the same as always, but now that Brit had taken the time to study her part-by-part, she could see gradual changes that she had never seen before. That the whites of her eyes were as yellowy as an old dog's, and that her hair was coming in milk white and so wiry it gave her a dandelion look from the back.

Of all things Brit ought to have noticed that last. After all, it was she who washed her hair for her twice a week. The tip of her braid had always touched her butt, but lately it had got so thin that Brit could work it into a knot the size of a tin cup.

"Next thin' I know he's tellin' me he's got to dig up the grave!" Suddenly all the sheriff's listeners became as alert as dogs about to be tossed a bone.

"Dig up the grave?"

"No!"

"Yer kiddin'."

"I ain't! An' that's exactly what he did, by golly. I stood right there an' watched 'im!"

"Lordy!"

"Imagine that!"

"How did the dead body look?"

There was complete silence and everyone looked at the blind girl. "For pity's sake, Markie!"

"Whut?"

"Listen to you!"

"I was jus' wonderin' what the dead body looked like . . ."

"Well, don't."

"Why not?"

"It ain't fittin', that's why not. Now you jus' hush about stuff like that! I swan!"

The little girl twisted her lips and looked disappointed as heck. Made Sheriff Goodman wonder: How does a blind person picture something anyway? Be pretty damn hard to imagine a dead person when you ain't never seen a live one!

"Was it his brother?"

"That's what he said."

"Mm-mm!"

"I just wanted to know what it looked like."

"Lord, how he must've felt!"

"We parted after fillin' in the grave. But instead of goin' home to bed, like I tole him to, he goes over to the cantina and sure as heck, there's ol' Gil and ol' Earl, ah, restin' up in back."

The sheriff saw Evie's raised brows but since he was only slightly less intuitive than a rock, he continued to struggle along with the story.

It ain't easy, he thought, talkin' about whorehouses and nakkid people around young unmarried ladies.

"When McDuff found his brother's watch in Gil Daggert's pocket, he tried to make Daggert confess to the deed. Unfortunately unbeknownst to him, Earl Daggert had heard the ruckus an' was standin' in the open doorway armed with a gun of his own. What happened next is blurry but when the dust settled, McDuff had a ball in his back an' Gil Daggert had one square twixt his eyes."

Brit was surprised to hear her own voice. "Couldn't Daggert's shooting have made the doctor fire without really meaning to?"

"Sounds reasonable to me but who knows what'll sound reasonable to the judge." Goodman sighed. "Everythin' would've been a lot simpler if he'da jus' come to get me insteada goin' over there an' bracin' Daggert hisself. It's likely I woulda got to the bottom of the whole thin'. Now he'll probably stand trial for murder . . . If he lives long enough."

"You'd hang a man for killing a Daggert?" Irish had her lip curled.

"I'd have no choice in the matter."

"Hangin' ain't so bad," said Evie. "As deaths go."

"Oh, Maw!"

"Euu!"

"Well, at least it's a dry one, an' the person gets to keep all their parts."

A hanging! thought Brit as she looked down at the man. She had witnessed one soon after they came to Sweet Home. She had been about Markie's age but she remembered it well.

The accused man had misjudged the character of his companion and boasted about a forcing. (A forcing, she had been told, was when someone made someone else do something they did not want to do.) He was arrested and insisted on a trial and a chance to tell his side of the story. He got his trial, all right, and by sundown he was hanging from the elm under which it had been held.

She had been too scared to look at the man's face but she would never forget the way his head was knocked on its side and how his feet speared for the ground.

"No one in Sweet Home'll try this man for killin' a Daggert," said Evie.

"Don't be so sure! The man who'll decide everythin' don't know Daggert from dawn."

"The new judge?"

"The new judge."

"Who asked for him anyway?" Evie just naturally distrusted a stranger butting into other peoples' business.

Goodman explained that Mexico City had recently declared that Sweet Home was an *estado distrito federale* and had assigned Judge Frederico de la Barca to its bench. Colonists would be able to have their legal business tended to there, in Sweet Home, instead of traveling all the way to Mexico City.

"Once things're up an' runnin', all the cases in the province're supposed be heard in Sweet Home an' I'll be takin' my orders from Barca."

"Is that a fact?"

"It is. An' when the judge tells me to bring McDuff in, I bring 'im in. Or it's adios amigos for me."

By then Goldie had returned with the doctor's bags. "I couldn't tell which was the right one so I brought 'em all."

McDuff was clearly in terrible pain. "That one." He barely had the strength to indicate a small bag made out of black leather. "Please . . . bring it closer."

Brit had to grab the back of her sister's nightdress in order to get to the bag first. Which made Irish flash on the time she ran her neck into a clothesline and which made her cough a little and give her sister a look and wonder: what on earth's gotten into her?

Carrying it carefully, Brit set the bag on a chair and then allowed her hand to linger on the black pebbly leather. She had seen many things made from leather but she had never seen anything as fine as that bag.

The sheriff and Goldie had moved McDuff—and the tarp—to the low bed where Evie had brought him around with a vinegar-doused rag. Brit followed with the bag and aligned it just so. It opened in the center and then laid flat out. Tiny straps held shiny gold and silver objects in neat rows and little pockets anchored dozens of small murky bottles.

"Well, Frenchie, there's your stuff. Now what?"

McDuff looked at Brit through a veil of hair. "Please . . ." A spasm of pain crossed his face. " . . . my hair . . . can't see . . ."

Brit pulled the strip of rawhide off the end of her braid and drew her fingers though his hair. It was thick and unruly and fell handsomely to his shoulders. Sweat or a fever had formed limp little curls on the ends. Imagine that! Curls!

She sat back on her heels and clasped her hands in her lap. If the rooster hadn't crowed right when it did she might have left her hands in his hair forever.

"Merci." He moved his head like there was a cup of water on it and lifted one brow. "Well, Madame Dare . . . Are you ready?"

"I guess. What's first?"

"You have water boiling."

A voice replied, "It's all ready."

"And a good fire going."

The same voice said, "Ready too. And there's clean rags right there beside you."

The shadow that fell over him became the lovely vision he had seen earlier. One hand was outstretched, as if she had been about to touch him. It was a gesture devoutly to be wished. Her fingers on his brow had been as cool and comforting as any touch he had ever known.

Coming around to her mother's side had put Brit in his line of sight. As she glanced up she went stiff as stove wood, pinned again by that look.

Evie Dare looked from her daughter to the man and back. "This is my daughter Brit, an' yonder's her twin Irish, an' this young'un is Miss Markie Dare."

A small face was thrust into his. "I'm nine an' I'm blind an' I can chin myself ten times without slowin' . . ."

"Enchanté."

"Goldie over there is my middle son."

The shadowy figure nodded and said, "I hear you met my kid brother."

The sheriff snickered at that. Only a Dare could get away with calling Blue Jack Dare "kid."

But Evie could tell that the doctor was barely hanging on. "Enough. We best get at it . . ."

"Good. I fear I do not have much time. The thin knife and those narrow tongs . . . yes . . . into boiling water first . . . then thoroughly wash the wound with what is in that bottle." He pointed and then nodded when Evie held up a bottle. *"Oui.* That's it."

Irish laid the knife and tongs in the three-legged caldron while her mother cleaned the wound. After Evie finished, she sniffed the bottle and then held it up to the light. "This stuff has stopped the bleedin' like a cork."

Everyone leaned closer in order to see the small round hole in his back. Goldie took a good look and then met his mother's gaze. It was already puffy around the edges. Jean caught their exchange. "What is it?"

"The wound's startin' to turn."

Jean was not surprised. The weather was warm and the land was alive with flies and insects. "You must cut that skin away. As soon as you get the ball out. If you get it out."

"Oh, we'll get it out, all right. The question is, what condition you're gonna be in when we're done?"

"That remains to be seen." His mouth quirked up on one side. "It is my sincere hope that I will be here to find out."

Irish looked over her shoulder at him. "These're as hot as they'll get."

"Bien! We begin."

"With this?" Evie held up a reed-thin knife.

"Yes. First probe for the ball, then carefully widen its path . . ."

"Hold on," Evie said. "What's that mean . . . probe."

For obvious reasons Jean hesitated to use the word "poke." Perhaps "feel" . . . Yes, feel was a much less distressing word.

"First you must feel for the ball with the tip of the knife. Once you know where it is, you will, I hope, be able to widen its path just enough to slip those tongs in, grasp it and pull it out."

Evie nodded. "Mister, you gonna take anything for the pain?"

"I can hardly do that if I am to be of any help to you."

"Whatever you say. Well . . ." She looked around then motioned something to Goldie. He pulled the heavy table closer to the bed.

McDuff gave him a crooked grin. "Merci!" And then he wrapped one hand around each of the table legs.

"Well . . ." Evie said again. "Then I guess I'm ready to begin."

"*Bien!* Good hunting, madam."

Irish handed her mother the knife and shut her eyes. Goldie stood by the man's head so he could hold him still when necessary and Brit stood nearby with clean rags and the tongs. Everyone stopped breathing while Evie put the point of the knife on the edge of the hole and then slid it in. McDuff made no sound but buried his teeth in the pillow and pulled on the table legs like he was trying to make them meet. His hands turned white and his shoulder muscles bulged. Veins rose in his neck and arms and made Brit think of a story Miss Mapes had told them about a strong man who tore the temple of Dagon down on himself so he could kill all the Philistines inside. Samson. Yes, that's who it was. Samson must have been a lot like this man, only this man had no intention of dying.

Silence smothered the room like a blanket and made every minute an hour. The tart smell of blood and sweat was sharp in Brit's nose and the rank odor of the bear-fat candle hung thick in the air. A fine sheen of sweat had gathered on the doctor's back and made it look oiled, and as she wiped the sweat away she kept wishing she could close her ears to the tiny sound her mother was making with the knife.

It was into that dead silence that Goldie tossed what sounded like a ten-pound log on the fire. Everyone jumped and glared at him.

"Gol-durnit, man!"

"For pity's sake, Goldie!"

"Can't you jus' set the logs in!"

"Mah! Goali cared me an' ade me bye muh hung!"

"Will everybody jus . . . shut . . . up!" Evie withdrew the knife and blood welled behind it. "I can't feel a thin'!"

She spoke to herself more than to the others and everyone was startled when the doctor said, "To your right. And deeper."

"Good God, man! I'm about to the hilt now!"

But she had spoken to an unconscious man. She shook her head. "This fella's got enough grit to be a Dare!" Goldie nodded and oddly enough Brit felt proud.

Once again Evie began then drew back. "Irish!"

"What?"

"Watch what you're doin'! Me gettin' the ball outa him ain't gonna do a lick a good if you've let the poor man smother to death!"

"Maw, I'm tryin' but . . ."

"Don't try. Jus' do it . . ."

Irish turned his head to the side. Which was what she would like to do . . . look somewhere else.

She hated the sights and sounds of doctoring. It made her eyes feel hairy and her upper lip damp. She would have stoppered her ears if she could have figured a way to hold the candle too. Her mother had started in again and oh, God how she hated that slurping sound! Made icy water run down her spine.

The next minutes seemed like a year, and Brit couldn't

begin to imagine how it must have been for McDuff. He ought to be able to take *something* for the pain. A few swigs of corn liquor worked for her brothers. She even knew where Blue had some put away. It was in a stone crock that was hung in the well.

Blue called it wild mare's milk. Said it would not only make a man forget his pain but his name, his game and whatever else he had ever known.

He ought to know. Between run-ins with the Indians and his one-night declarations of war in town there were areas on her brother's body that looked like a quilt.

"Ah!" Evie leaned closer. "I think I felt somethin' jus' then." She moved the knife up and down the path of the ball and everyone waited and hoped but pretty soon she gave a disgusted sound and stood up . . . which sent Irish from the room with her hand over her mouth. It looked like someone had tossed a bucket of blood on her front.

"He can't stand to lose much more blood."

"No. If he's to live, we've got to finish an' do it fast. Brit, you're gonna have to take over. My fingers've set up on me."

"Me, Maw? I can't . . ."

"You got no choice. I can't an' Irish can't an' Goldie's too ham-handed an' the sheriff here . . ."

"Heck, don't look at me!"

"Well, I sure can't!" said Markie.

Markie covered her grin with her hand and listened closely but nobody was chuckling, not even Goldie who almost always laughed at the stuff she said.

She walked to the fire and sat down to chasten herself. She wished she would quit doing that—making a joke whenever she got nervous. There were times when people did not want to laugh and she should have known that this would be one of them. But right there was her biggest problem. Sometimes it seemed like she could be as blind in her mind as she was in her sight.

"Maw," said Brit. "I haven't done anything like this before."

"You won't be doin' it alone. I am gonna guide you. All the way."

It had come as a surprise to Evie to learn that Brit was the best help to her in situations like this. The girl had a cast-iron stomach and unflinching hands, while Irish, who was so good at so many womanly things, would immediately go faunchy at the sight of human blood.

Brit knelt beside the pallet and willed her hands to be steady while inwardly she groaned. She did *not* want to do this!

But she no sooner had that thought than she realized that her mother was right. She had no choice. Either she tried or he died.

Four

Die was exactly what they expected him to do, but one day passed and then another and he still lived! Evie was frankly surprised, knowing how much of him they had torn up while trying to get the ball out and she told her girls that the man either had the stamina of a bull or he was one of the most willful people she had ever come across. She did not, however, allow them to get their hopes up. "It jus' ain't likely that he'll make it."

But then, when he was still alive on the fourth day she was forced to hedge her bet. "Now, I don't know. Mebbe the Lord's gonna take a hand in this."

As might be expected, a fever set in. Not the raving kind—at least, not at first—but the kind where the ill one lies motionless and burning.

After the bullet's removal, and before his mind went wandering, McDuff told them that someone had to give the wound a good scrubbing at least twice a day. He stressed that this was very important, so that the wound would not putrefy and so it would heal from the inside out. It fell to Brit to do that, every morning and night, worrying the entire time about how much she was hurting him, though she could have saved herself the trouble. In his fevered state of mind he probably would not have known if she had taken an axe to his arm. She told herself that, but it didn't stop her from crooning to him like he was a hurt child.

It was also Brit who dressed his wound, first with the solution he had pointed out in his case and then, when that was gone, with the crushed sage and shaved cotton-wood bark concoction that her maw had boiled down to a paste.

And it was she who drew a cool rag across the back of his neck and dropped water on his parched lips and brushed and retied his hair and washed his soiled linens . . . after her mother or one of her brothers had removed them from his body.

They had him propped on one side so his wound would drain and so they could try and feed him, and Brit did that too, but not with a lot of success and while he grew pale and weak-looking, so did she. But was it any wonder? She was so worried about him she could scarcely eat a bite!

No one—least of all Brit Dare—questioned her dedication to this man over all the others who had been cared for at their farm. After all, it was she who had dug the ball out of his back.

And so it was that most of her sleeping time was spent sitting beside his bed instead of sleeping in her own, and often the eastern horizon would be streaked with light before she would climb into bed and she would spend another day fuzzy-headed and bleary-eyed. But come the next sundown, there she was again, washing and crooning and dribbling water.

During the days when there was no school she would often drop what she was doing and run back to the cabin just to make sure he was still breathing in and out. Sometimes she would find him in a fitful state with his skin as hot as hades. Other times he would be as clay-like and stiff as a corpse and she could not decide which she hated the most.

For ease of tending his wound he wore only a pair of Blue's worn long johns, cut off at the waist and held closed by a string. She would wipe the sweat off his shoulders and then from the deep valley that ran down his back and she could wonder at the obvious strength in his chest and arms. And him a doctor, she would think. Imagine that!

Pretty soon there wasn't an inch of his body—except for the covered part—that she did not touch and look at to her heart's content. His back. Which was both smooth and lumpy and hard and soft. And his chest. Which was as wide on the top as it was narrow in the middle and which was spanned by a wedge of curly black hair. And his feet. Which were long and bony and white as a fish belly. She discovered that his second toe was longer than his big toe on both feet. And she found a birthmark beneath his left ear and counted the freckles on his shoulders and she put her finger on a dimple on his chin.

She was beginning to think she knew his body better than her own, until something happened that made her change her mind. He spoke out loud one night and about scared the dickens out of her. "Ah, my chéri . . . ," he said. "Ah want your 'ands on me forevair."

His eyes were feverish but his words had been clear as a bell.

She put her face next to his and said, " 'lo?" and he laid his hand on her breast. She squeaked like a rat but she didn't move because she couldn't. The universe had become centered on his palm and the almost painfully taut tip of her breast. Her eyelids fluttered and drifted closed as he gently squeezed and then massaged. First one way. Now the other. She moaned out loud and leaned into it. And kept on leaning until she found herself sprawled on top of him because his hand had dropped to the pallet. She sat up and looked at him but just that fast, he was gone again and she was left holding her own heart and staring at him.

Jiminy! What was that all about? Nothing she had ever felt before, that's for dang sure. Her breath had stopped and then her heart had fluttered and seemed to quit beating entirely.

Good Lord! Was that it? Could that be what Maw had been talking about when she told them about that passion between a man and a woman? Was that the most powerful feeling a human being can experience?

Neither girl had believed her. Not really. Brit did now and she racked her mind to recall what else she had said. That passion had no rhyme or reason and followed no set rule. That it would hit some people like a hoe handle, square between their eyes. That others could go along twenty years, seeing the same person day in and day out and then . . . on a day that was exactly like any other . . . Blam. There they were.

She told them how rare and fine it could be. And how fleeting and hurtful. How it could take hold of some people and turn them against life itself. Or make a person's spirit soar with the eagles.

And then she had warned them . . . Oh, yeah. Brit definitely remembered her saying that there could be a great deal of heartache in store for anyone who went against the laws of God or nature.

They had interrupted her there and asked: such as what? Such as having a great passion for another person's spouse, she replied, and they had been shocked! Who, they cried, would ever do such a terrible thing! She said hah! She had personally known plenty of God-fearing people who had committed terrible wrongs in the name of passion. She had heard that it had always been so. Some people had started wars and killed others or killed themselves. Some had even killed the object of their desire. No, Lordy, a person ought never, ever underestimate the power of passion!

She told them that she could have benefitted from just

such a frank and elemental talk back when she was their age. Unfortunately, she had come from a very small family, all males, and nobody had bothered to tell her a blessed thing. Which was why there had been such a terrific hullabaloo on her wedding night.

She reminded them that she had married their father, Otis Dare, when she was scarcely fifteen and green as grass. Of course, the first thing he wanted to do was get her clothes off her and of course he succeeded. Mostly because he distracted her with his hot roving hands and mind-stealing kisses. Oh, yeah, he was a smooth one, that Otis Dare. Why, she had not even known she was naked until she felt the lick of a cool breeze from the open window. (But by then Otis Dare'd had her nipple in his mouth and her will in the palm of his hand.)

Naturally, he had his way with her—sly devil that he was—and their wedding night produced their eldest child, Black Jack, nine months later. Ignorant and proud of it, she said. That was how she described herself back then.

She said the next day she was full of guilt about the pleasure she had experienced with her strong and highly spirited husband. Surely that had been wrong. It just *had* to be wrong. Goodness, if everybody felt like she had felt they would be talking about it night and day!

Talkin' about it, heck! They'd be doin' it! Mornin', noon an' night!

There was no one to ask except a certain preacher man who lived four miles distant. So she wrapped up a piece of ham and filled a jug with water and walked over to see him.

She said that Preacher Boggs was a reed of a man who spoke in a weak whisper until he was filled with Jesus and then he could howl louder than a hurt dog. Said she had heard him preach a few times before, but his sermons had not moved her because of their content, which was mostly temptation, and she had never been tempted that she could recall. But she was then. Oh, yeah. Tempted mighty bad.

The preacher fixed her with his pale weak eyes and told her that her eternal soul was at stake. Right here. Right now. That pleasures of the flesh were, he said, the root of all evil and the cause of more eternal souls being lost to the devil than any other sin and that was why congress between married people should only occur when they wished to have a child. And that was why she must hold Otis Dare at bay.

She promised the preacher that she would try but she had a feeling that Otis would be after her day and night and she just didn't know how strong she could be!

The degree of her self-doubt she kept to herself, but she had never quit thinking about how it had been between them. Not once during that entire walk over to the preacher's place. Not for a minute.

The preacher called on the Lord's help, praying over her so long and so hard that his sweat rained onto her head and his bony fingers left marks on her arms and then he sent her home. There she told Otis what the preacher told her to tell him. That she believed they should only have sexual congress when they were ready to make a child and since she was not ready to make a child, they should not be doing it any more—at least not for a spell—but that she would sure let him know when she was ready.

If she had been older and wiser she might have seen the twinkle in her young husband's eyes and recognized it for what it was. No Dare could ever pass up a challenge.

Naturally he would wear her down, but it was not easy and he never forgave that preacher. Took almost three years before she got Otis Dare to step foot inside a church again!

Otis had his work cut out for him, but she said he kept at her and kept at her . . . Said it seemed to her like he could find a hundred excuses for putting his hands on her. He'd say lemme give yuh a hand with that and then he would give her one all right, sliding it down her rear or brushing it across her chest. She said she could not recall the number of times she would have to quit whatever it was she had been doing and walk away fast . . . just so he would not hear her catch her breath.

She told the twins that their father'd had a fine manly figure to look at and that he made sure she had plenty of chances to look, pulling off his shirt and rolling his great muscles at her. Popped her eyes so many times she started to worry about them coming unhinged!

Here their mother had smiled a little smile and her hands had stilled in her lap. Then she told them about a certain high summer day when her eternal soul had been the last thing on her mind.

They were both using a grub hoe in the bean field, him in one row and her beside him in another when suddenly it was as if there had been some silent signal because they both stopped and looked at each other. It was a good long look. Time enough for her to watch a bead of sweat that fell from a spike of hair on his forehead to the swell of his chest, to the flat of his belly.

She remembered licking her lips and raising her eyes from the little dark spot that the sweat had made on his waistband, and then she remembered meeting his gaze . . .

And the next thing she knew she was on her back, stiff-legged as a dead sheep and screaming like an Indian!

They had a wonderful time making twelve children together but Otis Dare would die tragically and unexpectedly shortly after Markie was born. His death was so sudden that she had sat stunned for a month and for her the world had not been right since. She missed him still—especially in her bed. Lordy, if that preacher only knew how they had been together! And would be again, if only Otis were still alive.

If only Otis were still alive. Oh, if only he were!

The girls then asked her to tell them how she had known that Otis Dare was the man for her and she replied that the knowing part had been easy because she had been one of those people that passion had hit like a hoe handle. Matter of fact, all it took was one good look and she was gone. She said she would never forget that day. She had taken a dish of greens over to ol' Miz Barton, who had been feeling poorly and the first thing Miz Barton did was warn her that Otis Dare—that big harum scarum fella—was there, taking down some dead trees for her.

Well, since Otis Dare had a reputation for being the sorta fella who ate little skinny-ass girls like Evie Ellis for breakfast, she kept a wary eye out for him. But she did not see him until she got ready to leave.

She had just stepped out onto the porch and there he was, bent double in the yard. He had pulled a bucket of water out of the well and was about to toss the water over his head. She saw his strong back and shoulders and his long legs and big feet and the shape of his head and his gleaming black hair and she couldn't take her eyes off him. The way the sun struck him, the way he held himself so straight and proud. Right then was when she knew. She had to have Otis Dare for her man. If she knew nothing else in her life, she knew that much. So she set her cap for him.

Their maw had paused that day to bite off some thread—which took a lot of time because her teeth were so few and so widely spaced—and then she apparently forgot her place because a really long silence followed. Brit remembered scratching a chigger bite on her leg and thinking about going for a swim. It had been hot that day, the kind of summer day where a wise person will move real slow or not at all. Flies droned and bees buzzed in the tall grass that surrounded the clearing. The vast stretch of blue sky above them had held a circling hawk, slowly soaring on its uplifted wings. Sunlight glistened on the leaves and hummingbirds darted around the honeysuckle. She yawned. It wasn't that she questioned what her mother said but she was having a hard time believing that such a thing could happen to ordinary people like herself or like, for instance, the Garlocks. As she would say to Irish later: can you imagine ol' Mrs. Garlock looking at little skinny Mr. Garlock and feeling something like that? No, said Irish. It's not possible.

Yet neither girl had any trouble believing that it had happened to their mother like she said because they considered their maw anything but ordinary. And yet, when she went on it was obvious that that wasn't the way she thought about herself because she said she didn't know what possessed her, thinking she could get a fine man like Otis Dare. All that kept running through her mind was something her Granny had told her about the power of dreaming. How a smart girl can make a man notice her by putting her mind to it because it ain't hardly possible for one person to want another person that much and not have the other person feel it.

She said she knew it would not be easy. Said she knew she would have to think about nothing but him. First thing in the morning. Last thing at night. All the time in between. But a girl who did that might . . . just might . . . dream the man she wanted to her side.

For something really great to happen, it takes a great dream. That's what their Great-granny said.

So dream was what little Evie Ellis would do. A hundred, two hundred times a day she would shut her eyes and will him to see her. Not just *look* at her but *see* her.

And that's all it took? Irish asked.

All! their maw cried. It was a lot of work! I did not jus' go stick him in a bag, you know.

But to Brit the whole thing had sounded a lot less like dreaming and a lot more like foretelling because the way she did it was to imagine what would happen the next time they met. Say on a warm, quiet day when she would be walking into the village and she would see him coming toward her and he would be on one side of the road and she would be on the other and when he was about to pass her he would lift his hat a little . . . like always and she would give a little nod . . . like always, but instead of going on, like he always did, he would stop and turn around so he could watch her walk away. And then, that was when he would begin to see things about her that he had never seen before. Her strong back and shoulders and that she had a nice round behind, and how straight and long her legs were for her size and how clean she kept herself and that her clothes were mended . . .

And it worked! Like she had said before, she was so ignorant she didn't have enough sense to realize that it shouldn't! But for whatever reason, it did work! On one of the happiest days of her life Otis Dare would tell her that her eyes had talked to his heart. He said that all his heart had to do was stop beating and listen. And there had been tears in her eyes when she told them that.

The last thing she said to them—right before she told them it was time for chores—was that the love of a good person is God's little glimpse of heaven. His way of compensating for all the other hardships and losses a person must endure while they are earthly beings.

Brit only woke to her surroundings when she shivered from the cold. First she checked McDuff and found him sleeping quietly and then she added a log to the fire and sat staring into the flames. *If this is passion, then it is no wonder poor Jack is so miserable!*

She had never imagined she might end up like her brother—in love with someone who did not love her back. But maybe that choice was no longer hers to make. Maybe she was already gone! Was she? With her mother it had only taken one look. Could it also only take a touch?

It figured. If there was a path to true love that fit the Dare nature, the hoe handle between the eyes was it.

But he was so far above her. What had she to interest a man like Jean McDuff?

Maw had not worried about such piddle!

But Maw and Otis Dare were at least from the same world.

There was no earthly reason not to try, because only she would know if she failed.

It's true. So why not try? Heck, she could dream anything she wanted and nobody need ever know. That was the nice thing about dreams. Suddenly she was trembling with purpose.

All right then. I'll do it!

Hold on, said that other voice. What about going against the laws of God?

Right. She did not want the great heartache that was in store for anyone who went against God's laws. Somehow she would have to find out if he was already married or promised to another, but if he wasn't, then . . .

It wouldn't work. She just knew it wouldn't.

But for something really great to happen, it takes a great dream.

And so the argument went. First one side and then the other. Back and forth in her mind.

She looked off for a long time and then she looked at the lump that was McDuff and deep inside a voice whispered that it would sure be a shame never to kiss the man of your dreams. And then: if it felt like that when he touched her, wonder what it would feel like if she touched him?

Before she knew what she was doing, she had her hands on him, moving through his long silky hair, across his raspy jaw and stubbled chin, trailing down through the hair between his nipples then on further to his waistband and then lower still until her palm rested between his thighs. He moaned deep in his throat and beneath her palm something jerked like a snake. Her mouth went dry and her head felt light but she was going on with it no matter what. She drew a shaky breath and leaned close. She hovered over him for an instant and then she touched her lips to his. His lips were dry and warm, soft but firm . . .

But she was a little disappointed in the lack of reaction within herself, which was nothing like when he had touched her chest. Nevertheless, she settled in, perfectly willing to stay as she was, forever . . . only the wind caught the shed door right then and slammed it and she was upstairs and in her bed before she realized she had moved.

Good Lord! What had gotten into her? Taking her life into her own hands like that? She did not even want to think about what her brothers would do if they had walked in and caught her doing what she had just been doing.

Five

In the daytime Brit had to share McDuff with her sister because for as long as the fever had the doctor in its grips, little Markie had her ear stuck to his lips, trying her damnedest to make sense out of his mutterings. She was just certain that he'd had a wild and reckless past and she was quite vocal about her disappointment that he never spoke in American or Mexican so she could learn everything about it.

Actually they were all disappointed. Aside from what Sheriff Goodman had told them, they knew only what they could see; namely that he was a town man, well dressed, well schooled and very well heeled.

Why, when Evie went to wash his blood-soaked pants she said she found more walking around money in his pockets than most people saw in two lifetimes!

A person can't root around in another person's back without learning something about them and what Evie Dare learned about McDuff had made her change her mind about him. There was a time during that night of pain when she had looked deep into his eyes and she had seen the glitter of steel and that was when she knew that this man had the grit to make it in Tejas . . . if that was what he decided he wanted to do.

"That is just the sorta fella Sweet Home needs." She and Goldie were changing his bedding. "Probably doesn't know a deer from a elk but there are plenty of men around here who do an' there ain't nobody who can doctor anything bigger than a dog."

Brit, who was sweeping the dirt out the back door, had heard Goldie agree about the need for a healer in the area but he said that he doubted there was much chance of McDuff's staying. "Sweet Home doesn't have a lot to offer a fella like him."

In her mind Brit had to agree with her brother but in her heart that tiny voice was singing *There's me! Sweet Home has me!*

She had been dreaming her fool heart out. In her latest one, she had him waking one day well and clear-headed and, as luck would have it, the first thing he saw was herself, kneeling beside him praying. Her eyes and her hands were pointed heavenward and he would think . . . oho! an angel! and with his first words he would tell her how beautiful she was, that he knew that she had saved his life and that he was eternally in her debt . . . so much so that in return for his life, he was pledging it to her! She protested (but not too strongly) about what . . . or who . . . might be waiting for him in his own country and then she waited, sly fox that she was, for him to tell her everything she wanted to know.

But my life only began an instant ago! he cried as he took her hand and pressed his warm lips to her wrist. "How can I go forward when my heart is here?"

The words were from a story Miss Mapes had read to them in class one day. It was called *Romeo and Juliet* and had been written by a man who had lived long ago and far away.

From the way her eyes had kept blearing on her it was obvious that Miss Mapes had really liked that Romeo and Juliet story. Brit had liked it too but Miss Mapes sorta took away from the good parts by stopping all the time in order to blow her nose and mop her eyes.

That was one thing about Miss Mapes. A person need never wonder how she felt about something. Her face read like a track in the mud.

After she finished reading the story, Miss Mapes had called on each of them to ask what they thought. Zick Simmons said that he had especially liked the part about Juliet's quivering thigh and Miss Mapes' cheeks got red circles and she hurriedly called on Irish who said that she thought the story was all right, but Brit watched little Miss Mapes' mouth turn into a horseshoe when Irish said she would just as soon play leapfrog as hear it again. So, when it was her turn she said she liked it a whole lot—which was true. Also true was that she'd understood about one word in ten!

Oddly enough, in her dream she not only understood it, she could recite whole parts of it word for word. Like the part when Juliet told Romeo that if he did not let her leave, her maw was going to kill her and Romeo replied . . .

> My bounty is boundless as the sea,
> My love as deep; the more I give to thee
> Wilt thou leave me so unsatisfied?
> What satisfaction canst thou have tonight.
> The exchange of thy love's faithful vow for mine.

At the time she had thought it was impossible that there had once been real people like those in that story. And then Jean McDuff came and now she knew that it was true. There were places in the world where the people talk and dress like kings.

Unfortunately those places were not Sweet Home, Tejas.

She could make herself miserable ten times a day and did. Just like that. She would tell herself to remember how her mother got Otis Dare and her heart would soar. Then that other voice would say that she had gotten herself all worked up over nothing, and her heart would drop like a shot bird.

Her maw had been right. Passion caused a lot of heartache. But to her thinking, dreams were worse because dreams that do not come true hurt worse than the devil!

Besides the pain there was all that work. Lord, it was a terrible lot of work! She had been doing so much concentrated thinking that her stomach was sore!

First off, it was not exactly easy to slip away from Irish and Blue and Markie and Maw and Goldie and Jack, but if she managed that, then she had a favorite spot which was near a forked oak that stood in the center of a clearing in the woods. She would press her back against the tree trunk, lock her knees and clench her stomach and with her eyes tightly closed and her arms Christlike at her sides, she would imagine how it would be the first time he truly saw her as the person for him.

Or how it would be the first time they spoke.

Or the first time they touched.

And then she would will him to think about her! To *see* her! Now!

Jean hovered in a state of fever-induced confusion, and in that half-awake, half-asleep condition he had a dream. It was a dim and murky vision for which he had no interest initially, but it would soon hold him riveted.

He was someplace warm, even tropical, in a thick forest of trees with huge trunks and moss hung limbs. Colorful birds flitted from branch to branch and beyond the leafy glade there was a cascade of sparkling water that beckoned invitingly.

But this was only half a paradise. Drifting between the trees was a tattered fog that shadowed the lower ground leaving half of the forest bright and sunny and the other half menacing and ominous.

This place could be dangerous for him. He knew that, and yet he stood there tensely waiting, weaponless and vulnerable, and it seemed to him that the world was holding its breath and waiting too.

One minute he was alone; the next minute a young woman was there. They stared at each other for a time and then she smiled and he was lost to all else but her. The threat of danger was lifted. Instead anticipation ran through him with surprising intensity.

Lord, but she was a lush-looking little thing! A wild-haired woman/child barely clothed in a gauzy something that was scarcely longer than her knees. Her feet were bare and her hair unpinned and swirling at her waist. Ripe breasts pointed at him like arrows.

She smiled at him sideways, a fascinating smile with a child-like quality and he felt a wave of shame. She was erotic-looking but innocent. Too young and too sweet for a libertine like himself. Then she moved enticingly and revealed the taut curvature of her thighs and the tangled blackness between them and all thought of shame was gone. Instead his mind filled with his most carnal fantasies.

Somehow they were mere inches apart. He saw a teasing sparkle in her large wide eyes and then as he watched, he saw it replaced by a hunger the likes of which he had never seen before.

While her eyes talked to his soul, her soft hands reached out and touched him where it counted!

"Ah my chéri . . . I would have your hands on me forever!"

God knows he was trying to resist her, but the moist proximity of her mouth was too much. He was powerless against the greedy lust that rose within him. He kissed her lips and that easily did she capture him completely. He had never experienced such a swelling appetite for a female. Waves of desire rocked him as he kissed her slowly and deeply. She strained against him and their tongues danced feverishly.

Finally he broke away. He gave her a slow knowing smile. She gave him one back. He bent to kiss her left breast. She pulled her bodice aside to give him greater access and then twisted her fingers in his hair and bit his ear.

In seconds they were on the ground, he with his toes dug into the dirt and she with her heels drumming on his back. A witness as well as a participant, he watched himself as he reared back and plunged. Again. And again. And again. God, he was an animal! But a magnificent one!

They were both relentless, wallowing, grunting and pressing, crying and urging one another on, oblivious to everything but their quest for mutual fulfillment. It was incredibly wild and unspeakably primitive. Needless to say, it was the best sex he had ever had. And he wanted more.

On several occasions he did try to restrain himself in order to prolong their mutual pleasure, but each time it was she who would become shamelessly insatiable, exhorting him until once again, he was snorting and rutting like a crazed beast.

Then it came. And so did he, in a moment of such sheer ecstasy and such exquisite pleasure that he knew he had just died and passed into heaven.

But the instant that wondrous feeling subsided, the girl was gone. Vanished into thin air.

Jarring reality returned. Dirt and grass was stuck to his body and a sharp rock poked him under his ribs. God it was hotter than hades! He was dying of thirst.

The dream kept recurring, always confusing and always difficult to follow in the beginning but always ending in the same sizzling episode of sex.

She was the most beautiful and the most passionate female in the universe and she gave him everything he wanted, but it was never enough. He was always left unsatisfied in the end.

With the incongruity of a dream he spent the times without her at his country villa where he sulked and became short-tempered with the servants, and as the time between their interludes grew so did his personal deterioration. He became negligent in his grooming. Erstwhile companions shunned him and he was an outcast. He lost in the gaming houses, and even ugly women found him repulsive.

Of course it was all that girl's fault. Why did she always have to run away? God, it had been so good between them!

In his silent solitude he would torture himself with the memory of every inch of her body and want her as he had never wanted any other. And even that strange self-abuse was good!

Once for the briefest of moments he realized he was actually more awake than asleep and he caught a glimpse of the nymph of his dream. She was kneeling beside him, so close that he could actually see her unusually narrow waist, a pair of particularly inviting breasts and a round, well-shaped derrière.

His dream had become reality! He reached out to her and touched her lovingly, softly but once again she disappeared and he grasped only air.

He slowly drifted back into oblivion and his only companion was consummate disappointment.

Six

The first time Jean regained consciousness he felt so unlike himself he was certain he was dead. He lay unmoving and slowly his senses returned.

He was first aware of a shaft of sunlight that warmed his face and then of certain noises . . . the buzzing of bugs and the caw of a crow, the staccato tap of a woodpecker and from somewhere close by, the soft sound of a woman humming. The sounds soothed and comforted him until suddenly a terrible pounding shattered the air. His head took up the beat and throbbed in tandem. Slowly he turned toward the noise and through slitted eyes he saw an old woman with a mallet, beating a leather bag like it was a snake. "Madame, please!" he croaked. "Have mercy!"

"He's baaack!"

The yell had come mere inches from his ear, from a young girl who now cupped her mouth and bellered, "Maaaw! He's back!" She hitched her chair closer. "My name's Markie and I've been waiting to read you a story from this dot board here, see it? Ooops! Sorry!"

How could he not see "it" since "it" had rapped him smartly on the forehead?

"It slipped. Don't get mad now. I'm blind, you know."

He lifted trembling fingers to palpate the rising lump

on his forehead. He was alive. He was in a sort of hell but he was alive.

Unfortunately with that realization came a wave of ambivalence. He was naturally glad to have been plucked from the jaws of death but he also felt incredibly disappointed, because when the fever left him, something else did as well . . . only he had no idea what that something was!

Or did he? Something was lurking just beyond the grasp of his mental facilities, the thread of a wispy memory that led to . . . what? If only he could take hold of it. Perhaps with complete quiet he could concentrate long enough to . . .

In the time it took him to have these thoughts, several grinning people had crowded around him.

Ah! Now he remembered. These were the Dares. He had met one of the three brothers the night he arrived in Sweet Home but their features were so similar he could not now say which man it had been. Of course he remembered the old woman. And who could forget the blind girl! And finally there were the twins . . . two lovely young women who brought several things to mind, most of which were surprisingly lewd and extremely ill-mannered . . . even for him!

Mixed in with all that was something else, a bittersweet memory that was haunting and elusive and unfortunately, quickly fading from his mind.

To say that he was experiencing a great deal of difficulty in sorting out his thoughts was a huge understatement. About the only thing he knew for sure was that he had been brought here . . . to this remote farm . . . to die.

"How do you feel?"

He looked up at the old woman. "I'm . . . not sure. I think my left leg is numb."

"That may change. Then again, it may not."

"Thank you. And the bullet?"

"It's out but we had to cut a path wide enough to drive an ox through. Girls, run go get the coffee pot and fire up the stove. I'll bet you're starved!"

She offered him her tin of coffee and his gaze dropped to the hands which were wrapped around the cup. They were root-like hands with long, spatulate fingers and rough callused palms.

There had been something about hands during his fever. Warm soft ones that had touched him with great tenderness . . . and with white hot passion. Not these hands, which might have been a man's. "Who cared for me when I was not myself?"

"My daughter did. Waited on you day an' night. Wouldn't allow nobody else to lay a finger on you."

How interesting, he thought.

"Took out the bullet too, after my hands set up on me. Here drink some of this. It'll either cure yuh or kill yuh."

He took a sip and made some croaked comment about its strength. Evie thanked him and said she liked it too. She said she had recently taken to stretching her coffee with blanched jalapeño seeds to see if she could give it a bit more bite.

Any more bite, he thought, and I will be bleeding from the tongue.

"You recall how you got shot?"

He placed the speaker now as Blue, the Dare brother he had met the night he arrived in town. He had also been one of the last people to see Duncan alive.

"I remember."

And so he did. Everything, the graveyard, the cantina, the murderer and the pain . . . especially the pain.

But beyond that, what else? There was something more, waiting on the fringes of his sanity, something that was far removed from his last lucid hours when he had been searching out and confronting his brother's killer. He strained his powers of recall but whatever it was remained just beyond his reach.

"This here's Goldie and Jack. My other sons."

"Gentlemen."

"McDuff."

"The sheriff wanted us to tell him when you came around," Blue said.

"Please tell him that I am awake and that I await his pleasure."

"That's the way," said Goldie, nodding. "Might as well come at this thing head on."

"What thing?" Maybe he recalled less than he thought.

"The Daggert thing. You know. They shot you. You shot them. Goodman'll want to clear it up."

Jean had not thought about the legal consequences of his act.

"I doubt that Goodman will come to get you any time soon. He knows you ain't goin' no place."

"Rest for now," said Mrs. Dare. "I'll fix you somethin' to eat."

"Thank you."

"As for the rest of us," the mother laid a hard eye on her sons, "work's waitin' an' you girls don't have much time to spare."

"We'll talk later, McDuff."

"I'll be here."

"I expect you will!"

The three brothers shook the floor as they headed for the front door and the outside. The twins followed their mother to a side door that obviously led to a cooking area, for he could see a primitive clay oven just beyond.

At the threshold both girls turned and looked at him. The whole family had the same jaw. On the males it looked determined, on the females it looked passionate and willful. A line formed between his brows as once again he pondered whatever it was that kept eluding him.

One girl's lips spread in a generous smile, while the other's quirked in tandem with her brow. The former had the calm square gaze of a duelist; the latter the gaze of a sultry siren. The duelist went on out to join her mother but the siren stood silhouetted in gold against the morning sun. Jean raised his brows in silent question but she simply stared at him. Her *café noir* eyes were shrewd and alert, and as vigilant as a wolf. He felt a stab of desire of startling strength.

He had heard about two strangers becoming entranced with one another after an exchange of glances across a crowded room and he had always thought it was silly romantic folderol. He did not anymore. She had completely captured his attention. More than that if the truth were known. He could not have looked away on a bet.

During the particularly long moment that followed, he received as intense a scrutiny as he had ever received from one of her gender.

Challenged and a little annoyed, he was returning the favor, stare for stare, when suddenly reality blurred and a familiar figure emerged.

It was as if some part of him had stayed in his dream, for it was showing itself to him in bits and pieces, like a landscape that is viewed through a tattered cloth. He saw how the sunlight shone on the girl's hair and remembered how firelight had done the same. He felt soft hands touch his face and chest then urgent ones that clawed and demanded. Tender fingers riffed through his hair and then tangled in it and pulled him where they wanted his mouth to be. Innocent lips pressed against his while a not so innocent hand stroked his crotch like a favored pet!

He was physically stimulated, but he was also confused. He felt like he had taken hold of an unraveling thread and had pulled a tangled wall of wool over himself. The result was smothering.

Suddenly a blast of sunlight struck his face. His mind

cleared and the breath left his body as if he had sustained a blow.

It had been she! The girl standing in the doorway and that writhing embodiment of passion were one and the same.

He knew he had seen that lovely face before! Not smooth and placid as it was now but tight and slick with sweat as it had strained for completion! Desire ran through him like a sword but he still could not see it all. He rubbed his eyes with his fingertips and when he looked again, he saw that the opening was empty.

Actually everything was empty. The doorway. The world. His life. Yes, definitely that.

He lay back feeling weak and ill and utterly drained. He had never experienced anything quite like the bleak feeling that remained.

Long after she was gone the fantasy image remained. She would not leave his mind. Nor did he want her to.

Within himself something had been changed. Whether it was for better or for worse remained to be seen but plainly, something within him was changed.

Unfortunately, aside from that irrefutable fact and his name, he knew nothing else. He squeezed the bridge of his nose between his fingers and thought: What in hell is going on here?

Brit pressed her back against the wall and tried to get her heart back where it belonged. She had scarcely been able to stumble out of his sight after that look he had given her! Like he would like to suck her spirit right out of her! And she had been willing to let him. Oh, yes. In a minute.

Oh, she'd had no idea he would look at her like that!

Silly girl, that other voice said. Of course he has to look at you if he is going to see you.

True, but she had not known what it would do to her insides! This is not going to be easy. Not a bit easy . . .

Nothing worthwhile ever is.

She pushed herself away from the wall and smoothed her hair. Right. Remember that. Nothing worthwhile is ever easy.

The blind girl was still sitting beside him.

"Markie."

She turned her head toward the unseen caller. "Yeah?"

"Time to go."

"Is it? Oh, drat. Well . . ."

"Where are you going?"

"To school. Me an' my sisters . . . My sisters and I . . . go to school." She had spoken over her shoulder. Now she returned to stand at his side. "Say, are you all right?"

"Yes. Why?"

"When I said school you made a sorta strangled sound . . ."

"It was just a, um, twinge."

"What's that? A twinge?"

"Markie!"

"Comin'! Hot blast it!"

"It is a slight feeling of pain."

"Oh, boy!" She grinned. "Good thing you were out when you were healin'. Wouldn't any of us have gotten a moment's sleep."

"You better run along. You don't want to be late."

"Yeah. Well, bye. See you tonight!"

School! His siren . . . an innocent schoolgirl? Impossible! He heard horses' hooves and a feminine voice that sounded very familiar but he shook his head. No! No, no. Never!

Seven

The Dare girls had just finished school for the day and now sat on their horses at the turn off that led to the mill road. Brit and Markie rode old Goat while Irish was on Spots. Markie and Brit were headed home. Irish was going to the Schumachers to see if Mr. Schumacher wanted her to watch his son that day. The Schumachers owned the new mill, a two-story stone building that sat backed up to the creek.

It was late in the day and the town drowsed in the afternoon quiet. From where they sat, Brit could see that Bowie Garlock was standing outside his store, talking to a man who had his hands rammed into his belt in back. Behind the boarding house Maude Stone had stretched a rope between two trees and was beating heck out of a rug. A small black dog ran around her barking and acting like it was all a game. Beside the well there was a Mexican woman who held a clay jug balanced on her head while she talked to the mission priest, Father Guerril.

A wagon rattled by, then quiet descended again. Birds fluttered in the bushes and bees buzzed here and there. Markie yawned and laid her head against Brit's shoulder.

"Well, we'll see you in a couple of hours."

"I guess."

It was the sound of her sister's voice that made Brit look at her.

"Irish . . ."

"Yeah?"

"You still like it, don't you?"

"Oh, yeah." She shrugged. "I still like it all right. Why?"

Between the trees she could see the mill and a wagon load of grain that waited outside, and even from where she sat she could smell grain and the scent of new sawn lumber. "I thought maybe something was wrong."

"Nothing's wrong. Who said anything was wrong?"

Irish was bringing home fifty cents every time she took care of the Schumacher baby. Earning money just like the men. Made sure nobody forgot it either. Dropping the money in the coin jar and rattling it around.

Oh, to get paid for working in that beautiful house. What a place it was!

Everybody in town had seen the outside of the Schumachers' big two-story frame house with its deep, pillared porch and split-wood roof, but Irish was one of very few people who had ever been inside.

First off, she had told them that everything everybody had ever said about the place was absolutely true. Why, she had never imagined that a house for ordinary people could be so fancy! Everything had been painted, even the porch floor. She said it was a moss green and looked clean enough to eat off of. But, like Irish said, who in their right mind would paint a floor? Then there was this one little room that seemed to have little purpose other than as a space set aside for the staircase to begin! And she had told them how that room was long and narrow and how it had four doors that faced each other across a shiny wood floor. That on one side there was a spindly-legged chair with a cloth seat and back, and on the other there was a narrow looking-glass, edged with something curly and yellow. Tall wide stairs wound their way up the back wall and the whole place seemed to always smell like beeswax.

Irish had been working there for a few weeks now and she really liked it. At least Brit had thought that she did.

People said that Schumacher's wife was very ill, which was why he was often seen carting his red-cheeked little boy around with him. But other than that—and the fact that he was running the sorely needed lumber mill and a grist mill—nobody knew much about them. They had kept to themselves and had not had much to do with others yet, but this had seemed reasonable to the townspeople so far, what with the time it had taken to build a new home and to set up the mill and all.

One thing was certain—they did not want for money. Schumacher never bartered for anything he bought, but paid for every item with cash on the barrelhead.

Brit looked at her sister. She didn't know why Irish was blue but she certainly knew why *she* was. They'd had a geography lesson in school and one question from Brit was all it took for Miss Mapes to tell them more than Brit had ever wanted to know about France. That it was *the* most beautiful country in the world. The capital of art and learning. The hub of the universe. The heart of the Continent and Europe's crown jewel. That its capital city was called the City of Light, and that its people were world famous for their enjoyment of life. They just have fun, all day long. Fun. Fun. Fun. Nobody in their right mind would ever want to live anyplace else!

Oh, yeah, she knew why she was miserable, all right!

"Well, bye for now."

"Bye."

Because Brit was watching her sister walk the pony up the road she did not notice Pick Anderson until he was right beside them. "Hey!" he said and she jerked like a snake.

"Oh, hi, Pick. You startled me."

"Markie heard me, didn't yuh, Markie. Waved and everything."

"Why didn't you say something, Markie?"

"I did. I said: Hey Pick!"

"I didn't hear you."

"Mind in the clouds, huh?" Pick squinted up at her.

"I guess so." Brit didn't like Pick much, though she had no real reason not to. He was young enough and clean enough and a good hard worker. He also had a real nice piece of land south of town on which he had built a small solid cabin.

But it seemed to her that he always caged his eyes, like there was something in them that he never wanted her to see.

"How about if I come out tonight?"

He was grinning up at her and she was wondering why she had never noticed his pulpy lips before.

"Better not, Pick. We have a sick man staying with us."

"But Brit, he's a lot better no- . . . Ow!"

Brit's heel had met Markie's leg.

"He's still too sick for company, Markie. Maybe next week, Pick."

"Awright. I'll be lookin' forward to it."

It was silly, she thought. These reasons she had for not paying him much mind but he had put his hat back on. He wore it far back, so the brim was almost between his shoulder blades, and even that bothered her.

As they rode on, Markie had to know why she got kicked in the ankle and Brit told her, it was because she didn't want to encourage Pick Anderson to come out and hang around the house.

"Oh," said Markie. "Well then, why don't you just tell him so?"

"Because it wouldn't be polite."

Markie thought about that. Then, "Which would be the worst sin. To lie? Or not to be polite?"

"To lie."

"Then . . ."

"Markie, please. Let's just enjoy the ride home."

"I am enjoyin' the ride home."

"Then let me enjoy the ride home."

"But I was jus' wonderin' . . ."

"Markie!"

"All right. All right."

Markie wrapped her arms around her sister's waist and they rode on.

"I'm gonna read the doctor some of my stories."

"Good."

"We don't go to school tomorrow, do we?"

"No."

"Good. Then I'll read him my stories tomorrow."

Markie fell silent. She could tell her sister's mind was about seventy 'leven miles away and she wondered why, but pretty soon she rested her head on her sister's shoulder and dozed like that until they got home.

"I'll keep him occupied," Markie yelled. "Y'all jus' go on about your chores. Drat! Now I've got these all turned around! Well, that's all right."

The blind girl was pulling her chair closer to his pallet and Jean couldn't help but flinch for fear of getting brained again.

"I figured I'd read a bit first then I thought you'd probably like to hear some highly interestin' stories I know . . ."

The mother stuck her head in the back door. "Markie Dare!"

She stood up. "Ma'am?"

"You mind what I told you."

"Yessum." She sat and started shuffling her boards around. "Maw's always after me for talkin' too much. Says it jus' drives people nuts! Now this here is a story called 'The Lion and the Mouse' and it was written by a fella named A-Sop who lived . . ."

She put on a very remarkable demonstration—this little blind girl—and he listened with interest to her explanation of how it all came about. How her brother Goldie had made the board from which she learned the alphabet and how her teacher had fixed the story onto it. Unfortunately he was often distracted by some of the other things that were going on around them. But he supplied an occasional *ah* or *mm* and Markie was unaware that much of his attention was riveted on the area beyond the open door where Evie Dare and her daughters were chopping meat on a stump and drizzling something into a pot, stirring and bending to take a taste. Good smells soon started drifting into the cabin and his stomach clenched with hunger.

In time one of the twins came in. She saw him watching her and grinned at him. As the blind girl read on, the girl went to a bank of shelves that apparently stored the family's staples. He could see some baskets full of what looked like dried fruits and raisins, some lumpy bags that spilled potatoes and unshelled pecans and a row of jugs that appeared to contain things like sorghum, molasses, honey and melted fat.

The twin clinked some jars around until she found the one she wanted and then she started back outside. At the door she paused and looked at him and then she smiled. "Doin' all right, mister?"

"Yes, I am fine. Thank you."

The blind girl slapped the wood tablet in her lap. "Irish, I have ast you an' ast you not to interrupt me when I'm readin'!"

"Sorry."

"Now I have to start that part all over again."

Irish was chastened. "Gol, Markie, I said I was sorry."

"That's the thing with you, Irish. You always say you are sorry an' then you always do it again."

Markie sighed and sniffed and then settled into reading again.

Jean lay on his side with his head propped on his fist. As he stared at a knothole on the floor his face had a crafty look to it and there was a satisfied quirk to his lips.

So, he thought, my little siren is the other one. Brit.

Eight

Sheriff Goodman came out on Jean's next day of lucidity. "Pardon me if I don't stand," said Jean.

Goodman shook his hand then sat on the floor with his back against the wall. "No need to apologize to me. I'm at the age where the more boundin' around the other fella does, the worse I feel."

Evie Dare brought the sheriff a bowl of venison stew and in spite of Jean's having eaten only an hour earlier, she handed him a bowlful as well.

For breakfast he had eaten fried eggs on top of a wide wedge of fried ham, fried potatoes, fried okra, fried grits and refried beans.

"Eat!" She first pointed at the sheriff. "I know how you bachelors cook. And as for you . . . why, you ain't got enough blood for a bird."

"Yep. Bird blood. That's all you got left!"

"Markie!"

"Yessum?"

"You get on with your chores."

"But . . ."

"Scat!"

Bird blood! thought Jean. Perhaps that is why I feel so weak-kneed around a certain female.

Dutiful as toddlers he and the sheriff ate. Evie watched them for a minute and then left them alone.

Jean's pallet was in the main room, which was the center of the structure and the center of the family's activities. Skins covered the greater part of the plank floor lending a certain harmony and muting all the moccasin covered feet that crossed the room a hundred times a day.

On the north wall was a deep fireplace that had been built with river rocks and chinked with mud, and over the smoke-stained ledge that served as its mantel, hung assorted weapons on a deer-horn rack.

Here and there were several chairs made of stretched cowhide. Two benches and the long table where everyone ate were pushed against one wall when not in use.

Though far from the refined living to which Jean was accustomed, the rough-cut cabin was a snug, well-built and well-fortified structure. Efficient. Well thought out. Homey. And while he waited for Sheriff Goodman to finish eating, he wondered how long he would be allowed to remain in it. The sheriff had not made the long ride from town for his health. Perhaps he would take him into town today. The thought brought a stab of disappointment. For purely selfish reasons he was hoping to stay until he could sort out this thing with the girl . . . especially now that he had his wits about him. Which reminded him: he had not seen her yet that day and wondered where she had gotten to. He could not see the yard from where he lay but he could hear the birds calling and the hens cackling. The weary creak of the windlass blended with the sound of thunder, far in the distance. He tried to move slightly and a knife twisted in his back. Meanwhile Goodman had mopped his bowl shiny with his bread and set it aside.

"Well," he said and looked at Jean. "I hate to say I tole yuh so, but I tole yuh so. Now you're in a fine kettle of fish."

Jean shrugged. "I acted impulsively, but even knowing then what I know now I am not sure I would do anything different."

"That's what I want to know. Exactly what did you do that night?"

"You know what happened."

"No, now I don't. Not really. Suppose you tell me your side of it. Start with the last time I saw you, when you were headed for Maude Stone's boardin' house."

Jean stared at the floor but he was remembering the road with its center ruff of weeds and the cemetery with its tired wood crosses canted at odds with one another. But most of all he was remembering a simple pine casket and a smell of decay that was so powerful it was like an attack to the senses. A spear of moonlight had lit his brother's face well enough to see those familiar teeth, bared in a rigored grin. The death mask. It had been like a glimpse into hell.

When Jean lit his pipe he was not surprised to see that his fingers trembled. "I knew I would not sleep that night so after I left you I found myself aimlessly wandering through town. I felt dazed. I had seen Duncan dead with my own eyes, but my mind still would not accept the reality. I saw a light in the cantina and I wondered if someone could have remembered something more . . ."

He told the sheriff about talking to Dulce and how a few coins had gotten him the names of the men who had been in the cantina on the night his brother was murdered.

"She verified the other girl's story about the disagreement that had occurred between Gil Daggert and my brother, and the longer she talked the more convinced I became. I don't know why, but I might have witnessed the act myself . . . it was that irrefutable in my mind." He looked up and saw the sheriff's puzzled expression. "For some reason I was sure that Gil Daggert was my brother's killer."

"Go on."

"Well, when I learned he was only a few feet away I had

no choice . . . I had to confront him . . ." He shrugged.
"And you know what happened then."

"That the same story you're gonna tell the judge?"

He shrugged. "Of course! It is the truth."

"Huh! Well." Goodman took a sharpened stick from his
pocket and started methodically picking his teeth. "The
judge tole me he's gonna finish gettin' his house built
before he starts work. I tole 'im I thought it'd be best to
leave you out here 'til he's ready. Probably two or three
weeks."

"Two or three weeks . . . I can't possibly impose on the
Dares for that long . . ."

Outside someone called to another and was answered.
The voices were distinctly female but the precise words
were carried off on the breeze. He shifted impatiently.
Goodman's boots against the door were keeping it half
closed.

"Evie said they're glad to have you. Salt of the earth,
you know, the Dares."

"I realize that, but . . ."

"Best thing for the both of us. If you were in town I'd
have to keep Earl Daggert from doin' you in, which would
mean puttin' a guard on you night an' day. Which . . .
since I don't have any money for a guard . . . would mean
me sittin' up night an' day or . . ." Here he shot Jean a
teasing look. "I suppose I could let Daggert an' his pals
hold their own trial."

Jean inclined his head. "Since you put it that way . . ."

"A wise decision! I told Judge Barca that you were under
house arrest here in the care of two law enforcement of-
ficers, an' that I'd bring you in whenever he's ready to go
to work. By the way . . ." He stretched his leg to give him
access to his pocket. "I got somethin' here that belongs
to you. Picked it up off the bed that night."

The sight of his brother's watch brought Jean's anger

back in a rush. "What about Earl Daggert? Has he suffered no consequences for shooting me in the back?"

Goodman shook his head. "He claimed he was tryin' to save his brother from bein' murdered. Judge just flapped his hand at me when I tole him that." Goodman waited for Jean to finish cursing before he went on. "McDuff, I think if I was you I'd have myself a little talk with Abel O'Neal."

"O'Neal?"

"Wouldn't hurt. He's that lawyer fella from Philadelphia. I mentioned him to Miz Dare."

"Ah yes. She said something about him."

"Well, here's the thing. He's new at it, but they say he's upright in his dealings and sharp as mustard. I don't know but I've heard him talk that lawyer lingo an' he sounds pretty good to me."

"I met him at Maude Stone's."

"It don't hurt to get his opinion on things. You know what I mean?"

"All right."

"This ain't the States, you know. Hell, we don't even know how the law works down here. Nobody's been here long enough to find out. Now we have this judge who's gonna tell us what to do. Provided he ever gets ready. Meanwhile, we wait."

Goodman half stood—an apparently painful process. "Are you all right, Sheriff?"

"Yeah, it's jus' my bones. Too dang many years drivin' freight!"

Recalling his ride into Sweet Home, Jean held up his hand, "Say no more!"

"I can ask O'Neal to ride out sometime, if you want. He's got plenty of time on his hands."

"I would be obliged."

Evie came in then, wiping her hands on a cloth. "More stew anybody?"

"No, I best get on back. You know, somebody tried to fire the town last night!"

"What?"

"Yeah, I think it was some road toughs that blew in a coupla days back. The usual. Well armed and ill tempered, wild as javalinas."

"Who are they?"

"Claimed they were hide hunters but I didn't see any hides for sale. One calls hisself Clabe an' another one's Nob. The third fella says his name's Tuck, short for Kintuck." He laughed mirthlessly. "Bothers me when a fella ain't got but one name."

"Most men come to Tejas 'cause they've been run off from someplace else."

The sheriff ignored Evie and looked off with a frown creasing his brow. "There's a fella I heard about who beat a man to death with a wagon spoke. They say the killer had a nose like a lump of clay jus' like the hider who calls hisself Nob. Wish he'd jus' tell me if he's the same fella, but . . . since he ain't likely to do that, I guess I better get on back an' keep my eyes peeled." The sheriff plopped on his hat and tugged it into place. "Well, you'll see me when you see me, McDuff."

After the sheriff left for town and Evie had cleaned his wound Jean was left alone. Thunder grumbled again and soon a hard rain pocked the packed dirt in the yard and sent the chickens in search of shelter. The wind moaned in the chimney and mixed hearth smoke with that of wet dirt. It was a heavy but not an unpleasant smell.

With his chin on his folded hands he lay staring into the gray light of the dying day and he thought about the sheriff and the others like him. Hap Pettijohn. The Dares. He had to admit these Texians fascinated him. Hard-bitten and fearless. Adventuresome and restless as the wind. A breed in absolute apposition to his world of perfumed, bejeweled men and painted pomaded women.

And apparently the females of Tejas were every bit as hardy as the men! Only the night before he had sat talking to the three brothers and after he had answered all their questions he had asked some general ones of his own— more to be polite than anything—but the brothers had obliged by telling him some hair-raising tales about Indians and banditos and general no-goods.

The story that had stuck in his mind was one about a girl who had been lanced by the Indians and survived. The girl had been carrying her two-year-old sister at the time of the attack and had run with her across the prairie with the Indians in hot pursuit. By twisting her body this way and that she managed to protect the baby from the Indians' lances but had suffered three glancing cuts and one puncture wound herself. Jack said she would have been scalped if her father had not heard her cries and come running.

The family was well known by the Dares; the girl's brother was the unfortunate Cootie about whom Markie had said: dumb as dirt. She did not, however, speak with disdain about his sister.

Good Lord, he had thought. Was such uncommon valor bred right into them?

By evening his back had begun to ache and he slept early, and as he slept he dreamt. Only this time there were no sizzling sexual encounters. This time he dreamt about his brother's murder.

Dark shadows slowly turning gray revealed the back door of the cantina to him. It opened and he saw Duncan step out into the hushed gray-black morning. Duncan looked around, taking note of the line of light on the eastern horizon and the twists of smoke that curled from a few cabin roofs. The air was damp and cool. A dog barked on the other side of town, but otherwise the streets were silent and empty. Unsuspecting, Duncan paused to light his pipe. Suddenly an arm encircled his neck from behind. A knife blade flashed and in one quick motion it was over and he slid to the ground, killed over a whore that he would not have remembered had he lived another month.

Jean woke with a start, and the expectation of personal danger but he heard only a soft snore that came from the alcove where the old woman slept.

He remained tense and alert for a long moment and then he lay back, spent. He pressed the heels of his hands to his eyes, incredibly saddened by the useless waste of a life that had been so young and so vital.

The low-burning candle guttered in a sudden gust of wind. A log fell on the grate with a loud *thunk* and the snoring ceased. Jean lay marking time until it resumed its measured cadence. Unfortunately he knew there would be no similar resumption of sleep for him.

As he watched the moon throw shadows onto the wall he allowed his thoughts to sink deep into the past. It was a painful place and not one he visited on a whim. The only reason why he did so now was because of the chore at hand. Tomorrow he must write their mother and tell her that the wrong son had died.

Their mother. As incongruous as it seemed, she was probably the only thing that Duncan and Jean McDuff had held in common.

Nine

Twenty-nine years ago Jean Pierre had been born to Rochelle McDuff, the Scottish mistress of one of the most powerful aristocrats in France, the Marquis de Montceau. Their liaison was a love match for over fifteen years, one for which his mother had willingly given up a promising career in the opera. In return the marquis gave Rochelle McDuff everything she desired . . . except a contract of marriage.

The marquis's first wife died when Jean was six. Though normally remote and somewhat aloof, Rochelle assumed a hopeful and expectant attitude but when the marquis married another much younger and equally wealthy woman of the aristocracy, Rochelle became an embittered woman. She drank more, and more often and though she acted serene in the marquis's presence, she was a screaming harridan when he left. Because he was the image of his father, Jean bore the brunt of her anger.

Of course, for years he did not understand the reason for her animosity. The only thing that was painfully obvious to him was that he loved his mother and his mother no longer loved him. He began to doubt that she ever had.

The marquis's visits started to dwindle and within a few years the long-standing affair was over. Rochelle McDuff was pensioned off to Scotland, where she eventually married and in due time produced a legitimate son named Duncan.

Jean had expected to go along with his mother when she left France, but on the day of her departure he was abruptly informed that he would not be allowed to do so. In hindsight he should have been grateful—it would have been far easier and far less expensive for his father to have sent him away. Instead Jean was forced to stay in France in order to continue his education at Louis le Grand.

Left behind and alone, it was not long before Jean's feelings of abandonment became anger. With the contrariness of youth, he disparaged the elegance of the large flat that overlooked the Seine and barely tolerated its staff . . . the housekeeper and surrogate mother who cooked like an angel, her husband who served as his valet. Years later he would cringe when he remembered how he had acted toward the kindly old couple but in defense of himself he would argue that he was only ten and that he sorely missed his mother.

During the ensuing years he saw his father only rarely and then only for minutes at a time, but he would always remember him through the eyes of a child. That he was a stern thin-lipped man with dark expressionless eyes. That he had long fingers on which he wore several rings, including one of a gold lion's head with emerald eyes. The scent of the peculiar-smelling tobacco to which he was particularly partial. The silver-buckled shoes and the heavily brocaded coats.

But other than those things, Jean remembered little about him. Only that as far as he could recall, his father had never touched him. Not in anger nor in tenderness. Certainly never in love.

After his mother left, Jean's dealings with his father were conducted through his father's representative, Monsieur La Farge, who spent exactly a half an hour with him on the third Monday of each month.

A precise distance of three feet would separate the two stiff-backed chairs on which they would sit, La Farge with his legs crossed and a single creased piece of paper on his lap. Jean sprawled and petulant.

La Farge was a round-shouldered man with close-set, popped eyes and a great nose that was curved like an executioner's axe. Jean hadn't a clue as to his age. As the years passed he continued to look precisely as he had on the first day they met.

All of their interviews began with the same question. What would you like to tell your father this month? For several sessions Jean had merely shrugged and said nothing, until one day he realized that the only person he was punishing with his sullen attitude was himself, and after that, he started asking for small things—more pocket money, a certain plaything, a better mount—and he received them all.

One month he added the request that he be allowed to visit his mother and meet his half brother, and after a time his request was granted. He was to be allowed to visit Scotland—in the company of Monsieur La Farge, of course.

Unfortunately, it would not be the reunion for which he had hoped.

He remembered how his eyes had searched the dock for his mum, and the disappointment he had felt when he realized that they were being met by her emissary instead—a toothless old man who smelled of damp wool and cheap whiskey. The old man pointed to the rickety straw-filled cart that had been provided to convey them to his mother's new home. As might have been expected, La Farge refused to place his august personage on such a "thing" which prompted an interminable wait while a carriage, horses and a driver were arranged.

When Jean saw his mother at last, she was standing on the steps of a gray stone building. He leapt from the carriage and ran to her. (God, how he hated that memory now!) And it was fully a minute before he realized that while he was hugging for all he was worth, his mum's arms hung loosely at her sides.

She didn't say much but then she didn't have to. Her bastard son was an embarrassment to her, now that she had her tweedy husband, her legitimate child and her small but elegant country home.

Something else soon became obvious; namely that it had been she—and not his father—who had insisted that he remain in France. She had never wanted him. She thought he was the reason the marquis's affections had cooled. Ever sensitive to her feelings, Jean made himself scarce when her new husband appeared but the relationship he had hoped to re-establish with her never materialized.

He was supposed to have spent two months in Scotland, and now the time stretched unending. But pride would not allow him to send word to his father nor would it allow him to tell La Farge that he wished to cut the trip short. Stuck, he turned to his half brother Duncan for distraction and received—for the first and only time in his life—unconditional affection.

It would have been easy to hate Duncan, the child his mother adored. Instead he learned to care for him as he had for no other human being. Duncan was everything he was not. Innocent and guileless. Giving and forgiving. Lighthearted and eternally idealistic.

Any person who spent time with Duncan had to be willing to overlook certain flaws, such as restless energy, relentless curiosity and an addiction to practical jokes, but those few foibles aside, Duncan was a winning, intelligent child, and as the weeks of that interminable summer wore on, he became Jean's sole companion.

As an infant, Duncan had suffered from a weakness of the heart that might have killed a less stubborn child. A physician once told him that he would outgrow the disease, a prognostication that he probably believed to his dying day. But he still would have debilitating days when it was all he could do to get out of bed. The last such episode had occurred in New Orleans.

Duncan's illness was the reason why Jean had agreed to make the trip to America in the first place and why, as an afterthought, he had decided to bring his medical bag along, for Duncan refused to coddle himself. Quite the contrary. That much had been apparent to Jean from the first moment he saw him.

He would never forget that day. The carriage had been following a path along the water when suddenly a slim boy in short pants appeared on the top of the hill leading to the beach and immediately hurled himself down the grassy slope toward them. He fell, of course, and rolled downhill ass over teakettle. But when he finally landed, it was on his feet and he immediately bowed his back and flung his arms wide as if to cry: Now, there! What do you think of that?

That act of bravado—that instant of reckless bravery— had always exemplified Duncan to Jean. He aged but never changed.

Eventually Jean returned to France and sometime between the age of fourteen and sixteen he discovered women and the power of a well-turned phrase. It was a revelation that would reshape his destiny and change his outlook on life. The sullen boy became a congenial opportunist with a new objective in life: the pursuit of pleasure. He soon met many young men with similar interests and they slogged through school together, either drunk or about to be. From there he ran with a charming gregarious crowd of idiots, many of whom would die young, in sudden circumstances and of odd causes.

When the marquis died he left Jean with enough money to maintain a modest life style in Paris . . . or an extravagant one anywhere else . . . and instructions that he was to attend the Medical College at the University of Edinburgh for a minimum period of five years. No compliance meant no money.

The mandate amazed Jean. Years before, he had been briefly inclined toward science and on a whim he had mentioned his interest to La Farge. It was remarkable that La Farge would have relayed such a passing fancy to his father. Even more remarkable was the fact that the marquis had remembered. At the time of his father's death, Jean had not seen him for seven years.

In any event, since a nominal medical career was preferable over a commission in the army—and wealth was most definitely preferable to abject poverty—he accepted his father's conditions. It had nothing to do with selfless dedication to humanity. As far as Jean was concerned, being a doctor was not an opportunity to help mankind but a way to meet willing womankind.

He completed his studies well and might have been an outstanding physician, but he judged himself harshly and decided that he was lacking that special calling that set those few truly dedicated healers apart from all others. No matter. A man has to have some goal in life, and his was the pursuit of sensual pleasure. To be invited into the right parlors . . . and subsequently into the right beds . . . a man needed money and social standing. Fortunately, Jean had both. And would acquire more as he honed certain skills at games of chance. Most everything else became secondary.

Over the ensuing years Duncan visited him twice and they got on famously together. Then Duncan's father died and passed on to Duncan a piece of land which he had inherited from a black sheep brother who had been living in America. Duncan asked Jean to accompany him to Louisiana to dispose of the property. On a lark—and to get out of a certain female's tightening clutches—he accepted.

And now the only person he had cared a whit about was dead and here he was—stuck in this hellhole of a place, waiting to recuperate from attempted murder so he could be tried for murder! Given the pattern of his life to date, it was singularly revolting but entirely fitting.

A rooster crowed first and then he heard sounds of stirring. A small cough, a whisper, then soft steps overhead.

From somewhere came the deep-throated bray of a donkey, muted by distance but still an affront to the ears. And from the yard came the proud cackling of a hen and the fragrance of a wood fire. The paltry morning light breached the cheesecloth window cover and made a splattered pattern on the floor.

There had to be some way to turn this situation to his advantage . . .

As if an answer had come down from on high, two small narrow feet and some very shapely ankles began to descend the rawhide ladder that led from the loft.

As he watched, he lifted one brow and he thought: Well, well. Would it be appropriate to say . . . Ask and ye shall receive?

Ten

As her mother had warned, nine, blind Miss Markie Dare could talk the legs off a chair, but Jean had found her entertaining. So far. Within days he had heard quite a lot about an interesting array of subjects, but mostly he heard about his host family, the Dares.

It amazed him that Evie Dare was the mother of the three burly black-haired men who were as long-legged as she was short. Also amazing was the fact that there had once been twelve Dares, all birthed by the same rawboned and wind-burned female.

All the Dares bore a marked family resemblance, with square, strong-boned faces, high foreheads and determined jaws. They had long upper lips and full lower ones and bright, black eyes beneath thick, straight brows. However, in spite of these physical similarities, Jean had found it a simple matter to keep the brothers' names straight . . . because they were all named Jack.

He had asked their mother if that was so and she replied, "Why not? Jack's my favorite name."

"Of course!" he said and waved his hand as if to say: I am still addled with fever. "Why not indeed."

She went on to say that when someone had suggested that outsiders might have trouble telling her boys apart she decided to add her favorite colors, hence their first names: Black, Golden who was called Goldie, and Blue.

Black Jack was in love with Markie's school teacher, Miss Annie Mapes. Markie held her teacher in very high esteem and dearly wished that Miss Mapes loved her brother back because then Miss Mapes would marry Jack and become a Dare . . . but of all the rotten luck, Miss Mapes was already promised to marry another, namely Abel O'Neal, the young attorney Jean had met at Maude Stone's boarding house the first night he arrived in town.

Now Markie said her mother was worried that her eldest son would leave Tejas. Actually, her mother had said she would be surprised if he did not.

Apparently Black Jack Dare was not the sort to stay and watch another man live the life he wanted for himself.

Lately, Markie said, it had got so even she sometimes wished Jack would take himself elsewhere. The other day Goldie flat out told him that, and they "got into it" and now they scarcely saw their big brother any more and when they did he looked so mean and dirty that everybody just turned around and went the other way.

Abel O'Neal. Jean recalled the sheriff suggesting that he retain young O'Neal as his counsel when he was able to stand trial. The sheriff's recommendation was not necessarily on merit; by his own admission, O'Neal was the only attorney in town.

"The thing is," Markie was saying. "I plan to marry Abel O'Neal myself. Unless I die."

That last caught his attention. She looked like the picture of health. "Do you feel poorly?" he asked as he studied her. She wore her ebony hair in a single braid that was as shiny as her face.

"No, but if I die, I won't marry, now will I?"

"I . . . guess not."

She interested him, this intelligent and sensitive child. She had a sunny disposition and no apparent bitterness about her disability. Further, for a sightless person she was remarkably self-sufficient. Earlier her mother had dropped a sack of potatoes in her lap which she was deftly peeling and dropping into a bucket of water.

She had collected some eggs as well and they sat beside her, small brown speckled things that reposed on a bed of sawdust in a woven basket. His comment about the large number of them brought a rejoinder from her. Apparently she'd had trouble finding two hens' nests and would have to ask for her sister's help. Fortunately her sister knew just about everything there was to know about chickens.

"Of which sister do you speak?"

"Brit."

"Ah. Pray continue. You say that she knows just about everything there is to know about . . . chickens?"

"Mister, what Brit doesn't know about chickens has not been discovered yet."

"Really?"

"She can go outside in the morning, look at which chickens are roosting in the trees and which ones are perched on the fence posts and she can tell right where they've laid their eggs that day."

She paused to spit on a scrape on her knee and rubbed it in as she continued.

"Why, I've seen her name a chicken jus' by lookin' at the little crucifixes it leaves in the dirt."

"An invaluable talent."

"Yep. That Brit eats an' sleeps chickens. Rather talk about them than just about anything there is."

"Is that a fact?"

"Yep."

"Tell me . . ."

As it happened he was watching the subject of their conversation as he spoke. Brit had just appeared at the edge of the woods and was slowly moving toward them. Ahead of her she was gently prodding two stout and low-to-the-ground pigs. ". . . do people have trouble telling your sisters apart?"

It was merely idle conversation on his part, but Markie was encouraged to explain how she, being blind, had always told them apart by their natures and not by their faces.

"But Maw says it's easy once a person gets one thing straight . . ."

"And that is?"

"That all geese are swans to Irish and that all swans are geese to Brit. That's the key to the twins in a nutshell."

"I see," he said, although that was the furthest thing from the truth.

She went on to explain that Irish had a nature like Jack and Goldie while Brit was just the opposite. "Brit's more like Blue than anyone. You know what they call Blue in town?"

"I can't imagine."

"Hell Without the Fire."

"So she has a fiery temperament, eh." Jean found that arousing. Matter of fact, he was finding much to be aroused about these days. The more he healed the more he remembered, and he suspected Brit made sure of that by placing herself in front of him a dozen times a day. Bringing him his food, or clean bandages or a cool drink. She never spoke unless he spoke first, and then only about mundane matters. Never about shared intimacies. He found it amusing, this charade they played.

"See, it isn't so much the way the twins look but how they look at life. And what things they know the most about."

The girl was right. One look at those naturally swaying hips and suddenly even he had been able to tell which twin was which.

"Take Brit for example . . ."

Delighted, he thought.

"One time a king snake was crawling under the house and eating all of Lady Barbara's eggs."

"Lady Barbara?"

"Uh-huh. One of our very best layers. But Brit knew exactly what to do. First she found a rock that looked just like an egg and then she painted it white and then she set it in the nest alongside all the other eggs. That night the king snake ate it and choked to death. I heard its death strangle myself. Woke me from a dead sleep." She put her hands around her neck and let her tongue loll. "Akkk . . . Akkk. Akkk. Pfft!"

"That is the sound of a snake strangling?"

"Oh yeah. No doubt about that. I've heard lots of 'em. It's a real anogizing death."

"Agonizing."

"That too."

Brit was urging the pigs into an opening in a wood fence. "By the way, your sister Brit appears to be putting two pigs into a little wooden . . ."

"No! no!" Markie cried and stoppered her ears. "Don't tell me. Don't tell me what she's doin'!" A moment went by. She lowered her hands and opened her eyes . . . though why she needed to be concerned about the latter was unclear to him.

"All right. Tell me . . . does one of 'em have a pink circle around its left eye . . . ?"

"Well . . ."

"No! No! Don't tell me."

"Why, what is it?" She looked quite forlorn.

"I can't hardly eat ham any more. It still doesn't sit right with me, you know? Even after Blue told me the awful truth about pigs."

"Is there an awful truth about pigs?"

"Yes. They don't age at all. Soon as they get to be two or three years old they go crazy and must be put down for their own good."

"I did not know . . ."

"Yeah, it's true. Otherwise there's no tellin' what they'll

do. Blue told me there was a man who lived only three miles from our farm back in Tennessee. Fell and hit his head one day and a pig that he had hand-fed all its life ate off half his face! Right down to the ears. Blue said he saw him afterward. Said he wore a sorta melted-looking hat, trying to cover up his face . . . but Blue said it was near impossible to hide somethin' like that." She shook her head and shivered. "Boy, I'm glad I couldn't see 'im."

"Hand-fed it all its life?"

"Yep. Isn't that awful?"

"Hard to believe," he said, enthralled with her in spite of himself.

She shrugged. "Nothing can be done. Pigs are like humans that way. Some'll be bad no matter what, an' Blue says we jus' can't afford to take that chance."

"I see."

She selected another potato. "I'll bet I'm the only person you know who knows of somebody who's got only half a face."

"Come to think of it . . . you are right."

"An' I know two!" she crowed. "But . . ." She gave a superior sort of sniff. "That's another story for another day. I will say this much . . . it has to do with the people who own the sawmill. You know, Irish works for Mr. Schumacher a couple of times a week."

This sounded promising. Perhaps the twins shared appetites as well as appearances. "What does she do for him?"

"Run things I imagine. Maw says runnin' things is what Irish was made for. A big house. Ten kids. A sawmill. Anything no one else wants to tackle, that's the thing to give to Irish. You know how much she gets for takin' care of the Schumacher kid? Fifty cents a time . . ." She cocked her head. "Hear that?"

"What?" He looked around. "Hear what?"

"That." She hunkered down and with unfailing accuracy found a brown beetle that had somehow gotten itself upside down. It lay with its legs flailing and was buzzing like a saw. She righted it and then she returned to her seat and took up her work again.

"Don't you just love a june bug? I mean, how can something so little be so loud? That's what I'd like to know."

"They have very large mouths. Like some other little things I know."

"I know somebody who has the biggest big toes in the en-tire world."

"Who?"

"You!"

"Who says?"

"Brit!"

"Hah!" He resisted the urge to look down. "They are perfect for my size."

"Not according to Brit."

"I wonder how many big toes she has examined . . ."

"I'll ask her."

"Please do. What else did she say?"

"That you have black hair like us only it is kinda curly on the ends. And you have bushy brows and eyes the color of wild ginger. She says your nose is long and narrow and that you have full lips and freckles on your back an' a lotta scars . . ."

"She did, eh?"

"Must've been in a lotta fights, huh?"

"No, just accident prone."

"You are? Me too!" Markie waited but he had fallen silent. She shrugged. She had been hoping he would tell her about his accidents because then she could tell him about hers. She used to fall all the time but she almost never did any more.

A chunk fell in the fire and another potato hit the water with a plop, but Jean was staring sightlessly into the empty yard.

Actually two of his scars were from ladies. His former mistress had shot him when she learned he was ending their affair. Fortunately she was a better paramour than she had been a shot. She had formed a liaison with another protector faster than his flesh wound had formed a scab.

The other scar was from a fiery Italian actress who had attempted to stab him in the back while keeping her dress clean. Her odd stance had thrown her off balance and prevented the wound from being fatal. The other two scars were from duels. He had bled a bit, while his opponents had died. Such was the essence of his life back in Paris. Dueling. Women. Cards. Women. Dueling. Dice. Women . . . always plenty of women.

"Say, have you ever stuck a pea up your nose?"

Apparently he had lost the thread of the conversation. "What?"

"A pea. You know. Up your nose."

"Ah . . . no."

Jean was destined to be distracted further still. Brit had dumped something in to the now-penned pigs and stood shading her eyes in order to see something in the distance. As if hypnotized he stared at the gently curved shadow she made on the shed wall.

"I used to do that all the time. Maw got so fed up with me she said I'd have to wait till my nose holes grew big enough for the pea to roll out."

"Sounds reasonable to me," he said.

Now Brit was crossing the yard and a kindly breeze had pressed her shapeless work dress against her round, firm bosom and long, freely moving legs.

She had thick lustrous hair and beautiful skin but her true beauty lay in her eyes, which were wide apart, slanted and black as coal.

It was completely amazing to him . . . that such a truly beautiful female should be in this Godforsaken wilderness, let alone two!

"Say you aren't sleepin', are you?"

"Sorry."

"You sure got quiet all of a sudden."

"I think I may have become a bit feverish."

It was true. That vision of nubile beauty and the memory of his dream had made him quite "feverish" feeling. "Please go on. I am enrapt."

"Yer whut?"

"I am . . . very interested."

"About what?"

"The pea!"

"Oh, yeah, the pea. Well, Blue finally cured me of that business. Told me a person who'll do that makes their whole future chancy 'cause given half a chance a pea'll sprout an' grow upward into the person's brain . . . an' then the person has a pea brain the en-tire rest of their lives. I quit right then. I turned out pretty smart so far, don't you think?"

"Very." And relentless and painfully straightforward.

"All us Dares are smart. We were borned that way and Maw says onct you have all your smarts you can't ever lose 'em. Unless a mule kicks you in the head or you fall outa a tree."

Markie knew she had lost him again. She tilted her head and listened carefully. No question about it, the doctor was interested in something else much more than he was interested in talking to her, but the question was what?

Brit the beauty had returned to the yard. Now she had a basket crooked on one arm and was swinging an empty bucket by its rope handle. He watched the way the sun struck the honeyed planes of her face and then, until she had passed out of sight, the way the tuft of her braid brushed across the top of her rear.

"You don't have much to say for yourself, do you?"

"Sorry. What would you like me to say?"

She thought a minute. "Tell me what you did where you used to live."

"I concerned myself with my amusement." Dodging eager young virgins and marriage-bent mamas.

"Curin' sick people?"

"Perhaps a few." A more truthful answer would be: None. He had never really practiced medicine and, if it weren't for Duncan's illness, he would not have even brought his medical supplies with him. A wise move in hindsight.

"What sorta stuff did you cure? Arrow holes? Or bullet holes? Say, did you ever sew a scalp back on?"

"No." He gave her a curdled look which she, of course, could not see. "I mostly specialized in vapor fits and, ah, melancholia."

"What's that mean. Melan . . . colly?"

"Dissatisfaction with one's lot in life."

She snorted. "Heck, even I could cure that."

"How?"

"Change your life."

He sighed. "You know, I can't understand why I didn't see that. To think that I wasted all that time."

"Oh, well, can't be helped now."

"No. I suppose not. Too bad."

"Yeah. Too bad."

His treatment for melancholia had often been of a more . . . personal nature. Sometimes his being a physician was a useful means for conducting an assignation. But he could hardly tell his companion about those "cures" and so concocted a few tales of patients at death's door, cured by this odd thing or that and then he lamely finished with . . . "But lately I have been absorbed with research and so have treated very few individuals."

"Did you ever treat . . ." She lowered her voice and muttered darkly ". . . black tongue?"

"Black tongue?" She nodded. "Mm. Perhaps. I can't be sure."

"You haven't then. You'd know if you'd cured somebody with black tongue."

"Not necessarily. Perhaps in France it is known as . . . black gum." She was shaking her head. "Why not?"

"First off, 'cause the gums are not afflicted. Only the tongue. An' second off, cause it's so horrible you could never forget it if you ever saw it."

He was curious in spite of himself. "In what way is it so bad?"

"The tongue turns black and starts shrinkin'. Every day, little by little it gets smaller an' smaller till . . ." She scrunched her shoulders and pulled in her neck ". . . it is littler'n a goose tongue!"

"Mon Dieu! What happens then?"

"The poor person can't keep from swallowin' it an' so . . . they die."

He played along. "Any known survivors?"

"None known. There was one man who almost made it. Oh, it was a terribly sad case!"

"How so?"

"The poor fella thought he'd found the cure. Tied a string around his tongue to keep it from slippin' down his throat but he'd forgot one thing."

"What?"

"His cat."

"His cat?"

"Crept up on him when he was sleepin', saw the string hangin' outa his mouth an' thought it was somethin' to play with."

"Voilà! Instant death!"

She suspected he was silently laughing. "Well, not instant but it was over pretty quick."

"How does one get the black tongue?"

"Not *the* black tongue. Just black tongue."

"Sorry."

She must've been wrong about his poking fun because now he sounded seriously interested. "Dirt build-up."

"Ah!"

"Maw says people who don't clean their mouths good are the most liable to get it. That's how come I ask Maw to look at my tongue every mornin' to see if it looks clean or not." She stuck out her tongue. "Looks pretty good, huh?"

"Actually it looks a little blue."

"Blue? Oh, that's all right. That's just from some ol' berries I ate." A bit of time passed. She quartered two more potatoes but before she quartered another, she set the sack aside and said, "I'll be right back."

Half smiling, he folded his arm beneath his head and observed the yard through the open door.

Chickens, eh? A week ago he wasn't sure he would have recognized one in its natural state. Of course he knew about chicken pox and coq au vin but actually very little about just plain chickens.

No, wait a minute. That wasn't entirely correct. He did recall having seen an unplucked one on several occasions before, namely at a pub on the Thames. It had been painted on a sign alongside a huge pig. The Cock 'n' Boar. Yes, that was the place.

He felt measurably better despite the fact that the only time he could recall ever seeing a chicken in motion was when the sign was swinging in the wind.

"You know what Mr. Schumacher did all day yesterday?"

"No, what?"

Brit and Irish were kneading dough at the table.

"Planted trees!"

"Planted trees?"

The girls spoke quietly so they did not disturb the doctor. It was late afternoon and he appeared to be asleep.

"Yep. Apple trees."

"Goodness. All day?"

"Yep. His day off. Had Garlock get them for him. Twigs that stood about yeah high." She held a floury hand out over the floor. "Planted them all up and down the creek behind his place."

"I'll be."

"He said he just loves apples. Apple pie. Apple cobbler. Said he'll eat an apple over a biscuit any day."

"Really?"

"I thought I'd see if Maw'd mind if I took him a apple raisin pie."

"I'm sure she wouldn't."

"He's the nicest man!"

Brit noticed that her sister was smiling an odd little smile. "Is he?"

"Uh-huh. Nice but sad."

"Sad?"

"Mm. Even when he's doing things that should make him happy."

The one who sounded sad was her sister. "Because of his wife, you think?"

"I don't know. That has to be part of it."

"Maybe it's just his nature. Or it could be because of where he's from."

"He is different. No doubt about that."

Well, Brit could tell that from looking at him. Big, ruddy-faced fella, he was, with white blond hair and blue eyes. Strange speaking, of course, since he was from Germany. Which was not that far from France but which was real far from Tejas.

"You like it all right then?"

"I never said I didn't."

"Maybe not, but you acted like you didn't."

"I did not."

"Did too."

"Girls!"

Both girls looked over their shoulders at their mother and then back at their work and Brit whispered. "Did too!"

Eleven

Dusk that night found the family gathered on the porch, because it was a warm and clement night and because Evie thought they should partake of it. "Winter's nigh an' we'll be pokin' each other in the ribs soon enough." Goldie and Blue made a seat out of their arms and carried Jean outside as well.

As the night sky deepened from gray to black, the stars emerged and joined the pale yellow of the rising moon. Shadows streaked the yard and fireflies blinked among the tall grass. Birds twittered as they settled in for the night and then the crickets and frogs took up the slack. To Jean it was incredibly peaceful.

Evie sat in the stretched cowhide chair that she said had been made for her by her husband Otis. Markie sat on the stump that also served as a step. Irish leaned against the wall just under the window so the light would shine on the job at hand. She was straining honey into several crocks, the product of a bee tree that Goldie had robbed. Brit sat with the churn between her spread knees, methodically lifting and lowering, lifting and lowering . . . Jean rested on his pallet and admired the set of her down-bent head and the way her hair gleamed in the candlelight.

He was so enrapt with the pale ivory glow that the settling night had given her face, that he had to be spoken to twice.

"Jean. Jean!" Irish had scooped out a piece of dark honey with a deep golden comb and laid it on a piece of bark. "Here you go."

"Thank you!" he said and concentrated on keeping the primitive plate level.

"Who else wants some?"

"I do!" said Markie. "I do!"

"Better get some more while you can, Jean" said Goldie. "These girls'll suck up that stuff like water."

"Look who's talking!"

"It is sooo good! Mm-mm."

"Here, Brit."

"I can't stop right now. The butter's almost made."

"All right. Get ready."

Brit opened her mouth and her sister set some on her tongue. "Mm," she said. "Good."

"More?"

"Yes," she said and her eyes closed as her mouth did the same on the spoon. "Mm!"

When Irish pulled the spoon out there was a quick sucking noise that Jean would ever more remember as one of the most succulent sounds he had ever heard and Markie's head came up with a snap . . .

"Who made that big slurp?"

"I did," said Brit, giggling. "Irish didn't give me enough time to suck it off!"

Jean was unmindful of the honey that dripped off his fingers and onto his pallet because he couldn't quit looking at her. Her tongue snaked out to lick her lips and desire knifed through him. His skin tingled and his blood hummed.

"Did you speak, Doctor?"

Jean realized Evie was addressing him. "What?"

"Sounded like you growled."

"A twinge . . ."

"Another twinge, eh?"

"You must get about one a minute."

He shot Goldie a look and then returned to brooding. He could not decide if the girl was a coquettish siren or an innocent schoolgirl, but if she was the latter then he would be well to put Tejas far behind him. The desire he felt was not at all appropriate for a young ingenue. With that in mind he had already asked Blue to take a message to the sheriff; namely that his wound would soon be healed enough for him to travel but when Blue returned he said the sheriff wanted him to stay put. They could not hold a trial without a judge, and the sheriff had a "full plate" without having to be concerned with Jean's safety.

"Ah, tell me Madame Dare . . . what are you making?"

"A blanket," she replied. "I'm gonna sell it to the same fella who buys Goldie's stuff."

Blue said, "She makes 'em so tight they'll hold water." He took down a whetstone that was permanently hung on a nail near the door and commenced sharpening his knife. "Garlock offered her two dollars for the last one. Two dollars!"

"Garlock said she should stop everything she was doing and card sheep wool as fast as she could. Said he could sell everything that she could make." Jack was rubbing neatsfoot oil on a fancy Mexican saddle he had won in a dice game.

"As if I didn't have nothin' else to do." Her hands stilled and she looked away. "My cousin's wife taught me. Poor Ollie Ruth. Lord, I ain't thought of her in years. Had two cross-eyed kids, one right after the other."

"Maw, wasn't it Ollie Ruth who had the pet squirrel named Toonuta?"

"It was! Oh, Lord! I'd forgotten all about that!"

"I never heard of making a pet of a squirrel," said Jean.

Irish slapped a corncob stopper into the mouth of one jug and started on the next. "Ollie Ruth found the squirrel when it was just a baby an' raised it like one. I was pretty young but I remember how it would hold a pecan in its little hands and use its teeth to peel it around the middle. When it was finished it would take the two ends off and there would be two halves of perfect meat."

Blue picked up the story. "Ollie Ruth's son Hays would wait till the squirrel had one all peeled an' ready to eat and then he'd snatch it away an' eat it hisself."

Goldie pulled on his pipe. "Squirrel would get so blamed mad you could hear it chatterin' from a mile down the road."

"One time when Hays leaned in to get the pecan, Toonuta bit his finger clear to the bone. Hays let off a howl an' lit off after the squirrel with Ollie Ruth after him, hollerin' she'd kill him if he killed her squirrel."

"Never did move that joint again."

Jean was watching Brit. She had finished with the churning and was leaning back against one of the posts. She looked over at him then and their eyes locked and the others seemed to fade away somewhere leaving them alone in a silence that felt as weighty as a sodden blanket. He stared at her and she stared right back. God, she was a sensual-looking woman!

Evie felt like one of Ollie Ruth's cross-eyed kids, trying to keep one eye on her work and the other on the Frenchman. Oh, yeah, she had seen the way his gaze sought Brit out, the way his eyes always lingered on her face and form. Noticed it almost from the beginning.

Like most mothers, she was concerned that each of her girls find a good man and it was her considered opinion that the Frenchman was a good man for Brit. Clean and healthy. Wealthy and a doctor to boot! Seemed like somebody'd fixed them up to match, way her Brit liked doctoring and had learned so much about it. Evie smiled. Who knows? Something just might come of it. Something just might.

Irish said, "There's a circle around the moon tonight."

"Looks like a big wagon wheel," said Brit.

Then after a minute, Evie said, "Why not play a little, Markie."

"All right, but only if Goldie won't sing along."

"I won't, Goober."

Blue said, "Goldie sings like a saw."

"Can't carry a tune in a corked jug."

"I wouldn't mind, Goldie, but it throws me off."

"I said I won't." But his face was so full of devilment Jean was certain he would break his promise.

Markie brought out her fiddle and plucked the strings. Before she started to play she patted her foot and counted softly under her breath and the Dares exchanged looks and smiled. The tune was an Americanized version of "Yankee Doodle Dandy."

Jean had expected to have to fake enthusiasm for Markie's talent but in reality she was quite good. When she finished he complimented her and she pulled in her neck and blushed prettily.

In contrast to "Yankee Doodle" her next tune was soft and slow and almost sad sounding. At its end Jean asked the tune's name.

"I haven't thought of one yet."

"You wrote it?"

"No . . . not really. The tune went through my mind when I said the words to a poem I learned."

"Say the poem for us, Markie!"

"Yeah! Say it, Goober."

"Abel O'Neal taught it to me. Guess what happened the first time I heard it."

"I cannot imagine."

"My innards went funny on me."

"They did?"

"Uh-huh. At first I thought it was 'cause of the beauty of the poem but now I think it was on account of the sound of his voice." She ducked her head and played with a string hanging on her pocket. "I was afraid my innards might never be right again."

"Say it for us, Markie."

"It is a really famous poem about daffodils. Have you heard it, Doctor?"

Jean did a rapid . . . very rapid . . . inventory of his repertoire of poems but he could recall none about daffodils.

"Written by a man named Wordsworth . . ."

"Ah!" said Jean. "I was about to say it must be a Wordsworth work."

"Why?"

"The man was crazy about daffodils."

"He was?"

"Loved them. Talked about them all the time."

"He dee-ud?"

Irish rolled her eyes at him. "Say it, Markie."

> I wandered lonely as a cloud
> That floats on high o'er vales and hills,
> When all at once I saw a crowd,
> A host of golden daffodils;
> Beside the lake, beneath the trees
> Fluttering and dancing in the breeze.

"Mr. O'Neal told Markie about the poem but he never said its name." Markie opened her mouth to say something about Brit's comment but she got her foot stepped on so that "OW" came out instead. Irish looked at Brit and thought she had a real sly look in her eye. "Perhaps the doctor can tell us the poem's name?"

Bugger! Now everyone was watching him. "Of course. Let's see . . . what was that one called. It's . . . It's right on the tip of my tongue."

Brit twisted her lips. "Maybe you'll recall it in the morning."

"Maybe."

"Then again, maybe not. Maybe poems are not your speciality."

Why, the little tease! She knew full well what his specialty was!

"Time for bed. Markie, help your ol' maw up now."

The women retired but the men remained. Jack snuffed the candle so their faces were shadowed solely by the moon, and Goldie passed a jug of corn liquor while the talk went from whiskey to women to war. The Indian trouble was discussed. Apparently the last Comanche raid had resulted in the loss of a score of good ponies for several settlers to the west.

"The Comanche are good horsemen, aren't they?"

"The best," said Jack. "You see one on horseback, you don't know where the man ends and the pony begins."

"An' let there be no question about their courage."

The Dare men were in accord on that.

"Sonsabitches won't never quit."

"Fearless. Tireless."

Jack said he was in a fight once where a Comanche got his right arm broken by a musket ball. The Indian ran into a little clump of trees and Jack went in to finish him off. He found himself facing a drawn bow with an arrow pointed straight at his heart.

"Damn crazy Indian was holding the bow in his left hand and drawing back the arrow with his teeth. I was so amazed I almost didn't duck in time. Next thing I knew he had grabbed my horse an' was making his getaway. Damn arm floppin' around jus' like his hair."

Jean accepted the tobacco Goldie offered. "Is it true that only when an Indian is completely surprised can the white man best him in speed of arming his weapon?"

"It's true."

"Yeah." Blue nodded. "You gotta give 'em that."

"Then I have often wondered why the Indian does not keep his bow constantly strung. That way he could be ever ready."

"That's a good idea," said Jack. "Only problem is if a bow is kept constantly strung the stick will weaken and the arrow loses its force."

"An' they can sure shoot with force. I once saw a killed man who'd been arrow shot in the side. Went in one arm, clear across his middle and come out through the other arm."

Blue said that during the same fight a ranger had been killed with an arrow in the eye.

Not to be out-harrowed, Jean told about the famous king named Harold who had been killed the same way. "Happened at the Battle of Hastings in the year 1066."

"Hard way to go," said Goldie. "Don't much matter when it happens."

"I've seen harder." And then Blue told about a gut shot man who was in so much pain he used his bare hands in order to enlarge his wound and die quicker.

Out harrowed at last, Jean fell silent and reflective and struck by the conversation and its timeless quality. It seemed to him that a person might draw a parallel between their talk that night and thousands of similar ones throughout the ages. In tents and caves and in castles and keeps—wherever small gangs of men had been gathered together. All of it tied up with the struggle for survival and the strongest bond some men would ever know. While wenching or gaming in Paris he had never lacked for companions but he only now realized that he had never really known true companionship.

He also could not help but draw a comparison between the Dares' conversation and the drawing room prattle to which he was often subjected. And which had always bored him to distraction.

Suddenly a cow bawled as if it had been surprised, and all talk ceased while the Dares searched the timberline. Jean looked as well, but in a minute the air eased and the Dares returned to their tasks.

"How can you tell that it was nothing to be alarmed about?"

"Look yonder."

Goldie pointed under a bush where a cat had one leg stiff in the air and its nose buried under its tail and then over at an old mare who stood stock still in the corral. "The Indians're real good at creepin' an' crawlin' but they ain't that good."

In time the talk turned to Hap Pettijohn who was still after more men to ride his route. Jean described his ride from hell and everyone laughed softly.

Jack had finished with the saddle and before he put it away he showed Jean its silver conchos and fancy leather trapaderos and then he pointed out a scarred place on the cantle and told how the previous owner had been lucky enough to outrun some Kiowa a few weeks earlier.

"Unfortunately his partner would not have any luck if it weren't bad. We found 'im about three days later."

"Dirty bastards!" Blue spat. "There's no Indian worse'n a Kiowa."

The troop had followed the Indians and confronted them near a little stream but they "fought shy" and ran at first fire so the rangers split up to pursue them and that was when part of the troop had a strange encounter. Blue said that he and Jesse McIninch and Ed Cox rode into a swale and up and found a lone buck and a woman, watering their horses in a mott of alamos.

"Quick as spit the Indian drew his knife and killed his woman! Then he came at us like a damn crazy man! Took five balls to put him down. We three jus' stood there lookin' at that dead buck an his dead squaw an' we didn't know what to make of it. Come to find out he wasn't even one of the raiders we were after but a damn Kickapoo!"

"Why did he kill his woman?"

Blue shrugged. "Exactly what I asked He-Coon later. We had not increased our pace or raised our weapons but we did look like we were loaded for bear. He-Coon said the Kickapoo probably made a snap decision. Looked at us and figured we intended to kill him so we could outrage his woman. Since he had no chance of survivin', he decided to save his woman from us awful white men an' then go down fightin'."

Blue looked at Jean and the moon showed the perplexed expression on his face. "It ain't like any of us would've ill used that squaw! Hell, I wouldn't touch one with a ten-foot pole!"

"It don't stop you from lookin'."

"That's a damned lie!"

There was dead silence while Goldie and Blue stared at each other.

"Aw, unruffle your feathers, Blue," said Jack. "I heard the same damn thing."

Blue stood. "Then I'll say the same to you. That's a bald-faced lie. The day I look at a damn Cherokee squaw is the day I'll put my gun barrel in my mouth!"

"How'd you know we were talkin' about Jane Yellow Cat?"

"She's the only Indian lives in Sweet Home, ain't she?"

Blue was tense as a bow string but his brothers just looked at him with bland and unreadable expressions. After a long minute, he stomped off, kicking at twigs and muttering under his breath.

Jean had heard about the Cherokee girl named Jane Yellow Cat from Markie. Once a Comanche captive, she had been rescued by the troop some months back and had been taken in by Annie Mapes and her family.

There had been trouble about her attending school with

the other kids but Markie said Miss Mapes had put an end
to that. Said she would quit over it. Since the townspeople
had just gotten used to having a teacher, they did not want
Miss Mapes to do that.

Markie liked the Indian girl. She said what she didn't
know about bugs had not been discovered yet. And certain
insects were of particular interest to Markie at that time.
Especially those that sing, of which she had heard there
were more than ten thousand varieties. And doodle bugs.
She told him she was very interested in doodle bugs and
Jean had said whatever they were and Markie said she
would bring one to him. It made waking up worthwhile.

Apparently the Cherokee girl was quite attractive and
more than one single man had been giving her what
Goldie termed the "hairy eye." From the sound of the
slammed door on the brothers' cabin, it was obvious that
Blue did not intend to be included in that group.

Brit and Irish could hear the low hum of conversation
from the porch. The deep rumble of Goldie's laugh then
Blue's voice which they noticed because it sounded angry.

Their brothers often sat up late talking. Normally it
would not have kept them awake. To the contrary, it was
soothing to them, knowing that their brothers were awake
and watchful while they slept. Only, neither girl was sleeping. Brit was thinking about the way Jean had looked at
her earlier, savoring everything he had done and said.
There was so much she prized about him. Little things like
the way he threw back his head when he laughed, and the
line that formed between his brows when he listened. The
way he looked at Markie. With affection and perhaps a bit
of dismay.

She thought he was wonderful. Better than wonderful.
He was perfect.

Irish, on the other hand, was thinking about the only

secret she had ever had and wondering how long she could keep it a secret before it welled up and spilled out. Not long now. No, knowing herself, not long at all.

Twelve

Jean was being carted outside in the morning and carted back inside at night which was, as Goldie pointed out, not unlike the piss pot. Jean did not care what they compared him to. Observing the goings-on around him was a huge improvement over staring at a knife cut on the plank floor.

That's where he was on the morning following. It was shortly after dawn. A fog hung in the low areas but the air was crisp and promising. He was enjoying the acrid bite of his first pipe when he saw Brit come out of the hen house and walk toward him. He waited until she was about to pass him by then he cleared his throat and smiled invitingly. She paused. "You've got some eggs," he said and pointed at the basket she carried.

"Yes," she said and showed him the contents of the small basket which was mounded with several brown speckled eggs. Feathers and bits of chicken shit clung to a few.

She smiled and he smiled back but inwardly he was frowning. He could not help but think that there might be something amiss. No matter how superficial the relationship, there is generally a sort of counterfeit closeness affected by those who have shared intimacies, yet he could detect none with her. It made him stop and wonder if his dream was less real than he thought. But he knew that some of it had happened. He just knew that it had.

He glanced over his shoulder. The old woman worked

only a few feet away. Perhaps that was it. Perhaps she was constrained by her mother's presence. Unfortunately there was no way to know for sure. He cocked his head and studied her as she captured a strand of hair that blew across her face and tucked it behind her ear.

Interesting, he thought. She had the same square jaw, full lips and fierce black brows as her brothers but she had small ears, delicate of shape and flat to her head while her brothers' ears might levitate them in an upwardly moving wind.

He had never found ears to be particularly erotic but apparently they were now. He shifted, forgot his wound and grimaced.

"All right?"

"Yes, fine. Merely a twinge."

"That's good," she said and bent to pick up her basket. Mentally he scrambled for a means to prolong their encounter. "You know, I learned something very interesting today."

"Did you?"

He let her see the frank admiration in his eyes but she just stood gazing at him with that unnerving look of hers. Like she knew things about him he would prefer she didn't. "About chickens."

"Chickens?"

He pointed at the yard and smiled again. "I've long had an interest in them. Terribly indecisive creatures, aren't they?"

"I don't know. Are they?"

"They have always seemed so to me. Crazy things! For example, take that little gray one over there."

She looked. "Emma. A spotty layer."

"No wonder!"

"Why do you say that?"

"Since she cannot make up her mind whether she is

coming or going, I can easily see why she cannot nest long enough to do her business."

She looked over at the chicken and then she looked at him.

"She appears content now but if you had observed her earlier, you would see she is prone to extremely aberrant, er, highly irregular behavior . . ."

"Like what?" She stood holding her elbows, waiting.

"She seems to suffer from a nervous disorder of some sort. For no apparent reason she will suddenly jerk her head violently right then left followed immediately by a burst of frenzied running while squawking and flapping her wings in a most bizarre manner. Then . . . again for no visible reason . . . she will suddenly stop. Run. Stop. Run. She seems to consider flying. Decides not to and re-settles herself. Fluffs her feathers. Folds her wings and struts for a time. Then she returns to her previous preoc-cupation. Pecking and clucking." His eyes examined hers then he smiled. "I find them quite fascinating."

"If you say so."

"No, please. I would be interested in your opinion. What do you think?"

"I don't. At least not about chickens." She turned and walked off. A spotted dog fell in behind her and in a mo-ment they had rounded the corner of the cabin.

"Markie!" he muttered.

"Yeah?"

Her face appeared around the corner. She had her hand over her mouth. The little prankster! He modulated his tone. "Markie! How fortuitous! I was just thinking about you."

"You were?"

Her head was tilted to one side, as if she were listening to something.

"Come and let's talk for a moment . . . my little pet."

"Whut about?" Her eyes were vigilant and sly, like those of a denned fox.

"Nothing in particular. Let's just, you know, have one of our little chats."

She considered that for a minute and then she shook her head. "I don't think so. I think maybe I'll come back another time."

Merde, she was sharp!

That night Jean dreamt again, only this time it was more a nightmare than a dream, and unsettling in the extreme. He clearly saw himself back in France, only it was some years hence, for he was a much older man and God, he looked awful! An indolent slug with pouchy eyes and a sunken chest. Obviously he had returned to France and apparently picked up where he had left off, with a string of affairs and then a convenient marriage to Vivica De Marco.

Pale, glacial Vivica, a Plantagenet-like woman about whom everything cried: I am pure! I am chaste! Which had been precisely what she had said as she put up the requisite resistance to his attentions. Of course he eventually got her bodice to her waist and of course he found perfumed breasts and brightly rouged nipples.

Vivica had always endowed herself with an aura of secrecy, a practiced deception designed to hint at some hidden mystery. Unfortunately too little was hidden from him now!

The passage of time had not been kind to Vivica, who weighed twice what she had in her prime. Her expression had grown dull and lifeless. Her eyes were vapid and her nose long and as sharp as a knife. Most of her hair had fallen out, and all but of her two teeth.

Really, he was no prize but he was an Adonis in comparison!

They sat together in a room filled with tasseled lamps and embroidered pillows. Each had one gouty foot resting on a pettipoint hassock. He was reading. Ostensibly Vivica was knitting (!) only at that moment she was using the needle to scratch beneath her wig. Horrified, he watched as a little cloud of nits rose above her head and hovered there until she quit. She scratched, they rose. She quit, they settled.

Thus were they passing what appeared to be another typically peaceful evening at home.

Apparently the mantel clock's only purpose was ticking; its face was defaced so one could not tell the time, but the ticking kept growing louder and louder until he thought he would scream, then suddenly with a flash of light it was gone and it was late that night and they were in a canopied bed in a cold and airless room with cobwebbed corners and dog shit on the rug. Vivica's hairy legs were thewed across his back and her black soled feet were bouncing like stuffed puppets against his rear. Fat danced along her thighs and fell backward from her wrists. God, he was sweating over her, working like a dog, but apparently to no avail. He was impotent.

Unfortunately, he had not always been thus. A clearing mist revealed his progeny to him—a fat indolent son with bad skin and a high-pitched voice, and a sly insipid daughter who had her mother's nose and morals. Or lack of them. One brief look into their future and Jean's blood was curdled.

Unlike his sire, the boy would develop no aptitude for gaming and would lose the family fortune. Since he was unqualified for any other endeavor, he would become a politician, and from that realm would develop his talents toward violence and disorder. Arrested and tried as an anarchist, he would ultimately be hanged as a traitor to his country.

Jean's misery did not end there. At age fourteen his

second-born would become impregnated by the dwarf with a troop of traveling troubadours, and when she found parenthood not to her liking, she would abandon her son to his gran'pere and would never be heard from again.

The dream ended with his grandchild, now age seven, successfully setting Jean's home—and only remaining asset—on fire.

He saw himself framed in an upstairs window, staring with horror at the flames that licked the portières and he jerked awake, bathed in sweat.

Dawn had come and turned the land bloody. The rooster crowed, which was the signal for the mule to bray, which was the signal for the dogs to bark.

From the willow boundary along the creek came a hundred different bird songs and a clapper sounded somewhere, the indication that a cow was coming in to be milked.

He crawled outside and was rewarded with his first glimpse of Brit. She was a bucolic picture of grace and enchantment as she strolled along, swinging a bucket in one hand and a big spread-wing bird in the other. She smiled at him and would have passed on but he called to her.

"Wait!" he croaked.

"Yes?"

"Stay and visit with me."

"Visit . . . with you?"

"Yes, please. We can talk."

"About chickens?"

"No. Yes! Whatever you like." He looked at the bird. He looked at her and smiled winningly. He looked back at the bird and frowned. "What *is* that thing?"

"It's called a gobbler and, boy, it's a big one! Must be at least fifteen pounds."

"I thought it was a pterodactyl!"

"A what?"

"A prehistoric bird. Where on earth did you find it?"

"In one of our traps. We have some set up along both sides of the creek."

He wanted to impress her with the intelligence of his questions. He didn't know why that concerned him. His physical prowess should have been impressive enough. (Certainly it had been enough to impress him!) But now, whether it was irrational or not, he wanted an inspired tête-à-tête as well. He scoured his mind and lamely came up with a question about how the trap worked.

"The trap? Well . . ." She looked toward a small shed on the hill then back at him. "Suppose I get one and show you."

"Please do! I'd like that."

He watched her walk away and then glanced down. She had dropped the gobbler on the ground and it was a pathetic thing with its neck folded back on itself and one wing feather twisting in the breeze.

He raised his eyes and lowered his mind and thought of sex. It was a simple matter. All he needed to do was surrender to the images that kept coming to mind.

She brought a trap that her brother Goldie had just repaired and proceeded to show him how it worked. It was an ingenious thing fashioned from woven cane and baited with corn and apple cores. She told him that the traps produced something almost every day. Turkeys, prairie chickens, quail. Often they would produce one of their own chickens, and the errant fowl would have to be soundly scolded and then shooed back toward the cabin.

"Well, I better clean this bird if we're going to eat it tonight."

His smile wavered. "We are going to eat it tonight?"

"Yes." She said it would be stuffed with a spicy concoction of deer sausage and bread, seasoned with wild onions, mustard and sage, and slow roasted in the hearth or baked in the clay oven.

It would be one of the finest meals he would ever have
but of course, he could not have known that then.

He looked at her and she looked at him and then away
and a profound silence fell. She would soon go and he
very much wanted her to stay. "Allow me to help you prepare the, ah, gobbler."

"Really?"

"Yes, of course." He smiled again while thinking, God!
had he fallen so far? He looked at the gobbler and then
at the lissome girl and thought: Yes, apparently he had!

She studied him for a minute. "All right then." Again
she dropped the poor fowl in the dirt. "I'll be right back."

And she was. To pour steaming hot water over the bird.
A particularly noxious smell arose.

"Ugh!" she said with a little laugh. "Don't you hate the
smell of damp feathers?"

"With a passion."

With that she whipped out a knife and made two cuts
on each end of the bird, one to sever its head from its
body and the other to expose a fistful of entrails which
she pulled out and slapped into the nearby bucket. "Bait,"
she said and grinned.

"Great!" he said and grimaced. Though he had never
been this close to his next meal before—and did not care
to be ever again—he found he was willing to be as "native"
as necessary to get his hands on this minx again.

Every time he saw her she was even more alluring than
before. Her face. Her form. Lord, her form was enough
to drive a man insane! With his eyes he followed the curves
of her body beneath the soft fabric of her clothes and his
palms itched to touch her. He must have her again at any
cost. He considered the possibility with great pleasure.

She probably wore very little in the way of undergar-
ments. Maybe a pair of drawers that were soft and thin
from many washings. The prospect of removing them was
arousing him greatly. He remembered their lovemaking

and in his mind he once again felt the subtle smoothness of her buttocks and the tender sweetness of her lips . . .

Brit looked up and caught his eyes on her and he rattled her, looking at her like he did. But not as much as she could rattle herself by looking at him. It made no difference that he wore clothes all the time now—when she saw him, she still saw him naked—or almost—and her fingers itched to touch him again. Even if it was only to smooth his brow or to brush his hair back from his cheek.

He was still watching her. He was always watching her. Of course she had no one to blame but herself.

It had bothered her, the way she'd had to keep putting herself on display for him, but how was he going to *see* her unless he *saw* her?

She really had no choice, but the process made her very uncomfortable.

"I have not had an opportunity to thank you for caring for me when I was out of my mind."

His eyes gleamed into hers and his teeth brightened the rays of the sun. She looked away and her throat contracted like a closed fist. "I didn't do much."

"Ah, but you did. Your mother told me that it was you who sat up with me. Night after night. Often for the entire night. All alone."

He waited for either a denial or some acknowledgment of their intimacy but neither came. Instead she gave him an almost angry look.

"Are you going to pull those feathers or not?"

"What? Oh, yes. The feathers. Most certainly."

He tried to steer the conversation to personal subjects but she asked him about his home and then about Duncan and then from there she pursued other non-essential subjects such as his opinion of the weather, her brothers, Irish and Markie . . . especially Markie.

And he answered at length and with genuine animation, and that surprised him. He had thought he would have to make conversation as best he could but he found that she was amazingly easy to talk to.

And equally easy not to talk to. After a while a comfortable silence fell during which he turned his attention to his duty, albeit grudgingly. By that time there were so many feathers stuck to his hands that it felt like he was wearing gauntlets. He glanced up and found her solemnly looking at him and then she burst out in impetuous laughter. "What?"

"You! You have feathers in your hair and in your eyebrows and stuck on your cheeks and on your chin! What a mess!"

"I am intentionally sticking them there, eh? Look!" He stuck a feather on his forehead. "This way no one will have to chase all over the farm picking up unsightly feathers."

She threw back her head in full-throated mirth. He liked the sound of her laughter and then realized that he was also hearing his own.

I am laughing, he thought with a start. He couldn't remember the last time he had laughed out loud like that.

When the job was finally done she brought him a bucket so he could rid himself of the feathers, but as she handed him a dry cloth, he captured her hand and kept it. He looked at it and then he moved his thumb back and forth across the fragile bones of her wrist. He felt her pulse race and his own jumped in tandem and he thought: it will be fine. Everything will be just fine.

Brit watched him brush his thumb slowly across her hand and she trembled like a leaf in the breeze. He brought her hand to his lips and placed a soft kiss on her fingers and then turned her hand over and placed a light kiss on her palm and her heart started a wild gallop. Her eyes raised from their hands to his face and something stretched between them that was as taut as a wire.

"Brit!"

When her mother hollered she jumped a foot. "Comin'!" She held her wrist at her waist as if it were damaged and then she raised her brows in mock despair. "I have to go now."

He let his eyes drift over her face. "I understand." To Jean the most important word she had spoken was *now.* Unsaid but clearly implied was that she would return *later.* She picked up the gobbler which was particularly pathetic looking now.

"Oh, good! Here comes Irish." She waved. Irish waved back and slid off her pony. Brit said, "How'd it go this morning?"

"Fine." Irish was leading the pony to the corral.

"Anything wrong?"

"No." She smiled a little. "Everything's fine."

Brit watched her sister lower the top bar to the corral and then lead the pony inside. A line had formed between her brows. "Well . . ." She said to Jean. "Back to work."

As she walked away her mind was filled with the fact that he had held her hand and kissed it. She wanted to go to her secret place and think about it. She wanted to put her lips where he had pressed his and re-live every glorious minute.

She was definitely making progress. Oh, yes, that much was obvious. She ought to be overjoyed, but a niggling thought kept intruding: what was wrong with Irish?

She took the turkey to her mother, told her she would be right back and then headed for the corral.

All geese are swans to Irish and all swans are geese to Brit.

If she had heard that once she had heard it a thousand times, and if she had ever believed that it was not true, she did not any more. It was true.

Irish saw things other people did not. She had been known to walk outside on a bleak winter morning and cry, Jiminy! Look at that! And everybody would come roaring outside, thinking the worst, and there would be Irish, pointing at the old oak tree.

The same old tree that had always been right where it was. Always big and thick-trunked. Always wide and jagged-looking. Only, that particular morning Irish would have noticed that there was ice on it or raindrops on it or some blamed thing that had made it look entirely different . . . but only Irish would see it in just that way.

More than once she had wanted to throttle her, but the truth was, Brit did not think she would have seen half the pretty things in the world if Irish hadn't pointed them out to her first. Irish took the time to look. To Brit it was the time itself that counted. That alone was the biggest difference between them.

Oh, there were some other things. Irish was real open with her thoughts and almost never kept them to herself. She was like Markie in that regard. Whatever she was thinking was what she generally said. Brit, on the other hand, liked to keep her opinions to herself, although that wasn't easy to do when people were always poking you and asking you how come you were so quiet.

If there was another difference between them, it was in how they liked to spend their idle time.

Somehow, somewhere along the way Irish had been able to teach herself how to draw what she saw. She had started when she was still in three-cornered pants, making scratches on the walls and drawing in the dirt, but she had kept at it until by now she did it so well a person could look at one of her drawings and almost think they were looking at the real thing.

Nobody knew where she got that. The other Dare kids couldn't draw anything but water.

But none of that mattered now. What mattered now was just one thing: That *she* had always been the moody one and Irish had always been the good-natured one and that people ought not to go changing things like that without first checking with all the parties concerned! These were her thoughts as she found her sister shaking oats into the trough for Goat. Most of the Dare horses lived off the land like the Indian ponies did, but Goat and Spots were pets, and as such, they had been spoiled silly.

Brit watched her sister until she had finished and flipped her braid back and put the sack of oats in a bin. She was careful to hook the leather strap around a nail because Goat had figured out how to flip the lid and get to the oats.

Ol' Goat was old as dirt and almost blind but she was not dumb.

Only when she had finished did Irish turn to look at her and that was when Brit saw that she had been crying. Brit touched her sister's arm. "Maw's waiting on me now but we'll meet later, huh? Down at the creek?"

Irish looked at a place on her thumb and sniffed and then she nodded."Yeah, I guess we better."

Brit watched her walk away and fear eased up inside her. Something was terribly, terribly wrong.

Thirteen

Jean heard a rustle and thought: finally! As he came up on one elbow he fixed his face in what he hoped was a not too hungry expression, just in case she felt a little trepidation. He did not want to run her off after all the time it had taken to get her to come to him. However, "starved" was a pretty apt description of how he felt. He was actually surprised at the unexpected strength of his desire for her. And also the fact that he felt a little nervous, though not about his performance. He knew he could give a good account of himself there. What he was concerned about was noise and if their previous encounters were any indication, he had good reason. She had been very vocal in the woods.

Of course he was presupposing that the girl in the woods was not a figment of his imagination and then, that Brit Dare and the girl were one and the same. He would soon know at last!

He saw her feet descend the stairs and he smiled a self-satisfied smile and then he saw a second set of feet and his jaw fell open. A ménage à trois? Surely not!

He need not have worried because the twins never even glanced in his direction. Instead they continued on cat feet, across the cabin, out the door, and down the path that led to the creek.

"Well, I'll be damned," he muttered.

"You may well be," said a voice from the alcove. "But you might as well get a good night's sleep either way."

The twins headed for their favorite spot, which was a little set-in place that was between two stands of alamos alongside the creek. Irish sat on her heels and wrapped her nightdress around her legs. Brit looked around and shivered a little before she joined her. With dark came the sounds of the hunters. Coyotes howled in the hills and wolves in the prairie, and in the woods beyond the creek the night hawks and the owls were trying to scare something edible into giving its hiding place away.

"Well," Brit said. "Might as well go on and get it over with. You know you'll feel better once you do."

Will I? Irish wondered. Will I really? While it was true that she always told her sister everything and always felt better after she did, neither had ever told the other anything like this.

Irish laid her cheek against the rough cool wood of the oak and stared across the moon streaked creek where the bare branches of the trees were like jagged cracks in the sky.

Brit waited and after a while, Irish finally said, "Remember the time when Maw told us how she knew that Otis Dare was the man for her?"

That her sister would bring up something that she had just spent days thinking about herself was no surprise to Brit. That sort of thing happened to them all the time. "Yeah?"

"Well, what if that happened to me? What if I knew—sure as fire burns—who was the right man for me only . . . only he's married?"

"Married! God! Irish!"

"I know."

They stared at each other for a good minute and their faces were like pale cutouts on a black cloth.

"Mr. Schumacher!"

"Yes!"

"Oh, no!"

"Yes!"

"Oh, Irish!"

"I know. Believe me, I know."

"When? How?

"Remember the day those two men shot the dog?"

"Well, yes, sure."

"It started then."

"Clear back then?"

That had been one day last summer. A day so still that a person could hear the dry whirring of the grasshoppers and so hot the road shimmered in the glare.

They had been walking home with Markie. She was talking about school that day and about Miss Annie Mapes, their teacher. Markie thought quite a lot of their teacher, only she was a real stickler about talking in class and ladylike behavior, and both were areas in which Miss Mapes had told Markie she had room for improvement.

Irish had been watching a family of strangers who were coming into town. There were five of them. A kid who walked up front and gently prodded the two oxen along. A crooked old woman with a cane who walked alongside and on the wagon seat, a younger woman whose face was shaded by the funnel of her bonnet. Two more barefoot kids trailed the slow moving wagon with the family dog.

As she watched them, Irish had been wondering where they were from and if any of the kids would be going to school with them when suddenly there was a shot. Markie whipped her head around, crying, "What happened? What happened?" but Irish really didn't know at first.

Then she saw that a spotted mongrel lay dead in the

road and that two men, Bittercreek Clarke and Dutch Elliott, were standing outside Cooper's store, admiring a still-smoking musket.

Miss Mapes arrived from the school breathless and worried and a large blond man walked up. He was red-eyed mad and so was the squalling child he carried under his arm like a sack of grain. Irish knew who he was even before he said, "Who vass dat shooding in da street?"

It was Schumacher, the German millwright. Sweet Home's newest—and most valuable—settler.

Things happened fast after that. Schumacher told Bittercreek and Dutch Elliott that they could not fire their gun in the street and Bittercreek called him a turd kicker and Mr. Schumacher handed Irish his boy and dropped Bittercreek like a bad habit. Then their brother Blue was there and the mayor and then Jack. But in spite of the arrival of all these hostile people Dutch Elliott looked like he was going to do something so Blue rapped him smartly with his pistol.

When Clarke came around, he pointed at Schumacher and said he wasn't going to forget him, meaning he would be looking him up soon to even the score and Irish would never forget how Schumacher said, "Gut! Yew dew that!" And then he removed his hat and turned his head this way and that so Clarke could get a good look at him from every angle. (Just in case there was still any question in his mind Schumacher told Clarke where he could find him, meaning he would be looking forward to Clarke's looking him up.)

It was a tense time, no doubt about it and when Clarke and Elliott stalked off, everybody . . . the females anyway . . . let out a big sigh of relief.

Naturally the men acted disappointed, especially Mr. Schumacher who was jerking his jaw and muttering a string of nasty-sounding words.

Jack took still-crying Markie home, and Blue covered

the poor dog with a rag while he borrowed a shovel from Mr. Garlock.

Then came the moment that would stand out most in Irish's mind. When Emil Schumacher lifted his hat and showed her his white-blond hair and said, "Danke, little missy!" and she could not make a sound for the life of her. He stood tall above her smelling faintly of sawdust and leather and recently smoked tobacco and she just stood there with a stunned expression on her face and her heart in her throat.

And then she remembered that she still held the baby. His baby.

He took his son and plopped his hat back on and strode off but from that moment on Irish's life was changed . . . *she* was changed. So much so that it amazed her afterward to look at her reflection and see that she appeared the same because she felt that different.

The rest of that day went by a blur. Things happened she did not see, and people spoke to her that she did not hear. It wasn't as if she couldn't get him out of her mind, he *was* her mind! There was not another thought there except those about him.

Looking back there was one other thing she would never forget about that day, and that was the sharp stab of jealousy that she had felt when Brit turned to her and said she couldn't understand a word that Mr. Schumacher had said but that he sure was a handsome son of a gun.

She had never been jealous of her sister before, but she was then. Red-eyed jealous.

Afterwards she could not decide what had shocked her the most. Her reaction to Emil Schumacher's words of thanks—which might have been delivered with a hoe handle as well as a smile—or being jealous of her sister's sparkle for the first time in her memory. Oh, how she had wanted to sparkle for once. Just for once.

It had not surprised Irish that Brit had noticed boys first, because that was how it had always been with them. Brit had been a half step ahead of her all her life. She had walked a week earlier and talked a month earlier. She'd had her moon time first.

Nor was it surprising that the boys noticed Brit before they noticed her. Maw said that was because Brit sparkled and she glowed. Said it took more time to notice a glow.

By the time Irish met Emil Schumacher, Brit had been observing things like what she said about Mr. Schumacher for about six months. Most often it would be something about one of the boys in school. Sometimes it would be some little something about one of the men around town. A certain physical feature or a certain personal quirk that she would point out to Irish and that Irish would have never seen on her own. So no, it was not all that surprising that Brit had noticed Emil Schumacher first and pronounced him "a most manly looking man."

But by that incident with Schumacher, Irish's eyes had been opened too. No, more than just opened. More like . . . popped!

That day would be the beginning of her preoccupation with Emil Schumacher. She went out of her way to find out things about him. That he was the same age as her brother Jack. That he was from a town called Leipzig. That he was rich. That he had decided to build a sawmill as well as the grist mill. That he had a cooking room right inside his house. That his wife was mad as a hatter. And like a little squirrel in the autumn, she carefully stored those things away.

The next time she saw Mr. Schumacher (to speak to) was one day when she went to town with Goldie and he sprung on her the fact that he would be stopping at the new mill for a minute.

Now, she probably wouldn't have gone along with Goldie if she had known he was going to do that, but he only told her when they were already halfway there and by then she did not have much of a choice. It had been only a few days before, that she had convinced herself that she would be better off to stay away from Mr. Schumacher because she was not sure she cared for the strange sensations he had caused in her that day. But if she did have to see him for one thing or another, she would take herself away from him as soon as possible.

Well, they got to town and they stopped at the mill, but instead of staying in the wagon like she had told herself she would do, she followed Goldie right into the mill.

So much for her mind-making abilities.

And the next thing she knew Mr. Schumacher was asking her to tend his son once or twice a week while he tended to business that was better handled without a drooling baby under his arm, and she was accepting! She even offered to go to work on the spot by taking the child home and feeding him.

So much for her declarations.

Rumors about Mrs. Schumacher flew around Sweet Home like chaff. The latest . . . that business about her being a leper . . . was just ridiculous. Nevertheless, Irish had been very nervous about creeping around what appeared to be a completely deserted house. Balancing the baby on one hip, she had gone around the side of the house to the back door, which also stood ajar and found the kitchen room she had heard so much about. The floor was made out of smooth rocks and two of the walls were lined with shelves. For cooking there was both a shiny new Franklin stove and a fireplace that was shaped like a long-necked gourd with a hole punched in it.

She had been so busy looking around that she had not heard someone come up behind her, and the tap she felt on her shoulder almost sent her right out of her skin! She turned, expecting to see a horror and instead saw a middle-aged woman with a stern face and a chest that shot past her toes.

Irish told the woman that it was lucky she had a good hold on the baby 'cause she almost spit him out like a seed. Of course the woman wanted to know who she was and Irish told her she was supposed to help take care of the baby after school. The woman said she was Mrs. Von Blucker, the Schumachers' housekeeper.

Listening to her, Irish figured she must be German too. She had a thick accent and wore her gray hair braided into tight coils on either side of her head.

She was about to show Irish where the food was kept when an angry screech came tearing down the stairs. It was probably a human sound but Irish later told Brit that she sure would not know that by the sound of it.

An insulting tongue-lashing followed, which Mrs. Von Blucker ignored, and which Irish found near impossible to do. She could not keep her eyes from drifting to the source of the voice which was somewhere beyond the top of some narrow wood stairs. She had never heard such language before, not even from her brothers, not even when they did not know that she and Brit were listening outside their window.

Crazy, but none of it bothered Von Blucker in the least. All she said was that Mrs. Schumacher was very ill and that it was probably best if Irish did not go upstairs . . . which was just fine with Irish.

Ever since that day, Irish had gone over to take care of Emil Schumacher's son at least once or twice a week. She told Brit that she had grown to love the little cherry-cheeked child as if he was her own.

"But it's how I feel about his father that worries me now."

Brit watched her sit and stare at her hands. "You think you're in love with him!"

Irish nodded, miserable. "I know I am. Oh, Brit, he looked at me and my heart turned to water and I thought: I'm going to love him. Just like that. I'm going to love him and there's not a thing I can do about it. Married man or not, he's the one for me."

"What will you do?"

"I don't know." She turned her head and stared at the tree trunk as if she had never seen one before. "I can't help wondering why the Lord let this happen to me. He has to know I am the sort who will only love once."

What she said was true. She was a straightforward person and she knew herself. The simple fact was . . . she loved him. The fact that her love was shadowed by sorrow did not make it any less deep and abiding.

Brit patted her sister's arm while some nocturnal animal rustled the bushes and while the water hummed quietly along, and all she kept thinking was that her sister Irish was the last person she would have expected to go against the laws of God!

She was terribly worried. Exactly how bad was the "great heartache" that their mother had cautioned them about? And wasn't there something someone could do?

Fourteen

Not surprisingly, when Jean finally slept he dreamt of Brit, and as in the earlier dream he again saw himself at some future time, only now his spouse was not Vivica but Brit. The house was different too. Clean. Large. Very well decorated and well tended. French doors stood open to a terrace. Lace curtains moved in a soft breeze that smelled of honeysuckle.

They were seated at a table, eating in companionable silence. The meal was roasted chicken. The room was bright and airy but not formal.

He was well but casually dressed, as if he might take a stroll around the gardens after lunch. His hair was winged with gray but he was exceedingly fit-looking and had actually grown more handsome with age.

Brit was lovely. Her ravishing figure was clothed in green watered silk and her hair was simply coiffed, drawn up to her crown and then allowed to cascade freely down her back.

He noticed a half smile playing on her lips and asked her what she was thinking. She replied that she was thinking about a day twenty years earlier. What day, he asked. She looked at him with a familiar teasing glint in her eye. The day you tried to seduce me by helping me clean a turkey. Ah, he said and sniffed. I knew you would hold that against me! She laughed and described how odd his expression had been when she handed him the turkey ass side up, and how funny he had looked with feathers in his hair and hanging off his ears and eyebrows. He said he remembered kissing her hand that day and that he lost his heart in spite of the damp feather smell.

When they finished eating they walked arm in arm to the fire where he drew her onto his lap and kissed her with slow deliberate skill. She moaned softly. He slipped his fingers into her bodice and caressed her breasts then loosened the ties to her abdomen and worked his way down to her thighs until finally he was stroking her in her most secret places and making her quicken to his . . .

"What do you think you are the best at doing?"

"Mmft? Wha- . . . ?"

"It's me . . . Markie." He groaned and opened one eye. Damn! Indeed it was she. He took a moment to adjust himself and find a comfortable position. God, it was full daylight!

"Now take me, for example, I am best at climbing up a pecan tree and shaking down the nuts. How about you?"

"Dreaming," he said and yawned big.

"Dreamin'? You mean like . . . in the night?"

"Mm. Or in the day. Apparently."

"Huh!" Markie raised her brows and lowered them. Like her maw always said: there are a lotta queer ducks in this world.

"Are you awake now?"

"Most definitely. Yes."

"I've been waitin' for you to wake up so I could ask you a question."

"What?"

She pulled something from her pocket. "Mind tellin' me what color this rock is? Offhand."

Coming up to one elbow caused a sharp pain in his back but he took the stone, rolled it around and then held it up to the sunlight. "Offhand I would say it is a greenish blue."

"More green than blue? Or more blue than green?"

"Mm. Maybe more blue than green . . ."

"Drat! That's what I figured."

She dropped it back in her pocket and looked very disappointed. Jean shrugged. "It is still a pretty rock."

"Mebbe, but it's got to be green to be a curing stone."

"A curing stone?"

"Yeah. Don't you have them where you come from?"

"No."

"No?" She waited until she was sure he'd had time to notice her dropped jaw.

"All right." He sighed big. "Tell me what they do."

"Why, in the right hands, just about anythin'! But they're especially good for bites. Dog. Snake. Human."

"Good Lord!" He fell back onto his pillow and shut his eyes, but of course she went on . . . telling about how her Great-granny Ellis used to use one back in Tennessee and how it had saved the life of a boy who had been bit by a rabid dog.

"It happened pretty far from where Great-granny lived so that by the time she got there the boy was already makin' milk with his mouth, but she put her stone to the bite and it stuck and started sucking the poison out. Afterward Maw said she watched Great-granny clean the stone by soaking it in sweet milk. Said the poison drawn from that boy turned the milk green as grass."

"Did the boy survive?"

"Lived to have ten kids. By the way, Maw says that's something else a curing stone can do. Give kids to those who can't have 'em."

He wondered where one applied the stone for that result.

"You all right?"

"Yes. Why?"

"You moaned."

"Pray, do go on."

"Well, all right, but . . . can you keep a secret?"

"Oh, yes. Absolutely."

"Well, the best thin' about a curing stone is that . . ." She lowered her voice and spoke with delicious dread. " . . . you can use it to maim your enemies."

"Interesting."

"Yeah!"

"I suppose that would be useful."

"Oh, yeah!"

"You have many enemies so far?"

"Not so far, but my brothers do and I thought I'd learn to use my stone for them."

He caught himself nodding slowly, once again forgetting that she could not see. Then whatever he had been about to say was halted by what he felt, and then a second later, by what he saw. Brit had just appeared and the crazy thing was . . . he had known that she would. The air might have been lightning-struck. That's how acutely conscious he had suddenly been that she was nearby.

He stared at her as she walked closer. She had her skirt tail pulled through her legs and pinned up in front, which exposed her slim white calves to his view.

"Is it washday, Markie?"

"No. Why?"

"Nothing. Just wondering."

It wasn't the fact that she was trying to attract his attention that piqued his curiosity, but how well she was succeeding.

It was interesting to speculate on the reaction he was having to her. He couldn't help but think of a patient who had been presented for study at the university. The subject was a farrier, a hardworking man with a massive torso and hands like hams. He was obviously uncomfortable to be before such a large group of men, probably the sort who equated illness with weakness, though he looked anything but weak. Strangely enough the man's problem was the instantaneous physical reaction he would experience whenever he came within a hundred yards of a domestic cat. He had quite severe symptoms . . . a rush of warmth and a pounding heartbeat. Patchy skin and itching in odd places. Sneezing and wheezing of the diaphragm.

The man said he had sometimes suffered similar symptoms from certain smells but he did not say that he had ever had the reaction from contact with a human being.

Jean decided that somewhere along the line he had developed an affliction similar to that of the farrier because his instantaneous response to Brit's approach included all of the man's symptoms and several of his own including—but not limited to—tingling palms, standing arm hairs and twitching cods! Being of some—albeit minimal—scientific bent, it was only natural that his mind explore the causes.

Perhaps it was the phenomenon about which he had heard but never witnessed . . . namely the palpable presence that some people were purported to possess. He had known of a French actress who had been credited with that rare ability, namely the Divine Dianna De Blanc, who could, supposedly, walk onto a stage and merely by her presence command the attention of every eye in the room.

De Blanc had once appeared at a soirée he attended. Obviously he had been left unaffected, because he had been oblivious to her entrance and had continued to stare at a magnificent Da Vinci unfairly hung in a dimly lit corner. The Divine Dianna had stalked over to him and tapped him angrily on the shoulder. They were in bed within the hour and he was bored within half that time. By the end of the night they spent together, he was able unequivocally to state that she had showed him no more and no less "magnetism" than any other female with the appropriate equipment.

"Jean . . . ?"

"Mm?"

"It's me, Markie."

"So I see."

"Can I ask you something else?"

"Yes, of course."

"Sure you can keep a secret."

"Yes. I'm sure. What?"

"Well, what if somebody asked somebody else to find out somethin' about somebody but not to tell the somebody why, but that somebody's sister wouldn't tell why she needed to know what she needed to know . . . should that somebody find out what she wanted to know or not? I mean, what would you do?"

His brain was so strained his eyes ached. "Somebody wants you to ask me something but you are not supposed to tell me who that somebody is."

Her brow smoothed. "Yeah, that's it."

"What does Brit want to know?"

"She . . . Hey! You tricked me!"

"What?"

"You said Brit."

"I will wipe the name from my mind. All right?"

"Promise?"

"Yes!"

"All right then. Brit wants to know if you have anyone waiting for you at home."

Vivica's rouged breasts briefly flashed before his eyes. "No."

It was true. No promises had been made by either of them and even before he left for America they each had always been free to take other lovers.

And if he never returned, he knew that Vivica de Marco had too much sexual stamina to pine over him. Lovers would continue to come into her life and pass out of it, no doubt for as long as she was capable of attracting them.

"No," he repeated. "No one. Why does she want to know?"

"Exactly what I asked her myself . . ."

"And?"

"She said we might need to let someone know if . . . if you died."

"Why not just ask me for the name of my nearest kin?"

"Oh, no, Brit says we can't do that. You might believe we believed that you were gonna die and you might get discouraged and not get well."

"I feel as healthy as a horse."

That much was true. So far he had been making an unusually rapid recovery. Which raised another question. Perhaps she didn't think he was well enough to re-establish their affair. He most definitely was. Oh, yes. A little less athleticism on his part, a little more on hers and everything would be fine.

Unfortunately there had been little opportunity to speak to her alone. If the twins were home, so was his self-appointed watchdog and if Markie was off somewhere, the old woman was always nearby.

As a matter of fact, he had often felt the old woman's bead-bright eyes on him. Especially lately, and especially when the twins were around.

Brit had returned. She paused to shift a basket from one arm to the other, and then looking neither left nor right, she continued across the yard. He followed her as far as his eyes would stretch without chinning himself on the window ledge.

After Markie was called away, Jean lay there brooding. She was definitely flaunting herself in front of him. Back and forth across the yard. In and out of the cabin. Serving him his food. Bringing him fresh clothes. Tending his wound. Apparently, she delighted in teasing him but why deny them both what they wanted most? Could she be angling for a more permanent situation? It was an interesting idea, making Brit his mistress. Funny that he had never thought of it before but the more he thought about it, the greater its appeal. Why not? It was a very tantalizing thought. He touched his lower lip and recalled how she had sunk her sharp little teeth into it! Very tantalizing indeed.

Brit was everywhere. Collecting eggs, tending pigs, checking traps. Tearing to the edge of the woods, stopping so fast she would quiver like an arrow in a tree. Gulping air she would smooth her hair and wipe her brow. All so she could slowly stroll across the yard, and into Jean McDuff's line of sight.

She had drawn looks from her mother and Irish and point-blank questions from Markie. At that moment she and Markie were having a tug of war over the bucket used to fill the fire barrels.

"Drawing water is my job."

"I know, but I thought I'd do it for you today. You've been so busy with the doctor."

"Well, that's sure true." Markie relinquished the bucket. "Lately I've been so tired I've been makin' three tracks in the dirt."

"I know."

"I can barely haul my body to bed at night."

"I know."

"Well," She sniffed pitifully. "I guess I'd better get back in there."

Brit rolled her eyes. "Yes, you better."

"He depends on me. Poor fella."

"You're so good for him, Markie."

"I know."

Brit smiled as she watched her baby sister drag herself back to Jean's bedside, but when Markie disappeared, so did her smile. She chewed her thumbnail. Irish would not be as easy, and an hour later she could have congratulated herself for being right, but she was too busy.

"What on earth is wrong with you?" Irish asked.

"What?"

"What? You know what! You about trampled me getting to the woodpile this morning and now you've run me over to milk."

"I just want to do my fair share."

Irish narrowed her eyes. "I ain't givin' you nothin' that's mine."

"God, Irish, a person would never know you'd been to school."

"Never mind me. I want to make sure you understand me. Whatever it is that you're after, you ain't getting it. Nothing. Nada!"

Brit sniffed. "I don't want anything you've got."

"Nothing."

"Fine."

Irish stared at her and then she finally handed her the bucket. "All right. Here! You wanna milk . . . milk!"

"Irish . . ."

"What?"

Brit picked at the rope handle. "I'll give you a nickel."

"I knew it! I jus' knew it! For what?"

"I'll give you a nickel if you'll . . . let me turn the garden."

"Now, wait just a goldurned minute." Irish's eyes had all but disappeared. "You're gonna give me a whole nickel if I let you hoe the garden."

"Yeah."

She folded her arms and stared down her nose at her while Brit squirmed like a hooked worm. "Go get your nickel. I'll be waiting right here for you."

* * *

Irish showed up at the garden and helped her anyway.
They worked together silently until a little before supper,
moving up and down the rows, chopping up the dried
beanstalks and piling together whatever the pigs might eat.

At dusk Brit straightened and saw Irish standing at the
opposite end of the patch, staring off into the woods. She
went and stood beside her and draped her wrists on her
hoe. Off to the west there was a buzzard making circles
against the bruised looking sky. "Pretty sunset tonight."

"Yeah." She pulled her hoe close and rested her chin
on it. "Brit . . ."

"Yeah?"

She looked at her. "What is sinning in your heart?"

"Sinning in your heart? You mean like that traveling
preacher . . . ?"

"Yeah."

Brit pictured the tall thin man who'd had a gray beard
to his belt and who had gone on and on about that very
subject one Founder's Day, two or three years before. She
snorted. "Irish, you have not sinned in your heart. You
don't even know how to sin in your shoes yet."

"I think I'm learning."

"You're learning to sin?"

"Not on purpose but my mind'll just go off on its own
and I'll find myself pretending things."

"What things?"

"Strange things."

"Like what, for instance?"

"Like sometimes I'll pretend that Mrs. Schumacher's
house is my house. That her baby is my baby. Even that
her man is my man." She looked off for a time and then
she met Brit's eye. "How's that for sinning?"

"Oh, well, I don't see what harm that can do. If it's only,
ah, you know . . . play-like." Brit knew she didn't sound

very convincing but that was all right. Irish continued as if she had not heard her anyway.

"I couldn't quit anyhow. I tried to quit looking at him, but I just can't. I love to look at him. I think I could watch him for hours."

Brit saw Goldie ride in and saw Maw come out onto the porch to greet him. But Irish saw only what was inside her mind.

"One time he was talking to Goldie and he had his hand spread wide on the wall and I saw everything about it. If I close my eyes, I can still see it now. Which knuckle was skinned and every crease and freckle and hair. I wanted to lay my hand over his and measure it against my own. I wanted to press up against his back and put my nose in between his shoulders and smell him. I could see myself doing that and it was so real I almost wondered if I hadn't." She looked at Brit and her eyes were awash with tears. "It was crazy. I think I'm crazy."

Remembering how she was around Jean McDuff, Brit was fiercely shaking her head. "No, you're not a bit crazy. But I'm scared for you. Maybe you ought not to go back. What I mean is, maybe you should make up something and tell him you can't do it any more. Just to be safe." Irish was shaking her head. "Why not?"

Irish turned and walked off. "I have to go back. I'd rather kill myself than not go back."

Having remained behind, Brit stood and stared sightlessly off toward the still circling buzzard. After a bit she shook her head and whispered, "Jiminy!"

Jean was still alert to any opportunity to be alone with Brit but it would not happen that night. The Dare brothers were at home, and sat up until late smoking and talking.

They were worried about some looming political problems stemming from a recent visit by General Manuel

Mier y Teran. Apparently Teran had taken a tour of East
Texas and had not been pleased by the population mix
he had discovered; namely, over ninety percent anglo. In
order to solve the problem of too few Mexican families
in the district he was proposing to even things up by
bringing Mexican convict-soldiers and their families into
the area.

This did not please the Dares, who felt they had all they
could handle dealing with the bandits and Indians that
were already in their territory. Certainly they did not see
the need for imported law breakers from Mexico City.

There had also been a rumor that Mexico City was going
to restrict further Anglo immigration into Texas, which
the Dares also opposed and in addition, that Teran had
recently started reinforcing the garrisons at San Antonio,
La Bahia, Nacogdoches and Velasco. As Goldie said,
"Seems funny, their takin' all these steps to fortify against
their own citizens."

Blue said, "Makes me damned nervous, I'll tell you."

"Can't do much more'n wait an' see."

Conversation drifted from that point and Jean spent
the time thinking about Brit. Would the Dare boys object
if he made her his mistress? All were robust men who led
vigorous sex lives themselves. Perhaps they would be *sim-
patico* to such an arrangement. Liaisons such as he would
propose were made all the time in France. Surely they
were aware of such things. After all, this *was* 1828! Good
heavens, the area was remote, but they were not living in
the stone ages.

On the other hand, there was a definite feral side to the
Dares, a sort of familial protectiveness that was common
to certain primitive types. That was, however, an obstacle
for which he might have a ready solution: namely, a very
generous settlement.

Fortunately he was in a position to make them the sort
of princely settlement that only a fool would refuse, and

the Dares were definitely not fools. They were far from poor but they were not as well heeled as himself. How could they help but not appreciate the influx of a generous amount of gold? They could buy more land and cows than they had ever imagined.

It went without saying that he would freely support any progeny of the union. As his father before him, he knew his duty and he would do it. That was only right. And there was no reason why she could not marry when their *affaire* ended. His mother had done so and had been apparently quite happy with her lot.

He decided to bring the conversation around to the twins. It was really quite easy. One comment about their suitors and Goldie took it from there.

"Ol' Clyde's been after Brit for months."

"Yeah," said Blue. "Hangs around her like a damn breed bull."

Jean did not always appreciate the Dares' crude choice of words.

"She hardly seems that old." The brothers looked at him. "I mean to have been courted for years."

"I said months."

"Whichever."

"They're old enough, all right. Men started offerin' for 'em as long as two years ago."

"My God, two years ago they were little girls."

"Hah! Not in Tejas."

"Nobody's been rushin' 'em, you understand."

"Naw, we're lettin' 'em take their time."

"Do you have a type of brother-in-law in mind?" He was merely curious.

"A man who can take care of somebody other than himself."

"One who wants a woman for a wife."

So much for his idea.

"We've had a few lookin' for a bedmate for as long as they're in the territory."

"But not recently," said Blue.

"Naw," said Goldie. "Not since we laid down the law."

"I generally have a little talk with a fella when he first comes out." There was a snick-like sound and Blue's knife flashed in the moonlight. "I tell 'im I collect one-eyed worms in cold weather coats. Har har har!"

While the brothers were having a good laugh Jean was having a sudden chill. Thank God he had not declared his intentions. They probably would have killed him, very slowly and very painfully and afterward, as they were wiping their knives on the grass one would no doubt make a regretful remark about how much he had hated what they'd just had to do.

The Dare brothers went to bed and Jean slept two minutes after the candle was extinguished. It was the kind of exhausted sleep of one who had survived a close encounter with death. Which he felt like he had. Amazingly enough, it was also deep and completely dreamless.

Fifteen

Winter lagged. The frost that glistened on the grass was gone by breakfast, and the days changed little.

But squirrels scurried after acorns with vigorous enthusiasm and flocks of southward-bound birds filled the sky every day. Fair warning to less industrious humans of what waited around the corner.

Jean sat on a down-padded chair on the porch, thinking that there was something incredibly peaceful about the sounds of Tejas. The rhythmic ring of the windlass. The soft sound of birdsong that always filled the air. The lowing of cows and the occasional punctuative blat of the goat. Sounds that had once been so exotic and which were now so ordinary.

As he had these thoughts, it struck him that he did not think much about Paris any more and that when he did, he seemed to remember her at her very worst. The noise. It really was an incredibly noisy city. The filthy streets and the unclean air. The dank smell of the river. The ragged peddlers and the maimed beggars.

But these detractions aside, there was one huge positive: Paris was never boring, while Tejas, for all its supreme majesty, was phenomenally monotonous. Ah, well. Not that he couldn't see how men with simple needs might be perfectly content here. It was remarkably restful. Which was soon to be exemplified by his own behavior. It was only midmorning, but he found the ambience so soothing that he dozed.

And woke to a world of fury.

A storm had come up, one unlike any he had ever seen before. Thunder boomed like a cannon, and jagged spears of lightning ripped across the sky. He stood with difficulty, but he had to brace himself against a sudden wind that twisted the trees into macabre gargoyles and propelled things that stung his face like a slap. "I think it may rain."

He had made his remark to Jack, who had raced by with a rag tied across the lower half of his face, and as soon as he finished speaking he understood the purpose of the rag. He leaned and spat a mouthful of grit.

Blurred figures moved across in the yard, hurrying to let some stock free and to herd some others into their pens and corrals and Jean was wondering what he could do to help when a freezing rain hit like it had been thrown from a bucket and he found himself on his knees.

"That will be quite enough of that!" he muttered and crawled inside the cabin. Evie, the twins and Markie were already there. Brit and Irish had either loosed their hair or the wind had done it for them. They were sharing a towel and taking turns rubbing each other's head.

Evie had scooped live coals on a shovel and was carrying them to the hearth where Markie sat enveloped in a blanket that showed only her eyes. Someone might have posed her beside a sign that read: unwanted foundling.

He sat beside her and drew her close and he could hear her teeth clicking like knitting needles. He rubbed her arm and tucked the blanket under her feet and then he looked up and met Brit's gaze. As usual he searched her eyes for a message. She smiled. She looked at Markie then back at him and indeed, her gaze did hold a message. Unfortunately it was only thank you.

For an hour the rain poured off the porch roof like a

sheet of zinc. Wind-ripped limbs struck the cabin like a crusaders' siege on a battlement wall, and the thunder was so powerful, it rattled the jars on the shelves.

Then quite suddenly the storm was over, and with Markie to shore up one side Jean hobbled outside to view the carnage. Tree trunks glistened blackly and the ground shone with pools of water, but he had to blink from the sudden brightness. With shaded eyes he looked at the spot where the chicken coop and corn crib used to be. Then at a canted tree, a missing roof and listing cowpen fence. But once again, amid that amazing devastation, there was the customary chorus of chirring crickets, chattering squirrels and delirious singing from the bird kingdom.

Jack joined them and Irish came out and clapped a straw hat on Markie's head. "C'mon Goober. Maw says to go rinse and re-hang the wash."

As Jean watched grasshoppers fly out of the two sisters' path he said, "God, this is a strange country!"

Jack laughed. "Yeah, but you like it, dontcha? Hell, me, too! It's so damned . . ." He waved his arm expansively. "It's real . . ." He frowned.

"Exhilarating?"

"Yeah, that's it! Exhiliratin'."

Jack's black hair was slicked like an otter. He pulled his buckskin shirt over his head and twisted the water out of it before he hung it on the rail.

"You know, McDuff, you're all right." He slapped Jean on the back and water flew from somewhere. "Anybody who can tell weather like you has got a real foot up on things around here."

He slid a board out from under the porch and laid it across the mud near the step then he squinted skyward. "Sun's too bright to look at straight on, ain't it?"

Jean stared after him like he was a lunatic, but later, after he'd had an opportunity to think about it, he ac-

knowledged that Jack just might be right. He did like the
land and he did admire its people. He especially liked the
Dares.

Almost from the beginning there had been an estab-
lished ease between them and the longer he stayed with
them the more his appreciation for them had grown, particularly for their straightforward outlook on life. That was
never more apparent than when Markie asked him about
his friends back home and he could barely remember their
names. It was something he knew would never be true of
the Dares.

Theirs was not a life to envy—clearing the way for others—but he wondered if they would change it, even if
they could. He suspected they had been forced to prove
themselves for so long they would be lost without the
need to do so. Perhaps men of their ilk even searched
out wild and dangerous places in order to fulfill some
primitive need they had to confront and to conquer. Man
against man. Man against beast. Man against the ele-
ments.

The Dares were complex men, but strange as it seemed,
he understood them, and beyond that, he admired them.
Particularly for their fierce independence and adventure-
seeking spirit, and for the pleasure and pride with which
they had willingly pitted themselves against this land and
its inhabitants.

But he had never known such inconsistent characters.
Perversely obstinate one minute; precisely the opposite the
next. Violent and completely without mercy to their enemies. Overflowing with good spirits for their allies.

It was Goldie, the middle brother, that Jean knew best
because, as designated hunter and protector of the family,
it was Goldie who stayed closer to home. He often sat on
the porch and talked to Jean while he worked on a farm
implement or a weapon of some sort.

Goldie was a quiet and somewhat solitary man but Jean

found him to be extremely bright and very quick-witted. He was a fine woodworker and furniture maker and had been trading the things he made for those items that the Dares could not make themselves . . . axes, needles and cloth, pots and pans, gunpowder and salt.

Lately his talent had turned into a livelihood of sort. He had recently been asked to build a cabin for an Easterner who had money but no ability in that way. The man had been so pleased with Goldie's work that he asked him to build all his inside furniture and his barn as well. Goldie agreed and enlisted the help of his brothers when they weren't out on a scout. To facilitate matters further Goldie had recently worked a deal to have his wood cut by the German settler who had built a saw mill just outside of town. And with less fanfare than that, it looked like the Dares were about to venture into the home-building business.

Goldie said that not long after their two brothers were killed by the Kiowa, the alcalde, Lloyd Cooper, had offered all three of them jobs as ranging peacekeepers. The money was good, so they talked it over and decided they would take the mayor up on his offer but not all of them. Someone had to stay home to keep the larder stocked and protect the women, and since Goldie was the best shot of the lot and therefore the best hunter, Jack and Blue informed him that he ought to be the one. He disagreed and nominated Blue, seeing as he was the youngest and the weakest of the lot.

" 'Course there was hell to pay about that!" said Goldie, chuckling.

Jean asked him why he would prefer fighting Indians over what he was doing. Jean said to his thinking it would be much better to hunt fourlegged animals than two-legged ones, but Goldie shook his head. "We tossed sticks an' they cheated."

He might complain but he did his job well. The Dares—
and all their house guests—ate very well indeed.

Jean saw less of Jack or Blue because of their affiliation
with the peacekeepers, whose job, as described by Blue,
was to punish "all marauding Indians, larcenous ban-di-tos
or any other criminally inclined characters foolish enough
to wander into our territory."

Jean had heard stories in New Orleans about how the
Tejas immigrants were being imperiled by every imagin-
able natural disaster—droughts, floods, brush fires and
plagues. But from the beginning it was the natives who
had been the settlers' biggest problem, striking remote
farms with impunity and carrying off whatever—or whoever—they wanted. Cheap land was the lure of Tejas, but
the larger the farms the greater the distance between
them, and therefore the greater danger of an Indian attack. Sometimes someone would sight smoke on the horizon and be suspicious enough to investigate, but often
it would be days before some passerby found the carnage.
No matter how futile pursuit might seem, Jack Dare's
small troop would take up their arms and follow the per-
petrators' trail. Because they tracked the raiders deep into
their own territory, the Texians would often be gone for
days.

They were paid next to nothing—certainly not enough
to compensate for the risks they took—and even at that,
each man also had to supply his own mount and his own
weaponry. They had received no special training nor were
they particularly experienced in combat. Actually Goldie
had told him that when they weren't fighting Indians, they
lived the lives of ordinary men holding down ordinary
jobs.

Maybe it was Goldie's comments, maybe it was his own
imagination, but Jean had formed quite a different mental
picture of the troop from the one that he saw early one
morning.

Half sitting, half reclining on the porch, he was blowing ripples on a cup of boiled coffee that was still too hot to drink, when suddenly there was a shouted warning of approach. There followed the sound of horses' hooves beating the ground and wild barking by the dogs and a group of horsemen hove into view, a lean and hungry-looking lot astride muscular mounts of varying colors. They lined up in front of the porch, a half dozen sinister-looking faces below ragged slouch hats. The troop, he presumed, and they were anything but ordinary-looking to him.

Crisscrossing their chests were thin straps that held shot pouches and powder horns. Knife, hatchet and gun handles stuck out of belts and boots, and extra gun stocks were tied onto every saddle. Tin cups, water pouches and short-handled shovels hung off their pommels. Rolled and tied behind their cantles were mothy-looking blankets and extra clothes. One of the men, a Mexican by the looks of him, wore a high-crowned hat and had his blanket slung over his shoulder.

Now that Jean had taken a closer look, he was surprised to see that despite masculine handlebars and beards in various stages of growth, the men were incredibly young—closer to his brother Duncan's age than his own. But one look into their old-as-time eyes dispelled any notion of youth.

All but one of them were dressed in skins, an attire that lent even greater credence to their uncivilized appearance. But to Jean the fiercest looking man in the troop was their scout, a Tonkawa Indian named He-Coon. Here at last was the wild Indian Duncan had been so set on seeing!

He was a man of indeterminable age who wore only a long breech cloth, bison-hide moccasins and two bone necklaces. He had dark cunning eyes and an expressionless face made from some substance much harder than flesh. A ribbon of tattooed dots banded his forehead and crossed his bare chest just above his heart, and Jean would not have believed it, but his skin actually did have a coppery hue. He was also as hairless as an egg.

Word had come of a Kiowa raid to the west that had resulted in six deaths. The troop was needed to pursue the raiders, exact revenge and recapture the numerous horses that had been taken.

Blue and Jack both readied themselves in minutes and as Blue mounted up, he yelled, "All right, boys. Let's go chastise some Kiowa!" And with that the troop thundered off in a slurry of yips and howls and catcalls.

"One would not think that your sons were about to risk life and limb."

"Jack would jus' as soon make peace with the Indians, but not Blue." Evie watched them until they were out of sight and then turned to him. "More coffee?"

"No, thank you. Not now."

She stood looking off for awhile and then she started to speak. "I had six boys when we moved here. I'd lost three of my girls before they walked but I'd reared all my boys to be men. I thought I was gonna be lucky then . . . three of them were killed. And all within the space of a year!"

There was a long silence in which Jean thought he should say something but mere words of condolence seemed wholly inadequate. He finally murmured something but when she went on, it was as if she had not heard.

"Brown was felling a dead tree when it took a twist on him and struck him such a blow under his jaw that it snapped his neck like a twig. Happened right yonder, not twenty yards from the house."

She said she had not had time to gather herself from that burying when Red and Silver were killed by Kiowas. They had gone out after some horses that were missing. Maybe the horses wandered off. Maybe they were lured away. In either case, when the two men did not return, their brothers went looking for them. Unfortunately, they were too late.

"I was their own mother and I could not tell them apart. That's how bad they'd been cut. Blue was sixteen at the time and was with Goldie and Jack when they found the bodies." She stood and shook out her skirts. "We Dares're all pretty tight but Blue was real close to his brother, Red. Real close."

Sixteen

The troop returned two days later, starved, grim-faced and worn to the bone. But they had apparently been victorious. Slung across one man's back was an Indian lance and hung behind another's cantle was an elaborate shield made of stretched hide then decorated with feathers and fur.

Evie called, "Climb down, boys!" She pointed at a three-legged caldron on the hearth. "I got plenty of ham an' beans goin'."

As the men eased out of the saddles, Goldie collected their mounts' reins and called to Markie. "Come help me tend the horses, Goober."

The troop marched by Jean, which raised a massive amount of dust from the floorboards, and clinked the dishes on the shelves.

Blue had a bloody rag tied jauntily around his head. Another man had one around his leg. As they continued to stream by, Jean saw another who had been wounded in the shoulder and one who had been shot in the side. "Good God!" he exclaimed. "How often is it like this?"

"Hey, we won!"

"Yeah, y'all oughta see the other guys."

"All right," said Evie. "Anybody need fixin' afore food?"

Someone groaned softly and the two men nearest Jean laughed quietly. The one with a bloody rag tied around his shoulder leaned his way. "Jesse's worried Miz Dare's gonna do a job on his leg."

The man called Jesse shot the women a look and lowered his voice. "Miz Dare worked on my female-pleasin' finger last year." He stuck up his longest finger on his right hand. "Left it stiff as a board."

On a day previous Evie had shared some of her treatments with him. She was obviously a self-taught healer who had learned her skills through trial and error and so it had been difficult for Jean to determine the nucleus of her concoctions. But once he did it was quite an eye-opener. She was using some of the same components currently being touted by the finest physicians in Europe!

Unfortunately, for every viable concoction she had ten dubious ones. A broom across the door for colic. An onion peel in clabbered milk for runny bowels. Gunpowder for warts.

Gunpowder for warts, he had repeated and jokingly asked if the warted person ate the gunpowder or fired it. Quite seriously she said the latter.

She told him that once Goldie had been snake-bit on the thumb. Luckily he had been ahead of his age in size and the rattler had only been a little one and therefore not terribly poisonous. "I scarified the wound and then burned it good." But the scar turned into something that looked a lot like a wart. "Kept getting caught on stuff and would bleed if he looked at it."

It bothered him so much that he twice took a knife and cut it off but each time it grew back. One night he was cleaning his carbine and fancied a smoke before he went to bed. Unbeknownst to him, he had a residue of gunpowder on his hand and caught his hand afire. "Didn't hurt his hand much but it burned that wart-like place plumb off."

Evie said she had been burning them off ever since. "Bunions too," she added. "Provided the person'll hold

still. I will not do a bunion if a person will not hold still
for it."

The young trooper with the leg-wound cut another look
the women's way. "Say, McDuff . . . I hear you've done
some doctorin' here an' there."

"I have, but not here and not lately . . ."

Again the trooper checked over his shoulder. "Think
you could take a look at my leg?"

Inwardly Jean quavered but he could hardly say no. "If
you are sure you would like me to . . ."

"Sure I'm sure. Why not?"

Why not indeed?

"All right. Sit here in front of me."

Jean tried to unwind the bandage and found it stuck to
the wound. Before he could even lift his head, much less
his voice, a slender hand offered steaming water and a
clean rag. Brit.

"You could soak it off with this, Doctor."

Jean looked up at her but her attention was on the
wounded man. They were smiling at each other.

"Hey, Jesse!"

"Hey, Brit."

Jean cleared his throat and announced, "It appears that
the bullet has gone through without damage to either the
nerves or tendons."

"Thank you for the licorice."

"You're welcome."

"It appears to only require a thorough cleaning and
stitching."

Brit anticipated his need for needle and thread and offered his medical bag before he asked for it.

"I wish they'd had peppermint. I know that's your favorite."

"No, no. I like licorice just as . . ."

Jean shot a look between the two. "Miss Dare . . . Do
you mind holding this please?"

"Yes, Doctor."

"Ow!"

"Sorry."

McIninch gave a nervous little laugh then turned back to Brit. "So . . . what you been up to?"

"School and work. You know."

"Sorry I ain't been out to see you, but the sheriff said the doc was real sick an' I didn't want to cause a commotion. Now I see he's fit why I'll mosey on . . . Ow!"

"I am finished, Miss Dare. You may help your mother now."

"All right. See you soon, Jesse."

"Yessum, you sure will. I'll try to . . ."

"I am finished, Miss Dare." Jean ignored McIninch and his puzzled expression. "Next?"

Jean cleaned Blue's head wound which was only a graze and did not require stitching. Same with the side wound which was caused by an arrow that had dug a furrow across the only fat place on the young ranger's body. The shoulder wound was the most serious, but it too was soon cleaned out and stitched up.

Meanwhile Evie and the girls had started covering the table with pans of wheat bread and corn bread, jars of preserves and pitchers of sweet milk and jugs of cider. The troop found places at the table and then watched with hungry eyes while Irish and Brit ladled up the beans and ham.

Jean watched Brit carry the brimful bowls to each man, and he did not know what to make of her. Any self-respecting siren would revel in so much masculine attention but she kept her eyes downcast and her face a pleasant mask.

More than anyone, he knew that she was far from the shy innocent girl she had been impersonating during the last several days, but he had to admit that she was putting on a very good act. The question was: to what purpose? Was she a wanton or an angel? Or could she be a bit of both? Had she, for example, sampled physical amour with some oaf like McIninch and found the act to her liking but not the man?

No, she had obviously had more than one man. A girl with that big an appetite would have had many.

He looked at the faces around the room and wondered which of these men had been her lover, but he soon found that he had to quit. The exercise was beginning to sour his stomach.

The troop left and quiet descended. From his pallet Jean lay watching the women clean up. Jack and Blue sat on their spines with their coffee cups on their chests and their feet close enough to the fire to singe their toe hairs. Apparently they were interested in doing nothing more demanding than staring into the fire. Miss Markie Dare, however, had other things in mind.

"You'll never believe all the stuff that's happened to me!"

The look the two brothers exchanged, added the word: yet.

First, she said she had learned the words to three new songs which she would now play . . .

Blue interrupted her there. "Say, Goober . . ."

She paused, fiddle and chin lifted. "Yeah?"

"Please . . ."

She waited through a good minute while Jack poked Blue and Blue looked chagrined.

"Yeah?"

"Please . . . play that one you played the other night."

"Well, that's what I was fixin' to do 'til you stopped me."

"Sorry," said Blue. "What was that tune again?"

"There were three."

The first song was "Hey Diddle Diddle"—which was a good tune, all right, but she didn't think the words told a very believable story. Not like "Fiddle-De-Dee" which was about a fly that married a bumblebee.

Most days "Fiddle-De-Dee" was her most very favorite song, but there were some days when she just could not resist "Mr. Froggie Went A-Courting."

She sang them all three songs so they would decide which one was *their* favorite and when she had finished the men exchanged a look. Jack mouthed the word *three,* but Blue shook his head and held up his index finger: *one!* Jack shrugged and nodded.

" 'Hey Diddle Diddle.' "

" 'Mr. Froggie.' "

They scowled at each other. "Mr. Froggie was number three you butthead."

"Three hell! What does this finger mean to you . . . ?"

"What does *this* finger mean to you?"

Jean smiled. He was probably the only person in the room in a position to see what they were doing with their fingers.

Markie interrupted. "I better sing them again."

That shut them up.

They no doubt thought they were done once they managed to vote on the same song but they were wrong. "An' that's not the half of my new stuff," exclaimed Markie. "Listen to what else I learned!" She tapped her toe and swayed and recited . . . "One times one is one. Come with me and have some fun. Two times two is four. Come with me to shut the door . . .

"Four times seven is twenty-eight! Come with me and see me skate . . . Hey wait, Blue!" Blue had been trying to slip away. "I wasn't done yet."

"I thought you were."

"Goodness, no. I haven't done the alphabet yet."

Jack gave Blue a look. "The alphabet's what we been waitin' on, Goober."

"It is? Well, I suppose I could skip over . . ."

"Sure you could!"

"Oh, all right."

No matter how tired and battle weary the two men were, they were tolerant and loving toward their blind sister, but the display of such obvious closeness had saddened Jean. Even the affection he had had for Duncan was no comparison to the bond that existed between these Dares. He looked around at each shadowed face and for the first time in years he found himself longing for the family he had never had. A family like this one.

"Here I go . . . *A* is in always, but never in ever. It is in part, but never in sever. *B* is in bind, but not in tie. It is in bawl but not in cry . . .

"*Y* is in yawn but not in gape. It is in monkey, but not in ape . . ."

Jean noticed that by the time she reached the end, Jack and Blue's eyes were as fixed and unseeing as hers.

That night Jean lay listening to the restful sound of the crickets and the frogs. The fire's orange glow lit the cabin's interior but it was a dark night. The slivered moon was further dimmed by some ragged clouds that kept drifting across it.

Fog hung between the creek and along the rise that led to the cabin. It made everything look odd and vaguely off balance which was, all in all, exactly how he felt.

It had been an unsettling couple of days, partly due to his practicing medicine for the first time in years, and partly due to the admission he'd had to make to himself afterward . . . namely, that he had enjoyed it.

He knew he had done those men some good. Maybe he had not been as adept as a practicing physician who had kept his hand in, but they were clearly better off than when they rode up.

Of course Evie could have tended to them but from what he had seen, she had been wise to realize that her eyes and her hands were not what they used to be.

On the other hand, Brit would make a fine doctor. At first when she assisted him, he had thought she was anticipating his needs with uncanny accuracy. Now he believed she was supplying him with what she would have used herself. She was a born healer, if there was such a thing. Given the proper training and the right instruments, he was sure of it.

And there was the main reason for his malcontent. Finding out that she had more value than that he had placed on her made him feel like a shallow cad. Which was, of course, precisely what he was.

Apparently word had spread about his being fit enough to doctor the troop, and soon men of all shapes and sizes started showing up at the farm. They did not come for his services, but rather, to pay suit to the young ladies of the house. One by one they came and ranged in age from sixteen to sixty. Actually about the only thing they had in common was that all had a sort of choked ruddiness to their newly nicked faces. Some wore shirts with cuffs that hung over their knuckles. Some had sleeves that ended mid-arm. None had any sense of apparel at all. One poor boy turned to leave and presented them with the mark of flatiron scorched onto the back of his shirt.

The twins would sit under the live oak in plain view of their mother—and Jean—to entertain their callers. With brooding eyes Jean would watch them laugh and flirt and try to see if either twin showed a preference for one man over another. Without exception, all callers were encouraged to return, loudly and with much persuasive cajoling.

If he had not known better he would think that someone was employing the age-old female gambit, jealousy. It was so blatant and so adolescent. And so effective! Because there he sat, simmering with it. And why not? He was here first. If she was going to bestow her favors on someone, it ought to be him.

He was beginning to wonder if any part of the lovemaking had been real. Perhaps it had all been a figment of his imagination. Perhaps most patients who hover at death's door experience the same wildly realistic fantasies. God! It almost made his brush with death worthwhile. Then, just when he would decide that must be it . . . he'd had a case of delusions brought on by extreme fever—she would give him a look or move in a certain way and he would become convinced that he was right in the first place.

Indecisiveness was so alien to his nature he was beginning to wonder if he had sustained an injury to the head as well. Perhaps the sort of damage that had rendered him incapable of knowing his own mind.

A silent shadow padded by. Evie Dare.

"Madame Dare. Evie. A minute please . . ."

"Yeah?"

"On the night I was shot do you know if I hit my head?"

"Not that I know of."

"Mm."

"Why?"

"Nothing. Good night."

"Night."

Brit woke and found Irish's place beside her empty. She looked at the window and saw her sitting there, leaning against the wall.

She slid out of bed and went to her. Irish was holding her legs to her chest and her feet were turned in, as if she were afraid they would get trod upon. Brit sat on her heels beside her.

"Hey, Irish."

"Hey."

"What are you doing?"

"Nothing. Just sitting here."

"Can't you sleep?" Irish shook her head. "Huh. Well, wanna go down to the creek and talk?" She shook her head again. "Wanna talk here?"

"No."

"Well, what do you want to do?"

"Sit here. Alone."

Half mad Brit said, "Suit yourself!" and went back to bed. She punched up her pillow and jerked the covers.

Moony. She had heard someone called that once but she never thought she would ever use it to describe a Dare.

The next morning Brit was alone in the other room. Jean was alone, out on the porch. He called to her and asked for water. She drew it and brought it to him, fresh from the well.

"Merci," he said. "Wait . . ." He caught her hand when she would have withdrawn it. "Sit and visit with me for a minute."

She smiled. "All right."

She sank to the porch and tugged on her hand but he retained possession of it. He looked into her eyes and smiled lazily. "I have been hoping to have a chance to speak to you alone."

"You have?"

"Of course. For days. You must know that I have thought of you constantly."

Her mouth fell open. "You have?"

"Yes. Without ceasing."

Brit shut her mouth and tried to think of something to say other than what she had just been about to blurt: It works! My stars! She wanted to beller: Maw! It works!

"You have constantly been in my thoughts. And in my dreams."

"I have?"

"We must meet."

"Meet?"

"Yes. Please say yes."

"Well . . ."

He kissed the palm of her hand, which was a little damp, then he looked deep into her eyes. It got very quiet, and the longer they looked at each other the quieter it got.

Lord, she thought. The strength of his gaze! Why, a person could lose herself in it. And she promptly did.

"I have never forgotten how your hands felt on me."

Jean had fixed her with a strongly sensual look, well practiced and always successful. She could hardly miss the invitation in his eyes. Nor . . . if she was as experienced as he thought her to be . . . the protrusion between his thighs. The only problem was that she was staring at the porch floor!

"What is it?" Two red splotches had appeared on her cheeks. "What?"

"Markie Dare!"

The admonition was so unexpected that Jean flinched. Some unseen person had a reaction as well because a thump and a muffled "OW!" came from under the porch followed by a muttered, "Hot blast it!"

"Markie Dare!"

"Dang! You made me hit my head!"

Brit had stomped off the porch and was kneeling in the dirt. "Markie Dare, you get out from under there! Right this minute!"

Jean cursed. All he could see of Brit was her superbly rounded rear end bobbing above the porch floor. The rear was replaced by two faces . . . one dirt-streaked; one red with sisterly anger.

"Ouch! That hurt!"

"I'm gonna pinch you silly! Listening to other people's conversations! Wait 'til I tell Maw! Shame on you!"

This last, Jean barely heard because Brit was pushing her little sister up the stairs and apparently—from the yelps—adding a few well-placed pinches as she went.

He hoped her little behind would be black and blue from them.

He punched his pillow and cursed softly. For them to be alone he had to be able to walk . . . away from this place and away from that dratted kid!

Seventeen

When Jean had been sewing up Jesse McIninch's wound, he happened to glance up and notice that Jack Dare was paying especially close attention to what he was doing. At the time he had thought it was no more than an officer's concern for one of his men. However, early one morning he heard the slap of the men's cabin door and looked up to see Jack striding purposefully toward him.

Obviously he was right out of bed. His hair radiated from his head in stiff black spikes and he looked, as the natives would say, wild as a buck.

They exchanged grunts. Jack got coffee and returned. He stood there a minute then said, "You know, you did a pretty good job of doctorin' ol' Jesse an' the others."

"Thank you. I guess it must be one of those things one never forgets."

Jack looked off then looked back. "Wonder if you would look at a wound I got a few weeks back."

Again, he felt caught. He could hardly refuse his host and could only hope that it was not beyond his expertise. "Of course. If you think I can help . . ."

"I don't know if you can or not but it jus' ain't healing right. Lemme show you." Jack looked around. Goldie had just come out. "Goldie?"

"Yeah?" He scratched his crotch and yawned big and

Jean wondered if their cabin could be in some sort of wind tunnel.

"Stand watch there a minute."

"All right."

"I don't want Maw or the girls comin' out 'till we're done here."

"I said all right, didn't I?"

Jack grinned at Jean. "Goldie can be real cantankerous in the morning."

"So I see." And so he did! More than he cared to see, for without further ado, Jack had dropped his pants and was pointing at his cods.

For a second or two Jean thought he was being asked to treat a disease aptly named for the goddess of love, but then he saw a lump of scar tissue inches from the left testicle.

"Rubs when I ride an' itches like hell. It ain't seemly for a man to be scratchin' his vitals all the time."

Jean examined the place visually and then probed it with his finger. "I think there may be a shard of metal in there. Iron perhaps. Something."

"Well dig it outa there." He spraddled his legs.

"Now?"

"Unless you're too busy?"

"No. Not at all."

"Should I tell Maw to put your knife in water, Doc?"

"Yes, Goldie. Merci."

Minutes later, Jean had his nose in Jack Dare's groin. "Goodgawdamighty, man!" gritted Jack. "Ain't you done yet?"

"Almost."

Jean had worked with less distraction, what with Goldie telling an outlandish tale about a man who had been gelded and what with Blue yodeling in soprano.

"Jean?"

"Yes, Markie?"

For obvious reasons Markie was the only female Goldie had allowed out onto the porch while the surgery was in progress.

"Will you be forced to use maggots?" She spoke with delighted dread.

"Markie!"

Markie left her chair like a rock out of a slingshot. *Hot blast it! Maw must have been standing right next to the blamed window!*

"Whut?"

"You come inside here! Right now."

"Why?"

"I can't believe you! Askin' a crazy thing like that! You coulda throwed the doctor off."

"Oh, no!" Blue in his *sotto voce* soprano. "Don't throw the doctor off!"

"Maw, I was only gonna ask if I could listen."

Jean stopped probing and looked at her. So did everyone else. "Listen to what?"

"The maggots." She gave a delicious shiver. "Blue told me a person can hear 'em munchin' away the dead skin . . ."

"Blue Jack Dare! I swear you are worse'n any ten kids together! Why do you tell her such cockamamie stuff?"

Goldie said, "Blue was jus' leavin', Maw." It was true. Blue was at that moment trying to tiptoe off the porch.

"There!" Jean was extremely relieved. He had been starting to sweat.

Jack leaned close and saw a sliver of something bloody. "Is that it?"

"That is it. Who knows what it is or where it came from. But it is out now."

"Good. Lemme get another swig of that mare's milk and then you can start sewin' me up."

His mother called from inside the cabin. "Did I miss something, Jack?"

"It ain't nothin', Maw."

"It is too. I ain't doctorin' no more and that's final. I tole you I oughta quit a year ago. I cain't feel nothin' no more. Cain't see nothin' neither. I am too blamed old for anythin' any more."

"Yeah and your mind's gone too!"

"I can still swing a stick, Blue Jack Dare! A fat lot of good it's ever done me with you!"

Irish followed her mother outside. She was still muttering under her breath about Blue. Irish dumped water on the stump they used for cutting, and scrubbed it with a rag then she went inside and collected four onions and half a dozen potatoes, which she carried outside in her skirt. Her maw was coming out of the smokehouse with a loop of venison sausage. She laid the loop on the stump beside the vegetables and poured heated water in the cook pot.

"Maw?"

"Ayeh?"

"Don't take on about it. It wasn't your fault."

"Oh, it was too."

"Didn't you once say if a person does the best they can, can't nobody ask for more?"

"Ayeh."

"Did you do your best?"

"Ayeh. Hush now and chop. Are there any carrots?"

"I think so. Maw?"

"Ayeh?"

Irish cut her a side-eyed look and then sighed. "Nothing."

"What?"

"Nothing. Never mind."

* * *

Later that day Goldie presented Jean with a crutch that he had fashioned from a hickory limb then padded with a strip of bearskin. It was a bit odoriferous, but kind to his underarm, and after minimal practice he had been doing quite well. The crutch was most helpful when his leg suddenly went numb, as it was still wont to do.

It was a first step toward full recovery and perhaps to an assignation with a certain lady. In the interim, it would allow him to see more of the farm and to acquaint himself with its inhabitants. Unfortunately not all introductions were pleasant, particularly his meeting with an old blind mare who was called Goat because of her habit of butting people in the back. She apparently mistook him for Goldie because she trotted up behind him and knocked him flat on his face.

"She's looking for sorghum balls," said Goldie as he removed some of the sweets from his pocket and let Goat lip them off his palm. "Might not hurt to carry a few yourself."

Jean eyed the mare, who was so old she had tufts of white hair in her ears. He suggested shooting her, which earned him a hard steely look and a lengthy lecture on loyalty. Recognizing defeat, he obtained some of the sweet from Markie and would decoy the mare by tossing a few balls away from his path and then stepping lively.

Hap Pettijohn and Abel O'Neal rode in that afternoon and found Jean standing near the corral watching Goldie shoe a horse.

Abel O'Neal said he had interviewed everyone involved, and all pertinent witnesses, and it was the consensus of opinion that Jean shot Gil Daggert as he lay in bed only because Gil's brother Earl shot Jean in the back causing him to unintentionally squeeze the trigger.

Abel agilely sidestepped some animal scat. "I believe it will sound credible when you take the stand. You are simply telling the truth—namely that you intended to make a citizen's arrest and hand Gil Daggert over to the authorities, which in this instance is, ah, Sheriff Goodman. The rest of the trial will be a matter of going through the motions and then you will be free to do as you wish." He looked at Jean. "Are you planning to stay on in Sweet Home?"

"Good grief, no."

"Too bad. I think it is a splendid country."

Obviously O'Neal had never lived in the center of art and learning. Not that Jean much cared about art and learning but it made him feel better to think that he did.

O'Neal was saying, "I'm staying. Forever I hope. My only concern is, can I earn a living?"

"Not enough legal business?"

"Not so far. Of course, if I can ever master the Spanish language I have the potential of increasing my client capacity considerably. In the meantime, I am considering rangering."

O'Neal was a tall, alert-looking man in his early twenties with flaxen hair and blue eyes that held another's with an open, direct gaze.

"That seems a bit extreme to me."

"What?"

"Making a living by coming as close to dying as that."

O'Neal shrugged. "A man's got to eat. Besides, it will be good for me. Learning skills of survival and the like, although . . ." He frowned. "There are some survival skills I would just as soon not acquire. Like determining the height, weight and hair color of a certain traveler by fingering his horse's turds. I also don't care to be promoted."

"I can understand that business about the turds but what's wrong with getting promoted?"

"A troop joke. I've been told that every time the rangers go riding into the middle of a hostile encampment Jack Dare will holler . . . Any man killed will be promoted on the spot!"

"Ah." Jean chuckled. That sounded like Jack.

They walked on with Goat following along behind . . . just in case they dropped something edible.

"Tejas is not conducive to an easy life."

"That's a mouthful!" O'Neal sighed. "I'm afraid skills such as mine may not be in demand for many years. I would probably have been better off if I had forgone a legal career in favor of becoming a bull whacker."

"What in God's name is a bull whacker?"

He shrugged. "Who knows? But they are apparently in great demand. The other night a man told me that one of the richest men in the district got his start bull whacking."

"Ah, well. Remember that money isn't everything."

"What is?"

"A good repute. Public esteem. The favorable regard of your peers." He clapped him on the back. "Cheer up. No doubt someday someone will say that Abel O'Neal is the most beloved man in the territory."

"Did you ever know a beloved lawyer?"

"Hm. A point well taken."

They had reached the cabin just in time to be passed a heaping platter of roast turkey. Hap Pettijohn already had his face buried in a leg. He had not changed—literally. Jean recognized several of the stains that decorated his skin shirt.

"Ah! The lovely Miss Dare," O'Neal said and bowed to Irish. "And the lovely Miss Dare." He bowed to Brit. Both girls curtsied and grinned back.

"Hey, Mr. O'Neal!"

"Hello."

Jean remembered that the handsome young lawyer was betrothed to the school teacher, Miss Mapes—only one would never know it by looking at Brit, who was smiling at him and getting him a cup of cider and offering him a plate of food.

Suddenly a short stint in Tejas appealed to him. The trial would necessitate his staying for some undetermined time anyway and there really was no good reason for him to race back. He would probably never travel this way again. Might as well see a bit of the country while he was here. Maybe he would look around down south.

Hap was saying he had just asked Blue if he would be willing to ride guard on the runs between Brasoria and Sweet Home—when he was not out on a scout of course—and that Blue had agreed. "I hired young Charley Walters too. He's gonna drive."

"He is the one who drove Miss Mapes and her family down here from Pennsylvania," said Abel.

Hap nodded. "Yep. Good driver. Poor shot. But he's workin' on that."

Evie Dare said, "The boy's pretty green for that job, ain't he?"

"Like I tole Miss Mapes . . ." Hap had an awful choking fit, then went on, chewing and talking, both. "The boy's got to do somethin' to make a livin'. If it ain't this job it'll likely be another. An' the other might not be near as honest as mine is."

Jack said, "It's a risk."

Evie clicked her tongue. "Seems like things oughta be settlin' down insteada gettin' wilder!"

"I'll tell yuh, between the Indians and the banditos . . ." Hap shook his head and let the rest go.

Jean looked at Jack and lifted his brows. There had been at least one change in Hap Pettijohn in the last two weeks. He seemed to have aged about ten years.

O'Neal and Pettijohn stayed until after dark, talking about one thing and another, and then they prepared to ride back to town. Before they left Jean asked Hap if he would take a letter to Brasoria for him. Brit was cleaning up the table litter and Evie was probably the only one who noticed how hard she was listening.

"Give it to that whisker-faced saloon keeper. Tell him that promptly relaying the letter to New Orleans will mean another one of these for him." He added a gold coin to a small heap on the table.

Hap tapped the envelope. "Does it say on here who it goes to?"

"Yes. It is for a man who is staying at the Golden Eagle in New Orleans. His name is Remy Roudan."

"Who's that?"

"I swear, Markie, you are the nosiest person!"

"It's all right, Evie," said Jean. "Roudan is my, um, man."

"Your man? You mean like your slave?"

"No. Nothing like that. By 'man' I mean valet."

Jean looked at the others but they were just as blank-eyed as Markie. Only Abel O'Neal did not appear non-plussed.

"A valet is someone who looks after a gentleman's belongings and assists him to, um, dress . . ."

Markie's jaw unhinged then hinged. "You mean you can't get dressed by yourself yet? Gol, I've been doin' that ever since I was less'n one month old!"

He might have expected confusion over this. While O'Neal explained the purposes of a gentleman's gentleman, Jean found himself agreeing with Markie. In this context and in this place, a valet sounded utterly mad, yet in France a personal manservant was considered a requisite.

His letter instructed Remy to book passage to England immediately and from there to proceed to Scotland in order to deliver Jean's letter to his mother, informing her of Duncan's death. Jean's other instructions were for his Paris banker and solicitor, including instructions to sell his London home in Berkley Square.

He had been going to sell the London place for years. He was rarely in residence and it seemed a ridiculous luxury, paying for the upkeep of a home he never used.

At least these were the reasons he gave himself as he wrote out Remy's instructions.

The last thing Jean asked Remy to do was to pack up what belongings he had left in New Orleans—valises, his pistol case and his rapier—and arrange to transport everything to Sweet Home.

"You've decided to stay on then?"

His eyes went to Brit before he answered Evie Dare. "Only a bit beyond the trial but I don't want to leave my belongings in New Orleans untended for an extended period of time."

Brit felt his gaze and looked up. Lit solely by the hearth fire, the room was in heavy shadow but he had one brow quirked, as if he was asking her what she thought about it.

Abel O'Neal stood. "One more thing, Jean. The sheriff said to tell you he'll be out to take you in pretty quick now. End of the week at the latest."

"Fine." He made a little bow. "Tell him I await his pleasure."

Eighteen

And that was what he was doing on the day following, sitting on the porch, waiting for the sheriff and passing the time by watching Blue and Goldie replace some missing fence sections. They had been making good progress as they steadily moved northward along the winding road that led into Sweet Home.

Prior to beginning, Blue had said he could think of jobs that needed doing more but Goldie said that since they had to do it sooner or later, they might as well get at it. It had rained the night before and it is always easier to dig in the dirt when the ground is soft.

They were going about it in an orderly fashion, first hammering the sharpened end of a post into the ground with a maul, then walking off eight paces and hammering in another. Then they would nail two bars to each post so that when they moved on, the finished sections resembled a row of stretched X's.

Goldie's big booming laugh floated in with the wind and Jean smiled. Through slitted eyes he followed their shrinking figures until they were almost out of view and then he lazily let his eyes drift . . . to the slatted crib where corncobs were being dried for kindling, to the once sizeable and now barren garden area and then to the woodshed.

Through the leafless trees he could see how the sun sparkled on the water and on the far side of the creek the way the feed fields looked like brown checks on a board.

He saw all these things with his eyes but in his mind he was imagining the path a certain piece of soap was traveling right about now.

He had been thinking about leaving. Going into town with the sheriff and getting the Daggert business straightened out then arranging transport to Mexico City. Then he had seen Brit take the knife off the nail and slice off some soap and all thoughts of leaving had been wiped from his mind. Instead he imagined her sitting slick and wet in the water, slathering herself with soap, maybe singing a little under her breath.

Most of his dream might be fantasy but parts of it were real. He knew that for a fact. The question was: how much?

It was a question whose time had come. Without conscious thought, he pulled the padded crutch toward him and used it to lever himself to his feet, and when he rose and stepped off the porch, he moved as if he were a man in a trance.

The path to the creek was fraught with partially exposed roots and half-buried rocks, but the crutch helped him to navigate it fairly well, although still very slowly. Fortunately he had gone only midway when she came into sight, wearing a slightly damp dress and carrying a towel. She was naked under her dress. He could see that by the damp patch that clearly outlined one breast. She saw him and stopped. Alert but calm she stared back at him with none of the simpering shyness affected by so many young women he knew. A minute went by in silence though there were sounds all around them—birds and bugs, small animals that were moving around in the brush.

Brit was not surprised to see him. After all, she had been dreaming up a situation like this for days. She swallowed hard and spoke, "You'll be leaving soon."

"Yes, but I decided that there is something I need to do before I go."

She cocked her head. "Oh?"

A mockingbird's cry came from the trees above them. "I had to see you alone." He had not intended to blurt it like that.

"Me?" She steepled her hand on her chest, the picture of innocence. "Why?"

He moved a few feet closer. "I need to ask you about something that happened while I was sick."

"Yes?" She was looking curiously at him as if she didn't know what he was about. But she knew all right. Oh, yes. The little witch! "It was something very strange."

"Lots of strange things can happen with a fever."

"True and of course I realize I had all the usual symptoms. A rise in body temperature. A quickened pulse. Restlessness and emotional excitement. But in addition to all that, I might actually have also suffered some delirium . . ."

"Really? What's that?"

"Uh, wild and crazy thinking."

"Oh!"

"You see . . . I had this dream. A very vivid, very real dream." She stood staring at him but said nothing.

"It was raining. The air was damp and close and I recall thinking how terribly quiet it seemed. I had been sleeping but very fitfully and so I woke unrested and unsure of where I was. I lay there, waiting to sleep again when suddenly I sensed someone's presence. I strained my eyes trying to see who it was but it was too dark. I suppose I should have been afraid for my life, what with wild Indians and all, but for some reason I felt quite the contrary. Expectant. Excited. Like I could not wait for my guest to reveal herself to me. At last my visitor knelt beside me. She looked at me and smiled. God, she was beautiful! I willed my arms to move but they would not. I lay helpless before her."

Her eyes were still and very deep, the sort that would pull a man inside if he wasn't careful.

"The girl leaned forward and her hair fell to the floor, a silken shiny curtain of sable. She touched me with a lover's touch and then she kissed me and it was then that I knew my visitor's identity . . ." Gently he asked, "It was you, wasn't it?" Nothing. He walked closer. Something flickered in her eyes but she held her ground. "Wasn't it?"

"Yes."

He breathed a sigh of relief. At least that much of it had been real.

"Why did you do that?"

She seemed to consider the question for a minute and then she shrugged. "To see what would happen."

She had a husky graveness to her voice. "What did happen? My memory's spotty, you see."

"Well . . . not much."

Not much! Not according to his recollection of it! He gave a wry smile and thought: who was it who said candor was more refreshing than water in the desert. He looked up the path toward the house. He looked back to where she stood beneath the tree, big-eyed and beautiful. Light slanted through the limbs and dappled her face like a woodland doe. He smiled a little. "The conditions were less than ideal."

"Maybe so."

"Should we try it again now?"

"Why?"

She was still giving him that damn level look of hers. "To see if participation on my part will improve the results." He waited with his heart pounding against his ribs and finally she shrugged.

"If you like."

He supposed that wild enthusiasm was too much to expect but genteel interest would have been nice. He stood over her and was surprised to feel his limbs tremble. Apparently he had enough enthusiasm for them both! He cupped her head and gently coaxed her face up to his. It was a perfectly shaped face, immortal, like one would see in a museum. A master's rendering of someone either very wicked or very good.

God, the girl not only looked like a saint but she smelled like one as well. He inhaled none of the cloying perfumes so often used to poorly conceal unwashed clothes, but rather the sweet scent of sage and the sharp smell of strong soap.

Funny how his perceptions had changed. He no longer thought of beauty as a chalked face with black marks placed in a dozen tantalizing spots. Nor were perfect breasts those that were pushed so unnaturally high that they seemed to be rising from the collarbone.

Beauty had become a black-eyed girl with strong bones and good teeth and a way about her that was as elemental as water and yet as mysterious as the sphinx. An enchanting and a very beautiful riddle.

Her hair was loose and a little damp and he liked having his hands in it. He touched the tiny wet curls that coiled against her skin and then moved his thumbs across her high cheekbones which were wide and as pointed as arrowheads.

He could see himself reflected in her eyes and he was suddenly reminded of a childhood time when he had loved and thought he was loved in return. It had been an idyllic time. A time when he would not have changed his life for the world.

He held her gaze as he lowered his head to hers. Softly their lips met and her eyes drifted shut. He kissed her gently and very carefully but with the expertise learned in a thousand kisses.

He had intended to maintain a control of himself but found he could not. Instead of driving her crazy with soft caresses and gentle kisses, he had, it seemed, driven himself crazy instead. He was no longer thinking about seduction . . . he was no longer thinking, period. He had ceased to think of anything but how she felt in his arms. With a surge of feeling he did not bother to analyze, he deepened the kiss, parting her lips with his then angling his head and fitting his body to hers like a key in a lock. She leaned into him and kept leaning as she kissed him with the sweetest mouth in the universe. He slipped one leg between hers and her moan vibrated to his very core.

In an instant desire had made him as primitive as an animal in rut. He lifted her up and into him and it was not enough. Nothing would ever be enough. One arm spanned her back and brought his fingers near the curve of her breast. He touched her, cupped her and felt her nipple harden under his fingers. He kissed her ear and the place beneath it on her neck and spoke wild words against her skin.

His voice was rough and passionate and his body hard and hot against her. Brit felt like a leaf caught in a swift-moving stream, but she did not care. Her dream had become her life. He buried his face in her neck and she drew a deep shaky breath. Her heart danced with a crazy rhythm. His long-fingered hand was moving toward some place it was surely never meant to be but she was too helpless with pleasure to do anything about it.

With her head back and arching toward him she almost lost her footing when he suddenly pushed her away and backed up.

He stood looking at her in shock, blinking like a man who has been introduced to light after a long time in the dark. Primitive signals had just gone off in his brain and a warning voice had shrieked in his ear. He wanted to be wrong but he knew his instincts were right. This was not the sensual siren who had invaded his dreams. Far from it. This was an untried innocent. Not only had she never been with a man but she had never even been kissed by one! He would stake his life on that. Further, the reason why she kissed like a child was because she was one—at least with respect to things having to do with males, females and sexual gratification.

She stood immobile and stared back at him. "What is it?"

He looked at the bewilderment on her face and he rubbed his eyes. If he had ever kissed virgin lips, they were hers. Good God, it should not matter but it did. It mattered a lot.

She took a shaky breath. "What is it . . . what?"

"Brit. My dear girl, I must beg your pardon."

She looked at him for a minute and then she smiled a little. "We didn't do anything that bad, did we?"

"You misunderstand." He bowed a little. "I have made a . . . grievous mistake."

"You have?"

"Yes."

She stared at him. Swallowing once, she said, "What kind of mistake?"

"A grave error. I have made a grave error."

"Why? What's wrong?"

He rubbed his forehead. "Everything is wrong, but it is nothing you have done. It is my fault. All my fault."

"What is all your fault? Tell me so I can understand."

"Put quite simply, I mistook you for . . . someone else."

He thought she was someone else! What he meant to say was: he had thought she was Irish. Oh, God! It struck her like a hoe handle. He was in love with Irish!

Her eyes were wide and hurt and Jean felt wretched. The last thing he wanted to do was hurt her. He reached out for her but she was gone, bounding over a fallen log like a deer.

Naturally he was preoccupied and did not hear the tell-tale whuffle, until mere seconds before he was the recipient of a not very gentle butt in the back. In trying to fall without doing damage to his back wound, he twisted and slipped on a pile of wet leaves. Which brought the apex of his thighs slamming against a rock and which pounded his cods to peanuts. Cold wet lips touched the back of his neck and he rolled over in time to hear Goat trot off.

The pain was the sort that told him he had never really known what pain was before. He must have lost consciousness for a minute because when his vision returned there were three beard-roughened faces drawn together above him.

"Hey, McDuff!"

"How you doin'?"

"Swimmingly, thanks for inquiring." Jean spoke through gritted teeth.

"Then how come you're laying there like a shot man?"

"Clutchin' your gonads?"

"An' lookin' like hell."

"I suppose you could say that I have just suffered the meeting of a rock and a hard place. Will you tell me something . . ."

"Sure. What?"

"Is anything bleeding?"

"Not that I can see but I will say this: I have seen better color on a put out eye."

"What're you doin' out here anyway?"

"I was watching those ducks."

Blue shielded his eyes to look at the gray sky. "Uh-huh. Well. They're headed somewhere, I reckon. Which is more'n I can say for you."

"You wanna hand up or you wanna watch ducks some more?"

"I'll watch ducks."

The Dares left him to fend for himself. Unfortunately it was quite awhile before he was capable of getting to his feet, much less walking back to the cabin. It was just as well. He needed time to think . . . only, this time he vowed to use the head that sat on his shoulders.

Of course there was an obvious solution, and that was: the sooner he left, the better. He belonged where things were either black or white, and where he understood the rules of all the games.

But was that place Paris? He wasn't so sure anymore. His perception of female beauty had changed. Had his other opinions changed as well? Had tree-lined boulevards and moss-covered châteaux been supplanted by hard bright stars on an ebony sky? Or an eagle soaring above a sun-struck prairie?

Or perhaps a girl with a form to die for?

Good God! What was he thinking? It would be sheer folly. Marriage had apparently been her goal—there could be no other reason for an innocent to flirt with literal disaster—but of course, it was entirely out of the question. Two people could not be more ill-suited to each other. He paused on the path. Yes, of course he was right. They were terribly incompatible.

Ah, well. At least he had not imagined those veiled looks and steamy smiles. He recognized the ploy now as an attempt to seduce him into a proposal of marriage. Thank God he had seen it for what it was. Under certain conditions or given the right set of circumstances he might have relieved her of her virginity . . .

Call it late-developing moral principles or latent probity or a Lazarus-like resuscitation of a conscience. Whatever it was, he would not seduce the daughter and sister of these Dares. That was all there was to it. He would do one good thing in return for what the Dares had done for him. He would leave Brit alone. He would go into town tomorrow, straighten out this thing with the sheriff and leave the area immediately thereafter. Yes, that's what he would do. Tomorrow first thing . . .

But all his plans went to hell the moment he saw her again. She was standing on the porch with Markie, her face partially in shadow but grim and tight-looking. He stopped on the edge of the clearing and watched her and the sure knowledge that he must leave felt like a knife in his heart.

Brit had her work cut out for her, looking at Markie's rock without letting her know that she had been crying. She blinked in a vain attempt to clear the shimmering view and said, "It's a very pretty rock, Goober. Brown with yellowy streaks. It sort of reminds me of a butterfly wing."

Brit had not known a person could talk with a broken heart but apparently they could. Oh, what a fool she had been! A yoke of misery weighed on her shoulders. All that time that she had spent, trying to get him to notice her had been wasted. He had noticed Irish instead. Now everything was haywire. She wanted Jean, Jean wanted Irish, but Irish wanted Emil Schumacher. And she presumed Emil Schumacher wanted his wife. It was all an awful mess.

Brit picked up her sister's hand and laid the rock in it. "Here you go, Goober. I have to go get my chores done."

"Yeah I better, too."

Markie frowned after her sister's receding footsteps. Brit had not wanted her to know that she had been crying but she would have had to be blind *and* deaf not to hear her strangled voice and clogged nose holes.

So. Now. Markie figured it was up to her to find out who had made her sister cry and why. She narrowed her sightless eyes and went thin-lipped.

Whoever it was had better not have done it on purpose. That's all she had to say!

"Maw!"

Irish's voice had been so loud and so hard that Evie looked up at her. She was standing stiff and strange looking before her. Evie set down the basket of wet clothes and let her eyes run over her daughter. No wounds and no signs of distress, at least not physically.

"What is it?"

Irish looked at her mother and then at her brother's shirt. She stretched one sleeve out on a limb and then clasped her hands at her waist."Maw . . ."

"What?"

"Have you ever heard of somebody who liked to hurt themself?"

"What?"

"I mean hurt their body. Cut their arms or scratch their faces . . ."

"No, I never heard of such a crazy thing! Where did you?"

"From somebody. I don't know."

"You don't remember?"

"No."

Evie watched her slap another shirt around and then twist the water out of it. Irish looked sad. "You know, jus' because I ain't never heard of such a thing does not mean it ain't never happened. Girl, there's lotsa things I ain't never seen or heard."

"It could be possible, then."

Evie considered that and then shook her head. "I don't think so. A person would have to be a ravin' lunatic to do something like that!"

Irish looked sadder still. "That's what I thought."

Nineteen

The women had retired, Evie to her pallet behind a little wall in the main room and the girls to their beds upstairs. Jean had heard the creak of rawhide on wood as they ascended the ladder. Then through the open window he heard the sound of water being poured from one vessel to another, and in his mind he saw Brit stepping out of her garments and washing up for bed and the image recalled the satiny feel of her skin and the sweet scent of her hair. She was twenty feet away. That's all. A mere twenty feet.

"Dieu!" he muttered and folded the pillow over his ear.

By what magic did the taste of her still cling to his lips! He had made love to many women and had afterward given neither the event nor the woman more than a moment's thought. He was not twenty, but a mature man with a wealth of experience with females and their wiles. Yet here he lay, trapped like a fly ensnared in a web. And his captor was the beautiful Brit Dare.

Bringing her into his world would be like locking a young colt in a paneled drawing room. She would hate Paris. He intuitively knew that to be true. Now it was extremely important that he remember it.

That night his nightmare returned, and he found himself back in Paris, only at a time that was many years in

the future. He was incredibly old, with frozen vocal cords
and lifeless limbs, confined to an adult perambulator and
unable to move more than his eyes.

As if he had been painted on canvas, Jean saw himself
sitting alone, a solitary speck upon a flat landscape, a bent
and broken thing in the middle of a vast sea of nothing.
Limitless space stretched all around him, unpopulated by
people, empty even of birds or flowers or anything of substance or beauty.

He had not known it was possible to be so utterly alone.
Was this how his life would end? In this cavernous void?

Suddenly something appeared at the outer reaches of
his abyss. A small black dot that might have been a bug,
crawling slowly across the pure white canvas.

As the dot drew closer, his heart leapt with joy. It was
his grandson . . . come to give succor to his old papaw . . .
But his joy soon fled and it was replaced by craven terror,
for the dream's final image was that of his grandson, carefully placing sticks all around his chair.

He sat bolt upright, breathing like a blown horse. Too
debilitated to stand, he pulled himself across the floor to
the open door where he looked at the moon-struck fields
and breathed deeply of the night-cooled air. Tejas! He pil-
lowed his head on his arms and he almost sobbed with
relief.

He had never placed any credence in dreams. He had
always blamed the few he'd had on an extra after-dinner
port or that too rich sauce on the boeuf bourgignon. Not
anymore. He placed a lot of credence on what he had just
witnessed. That dream had been a warning. He knew it as
sure as he knew his name. He stood at a sort of crossroad.
The question was: to what? Was he supposed to choose
between returning to France and staying in Tejas? Ridiculous! Of course he would choose to return to civilization.
He would take his chances with his progeny if it came to
that. Better to die at an offspring's hand than by the knife

of some savage Indian. There really was no question in his mind about the direction of his future. It was east. Out of Tejas. Out of the Americas. In the meantime his only objective should be healing enough to be mobile.

He considered the string of imprudent acts that summed up his life and vowed vigilance lest he repeat that recklessness. As long as he remained in this land he would resist temptation hour by hour, and the days would take care of themselves. He would keep his mind and his eyes off that girl and put all thoughts of pleasure, gratification or sexual satisfaction out of his mind.

And then came the dawn.

He woke in a suspended state of sexual readiness, the worst since he had caught the greedy eye of the butcher's wife, Emma Ford.

Emma Ford, God love her! He had not thought of her in years. The woman who had driven his virginal thirteen-year-old body wild for weeks. First she had let him see her but not touch her. Then she had let him see her as she touched herself. But never ever—or so it seemed to him—would she allow him to touch her.

Otto Ford, the butcher, was a huge pig-eyed man with black hair growing out of his collar. He could have broken him like a twig, but Jean was beyond caring. Death . . . dismemberment . . . anything was preferable to never possessing Emma's plump pink body.

He was putty in her hands by the time she had playfully wrapped her apron strings around his wrists and something silky over his eyes. "Open," she had whispered then popped a hard hot nipple in his mouth.

Now as during that tortured time so long ago, everything he saw titillated him. And he saw a lot. It seemed the world must mate in front of him. His first sight that morning was that of three alert-looking male dogs trotting along behind a small sleek-haired female. The bitch was obviously in season—even Jean could see the appeal of her bright pink tongue and soft, liquid eyes.

Working in concert, the three males got her backed up against Goldie's work shed so that she was boxed on all sides. She could not possibly get away from them all. She knew she had to choose. She refused the black-faced dog and ignored the buff-colored one. Ah, the liver-spotted dog had caught her eye. Yes, clearly he was her choice. She moved toward him and then danced away . . . catch me if you can. Calm but determined, the male circled her and came closer and closer with each revolution. The female growled at him but her skin was rippling with telltale shivers of anticipation.

Suddenly the male feinted left and when she dodged, he locked his jaws on her loose neck-skin. Her yelp of protest drew a warning growl as he came around behind and tried to mount her. She struggled but he prevailed and finally entered her. She made a protesting sound but he quickly anchored himself and went to work. She struggled briefly and then she stopped and went-spraddle legged. The male dog bared his teeth in a canine grin and never slowed. Soon he was rewarded with low doggie hum from deep in the bitch's throat. The male hung on and on and on. Finally, he stopped and stood as straight as a man. His eyes went blank and his expression changed . . . reactions that were replicated by the human witness on the porch nearby and from that moment on, Jean lay in a state of arousal that was unlike any he had ever known before.

The dogs were only the beginning. Rampant fecundity surrounded him.

The cock, a lusty, brutal fellow, nailed four hens before breakfast. A calico cat with a long rat tail had a highly enjoyable interlude with a half-eared black tom, and by mid-afternoon the sleek-haired bitch—that shameless hussy—returned with her spotted lover and rendered an encore performance.

Half-drugged with need, Jean lay a helpless witness to a dozen such couplings. And if the matings of the animal kingdom were not torment enough, there was the ever-present display of human lust: Blue who always smelled of sex. The thwarted lover Jack, who often stomped around with the red-rimmed eyes of a bull.

At dusk, the Dares remained in the main room after the evening meal, while Jean went back onto the porch. Alone and finally at rest, he was staring off toward the woods, grateful that most animals slept at night and that those that did not were at least out of his field of vision. Then he happened to glance downward and see that two propagating ants had chosen to tryst mere inches from his nose. It was the final straw! The coup de grâce . . . The male ant had connected.

"Yesss!" he hissed. "That's the way, mate. Long strokes! Follow through. That's it! Good! Very good!"

He felt a presence and looked up. Goldie Dare stood over him, his mouth full of something.

Goldie knelt. He looked at the ants and then he looked at Jean. He noted his dark, half closed eyes, the sheen of sweat upon his face. He chewed and swallowed and said, "You up to a ride into town?"

"Am I up to it?" An interesting choice of words. "Yes. I am most definitely up to it."

Blue came out too. "What's up?"

Jean groaned.

"We were talking about takin' a little ride into town."

"Good!" said Blue. "I'll get the horses."

Goldie tossed a buckskin jacket at him. "You sure you feel strong enough . . ."

"I'll be fine. As long as there are sporting women there."

"Sporting women! Hell, we got women who can show you stuff you ain't never seen before."

"The same old stuff will be quite sufficient."

Irish and Markie fell asleep right away but Brit lay thinking. She had been doing a lot of that lately, and after due consideration, she had come to some very important conclusions about things having to do with Irish and herself and the mess they found themselves in.

First off, Irish fancied herself in love with a married man. And if that wasn't going against the laws of man and God, Brit didn't know what was.

Second, Jean McDuff was the best man to see a Tejas sunset in a long long time. Maybe ever. He was at least a hundred times better than any of their other beaus. And he wanted her sister. Now, if she told her sister that she wanted McDuff for herself then Irish would never even look at McDuff as marriage potential. But if she just kept quiet, Irish was bound to notice him sooner or later and she might—she just might—fall out of love with Emil Schumacher and fall in love with Jean McDuff.

Thus by her silence would Brit ruin her own life. But she would save her sister's immortal soul.

It was small recompense for dying of a broken heart but it was better than nothing.

She had also thought a lot about what had happened that day in the woods. She especially thought about what their mother had told them about the man being the key and the woman the lock, and about how McDuff had made her feel. And what Maw had said made sense to her now because her body had wanted something that day in the woods. Wanted it in the worst way and wanted it still.

What worried her was this: What if nobody could unlock her but Jean McDuff? This had occurred to her the day before and she had been stewing over it ever since. The possibility was very worrisome.

If McDuff was never going to be hers then she was going to start trying to get over him. Maybe she could do it. Maybe she couldn't. One thing for sure, it was going to take a long long time and even then it was chancy.

But what if she did finally get over him some day but nobody could unlock her but him? Oh, God, nothing could be much worse than spending one's entire life locked up inside. Big silent tears started to course down her cheeks and she wept herself to sleep.

Twenty

They allowed the half moon to rise high in the sky before they left, thinking the fewer people who saw him in town, the better.

"What some men won't do . . ." said Goldie with a chuckle.

Jean managed to find a comfortable position slightly forward in the saddle and they set off. The Dare brothers kept the pace slow.

It was a clear still night with a sky that was so low the stars looked like they could be rearranged by hand. Flanking trees threw long shadows across the road and the gentle breeze smelled dry and damp at once, as it will in the autumn when leaves are moldering on the ground and all else is dying on the vine.

Arriving around midnight, they sat their horses and looked at the score of houses and businesses that made up Sweet Home. Some of the buildings were whitewashed adobe and eerie-looking in the dark. The rest, which were clapboard or peeling log, blended right into the night.

A few lanterns still burned—one at Dirty Dave's and another in an upstairs window at the boarding house—but the moon lent enough light for Jean to re-acquaint himself with the town.

A single road halved it, with the barbershop/bath house, the apothecary's and the general store on one side and a narrow bank, a tinsmith's shed, and the land and assayer's office on the other. Beyond, near the edge of town, was a farrier's shop, and Hap Pettijohn's corral inhabited, as one might expect, by the owner's prized mules.

Blue turned to Goldie. "You comin' with us or are you gonna have a piece of, er, pie? Miss Maude serves an awful good piece of pie and I see that her light's still on."

"Shut up, Blue!" Goldie turned his horse. "We'll circle around. Come up on Dulce's from the creekside."

Blue heeded his brother's warning but Jean saw a slash of white across his face.

This was the first he had heard that the owner of the rooming house was Goldie's woman and he wondered if it meant more than sex to either of them.

Dulce's was set off by itself, a low-slung adobe building with a thatched roof and tall narrow openings for windows. From within came the low hum of conversation and the soft strumming of a guitar. They walked their horses around back, out of plain view of the street.

The cantina was one large room, floored by dirt and sparsely furnished. A blue haze of smoke obliterated the ceiling and combined with the strong smell of damp dirt, gamey bodies, and pungent beverages.

A dozen men sat shaking dice or playing cards. Half again that many lounged against the long bar, drinking. In one corner was a man in a sombrero, hunched over a guitar and squinting against the smoke of a small black cigar.

They were subjected to prolonged scrutiny by all the patrons, but most particularly by three men who stood at the plank bar. They were a particularly disreputable-looking group. A Mexican who wore slashed pants and a sombrero with a beehive crown and two anglo men clad in skins. The latter were so shaggy-faced they looked more like animals than men.

Someone called to the Dares from the rearmost table

and Goldie peered through the smoke. "Hey lookit! Yonder's ol' Hap Pettijohn."

"Let's sit with him. Hey, Gregorio! Amigo mio! Bring us a bottle over yonder, will yuh."

Hap greeted Jean with a hearty blow to the back and then remembered his wound. "Damn! I forgot!"

"No problem. Actually a kick in the rear would be more painful than a clap on the back."

"I'll remember that."

They were served tequila by the one-armed man called Gregorio who had a thumb through the jug handle and a hairy finger in each of their glasses. He set everything down in the center of the table and caught in midair the coin that Blue flipped him, all without lifting his eyes. When he left, Jean asked if there was some reason why the man looked so morose.

"Gregorio Alazar always looks like he's just learned that his sister's a whore. Well, speak of the devil . . ." Dulce had come to the table. Goldie pulled her onto his lap.

Jean had already met the owner the night he was shot. She was a full-figured woman with blue-black hair and a gold tooth that flashed when she smiled.

On that first night she had advertised her wares by pulling her blouse under one melon-sized breast. At the time he had been too preoccupied with finding his brother's murderer to take her up on her offer. Now, however, the image of her breast might have been tattooed on his eyelids.

Across the room, the other girl, Lucetta, was smiling at him over the edge of a whiskey glass. Goldie leaned close, "She sure looks willing."

"Hm." Unfortunately Jean's willingness was beginning to wane. He had just flashed on her the way he had seen her last; namely astride a man who would soon be dead.

Considering the fact that she was excited by blood-letting

she must have really enjoyed a night when her lover was killed and another man shot in the back.

After Dulce left to tend to some matter, Jean commented on her seemingly congenial nature, and Blue leaned close. "Lemme jus' tell you the difference between Dulce an' Lucetta . . ."

Goldie said, "I believe that I'm better qualified to provide that information than you."

"Hell, I don't see why, seein' as how I taught these gals about everything they know."

Goldie snorted. "I was fixin' to say that the biggest difference is style. Dulce is, for want of a better word, restful."

"Hah! You gonna put restful above a quim like a snappin' turtle?"

Jean wasn't sure that sounded all that appealing but he lit a small cigar and narrowed his eyes in a judicial squint. "And the others?"

"The others?"

"The other women."

"There ain't none."

"You mean there are only two sporting women for the entire town?" That was a bit more fraternal than he liked.

"Well . . . yeah."

Jean was about to respond, when an instinctive feeling of peril distracted him. He looked around.

He was sitting with his long legs stretched out in front of him. Goldie sat to his right and Blue to his left with his chair backed up to the wall . . . probably so he could not be come at from behind. Hap, who apparently had no concerns either way, sat with his back to the room at large.

These things were of interest to Jean only because of a broadbeamed man who was staring at them with dull animosity. Jean kept his face a mask of indifference and studied him in return.

The man had the build of a bare-fisted fighter, with thick shoulders and a massive neck, and he was wearing a tarpaulin coat that looked chewed. Other than those things there was nothing to distinguish him from the other men in the room yet he looked vaguely familiar. Finally, Jean nodded toward him and asked Blue who he was. Blue looked at him. "The possum-eyed fella is Doke Doyle. The close-bred lookin' fella with half a nose is his brother, Dempsey. Their place backs up to the Green's land on the north."

"The one named Doke looks familiar."

"Huh. Well, I suppose you coulda seen him the night you braced Gil Daggert about your brother. He's a particular friend of the Daggerts."

"Doke's a hard man to have a liking for even when he's sober," said Hap.

"Drunk he can barely be recognized as a human bein'."

"He's worse'n Dempsey but neither one's a prize."

Hap leaned and spat on the floor. "The Doyles've never had much luck with their partners. They claimed one man died from eatin' too many green pecans. Another one jus' up an' disappeared one day. Set off for Brasoria to buy a horse and never returned. Or so they claimed. Each time 'course the Doyle brothers got their partners' stock an' all their trappings. Migh-tee damn convenient, if you ask me."

Blue puffed on his pipe. "They've always had a surly reputation. They used to trade with a band of Caddos. One night they got drunk and Dempsey bet the Caddos that they could not steal his horse from him. Brought the horse right into the cabin and tied the reins to the bed post but the Caddos slipped in and took it anyway. As a gesture of good will, they returned the horse but Dempsey got so mad he shot it. Caddos quit tradin' with 'im after that. Said they would not deal with a crazy man."

Hard glittering hate flared in Dempsey's eyes and Goldie was returning it look for look. "Our run-in with the Doyles has to do with their eatin' a steer with a Dare slit in its ear."

"They claimed they didn't know it was ours," said Blue. "I told them they were lying dogs but we decided to let it go until the next time. Two days later somebody took a shot at me from behind some rocks. There were no tracks but I've always had a feeling it was them."

"We're gonna have it out with them one day, sure."

"Maybe sooner than you think," said Jean. Doyle was coming closer. There was food—or worse—down his front and the reek of whiskey radiated from his person like sun waves on a hot day.

"Wadn't you the cold-blooded coward what murdered Gil Daggert?"

"Don't go to the bait."

Jean gave up trying to make sense out of the man's words and considered Hap's advice. While he did not relish a bare-handed fight with a man whose knuckles were the size of peach pits, it was not in his nature to allow an insult to go unanswered. He appraised his physical condition and concluded that he could probably stand up for a round or two. A moot point; Dempsey and the Doyles' Mexican friend had spread out and were moving in as well.

Jean would later remember strange things about those moments. That the Mexican's spurs had rowels so large they were leaving rake marks in the dirt. That the guitarist never stopped strumming. That Lucetta's mouth was formed in a perfect O.

Drawing a deep breath Jean thought, so be it, and stood. "I take exception to your words," he said and backhanded Doke hard enough to knock his head to one side.

Doke had been looking for him to draw a weapon. The last thing he expected was to be slapped like a woman. It was the worst insult he had ever been dealt.

A worm of blood appeared at the corner of Doke's

mouth. He looked at Jean and grinned and Jean thought: Ah! Apparently I have gotten his attention.

The Mexican drew a knife and rushed Blue, which distracted him enough for Dempsey to grab a chair and try to crash it over Blue's head. Stunned but not hurt, Blue hit Dempsey square on the lump of gristle called an adam's apple and then brought doubled fists down on the back of his head. Dempsey spread out flat on the ground. While Blue was dealing with Dempsey, Goldie knocked the knife out of the Mexican's hand and they went down in a kicking mass as each man grappled for the other's eyeball.

Meanwhile Doke came at Jean like a bull but Jean stepped aside and buried his fist in Doke's stomach. Doke swung a meaty arm at Jean, which he ducked and answered with two quick jabs to the ribs.

Neither blow made the least impression on Doke. He drew a razor and while Jean easily parried his first thrust, the second sliced through his sleeve to neatly score the skin below.

That got Jean's attention. He cursed and drew the short double-edged rapier he kept in a sleeve scabbard and stabbed Doyle in the side.

Doke looked down at his wound, which was bleeding freely, and said, "He's killed me, boys." He sat heavily. "Killed me dead!"

"You will live. Unfortunately."

Jean cut off a piece of his shirt and used his teeth to tie it around his arm and then he releathered his knife. Hap would later tell Bowie Garlock that Jean looked almost disgusted when he took a rag to his knife.

The fight was over as fast as it began. The Mexican was a crumpled thing in the corner. Dempsey had come to and was crawling out the door. Hap was struggling with Doyle's dead weight, trying to help him follow his brother.

"Hang on an' I'll give you a hand," said Goldie who

was testing a molar between two fingers. Finding it still anchored to his satisfaction, he grabbed Doyle by the collar and dragged him like a sack of grain to the door where he used his boot heel to propel him out the door.

"There!" he said and went off to get a drink.

Evie met them at the corral when they rode in. She held her lantern high. Looked at Blue. Looked at Jean and then looked at Goldie.

"Doctor yourselves!"

"Yessum."

"Thank you, ma'am."

Morning found the three men on the porch licking their wounds. Goldie had a lumpy jaw, Blue limped from a stomped toe and Jean's arm was bandaged and tied tight to his side.

Nothing had been said, but they still felt every bit as foolish as Evie had intended them to feel. Jean felt worse than foolish. He had traveled to town to get a whore and got wounded, again, instead.

They saw a rider coming, and Goldie said, "Yonder comes the sheriff." He stood and so did Blue.

"Where are you going?" Jean shifted and grimaced. It was hard to find a comfortable position now, whether seated or reclining. His back wound had been reinjured and throbbed in tandem with his cut arm.

"I got stuff to see to," replied Goldie.

"Me too."

Jean was still muttering about what dirty cowards the Dares had turned out to be, when the sheriff clomped across the porch to where he sat. He fixed a foolish smile on his face. "Sheriff!"

"Well, McDuff, I hear you been at it again." He stood with his fists on his hips.

"At what again?"

"Incitin' the citizenry of Sweet Home."

"Now, Sheriff . . ."

"Aw cut the crap. I can see your damn arm's in a sling . . . is it busted?"

"Cut."

"An' your back?"

"Ah . . . only badly bruised."

"I suppose you think this is gonna give you some more time . . ."

"On the contrary. I welcome the opportunity to regain my freedom and stop sneaking around at all hours of the night . . ."

"Well, you regain it an' you ain't gonna have it for long . . . way you're goin'." He slapped his hat against his knee and a little cloud of dust appeared.

"You boys didn't pull the wool over anybody's eyes, yuh know."

"We, um, I realize that."

"I knew y'all was in town about five minutes after you rode in."

"That soon!"

"About the only thing's that's keepin' me from addin' more charges against you is Hap sayin' that you was forced into it. That an' the fact that no one was seriously wounded."

"I appreciate it, Sheriff. Thank you."

"The judge went to Mexico City for a relative's funeral. You got another three weeks afore he gets back."

"Three weeks!"

"You keep your nose clean, hear. You understand what that means? Keep your nose clean?"

"I understand perfectly."

"I'll pay my respects to Miz Dare and the young ladies an' then I'm gonna make that long ride back into town. I sure do hope that I do not have to make it again no time soon. If you get my meanin'."

"I do. Yes, I do. Thank you."

* * *

True to his vow to avoid Brit, Jean spent the next few days with Goldie, lending a hand here and there or helping with some of the less difficult chores.

After Goldie learned that Jean had no family to speak of, he tried to talk him into staying in Tejas and filing on some land. He claimed that a simple process would net a man a land grant of over four thousand acres at a cost that was mere pennies per acre. The head of a family need only apply for his "head right"—called a league and a labor—in order to receive one plot of four thousand four hundred and twenty eight acres, which was a league, and one plot of one hundred and seventy-seven, which was a labor. There was the little matter of becoming a Mexican citizen and a Catholic but that did not seem to bother the Dares. Nor did it bother Jean. He had been baptized a Catholic.

He found himself toying with the idea. It had become more appealing, the notion of staying and settling in Tejas. Perhaps he would found a dynasty. Of course he would have to marry and procreate. A man cannot found a dynasty without quite a lot of procreating.

He supposed Mexico City would be the place to find a wife. A widow perhaps, cultured and preferably landed, young enough to produce the requisite child or two, mature enough to tolerate a mistress. Details could be worked out later.

He would talk it over with Goldie. Tell him about his plans to find a wife and then seek his advice about traveling to Mexico City. If it did not work out, if he got bored with the woman or with Tejas, he could return to France alone. Others had done it before.

But in thinking of wives and dynasties, he could not help but think of Brit. Unwillingly he pictured her in five or ten years, married to Clyde Maxey or Jesse McIninch or one of the others, producing strong, sturdy sons and lovely black-eyed girls, and he had to quell the violent jealousy that stabbed through his gut.

He had to learn to force such inflammatory thoughts aside. Marrying Brit Dare would not be an arrangement. Marrying Brit would be a marriage and there would be no going back then. He would have to cut all ties to his old life.

A daunting thought, yet it had strange appeal. A fresh start. A new beginning. And of course there was the prize. Only he had no idea what the future held. At some point he would be declared fit enough to stand trial and then . . . who knew?

It was heartening that, in Goldie's opinion at least, he would be absolved of the killing of Gil Daggert, which would allow him to choose whether he wished to go or stay. Also, neither he nor Abel O'Neal thought he would actually go to jail or be executed for killing Gil Daggert, but he supposed that stranger things had happened.

It would not hurt to have an alternate plan in mind. Abel O'Neal could be the most alert, nimble-tongued attorney in Tejas but it was *his* neck that would be stretched. Having heard about the corruption of Mexican officials, he assumed that his release could be guaranteed with a bribe. Money spoke volumes in any language and he was not above bribery, if it came to that, and once the trial was finished there would be plenty of time to decide what to do with the rest of his life.

He thought he had made a decision not to make a decision. Instead he found that he could not leave it alone. He looked over at Goldie.

"What would I do here?"

"Hell, be a doctor I guess."

"Could a man make a living at it?"

"Depends on how much money you need to live. I'd say so though. Yeah, sure. Why not?"

"I don't know if I remember enough medicine to practice it."

"You did pretty good on Jack and the boys."

"Those were all simple problems."

"Ain't that ninety percent of doctorin'?"

"Yes, I suppose it is."

Goldie was working on a new axe handle. He blew on the wood then sighted down it. He looked at Jean. "You got somebody waitin' back home?"

"Yes and no."

"You gonna marry 'er?"

"She thinks that I am."

"But you ain't promised that you would."

"Good grief, no!"

"Huh. Well. You're a long way from that problem, ain't you. Hey! Mebbe they'll take you in the rangers. They can always use a good man."

Jean rubbed his jaw and pretended to consider the idea. "Fighting wild Indians for a living . . ." He punched his palm. "By God, that's it! The very livelihood toward which I have been working all my life."

"Hey, it ain't so bad. I don't think they've lost more'n three or four men."

"Out of less than a dozen!" Jean exclaimed but Goldie Dare strode off, laughing.

Twenty-one

"Irish!"

"Ma'am?"

"What on earth is keepin' your sister?"

Washday was a full day and started early, with a conflagratory fire that was laid in the backyard and kept burning all day. First everything that would hold water was put to that use, then all the clothes were boiled and scrubbed and then hauled to the creek to be rinsed and then hung on bushes to dry. It was hard, hot work that had to be done at least twice a week.

Irish straightened. Drawing her arm across her face left a streak of soap across her forehead. "I can't imagine." It had been quite a while since Brit had gone down to the creek.

"Well, run go find her, will you? We need her help."

It was a grateful girl who dried her hands on a sacking cloth and did as her mother said and as she headed for the creek, Irish was thinking that she could at least take a few minutes to cool off. Those pots threw a lot of heat, although a washday at this time of year was not near as bad as one during the summertime.

Sure enough, she found her sister there, sitting with her knees drawn up and her arms wrapped around them. She turned her face away but not before Irish had seen her shiny streaked cheeks. Irish sat on a rock and put her feet in the water. "Oh, my that feels good!" Irish purposely did not look at her sister until she heard her sniff and blow her nose and clear her throat.

Irish was at a loss for words. It was unusual for Brit to cry. It was unusual for any of them to cry. Well, except for Markie. Maw always claimed that's why Markie couldn't see: because where most people had the business part of an eyeball, Markie had water.

Something had been wrong with Brit for days, but Irish had not pressed her on it. Neither of them talked to others that freely, but sooner or later they always talked among themselves. But the thing was, Irish had plenty of problems of her own and Brit had been good enough not to badger her about them. The way she figured, she should at least do the same for Brit now.

Brit stood and walked to the water's edge. She had been trying to gather herself for an hour and was not having a lick of success. She hated herself like this . . . crying at nothing, crying at everything, but apparently there wasn't anything she could do about it. Even when her eyes were tearless she must be weeping in her heart because she could be doing most anything and get a threatening full-ness behind her eyes, and that was it . . . She would have to find a place to let loose or else!

She splashed water on her face and then used her hem to dry it. When she finished she stood looking at a point far away. "Irish . . ."

"Yeah?"

Brit wanted to ask her sister if she thought she could ever care for Jean McDuff but she could not bring herself to do it. It was almost like saying the words might make them come true. "Irish . . . I was thinking about getting married."

Irish looked at her sister but her face was turned away. "Are you really?" It explained so much. Her other-world gaze and disinterest in food. Her spurts of activity and pre-occupation with her person. "Oh, Brit, is it Clyde?"

"Clyde?" Brit had been about to say no. Instead she shrugged. "I like him."

What was there not to like about Clyde Maxey? A good, honest, hardworking man who hammered hot iron into horseshoes and plowshares. Only, how could she marry someone she only liked?

Which was exactly the sentiment her sister voiced. "I don't think a person ought to marry someone they only like."

"A person can't marry someone they hate and if they can't have the one they love, well, why not settle for like." Brit had a sudden thought. She looked at her sister. "Irish!"

"What?"

"Do you want Clyde?" A part of her pleaded: Say yes! Say yes!

She gave a hollow sounding laugh. "Nuh-uh. Not me."

Brit slumped back. "There's nothing wrong with him."

"Not a thing." Nor was there with any of the others. Tejas had fifty men for every female. The twins could have been homely toothless hags and still would have gotten plenty of suitors. Which was a large part of the problem. Too darn many to choose from. "You girls're almost seventeen!" their maw had cried. "I already had two young'uns by your age."

Their brothers complained about losing their peace of mind and peaceful nights. "One fella's got to bring his mouth harp, another his banjo. One does the jig while another one stands on his head. One does back flip-flops and one chins hisself to death." Then Evie had added, "My Lord, seems like every man in the district wants to marry my girls!"

Save one, Brit thought.

Before Jean McDuff came to their farm, Brit and Irish

would discuss their choices all the time. That so-and-so had nice-colored hair or that so-and-so had an especially pleasant smile. But nothing they saw had helped them make up their minds.

"Irish, do you remember Lura Pat?"

"Lura Pat? Goodness yes! How could I forget her!"

The poor girl had been promised to marry a boy one day in May, but a week before the wedding the boy got word that his father was seriously ill and that he was not expected to live and so Lura Pat's intended left for Kentucky immediately. Unfortunately for Lura Pat, her intended's father did not die but lingered and so did Lura Pat's intended and by the time he finally returned, poor Lura Pat was two weeks from a fat baby boy.

Irish was shocked. "Brit, you aren't . . . you didn't . . ."

"No, but now I can understand why some girls do."

"Who is it, Brit?"

"I . . . can't say yet."

"You can't say. What do you mean, you can't say?"

"Irish, you know I'd tell you before anyone but right now . . . I just can't say."

A face flashed in Irish's mind. It was Jean McDuff. That's who it was. She should have seen it before. She would have if she hadn't been so tied up in her own problems.

"Has he kissed you?" Brit's jerky move could've been yes or it could've been flies. "Did you kiss him?" Finally, she nodded. "Oh, Brit . . ."

"Oh, Irish, sometimes I think I better quick find somebody and marry him before I ruin myself."

"Lordamercy!" Irish shuddered with excitement. "How close did you come?"

Brit looked at her. "To what?"

"Ruination."

"Hah! I saw the world from the bottom up."

"Jiminy!" whispered Irish as she savored the thought. Then, "What does it feel like?"

"I have no name for it. All I know is that I near about died from it." She gave a little shiver. "Oh, Irish, it's like nothing I've ever known before."

Irish opened her mouth twice and shut it twice. She was feeling a bit foolish for telling her sister about the quirky little feelings she had been having about Emil Schumacher. Compared to what Brit had apparently experienced, her little quirks hardly seemed worth talking about.

"Why can't you tell me who it is?"

Brit shook her head. "I just can't. Some day I will." *Maybe in ten or twenty years.*

"You know . . ." Irish thought a minute. "If you're unsure about . . . things you could always talk to Jack. Lord knows, Jack can tell you what it's like to be in love."

"Irish, I cannot talk to Jack about something like this."

Irish nodded. Way their brother had been acting lately, a person could not ask him to pass the salt without getting their heads bit off.

"Well, then what about Miss Mapes?"

Brit gave her a look. "Oh, Irish, really! Miss Mapes is too much of a lady to know about things like that."

"Hah! That's what you think."

"What do you mean?"

"It just so happens I saw Jack and Miss Mapes in the woods one time."

"Oh, good!" This was wonderful news. Both girls loved Miss Mapes and wanted her to marry their brother in the worst way.

"He had her pressed up against a tree and he was talking low and soft to her and he, um, he had his, um, hand inside her top."

Brit covered her face. "Oh, God! Don't tell me! I can't stand it if you tell me!"

About a half a minute went by before she looked over. "Then what?"

Irish blushed. "Gol, Brit, you should've seen how they looked."

"Like how?"

"Miss Mapes' face was all blotchy and Jack's was tight and almost . . . grim-looking and she was draped over his arm like a rag!"

Brit moaned. She lowered her voice. "What else did they do?"

"I have no idea. I was too busy backing out of there."

Brit looked at her, frowning. "What?"

"Well, I couldn't watch my feet an' watch them too."

"You didn't stay and watch?"

"Watch?" Irish looked shocked then contrite. "Well, only for a minute but I was so blamed scared it was hardly worth it. I mean, what if Jack had caught me?"

"Oh, honest!" Brit sounded brave, but she didn't know if she could have stayed and watched them either. Just hearing about it had brought her the same pleasure-pain she had felt when she was riding McDuff's leg and he had been kissing her senseless. Then, as now, she was not sure she ever wanted to have that feeling again. Not because she didn't like it but because once it started she never wanted it to stop.

Their mother's annoyed bawl made the girls jump and hurry back up the path. "Brit, will you tell me if anything changes?"

"Yes."

"Promise."

"Yes, I promise."

Brit had wanted to ask Irish if Jean had spoken to her about love or if he had tried to kiss her but she couldn't bring herself to do it because she expected the worst, namely that he had, and then what little heart she had left would be crushed like a grape.

Sooner or later he was bound to ask Irish to marry him and she could not imagine what she would do then. Die of a broken heart, she supposed.

She hated to think of him locked in a jail but it was really hard seeing him all the time. Lounging around on the porch, talking to Blue, talking to Markie, talking to Maw. But whoever he was talking to, he was always watching her. Why? He had to know who she was by now. She had even started looping her braid, just in case he had any doubts. But he still looked at her like she was something to eat.

One day an awful thought came to her. Maybe he thought she was like one of Dulce's girls! Oh, God that would be terrible! Later, after she had settled down a bit, she decided she really couldn't blame him if he did, not after the flirty way she had acted around him. She was so ashamed! It got so she hated every time she had to see him. Used to be she went out of her way to put herself in his line of sight. Now whenever she saw him she went the other way. Fast.

Twenty-two

Brit was late, and sure enough, Irish was already waiting when she got there.

Earlier, she had been putting the plates on the table when Irish came in with the bread. Irish had shot a look at the porch where their brothers sat talking to Jean, and then back at Maw and Markie near the oven. Then she leaned close and told Brit she wanted to meet later at the creek. Brit had been about ready to leave for the creek when Pick Anderson rode in. She had only now managed to push him off on Blue and Goldie and had left them happily rolling some dice.

The two sisters walked a little ways off the path. Brit sat on a rock and studied her sister. Her face was flushed and she was pacing back and forth in front of her. Suddenly Irish covered her face with her hands. "Oh, Brit!"

Brit stood. "What is it? What's happened?"

Irish looked off and then at her sister. "I've seen Mrs. Schumacher."

"Oh, no! Is she . . ." Brit swallowed hard. "Is she a leper?"

"Hardly. Oh, Brit, she's so pretty you can't believe she's real. She looks just like an angel! She's got shiny silvery hair and big blue eyes and pale pale skin. You swear you could see right through if she was to stand right in the light."

"Did she act crazy?"

"She acted as right as rain. Talked as sane as you or me."

"But what about the ranting you heard?"

"I don't know. That's the only time I ever heard her take on like that and I don't even know if that was her. It's only Mrs. Von Blucker's word that it was."

"You doubt her? The housekeeper."

"I don't know."

"But why would she say it was Mrs. Schumacher if it wasn't?"

"I don't know. All I know is every time I've talked to Mrs. Schumacher she's been as nice as can be. She doesn't sound anything like the person I heard that day. She's got a soft sweet little voice that sounds like it's more for singing than for talking and she speaks very good English. She said her father was a British seaman."

Brit frowned. "How often have you talked to her?"

Irish looked at her hands then up. "I don't know. A lot I guess."

She said the first time it happened was a few weeks ago. She had the boy on a blanket down by the mill. Far enough so Emil Schumacher could not see them if he happened to look out the window, but close enough to hear the mill wheel spill water onto the tailrace.

"I just love that sound! I go there almost every day. I take my paper and pencils with me and I draw while the boy naps. It's so peaceful . . . Well, anyway, one day I saw a red bird in a clump of bushes growing back behind the house. I walked over there. I wasn't so far that I couldn't see the boy but I was in a place I had never been before. Anyway I watched the bird until it flew off and then I was walking back when something caught my eye. I glanced up and there she was, standing in front of a little window on the second floor. She sort of beckoned to me and when I came nearer she pointed at the boy and starting crying 'Oh, my baby!' she said. 'My sweet child!' And then she held out her arms and that's when I saw the ropes."

"Ropes?"

"Her arms were tied at her waist so she could only raise them just the littlest bit. Later I found out that there was another rope from her ankle to an iron bar on the wall. She told me her husband kept her tied up and that he beat her and would not ever let her see her son. She begged me to bring her son to her. I didn't, of course but I'll tell you, walking away from her was about the hardest thing I've ever done. She was crying and oh, you have never heard a more pitiful sound. Not loud but soft little whimpers with hiccups in between . . ."

"Oh, Irish! Do you think he does?"

"I don't know what to think, but somebody does. The next day her face was all scratched up and she had a big mouse on her eye."

"And she told you that he did it?"

"Yes! She did."

"Cripes! Do you believe her?"

"I don't know what to believe. I've been over it and over it in my mind. First off, a mentally sound person would never scream and curse like she did that day."

"If it was her."

Irish nodded. "If it was her and second, what about Mrs. Von Blucker?"

"What about her?"

"I just don't think she would work there if Schumacher was a wife beater. She's just not the sort to tolerate strange stuff from anybody." She shook her head. "I'll tell you, if I truly thought he was doing that, I'd go straight to the sheriff with it."

"But if he isn't doing it, then who is?"

"I don't know but I sorta asked Mrs. Von Blucker . . . not right out, mind you . . . and she sorta said something that made me think they were protecting Mrs. Schumacher from herself."

"You mean . . . ?"

"I don't know what I mean. Maybe that she did those things to herself."

"I never heard of such a thing."

"Me neither. I asked Maw if she ever had . . ."

"And?"

"No. She said no."

"Mm! So now what?"

"I guess wait and see what happens. I don't know what else to do." Irish looked up. A swooping bird had made a momentary shadow on the ground.

She was silent for a long time, and then she said, "One day I took the boy for a walk and when we came back there were some things left on the blanket."

"What things?"

"A charcoal pencil with squared edges and a large pad of paper."

"From him?"

"I guess. Apparently he had been watching us right along." She looked at her sister. "Oh, Brit, I just can't believe he can be as nice as he is to me and to Mrs. Von Blucker and to his son and then beat his poor wife like that."

Brit nodded but she was very worried about her sister.

"Irish, you have to try and keep from getting in over your head."

"I don't see how I can help it."

Brit didn't either. Irish was a Dare and if a Dare got stuck on somebody, they stayed stuck. "But he is a married man! Maw'll kill you."

"I know! I know!"

They linked arms and started walking back to the cabin. Their lives used to be so simple. Now nothing was simple any more. Brit wondered if anything would ever be again.

After a time, Irish said, "I thought about your idea."

"Which idea was that?"

"That maybe we should both marry the first men who will have us."

"I've re-thought that."

"Me too and I decided I'm not going to do that."

"But, Irish, a girl has to get married."

"Why?"

"I don't know. She just does."

"Not me." said Irish. "I know I'll never marry anyone else. I'll stay with Maw and Markie and I will live but my heart will die. I'll grow old before my time and people'll point at me and say: look at that poor and pitiful thing!"

Brit sobbed. "Oh, it's so sad!"

Twenty-three

Jean's vivid fantasies returned that night, only this time it was a dream that was more to his liking than the last one had been. Again he saw himself in the evening of his life. This time he was a tall, straightstanding man, surrounded by thousands of acres of sun-drenched land. A half dozen offspring stood by his side. Three box-jawed sons with long limbs and far-looking gazes and three lovely girls with clear eyes and happy faces. He woke abruptly and in complete consciousness.

It was still dark outside, but when further sleep eluded him he lay brooding into the coals in the fireplace and listening to the creaking of rawhide and the rustling of corn husks as people around him shifted in their sleep.

Suddenly from somewhere outside came the quavering call of a night bird. It was a sad and solitary cry, one that begged for an answer, but one that got none and soon he was filled with a restless yearning. It was a feeling he recognized intuitively, rather than an emotion he had ever experienced before. Deep within himself something existed that hungered for something. Not land or more money. He could have all he wanted of that. What then? Some person? The proverbial soulmate of his destiny? The one person in all the universe who could bring peace and contentment to his life?

He had heard about such queer notions but luckily he'd

had the good sense to see them for what they really were. Visionary fairy tales that were only appropriate for the very young or very naive and only at bedtime.

Not that he would not like to believe in fairy tales. Who wouldn't? Unfortunately he just didn't have it in him. Even when he was a child he had been a cynic about such claptrap. It was sad but it was true.

His low mood stayed with him beyond sunrise, when Blue came out to smoke his morning pipe. Jean offered his tobacco pouch . . . which Blue declined and Blue offered Jean a cut off a loop of deer sausage . . . which Jean declined. With those amenities observed, they smoked in a silence that was accentuated solely by the singing of bobolinks and larks.

Evie came outside and wordlessly handed them each a tin of coffee, then she stood there and looked at the fog that was creeping across the meadow. The morning was cold and damp and they would have been able to see their breath even if they weren't smoking.

"Foggy again!"

"It'll be gone in an hour."

Having made that proclamation, she returned to her chores and silence descended.

All the brothers liked a pipe. So did their mother, though her true preference was for tobacco that had been rolled in the soft underleaf of a corn husk. As for Jean, he was particularly partial to a small cigarillo that was cured and rolled by an Armenian tobacconist who had a shop near his home in Paris. He still had plenty of tobacco, but no more papers and did not relish his inevitable decline to a corn husk wrapper. He had therefore been especially pleased when Goldie had presented him with a pipe of his own. The bowl was red clay, with a stem that had been made from a deer-bone that had been hollowed out then wrapped with twisted rawhide to protect the smoker's fingers. It was crude and primitive, and yet amazingly, he had never owned a better-drawing pipe. In return, he presented the Dares with a tin of very strong, very costly Turkish tobacco. With their penchant for things with "bite" it was not surprising that they declared it to be the best tobacco they had ever smoked.

Jean sat with one leg raised and his back to the wall. Blue stood at ease with one shoulder against the oak post.

As he looked at his companion, Jean couldn't help but notice that he was sporting a yellowy left eye and a lopsided lower lip, but then he often displayed the effects of some recent combat.

He must have sensed Jean's gaze because he rubbed his hard chin and said, "I know what you're thinkin'." He slid down the post. "I swear, sometimes it seems like there ain't a pleasant person left in this en-tire country!"

"Trouble in town?"

"Well, hell, jus' a little run in with some hiders."

"Let me guess. Clabe, Tuck and Nob?"

"Hey, that's right!" Blue was looking at him. "How'd you know about them?"

"The sheriff mentioned them. It is funny how their names stuck in my mind. I think because they reminded me of a nursery rhyme. By the way your face is not that bad."

"You shoulda seen the other guys!"

They laughed then Blue watched Jean add tobacco to his pipe and tamp it down with a stick. He liked him. When he had something to say, he said it, and Blue especially liked that. He could not abide a pussy-footed fella.

"You look like you've been in a few wars yourself, judgin' from all the hack marks on your body."

"Not wars so much as polite blood-lettings." Seeing Blue's puzzled look, he elaborated. "Among some Parisians it is fashionable to fight for unimportant reasons, the most common one being boredom."

"You mean that where you come from a man'll kill another for lack of somethin' better to do?"

"In a word: yes."

Blue snorted. "An' they call this an uncivilized land. Hell, we at least fight over somethin' important like . . ."

"Like . . . ?"

"I don't know. Wimmin or cards or horses or wimmin . . ." He grinned. "Mostly wimmin, now that I think about it."

Jean smiled to himself. Goldie had told him that a wise man will beware a windy day. *One too many blinks an' ol' Blue'll have his wife in bed.*

No man need be concerned on that day, which was so still and windless that it looked painted. The hills were silver-streaked by a pale sun that appeared to be far away and much weakened by the distance. As Jean watched, a covey of passenger pigeons rose from a clump of alamos and became like black dashes against the sky. "Markie told me you won a horse the other day."

"That damn mare was the root of all my trouble, but I asked for it. I intended to win her or take her by force. I cannot abide a man who'll mistreat a dumb animal."

"What happened?"

"A couple of us were sitting inside Dirty Dave's when these fellas rode in. I'd seen them around but I'd had no call to speak to 'em. I'd heard plenty about 'em an' none of it was good. Well, anyway, they were about to dismount, when a dog ran out an' caused one of the horses to shy. Fella called Tuck got off an' started beatin' the horse so I went outside an' gave him a few quirts so he could see how it felt to get whipped in the face . . . Ed Cox was holdin' a carbine on his friends, of course."

"Of course."

"Then I noticed that the mare'd been creased . . ."

"Creased? What does that mean?"

"Some men like to fast-tame a horse by shootin' it low

across its neck. I don't believe in it myself. Ruins more'n it tames. Especially if they miss their shot."

"I can see how it would."

Blue chuckled, remembering. "The fella threw some threats around. Said he was known high an' wide for his shootin' abilities. Claimed he could cut a string with a bullet at thirty paces. I tole 'im I ain't never shot at no string but I've shot at plenty of men an' had never missed a one. That settled him for a time but I figured it was only temporary. He did not like me an' vicey versa and you know how that goes."

Jean pictured two dogs that were circling and bristled out, and he nodded.

"Somebody suggested a game of chance and we shook some dice first an' then switched to cards. Tuck an' Nob got to drinkin' pretty heavy. Along about midnight neither one of 'em could tell the difference between whiskey an' water. Tuck pushed all his money in on three kings but I held a full house. Next hand he went crazy over aces and nines an' got beat with a flush. He was madder'n a jar of bees but he'd lost so much by then he had to do somethin' big to get even. Seein' as how I'd been talkin' up my horse, it was only natural that he should suggest a race . . . Loser loses his horse."

"That was deep betting."

Blue considered himself a horseman and had captured and tamed his string of ponies himself. His favorite mount was a sorrel gelding that he had taught to paw the ground on command and bob its head yes or no to certain questions.

"Only if you lose," he said, grinning. "That mare could've beat my horse but I had a feeling she'd rather die than run for that fella, an' it turned out I was right. Soon as he started whalin' the hell outa her you could just see her shorten her stride an' there she is." Blue nodded toward the far pasture. "Ain't she pretty?"

She was. Two shades of gray with a white face and mane. A smart-looking horse and graceful as a cloud.

"She looks fast. Is she?"

"Fast as hell an' mean as the devil. I'll tame her though." He held up one finger. "Tame, I said, not break, and then I'm gonna breed her to that stallion of Jack's."

"The black one?"

"Yeah. Hopeful."

Jean had admired the deep-chested horse with its long, muscular legs. He looked over at Blue. "Jack named his horse Hopeful?"

"'Cause that's how he always acts. Hopeful. You know?" He winked.

"Unfortunately I do. But you've got the mare penned up by herself."

"She bites. Anything an' anybody. Whatever an' whoever she can sink her teeth into." Blue grinned over at him. "They say there's some wimmen like that. So damned prickly only the most careful man can get close enough to get some." He blew smoke rings skyward. "I ain't never met none myself."

Blue's banter was earthy but Jean rather enjoyed the mixture of coarse vulgarity and masculine confidence.

"Speakin' of which . . ." Blue put his legs straight out and his hands behind his head. "I'm restless as a rat right now, but I'll wager I'm not near as restless as you."

Jean replied ruefully. "That's a bet you would win."

"We could try an' sneak you into town again but I'll tell you, if we get caught ol' Goodman'll throw a hissy. An' then there's still Daggert an' his pals. I hear they're just waitin' for you to ride in to town so they can put about a hundred holes in you."

"An uplifting thought."

"Hell, McDuff! You can get by a bit longer." No one had heard Goldie come out onto the porch.

"I imagine I can," he said but he was thinking about

what happened in the woods that day and how close he had come to tossing Brit on the ground and having at it. That was what he did not want to happen again. Aside from the fact that he valued his life, the last thing he wanted to do was repay the Dares' kindness by seducing their sister. No, leaving was what he should do and as soon as humanly possible. His unruly fantasies coupled with those vivid memories had sorely shaken his trust in himself. Especially since the mere sight of her would send his mind back to that afternoon in the woods. In his imagination he must have held her in his arms a hundred times.

There was one factor in his favor. She apparently had sensed how close they had been to crossing the Rubicon because as much as he had seen her before the incident in the woods was how little he saw her now. A part of him was relieved. Another part was sorely disappointed. It was that latter "part" that worried him.

A figure rode into view mounted on a good-looking bay and sitting easy in the saddle. Blue shaded his eyes and studied him. "Well, well. Yonder comes ol' Clyde. Headed for town, I'll bet."

The approaching man removed his slouch hat and waved it. Like most in these parts, he wore his hair long enough to cover his neck and was dressed entirely in skins. He was heavily armed even for a trip into town.

"Hey, Blue!"

Maxey was second in command of the ranger troop. He was purported to be a fine tinsmith, an adequate blacksmith and an all-around good fellow, yet there was something about him that Jean did not like. It had nothing to do with the fact that Maxey was Brit Dare's most persistent suitor.

"Hey, Clyde! You remember Doc McDuff here."

"I 'member." Maxey nodded. "McDuff."

Jean nodded. "Maxey." He could be as taciturn as anyone. Maxey lifted his hat, scratched around then pulled it back on. "Miss Brit around?"

"Nawhell. She run off with a Mexican fella passin' through." He turned to Jean. "Tuesday a week, wasn't it?"

"Wednesday I think."

Blue pretended to think. "You're right. It was Wednesday."

Clyde guffawed and scratched his beard, the value of which had always escaped Jean unless the poor devil had no chin. It was ginger-colored and made him look ten years older than his years.

"Well, guess I might as well go into town then. You up for a game?" Clyde addressed Blue.

Blue scowled. "T'hell you say! You still owe me two bucks from the last time we played!"

"Like hell I do . . ."

"Well, I guess I can recollect who owes me money an' who don't . . ."

In spite of their heated words, Clyde was following Blue into the nearest pasture and waiting while he caught a horse.

"That's Brit's special beau," said Markie. "Clyde Maxey."

Jean looked at her. She spoke around a half-eaten corn fritter.

"Want some?"

"What's that supposed to mean?"

"Do you want some corn fritter or do you want me to get you one of your own?"

God, she was infuriating at times. "I meant, what did you mean by saying that's Brit's special beau?"

"Oh, heck, I don't know."

"Well, who told you that?"

"Brit did."

"Oh."

It must mean that they had come to an understanding.

He doubted that she had given herself to him. No, he was quite certain of that. Nonetheless he looked at the tall Texan and decided to kill him.

Decided to kill him?

Was that what had just flashed through his mind? He rubbed his eyes. Insane! He was driving himself insane. Death at the hands of the Daggerts was preferable to this slow loss of his mental faculties.

Evie came out to toss some wash water over the rail, and paused to shade her eyes toward the pasture and the two men. Jean fixed his face in a smile and held it in place. "Markie says that is the fellow who may soon become a member of the family."

"That's him. Clyde Maxey." She wiped her hands on the sacking cloth apron at her waist. "Been after Brit to marry him for about a year now. I like 'im. Good man."

As the two men rode by, Blue flung out his arms Christ-like and yelled, "Once again I fight temptation an' once again I lose."

"The Lord did not put Hisself out on that one!" said his maw, but she was smiling. "Well, let's hope it is a peaceful night."

Markie interrupted then, and proudly said that her brother Blue could whip any three men in Tejas.

"Unfortunately for Blue," said his mother. "He always seems to get into it with five!"

Brit rounded the corner of the cabin just as the riders were disappearing up the road. As she looked after the retreating figures, Jean looked at her. He hated that he hardly ever saw her any more.

"Was that Clyde Maxey, Maw?"

"Ayeh."

"Didn't he want to see me?"

"He did but Blue tole him you'd run off with some Mexican fella."

"I swear one of these days I'm liable to do that! Just to fix Blue Jack Dare."

He watched annoyance flash in those poured chocolate eyes and grinned. As always, she enchanted him, even with her flares of temper.

So Clyde Maxey was about to declare for her. It did not surprise him. He would be a fool to think that he was the only male who had been bewitched by her. Who wouldn't jump at the chance to marry and bring forth a half dozen strong sturdy children with this girl? Not only was she sensuous and desirable, she was also witty, intelligent, amiable and exciting to be around. And let's not forget . . . what she did not know about chickens had not yet been discovered!

A man could do worse. He thought of Vivica and shuddered. God! A man could do a lot worse.

"At least we can be miserable together."

That was what Brit whispered to Irish that night. They were facing each other in bed. Markie lay sleeping right next to them but she was turned on her side and only the crown of her head showed above the quilt.

"I don't think I can take much more miserableness."

Irish had talked to Mrs. Schumacher again. This time she said she had climbed an old hickory tree and had seen her face to face.

She had told Brit that and then she had fallen silent. Brit nudged her. "Well . . . ?" Her sister's face was grim and incredibly sad. "What did she say?"

"She said he tried to drown her yesterday. She said he offered to take her down to the creek for a cool bath. It had been warm in her room and she wanted very much to go with him, but she was afraid he was going to try and trick her. She said he'll do that to her every chance he gets. She said she asked him if she could trust him.

She begged him not to hurt her again if she did and he swore he would not . . . He said he would let her go in the water by herself and that he would never hurt her again. He said he had turned over a new leaf. Or the same as that in German. But once he got her down to the water he pushed her in and tried to hold her head under. She said she screamed and fought him, but he was so much stronger, she was almost a goner. Then luckily she heard a wagon coming up to the mill and when he loosened his hold to see who it was, she got away. She ran back to the house and locked herself in her room."

"Where was the housekeeper all this time? Mrs. what's her name?"

"Von Blucker but he calls her Vonny. She had supposedly gone over to Garlock's for supplies but she might not have meddled between them no matter what he did. Von Blucker really likes Schumacher. You can tell by the way she talks about him. Ask the mister about that, she says. He'll know what to do. Or she'll say . . . the mister can fix that. He can fix anything."

"That's why Mrs. Schumacher hates her."

Irish nodded. "She says Von Blucker is worse than he is. She's the one who locks her up every night. She said Vonny would never help her because she is in his pay and on his side. Just like me."

"Don't say that."

"If it's true . . . if he's doing it . . . then I am just as bad as Von Blucker. Maybe worse."

"But is it true? There's the question."

"I can't believe it of him. I just can't."

Some coyotes had started yammering and one of the dogs gave a half bark before it caught itself. Brit squeezed Irish's hand and got a wobbly smile in return. Irish sniffed a little then went on, "Yesterday I took the boy down to the water. There's a little shallow place that runs several feet out. I took off his napkin and let him sit in there.

You should have seen him! Splashing and laughing. I don't know when I've ever seen a happier child, unless it was Markie when she was his age. Anyway, something made me look up and there was Mr. Schumacher, standing on a little hill across the way. He had a gun on his shoulder, going hunting I guess. I was gonna wave but he sorta . . . froze me. He just kept looking and looking. Johnny'd gotten my front wet but I couldn't even cover myself. It was like he could see right through my dress and through my drawers right down to my bare skin! Like I was, you know, naked before him. My skin started burning and oh, Brit I wanted him to stop looking but at the same time I wanted him to come down that hill and throw his things aside and . . . grab me!"

"Oh, Lord! Don't think about it! Don't talk about it! It kills me!"

"You? How do you think I feel? Wanting a prospective murderer to . . . to do whatever he wants to do."

Brit thought that things were going from bad to worse for both of them.

"Do you think he knows that you have been talking to Mrs. Schumacher?"

"No."

"So neither the mister nor the housekeeper have any reason to put on an act with you."

"I guess not. I don't know. I'm driving myself crazy wondering who's telling the truth."

Both girls were silent for a time, then Brit said, "Irish . . . ?"

"Yeah?"

"Does Jean ever talk to you?"

Irish looked at her, frowning. "Sure. All the time. When I see him."

"What does he talk about?"

"About all sorts of things. I don't know. The weather. Markie. Stuff like that."

"That's all?"

"No."

Brit's heart fell. "What else?"

"Yesterday we talked about you."

"Me?"

"He told me about helping you pluck a turkey. It was so funny!"

"What else did he . . ."

Markie sat up in bed. "Are y'all gonna ever go to sleep? I am worn to a frazzle . . ."

"Me, too!" said Evie downstairs. "An' that hummin' is drivin' me nuts! Sounds like a buncha bees in a tree!"

Oh, God! thought Brit. Thank goodness Jean had his pallet out on the porch!

But before she slept she thought about what Irish had said and she wondered why Jean would talk to Irish about her. Had Irish told him that she was crazy about Mr. Schumacher? No. As free as Irish was with her thoughts, she would never do that. Or would she?

No, it was more likely that he had probably figured it out for himself. Thinking was about all he did. Watching and listening and thinking. Maybe he had decided he might as well take her instead, seeing as how Irish was not interested and being the randy sort of man that he was. That sort of thing had happened before. Jesse McIninch had liked her before he switched to Irish and Clyde had been sparking Irish and then switched to her. She didn't think Irish had ever cared before—certainly she had not—but she sure cared now. Oh, yeah. A lot. She sniffed and turned onto her side. Second best. No Dare would ever stand for being second best.

Twenty-four

Jean was sitting on the porch, waiting for the sheriff to arrive and Markie was keeping him company and trying to distract him from the prospect of being tossed into jail. She had succeeded.

"Let me understand the question, eh? Can a person be kicked by a mule and not remember. Is that the question?"

"Yeah, right."

That's what Markie liked about the doctor. He never acted like her questions were stupid like some others she knew.

"Well, I guess that depends," he said at last.

"On what?"

"On whether or not the person were lying there with a . . . what did you say . . . an oatmeal brain? Then it's entirely possible that the person would not remember anything."

"She has all her senses."

"She?"

"It's Irish."

"Ah, Irish. Well then, I doubt it. Irish is the sort of person who would remember being kicked in the head by a mule."

"That's what I thought too, but Zick says that only a person who's been kicked in the head would keep working at the Schumacher place."

"Why? It sounds like a good thing to me." If he remembered correctly she was getting paid fifty cents "a time" to watch the mill owner's kid.

"But she's puttin' herself in danger every minute she's there!"

"What sort of danger?"

"Very perilous danger."

"Why?"

"It's Mrs. Schumacher."

She turned her head left then right—and prompted Jean to wonder where she picked up those gestures—then she lowered her voice. "She's got intensive leperitis."

That brought his head around. "Mrs. Schumacher's got what?"

"Intensive leperitis an' it's made her crazy as a bedbug. You wouldn't catch me going over there even if they paid me fifty cents an hour."

Jean raised his brows. "Markie . . ."

"It's the truth," she cried. "Honest! You can ask Zick's cousin if you don't believe me."

Jean chuckled. "Markie, leprosy is not that common in this part of the world. Africa or Egypt, yes, but not Tejas. I doubt if anyone even knows what leprosy looks like."

"Zick's cousin does."

He looked at her. "Who is this Zick anyway?"

"Ezekiel Simmons. He's in school with me but it was his cousin, True Purfule who actually saw them."

"True?"

"Yeah. True Purfule."

"He recognized the disease, eh?"

"Yeah. Wanna hear about it?"

He sighed. "Yes."

Markie's face said I thought you would! She walked her rear forward and leaned close. "One night True was coming along the creek road when he saw a buggy headed toward him. He had been gigging frogs down by the mill and did not want to be seen in case he ought not to be there so he threw himself in a gully quick and laid one eyeball above the edge. There was a bright moon that night so he could see that there were two people in the buggy. A man and a woman. The woman was wrapped up in something that covered her whole body and the man was Emil Schumacher. The wagon got to where he was hidin' an' True said he was sure hoping they couldn't hear those frogs, jumping around like crazy an' trying to get out of the sack when suddenly the wagon hit a bump an' something fell off the woman an' rolled onto the road." She leaned in and lowered her voice. "It was her eyeball!"

"No!"

"Yesss! Stopped less'n an inch from True's nose."

"So True actually saw her eyeball, um, eyeball to eyeball. In a manner of speaking."

"That is exactly key-rect."

"What happened then?

"Well, naturally the Schumachers got off the wagon and started lookin' for it."

"Naturally."

"She was stompin' around, fit to be tied. And you can just imagine the pickle poor True was in!"

"I can?"

"Well, yeah. 'Cause he knew that sooner or later they were gonna get over to his side of the road and see the eyeball and then see him and his frogs sooo . . . Lordy, he sure hated to do it, but he reached out and thumped the eyeball out into the center of the road."

"Dieu!"

"Euew?"

"No, I said Dieu!"

"That's what I thought and I didn't think they said Euew where you come from."

"Will you go on with it!"

"I was! I am! Anyway, Schumacher found the eyeball and went to glue it back on but she was carryin' on so, he couldn't."

"Kind of him to try, though. Don't you think?"

"It was the least he could do. I heard he is awful hard on her. Keeps her upstairs under lock an' key. Although I really don't see that he's got much choice. I mean, everybody knows how a leper gets toward the end."

"How do they get?"

"Why, they'll bite about anything they can set their teeth in! True said he heard about one that chewed clear through a door. Solid oak it was too!"

"Amazing."

Markie thought so too and would have been very hurt to know that Jean had not been commenting on the story. Brit was coming their way, wearing a straw hat and carrying a couple of cane poles. Crisscrossing her chest were two pieces of rawhide for a shot pouch and a powder horn, and she carried a long rifle.

For all her slenderness she must have a great deal of strength in her body. Jean had shot Goldie's carbine and had been surprised at its weight.

She looked magnificent, like a fierce female warrior of old. He shifted uneasily and searched the road from town. What was keeping the sheriff? The afternoon sun was already cresting the tops of the trees.

"Irish can peel an apple from stem to butt an' never break the peel."

Apparently he had lost the thread of the conversation. Again.

"I used to wear the peels when I was little, back before I knew any better. I'd string 'em around my neck an' pretend I was a princess. I never could figure why one day would spawn so many more flies than the next."

He threw back his head and laughed. "Markie, you are priceless."

"What's that mean?"

"That there'll never be another like you."

She rubbed her cheek on her shoulder, as if to remove the red. "I never met anyone like you neither."

"I am not so different."

"Oh yeah, you are."

"How?"

Brit had leaned the poles against the shed and disappeared behind it.

"Well, the biggest thing is how you speak American."

"I speak American very well."

"Hah! You hear how you jus' said nev-aire?"

"Nev-aire?"

"It's never. Nev-er."

"Nev-aire."

"Never"

"Nev-aire."

"Oh, never mind!"

"Nev-aire mind!"

"You cut that out!"

He had been laughing and then, abruptly, he quit. Markie had her head cocked, listening. "What is it?"

"Looks like Brit is coming for you."

"Oh, good. Say, how does she look?"

"Like a symphony."

"Like a what?"

"She looks like a song. She walks like a dancer. She is music." He looked at Markie. "Why do you ask?"

"'Cause she was crying last night."

"Crying?" His heart leapt. She was crying last night. He was leaving today. Was it too much of a coincidence? "Why?"

"I don't know."

"Can you find out?"

"Mebbe so. Mebbe no." Her voice changed. "What's it worth to you?"

"Why, you little squint!"

Brit's arrival deprived him of the opportunity to throttle her sister. She nodded. " 'lo."

"Hello." Her eyes did look pinched and tired. She looked away.

"Let's go, Goober. Maw says she's got her mouth all set for some fish."

Markie's face brightened. "We goin' fishin'?"

"Soon as you get a move on it." Brit called after her. "Don't forget your hat." She looked at Jean. "How are you, Doctor?"

"Very well, thank you. And you?"

"Fine, thanks." She looked away. She looked back. "I understand you could be going into town today."

"Yes, apparently."

"We'll miss having you around here."

"Not as much as I will miss being here. I have not seen much of you lately . . ."

Jack came around the side of the cabin with a saddle slung over one shoulder. "What's up?"

"Nothing." Brit raised her arm to pull her hair off her neck which outlined her full-bosomed figure and long straight legs. "Maw says she feels like fish for supper."

"Watch yourselves. Goldie says he saw some strange tracks a couple of days back."

"We will."

She looked at Jack and then her gaze fell on Jean and then it moved on. But not before he had seen that her eyes were remote and uninterested.

Ah, he thought. If he did not know better he would think she was employing that age-old female gambit . . . pretending that he does not exist.

Two could play that game. He shaded his eyes (though he sat under the eave of the porch) and looked down the road to town.

Evie returned with Markie and plopped her hat on her head. "All right then. Go get a big 'un."

Only when Brit turned and led her sister to the creek did Jean allow the unabashed appreciation to show in his eyes. Evie stood watching them go. "Wonder what's got into that girl."

"I am afraid I have annoyed her."

"Well, that ain't hard to do." She flapped her apron at a big green horse fly. "She can get touchy as a boil."

The two girls had disappeared into the trees. "Really?"

"Oh yeah. You don't have children, do you?"

"No, I do not." At least none that he knew of.

"It comes and goes. On girls especially. But it seems like it's gotten worse of late. I'll tell you, it is an awful concern to me, having pretty young daughters in a female-sparse place like this."

Evie was watching the doctor who was watching the spot where Brit had disappeared. "I can't wait 'till they're both wed. It's bound to do wonders for their dispositions an' I know it'll work wonders for mine. Take a big load offa my mind." She cut the doctor another look and saw that he was staring at the path to the creek and frowning. She smiled to herself. "They can quit all the folderol and get down to the business of bein' wimmin. Tendin' the needs of their man an' havin' their babies an' all."

Jean shifted again. Amazing, but he was finding the old woman's conversation stimulating. It was all that tendin' talk. Where was that blasted sheriff!

She looked at a place on her hand and then went on. "You know Jesse's been after her for months. I guess she told him jus' yesterday that she's ready to give it some serious thought."

He looked at her. "McIninch! I thought it was Maxey."

"It's one this week and another one the next. Been that way with both of 'em for a year. I'll tell yuh, it's about to drive me nuts . . ." Her voice trailed away as she went inside.

The ranger trooper's face formed in Jean's mind. While it was true that McIninch was handsome and well-formed he was also young. Terribly young. And disabled as well, if one counted his female-pleasing finger.

To his thinking, it was not too small a thing to ask . . . that Brit at least have a dexterous man who could switch from one digit to another.

His reflections were conjuring some very unappetizing images. He had to quit. He had to let it go. He had to let *her* go. Of course she would marry. A beautiful, nubile girl like Brit would have to, and he should not be concerned about which man she selected as long as he was a good one. That was what mattered in the end. Someone who would be kind to her. Someone gentle and tender. A good provider. A good lover. As for himself, the most he could ever hope to be to her was a benevolent friend.

Balls! Who was he trying to kid? The very thought of Brit married was unadulterated torture. The fact of the matter was, he wanted no one for her but himself. He hated the thought of another man's hands on her. He would rather be shot. Twice. He was an impostor. A hypocritical fake.

He rubbed his eyes. First Clyde Maxey, then Jesse McIninch. Next it could be anyone in the world and there wasn't a thing he could do about it.

He sat and stewed on it. He couldn't quit thinking about Brit in another man's arms. In another man's bed. His imagination was out of control. He had to put these thoughts aside. Where was that kid when you needed her? He grabbed his crutch and limped off the porch.

From the window Evie watched him until he had

crossed the yard and then, humming a spry little tune, she returned to her dinner preparations. She was pretty sure she had got to him just then. Oh yeah. Stuck him good.

Twenty-five

Goldie had shot a deer and hung it from a tree limb near his work shed. As Jean came up, there were half a dozen dogs milling around underneath the tree whining and snapping at each other, impatient for what might soon be tossed their way. Jean leaned against the top tier of the tied-log corral and watched as Goldie gathered his tools from his shed.

The shed was Goldie's domain. He built it, he used it and he kept it clean and tidy. Woe to any who removed his tools from it and did not return them as they found them . . . well oiled, sharpened and in their proper place.

The shed had sides made of wide-spaced posts, and a roof of wood for shade. Animal hides were tacked on its sides and a huge dried fish head was nailed to one of the posts. The monster catfish had been caught spring of the previous year and earlier Goldie had told him that it had been weighed by putting a long plank over a barrel and standing Markie on one end of the plank and laying the fish on the other. He said it had been something to watch the fish slowly elevate Markie who was, of course, squealing at the top of her lungs.

Across the shed roof was a huge snakeskin, with a horseshoe nail hammered through its great triangular head. The tail, which ended in a long set of horny rattles, hung six inches beyond the back of the shed. Goldie had told him that the snake had been seven feet long, with a body that was as big around as his arm.

Jean had looked at the hairy forearm that Goldie offered for his comparison and then up at the diamondback's skin and asked where it had been killed. Goldie had looked at him with his John the Baptist eyes and replied . . . right where you're standin'!

Jean would have paid a lot not to have looked down at his feet right then. Or, for that matter, up at Goldie, because he was slapping his thigh and snorting like a pig.

"Hey, J. P."

"Hey, Goldie. The girls went fishing."

He looked up from honing his knife. "Brit and Markie?"

"Yes. Aren't they supposed to be in school today?"

"There is no school in October."

"No school in October."

"No, and you know that little Markie'd rather fish 'n eat! She's good at it too. Feels even the smallest nibbles." He gave his knife a few last strokes. "Hope Maw makes cornbread. Jack likes plain bread with fish. Blah! Gimme a hunka cornbread with a layer of apple butter about yea thick an' mm-mm . . ."

"Both sound delicious to me but I doubt that I will be here for either."

"Hey, cheer up, McDuff. Maybe Goodman'll stay for supper."

"Perhaps . . . the way the day is going, it will be breakfast tomorrow."

"Hey! What do you care, right?"

"Right," said Jean as he cast a doleful eye toward the creek.

The boat had been made out of pine staves sealed with pitch and was shaped like an Indian dugout. Upended against the rain, it was kept wedged between the roots of a live oak a little ways south of the path. Brit righted it and set the bait in it and then the poles. As she held it steady, she said, "All right, Markie, climb in."

Markie did so and settled herself. "Where's the bait?"

"It's there."

"And the poles?"

"They're there."

"Well, what's the hold-up then?"

Brit made an exasperated sound. Having already tucked up her skirt, she waded in, gave a great heave and threw herself in belly first.

"We're off!"

"Shh! You'll scare the fish!"

"Me? You're the magpie!"

Brit paddled upstream, following the creek as it curved into the woods, and staying just far enough from shore to miss any low-slung branches.

There was a certain spot where they liked to start, because from there they could stow the paddle and drift downstream at a speed that was particularly irresistible to certain large fish.

Brit shivered a little. In places the creek was so narrow that the leaning trees formed a bower across it and although most of the branches were leafless now but they still lent enough shade to cool the air considerably.

While Brit paddled, Markie threaded sun-seasoned chicken guts on the two bent nails. She spit on her hook then dropped both lines overboard.

Normally Brit would love to be fishing on such a quiet, peaceful day, but she couldn't quit thinking about what was probably taking place back at the cabin.

Sheriff Goodman had probably arrived by now. Why, Jean and the sheriff could already be on their way into town.

It was entirely possible that she might never see Jean

McDuff again because as far as she knew, he intended to have his trial and leave town immediately thereafter.

She pictured him as she had last seen him, lounging on the porch as he waited for the sheriff, and she told herself it was a picture that would have to last her the whole rest of her life. She choked back a sob.

This was why she had stayed away from him. It hurt her heart too much. Right now it was aching like a bad tooth, exactly as she had known it would . . . because the same blamed thing happened every time she saw him.

She should have just stayed away. She could sometimes go ten or fifteen minutes without thinking of him if she did. She had proved that to herself time and again over the last several days, but no, she'd had to walk right up there and . . .

"I got a bite already!" Markie set the hook. "Got 'im!" she cried and started pulling her line in hand over hand.

"Don't horse 'im!"

"I ain't!"

Intent on the swirl beneath the surface, Brit did not notice when some blackbirds took flight but she looked up when a drinking deer bolted.

"What was that?" asked Markie.

"A deer I think."

"Did we scare it?"

"I guess so."

Brit had a strong sense of foreboding and had the carbine in hand before the men stepped out of the trees. There were three of them, shaggy and dirty men who spread out so they were no more than twenty feet away from where the creek met a sandy shoal. She snagged an overhead branch and thanked God when it held. "Hold us here, Markie."

"How many are they?"

"Three."

"Phew!"

"I know."

Brit had to get Markie to safety. She quickly considered her options. Firing into the air would let the others at the cabin know that they were in trouble, but then she would have shot her wad and any one of the three men would have time to wade out to them before she would have the time to re-load. They could definitely get to them before Goldie or Blue could.

No, she would not fire unless she made the bullet count. She did not doubt that they were up to no good; they would have called out a friendly warning if they weren't. Still, before she killed one of them she would like for them to prove it to her. There was the outside chance that they did not know the customs of the land. Maybe they were foreigners or something.

All these thoughts took only seconds and she still wasn't sure what to do. Meanwhile one of the men had walked out on a long log that brought him within jumping distance of the opposite shore. He grinned at them. "Hey, little girls!"

So much for her foreigner idea. His accent was the familiar nasal twang of the Tennessee hill country.

"Brit?"

"What?"

"Why don't we holler for help?"

"I think they can get to us before help can."

And hollering might set them in motion. She was scared to death to take her eyes off them. One had a face like a squashed toad with eyes so deep set they looked like they were being pulled on from behind. One had a hairless skull above a ginger-colored horseshoe of hair, an unnatural condition almost certainly made by some Indian's knife. He had come close to losing his eye too. A long scar lay across his face like a quirt weal.

The third man stood in the shadows so that she could

not see him but he had on a fox-skin hat and wore the
tail over his shoulder like a girl with fancy airs.

Brit shot a look her sister's way. One hand had a death
grip on the limb and the other held her knife. "Markie,
I'm getting in the water and taking the gun with me. Soon
as I say let go, you let go of the tree and paddle downstream
fast as you can." Markie was shaking her head hard enough
to sling her braids. "Yes! Let go the tree, Markie!"

"No!"

One of the men pointed at Markie. "Hey, Tuck! Look
at that knife the little one's got."

"I see it."

"Ain't that about t'cutest thin'?"

Markie tucked her chin and hoped it shaded her sightless eyes. "It may be little but I'd rather be on my side of
it than yours."

"Oh, ho!" said one and called Markie a word that neither girl had ever heard before.

"Look at you!" said Scar to Brit. "Pointin' that big gun
at us."

"Yeah, c'mon girls. We was jus' gonna get us a drink of
water."

"If you have to get that far in the water you must drink
through your belly button."

"Honey catches more flies 'n vinegar."

"You ain't no fly, mister. I recognize a rat when I see
one."

The hairless one drew a fighting knife as wide as it was
long. He was ten feet distant, close enough for her to smell
the whiskey reek of his clothes and what's worse, close
enough to look into his watery sun-faded eyes and see that
they were mean as a trapped weasel. She sighted the barrel
of her gun between them.

"C'mon now, girley. You don't wanna shoot me!" He
smiled and it was the ugliest smile Brit had ever seen.

"This is gonna go easier on yuh if yuh don't make no trouble."

"Yeah. What we got in mind ain't gonna do you no harm."

"Might do yuh some good!"

"That's right. Think of it that way."

Goldie was finally ready to clean the deer.

" 'Course I go for a head or a neck shot. I hate the mess of a chest kill an' I usually will not skin a deer on the spot. Too messy to move an' the raw meat draws so blamed many flies. No, I generally like to wait an' . . ."

It was not like he was going to skin deer for a living, but that was the way Goldie talked. Slow and careful, so Jean would understand everything he said.

While he listened to Goldie with half an ear, he watched the way the leaves were being moved along by the soft easterly breeze, slowly spinning to the edge of the hill and then over, toward the creek where the girls were fishing.

". . . cut like so an' then I draw a line down each back leg like this . . ."

Jean walked to the ledge to brood, but the ambience of Tejas foiled him. The sun felt warm across his shoulders and the air smelled of sweet hay and sun-ripened manure. Two birds vied for dominance in the branches overhead and Goat snuffled contentedly, happy with the bribe he had tossed her.

". . . take each hind quarter like so an' then I like to make a cut right about . . ."

Jean saw the trees mirrored in the creek and then he heard Brit's voice and suddenly he felt a cutting loneliness.

He was suddenly jerked out of his reverie. Her words were indistinct sounds carried off on the breeze but in his state of heightened sensitivity he imagined that she had called to him. A fantasy, no doubt, but one as compelling as any he had ever known. He had not intended to descend to the water but the next thing he knew he was hobbling down the path that led there.

Still above the creek he paused and searched the water for any sign of the two girls but he saw nothing of them. Then suddenly a half dozen blackbirds rose above the trees and a heartbeat later a stranger slouched into view, looking left and right and moving slow . . . like a crane that was stalking a fish.

Jean glanced behind him but Goldie was out of sight, hidden by a copse of trees and then he realized he could not alert Goldie without also alerting the man below. Suddenly he heard Markie shout and he forgot everything but getting to the girls as fast as the terrain—and his wounds—would allow.

The trail broke off to the right and he stayed with it until he came into a little clearing and there he saw two men, one standing in the water and the other standing on a log that jutted into the water. Both were laughing.

The Dare girls were backed up against the opposite bank. Markie's face was scared but grim. Brit was waist-deep in the water, bent at an odd angle against the boat. She looked like she was trying to push her sister downstream without taking her eyes off the men and without getting her weapon wet.

She saw Jean and her eyes widened and flared in fear. Jean raised his crutch and launched himself at the closest man who heard him at the last minute and pulled his musket and fired at point blank range. Jean felt a searing pain across his temple and then heard a roaring noise . . . which he assumed was blood rushing out of the massive hole in his head . . . nonetheless he also heard a resounding crack as his crutch met with the man's head.

"Run!" he cried but instead Brit raised her carbine and fired, and a man fell dead at his feet, shot square between the eyes. Dazed, Jean stared down at the man who had apparently been about to shoot him in the back.

Brit screamed a warning as a third man fired and Jean went to one knee, hit again. Suddenly there was a blur and Goldie was there, knocking the shooter down with his fist. The man tackled him around the legs and together they rolled behind some brush.

Through a red haze Jean watched the man he had hit with his crutch. He was getting up rump first, like a cow, holding one hand to his head and peering through streams of blood. Jean lay helpless as a babe as the man pulled a musket and pointed it at his head . . . but the gun misfired!

Cursing, the man flung it aside and unsheathed a knife and came toward him.

"Nob!"

Blue Jack Dare came crashing through the trees and stopped twenty feet away. Softly he said, "Hey, Nob" and smiled.

Goldie emerged from the brush alone and joined his brother and they both stood staring at the man called Nob. Blue sprouted weapons like a hedgehog. Goldie had his lips rolled back like a hound who had just smelled a bloodied sack.

Nob looked at his comrade who lay motionless on the ground and then at the Dare brothers, and Jean knew he was thinking that he would have to kill both of the Dares if he was going to live.

He opened his fingers and let the knife fall to the ground and said, "Hey, boys, y'all've taken this whole thin' wrong. We didn't mean nothin' by it. Honest."

As if he would give the universal signal of peace, Nob slowly lifted one hand. When he had it ear level, Blue shot him and then he went to him and pulled out the knife that he'd had in a hidden scabbard that rested between his shoulder blades.

Brit tossed the carbine in the boat and piled in. "Markie, let go now so I can paddle us to shore."

"Is everyone all right?"

"Blue and Goldie are fine but Jean took two bullets."

"Is he all right?"

"He's . . . very still."

By the time they reached shore Evie had arrived and was kneeling beside Jean. "The head wound's just a scratch but I ain't so sure about the arm. Cut off that sleeve, Goldie."

There was a perfectly round hole bored in Jean's arm. Arranged like an eyebrow above it were three smaller, equally perfect holes.

He had been shot with an escopeta, a short Mexican musket called a buck and ball by the Texians. The charge was an ounce ball with three buckshot behind it, hence the four wounds. The larger, lower ball had broken the bone.

"I think the arm's busted," said Blue.

"I think it is too," said Jean. The diagnosis was intuition on his part. He could barely lift his eyelids.

"Why in hell would you come down here without a weapon?" said Goldie angrily. "You gonna fight 'em bare-handed?"

Jean's response got trapped in his throat because a few feet away Brit was rising from the water and the wet fabric of her dress was like a second skin that cupped the dark mound at the apex of her legs and detailed the brown circles that were her nipples and Jean's tongue felt forever stuck to the roof of his mouth. Then his wound prevailed and his eyes drifted shut and his mind slept . . . but the most beautiful sight he had ever seen would remain etched on his lids forever.

Goldie stood looking down at him. "What'd he say before he went off?"

"Sounded like . . . amazing!"

"That's it," crowed Markie. "He says that a lot. Ah-maz-eeng! It's about his favorite word."

Evie and Brit went ahead to get things ready and to send Irish back to the creek with a tarp for her brothers to use to carry Jean back on.

Brit had set water to boil and was waiting on the porch with an outer calm that masked an inner storm. Then her brothers and their cargo appeared and her heart leapt. Markie followed with the crutch, although, like she said, she didn't know why she bothered since it was about busted to bits.

Evie pointed. "Lay him on the ground, boys. Lordy, his head's bleeding like a pig." Brit glared at her mother. She had been trying very hard to ignore the coils of blood in the dirt.

Jean opened his eyes and lay gazing up at a sky that looked like rippling blue water. Flying too high to identify was a lone bird. Lower down was a monarch butterfly. Surely the last of the season.

Also probably the last of his life for he had no doubt that his end was near and that these were the things that all men see right before the end. A beautiful woman. A spectacular sky. A last butterfly. A lone bird.

Of course a man could die inside, in a room. Then he would see far different things. A water spot on the plaster. A cobweb. A crack.

No, he much preferred to die where he was. Here beneath the wide Tejas sky. It was a fine place to die. It was the only place to die.

"Boy, you'll do about anythin', won't you?"

By moving his eyes a little to the right Jean could see a crotch and a belt buckle and an overhanging gut that he would recognize anywhere. Sheriff Goodman. Unfortunately he was too tired to respond and was glad that Evie did it for him.

"What on earth're you talkin' about, Sheriff?"

"I'm talkin' about the lengths this man'll go to so he can stay outa jail. That's what I'm talkin' about."

Jean started to chuckle and almost passed out from the pain.

"Honestly, Sheriff!"

Goldie snorted. "You think he got shot so he could keep outa jail?" Goldie gave an incredulous snort and Jean wanted to kiss him.

"He more'n likely saved the girls' lives, you know!"

And Blue. He had always liked Blue.

"Hell's bells! Pardon my French, ladies, but this is the third time I've come out here to pick this fella up only to find he's jus' got the you-know-what shot outa him. Again. You think I like makin' this ride for nothin'?"

"You can stay to supper."

"Well, in that case . . ."

"An' then you can haul those bodies back with you."

"Three bodies."

"Clabe, Tuck and Nob."

"Uh-oh!"

"Yeah, there's two down by the creek and one in the bushes."

"Mm-mm. Well, then I guess I will stay after all and thank you, Evie, for the offer. As far as any haulin' goes, I commandeer you, Blue Jack Dare, to help me get 'em into town. Since you have been such a big help puttin' 'em down."

"Hah! You can leave 'em rot where they lay, far as I'm concerned . . ."

"Phew!" said Markie. "They smell bad enough already!"

The voices ebbed and flowed and Jean went back to studying the sky. The bird was still there. Hovering. Was it waiting? Could it be waiting for him? "What is that bird?"

Brit glanced up. "It's a dove. Please don't try to talk now."

Markie took the hand on the end of his unbroken arm. "I know a story about how the mourning dove got its name."

Bless her! Dear little Markie was trying to take his mind off Evie putting her arm through the hole in his head. He had always wondered what scarify meant.

"The story starts when Noah was on the ark with two of every animal and bird in the world. He was looking for land, see, but there was no land to be found and it was gettin' very serious. They were almost out of food and water and all the animals could die! One day he called all the birds together and asked for one of them to volunteer to fly off and find some land so the rest of the world's creatures could live. The buzzard said . . . heck, I ain't riskin' my neck fer no ol' gator, and the eagle said he thought the sparrow ought to go. Finally, the mourning dove stepped forward and said he'd go and boy, ol' Noah was sooo glad that he told the dove that if he would do this very important job for him, he would give the dove enough money so it could get a good start in the new land. Well, the mourning dove said all right. I'll do it. So off it flew and it flew and it flew until its little wings were about ready to fall off. It was this close to giving up when it finally saw land. Hallelujah! it said. Thank you, baby Jesus! it cried. And it made a bee line for shore. Of course, the first thing it did was drink eight buckets of water and eat seventy 'leven worms but, after it had rested up good, it collected an olive branch and brought it back to Noah to prove that he had found shore. Noah turned in the direction the dove said and sure enough they found it and soon all the animals were safe and sound and happy in their new home. All except for the poor dove. Why, you're wonderin'? 'Cause that dirty rotten low-down Noah hedged on his bet and refused to pay the mourning dove! Which left the poor dove poor as dirt and sad-sounding forever after. An' that's why if you listen to the mourning dove's cry you can hear that it is saying 'Pay me No-ah, Pay meee No-ah.' How's that for a great story, Jean? Jean!"

"Markie, I think he's gone."

Her breath caught. "He's . . . he's dead?"

"No, just resting."

"Hot blast it, Maw! You scared me half to death!"

Irish said, "That was a real nice story, Goob."

"Yeah, but now I have to tell it all over again!"

"No, you won't." Jean opened one eye. "I heard everything. I condemn Noah as a liar and a cheat and I will tell him exactly what a swindler he is. As soon as I see him." With that he closed his eyes and prepared himself to die. And by the time Evie had seared his wounds with the flat of a hot knife and then set his arm in a clay cast, he would wish that he had. The excruciating pain so befogged his mind that he could not think. Nevertheless, some parts of him were still aware. His memory for one. The last thing he thought before he lost consciousness was how beautiful Brit had looked coming up out of the water.

The sheriff stayed for supper, which was a somewhat somber meal. After all, three men were dead and nobody took that lightly.

The sheriff did a lot of muttering about the doctor and still acted as if he had intentionally thrown himself in harm's way in order to delay going into town for trial. Brit knew the exact opposite was true. All week she had sensed how anxious he was to leave and much as she wanted him to go, it had hurt her that he wanted the same thing.

She had been hoping that the old saying "out of sight out of mind" was going to work for her although it hadn't so far. She had been everywhere but where he was for a week and wherever she was, she had thought of him. Now he was down again, muttering and hot to the touch, and she was beside herself with worry.

Jean slept and as he slept he dreamt that he was adrift in an endless ocean. He had been for a long long time. The sun was relentless and he had no shade. What's worse, he had no water. His throat was sand-coated and his lips were cracked and bleeding when suddenly a shadow passed over him and offered one brief instant of blessed relief from the sun's searing rays. He squinted up and saw a bird.

A bird! Land! It must be land. Every sailor knows that a bird means land and land means birds.

He paddled with renewed fervor, trying to keep the bird in sight, but it was quickly outdistancing him! He paddled and paddled . . . until his arms were wood stumps and his shoulders were frozen in their sockets. Finally he put his head on his knees and he cried, "Wait, please wait."

Of course the bird was too far away to hear him. He was done for. He had mere minutes to live. He raised his head for one last look and through bleared eyes he saw the bird far, far away.

Slowly, very slowly the bird wheeled and what had been a black speck became increasingly larger . . . and larger! The bird was returning for him. Finally the huge bird hovered directly over his raft.

Thank God! he said. He was saved!

And then he saw that the bird's body had feathers and wings but that its head was that of his grandson, the fire starter. He smiled down and Jean saw his black goose-sized tongue . . .

The sound of running woke him.

"What is it?" Evie asked.

"What? What is what?"

"Why did you scream?"

"Scream?"

"You jus' hollered somethin' awful!"

"It was nothing." He waved. "A sudden pain."

The others left but Goldie stood grinning down at him. "I'll say this much, Jean. You ever get captured by Indians you better pray you can swaller your tongue. They'll keep a good screamer alive for a week!"

Twenty-six

A few days later Jean was once again well enough to be conveyed out onto the porch, where he was watching the Dares prepare to leave for Sweet Home. They were going to attend an event called Founder's Day, an outdoor prayer meeting which would feature the town's newest settler, the Reverend Hollis, and which would be followed by contests of shooting, riding and drinking skills, and then a barbecue and a dance.

Jean was not going. He could hobble around on his own but he did so very slowly and very painfully. His left arm was splinted from elbow to wrist and his head was bound like a pasha's. His right arm was barely mobile and his back muscles had just quit going in and out of violent contractions. He was, as they say in Tejas, weak as a cat. It was a condition he particularly regretted on that day, because for an autumn day this was an especially nice one, cool in the morning and steadily warming as the day wore on. By the time the sun had topped the trees, the land was bathed in gold and the tree line looked etched onto a cloudless blue-white sky that was as clear as glass. For once the wind was non-existent.

The Dares' departure was nigh. Goldie had hitched the team to a large wagon that had wooden bows but no cover and Brit and Irish had helped their mother carry cooked dishes to the back of the wagon, where they were carefully placed on a cushion of straw and then covered with clean sacking cloths.

Earlier everyone had spent a great deal of time on their toilette. Dresses and shirts had been boiled, scrubbed and mended. Boots and shoes had been greased and re-stitched. Buckskins had been well brushed out and, in Blue's case, the beading had been repaired. Then that morning the men trooped down to the creek and returned with red jaws and slicked glossy heads that could not be distinguished from drakes' tails.

The girls had bathed earlier and then helped each other with their hair. Markie had sat on the step below Brit while she braided her hair. Which put Brit in profile to Jean and which allowed him the unfettered view of her smooth cheek and narrow nose, her strong chin, and the dimple that appeared and disappeared in her cheek . . .

I must have her or die!

That insane thought had flashed through his mind like lightning across the sky and he'd had to shake himself mentally. These aberrant notions were occurring all too frequently. Wild ideas and strange suggestions kept popping into mind at the oddest moments. It must have been the blow to his head. He had to take himself in hand and set his mind on something else . . . the events of the preceding evening for instance.

Yes, that would work. For example, remembering how interesting it had been to hear each person voice their expectations for this year's Founder's Day event.

Markie had pinned her hopes on one thing . . . namely that Electra Cooper would urp again. The mayor's daughter had never disappointed Markie before but, like her mother so often said, there are no sure things in life.

Apparently the unfortunate child could always be badgered into being "it" for crack-the-whip. Chances were slim that she would suddenly equate crack-the-whip with her bilious episodes—the mayor's daughter was not known for

being especially "deep in the mind"—but Markie was prepared for the worst and what would obviously be a crushing
disappointment.

Irish said she hoped Mr. Schumacher and his son would
be able to come, a small wish that drew Jean's attention
because of the way she had sounded when she said it. She
said the baby had had a cold and was teething to boot,
and Mrs. Von Blucker had told her that the last week Mr.
Schumacher had been up every night, walking the boy for
hours on end, trying to quiet him so that he would sleep.

"Mr. Schumacher looked so tired. I told him I thought
it would do him good to, um, you know, get away . . ."

Studying her, Jean had noted her downcast eyes and
cherry-like cheeks and he thought: Oho! what's this? Had
Irish—seemingly oblivious to the opposite gender—had
an awakening of sorts?

Jack was characteristically silent and only voiced his desire to win money at various feats of skill. Goldie said he
hoped the ol' Indian woman who made the best green
chili tamales in Tejas would be there, and Blue hoped a
certain knife maker would be able to replace a blade
scored by a Mexican bandito's bullet.

Their mother said she hoped they could get through
the day without too much letting of their own blood. Only
Brit, the one whose desires he most wished to know, had
remained silent.

She had changed since the incident at the creek. She
had become much more reserved and serious acting. He
hated to see her that way, for she was a girl whose face
had been made for laughter.

However as he looked at her he was frowning because
nothing about her said serious to him now. Rather the
words that came to mind were carnal, libidinous, erotic,
passionate and sensual.

She wore a plain-cut frock that was mostly blue with tiny

white flowers, and she looked lush and nubile and ripe as a peach. Ripe for the plucking.

At this moment, seeing her innate allure and knowing first hand about her desirability, he could easily see that some young stud might get the wrong idea. Who knew what sort of ruffians would be attending this thing? Maybe he should caution her mother. Maybe a word to her brothers.

They were almost ready to leave when Jack brought out two carbines and stacked them against the wall beside him. "What's this?"

"In case of Indians." He laid a shot pouch and powder horn on the table.

"Indians!" Jean sat straighter. "You expect trouble?"

"Don't hurt to be cautious. They may figure we forgot what happened five years ago."

"What happened five years ago?" Jean scanned the tree line as he spoke.

"Comanches hit all the farms where people had stayed at home insteada goin' into town for the shindig. Musta had a spy watching each place. Sonsabitches planned it an' pulled it off, slick as snot." He looked off, remembering. "You know, I've heard people claim that a red man's just naturally dumber'n a white man, but I personally have never met an Indian that wasn't sly as a fox."

"Was anyone hurt?"

"Well, hell yes, people were hurt. Damn Comanch' didn't ride all that way to throw eggs at us."

Jean cursed himself for asking but he was powerless over the need to know. "How bad was it?"

"Well, lessee now," He looked skyward. "If I recollect correctly there was nine killed an' one wounded, which was ol' lady Palmer. Yeah, Lacey Palmer. That was her name. She's since gone beyond the river. Hell, at that time she was, oh, I suppose ninety somethin'. Anyway, she'd claimed she was too crippled up to stand the trip into town but when the Indians attacked she crawled up onto the roof and threw burnin' wood down on 'em. Indians saw her hoppin' around up there and figured she was crazy so they rode off an' let her live. When we came on her she'd stripped off her smolderin' clothes and stood buck nakkid. She'd doused herself head to toe with a bucket of water and looked like a plucked goose. Had a chest as flat as a starved man. Nipples clear down around her waist. Mm, I'll tell you, it was a helluva sight. You ever see a soppin' wet ninety-year-old female, you'll know what I mean."

"I may go after all."

"Go?"

"To this Founder's Day thing."

"An' do what? Hell, look at yuh! Bandaged head an' both arms, walkin' with a crutch. You're so pitiful an' sorry lookin' yuh might as well throw cold water on the en-tire town. All the ladies'd be cryin' . . ."

"All right. All right."

Jack threw back his head and laughed. "Hell, you oughta be safe enough." He used his chin to indicate the bell hanging from a crooked nail by the front door. "See that yonder?"

"Yes . . ."

"You see any Indians, you ring hell outa that bell."

"Can you hear it in town?"

"Nawhell! But it'll help keep your spirits up." Jack's ox-bow mustache lifted in a smile. "Which I understand is damn hard to do, hanging head down over a roastin' fire."

A Texian's idea of humor took time to appreciate. More time than Jean had.

"Here . . ." Jack had whipped out a knife with a blade as wide as his brim and was offering it, elk-horn handle first. "Take this as well."

"No, no. I would not think of depriving you of your knife."

"Hell, I carry two others."

"Well, in that case."

As Jack sawed his hat on, Jean glanced at the wagon where the females sat waiting. "Say, I was thinking . . ."

"Yeah?"

He wanted to say something about Brit and all those ravenous men, but there didn't appear to be enough time. "Never mind."

Jack looked at him. He liked the man but he didn't understand him. "Well, mebbe I'll see yuh tonight. If you're still alive an' kickin'."

"I sincerely hope to be and may I say that it has been particularly pleasant talking to you!"

Jack had started off. Now he returned. "Say, that reminds me. Blue heard that Doke Doyle's mendin' nicely."

"I was up nights about that!"

Another hearty laugh floated back to him as Jack strode to his steed and flung himself on. One of the brothers must have given an unspoken signal because suddenly they were tearing off across the field, flailing their horses rumps with their hats and yelling like banshees.

The team pulling the wagon responded with an impatient little dance and Evie yelled, "Sah in there you horses!" Then she climbed up on the seat and took up the reins. Markie sat beside her and the twins sat facing Goat, who did not look happy about being tied on back.

"Well, awright. Are we ready, girls?"

"Ready, Maw!"

"Grab a holta those pots!"

"Got 'em!"

"YEEE-HAA!"

Good Lord! Now they too acted like they were in a race, even though it was one in which they were the only contestant. He saw air between every bottom and then he didn't and once again he felt every rock between Brasoria and Sweet Home!

As they neared the creek Markie turned and waved at

him. He raised his arm and waved back, and felt like a fool.

He watched them until they were out of sight, and longer, looking at the place where dust rolled off the road like a balloon. Finally the leaves settled and birds renewed their twittering in the brush and he took a deep breath and told himself how much he was going to enjoy the solitude. It was a flagrant lie. If it weren't for the potential of an Indian attack he would have been bored to tears already. A cowbell jangled, and for the first time it seemed a sad sound to him. Brit's face came to mind.

Hell, he was lonely. Damn lonely. He had always been alone before. It was how he spent all his time lately. Pensive and alone and lonely feeling. He felt wistful and needy and a hollowness grew within him like a hunger.

It was full day now. He could feel the heat of the sun where his legs extended beyond the roof line and the sleepy silence was so profound he could hear the string of dried peppers rattling in the breeze.

Maybe it was too quiet. Made him think of one of those bedtime stories the Dares were always telling. One in particular. The one about the time the troop had come to a burned patch of ground where there used to be a cabin. The Dares had told him about the quiet and how all the white men had thought the Indians had gone but then He-Coon had told them to listen very closely and they did and after a long time they agreed amongst themselves that it was a strange and unnatural sounding silence. Then a gust of wind blew up and stirred the trees and then it died and suddenly the air was rent with arrows and bullets and a score of screaming Indians appeared as if they had come up out of the ground.

Obviously that was not the best story to call up at that time, because he spent the next couple of hours staring into the woods and seizing up every time a bird took flight.

But as more time passed and as the sun moved and little else, he began to relax and his thoughts rambled.

He had never seen Jack act so amiable, like a man who'd had a huge weight removed from his shoulders.

Or perhaps like a man who had looked at his choices and made a decision. Perhaps Jack had decided to give up on his quest of the elusive little schoolmarm. Could be it was as simple as that.

Oh, well. Jean scratched around and yawned. He supposed he would find out soon enough.

His eyes found a lazy hawk and followed it as it slowly circled the sky, and then a billowy cloud that was a perfectly shaped breast, white and pink-tipped, soft and satin-y looking. The lovely image stayed on his eyelids and soon, in spite of his intention to remain vigilant, he fell asleep.

Long shadows streaked the yard when he woke. He stretched then gave a little shiver. The setting sun had taken the day's warmth with it. Odd, but it was almost as if something had awakened him. He scanned the horizon and the shadowy line of the trees. Crows called in the bushes and some small animal rustled around under the porch, but thankfully there were still no Indians in sight.

He had fixed his pipe and lit it when suddenly there was a wagon tearing up the path. The Dares back so early? No, this wagon did not have the bars across the top.

Yet that was Jack riding alongside, and it looked like Brit up behind him!

Using his new crutch Jean descended the stairs then had to jump for his life when it appeared that the wagon wasn't going to stop!

He soon saw the reason for all the hurry. Thrashing around on the flatbed was a boy, eight, maybe nine years old with a four-inch splinter impaled in the sole of his left foot. The boy's mother and his sister were sitting beside him and both looked like they had been in a wrestling match with a wildcat. The mother was trying to subdue the boy but he was writhing like a snake. The pain had to be excruciating.

"These are the Biegels, Doc. Walt and Mavis." Jack carried the boy up onto the porch. "An' this here's their boy, Lark."

"Please help him," said the mother. "He's in so much pain."

"I don't know how it could've happened," said the father. "One minute he was walking along and the next . . ."

"It doesn't matter." Jean looked up at the father who had pulled off his hat and was trying to tie it in a knot. "The only thing that matters now is getting it out." He turned, intending to ask for his bag and found that Brit was holding it out for him. He selected a bottle of nitrous oxide and she handed him a clean cloth.

"I tried to pull it out but he yelled so . . ."

Jean looked up at the mother then at the little girl who had her arms buried in her mother's skirts. Huge brown eyes stared at him over a thoroughly sucked thumb.

"I'll heat some water."

"Thank you."

"I brought Brit along," said Jack. "I figured she could help."

"Indeed. I could not ask for better."

He could tell she had heard his comment by the color of her cheeks. As he had intended.

As Jean tapped a couple of drops of liquid onto the cloth, he said, "Son, I am going to give you something that will make you sleepy." The boy glanced at him then away. His eyes were wild and slitted with pain. "Then when I take out the splinter you will not feel a thing." Jean held the cloth over the boy's face and the boy's gyrations slowed then ended. Soon his fists had unclenched and his breathing became deep and heavy.

The Biegels were a family of redheads, ranging from the father's deep mahogany to the girl's carrot color, but the boy was the only one with a redhead's complexion as well. Freckles were scattered across his stubbed nose and thin cheeks like a rusty bat wing.

The mother slumped against the post. "Thank God," she said. "I don't think I could have stood another minute."

Jean looked at her. "It might be best if you took your daughter for a little walk." She looked at him and then at her husband. She was obviously reluctant to leave. Jean put a hand on her arm. "It's best that the little one not watch."

"You're right. Yes, all right." She looked at Jean and whispered, "Try . . . please try not to hurt him."

"I will not hurt him."

"Will he be all right, Doc?"

"If we can get all the wood out and if an infection does not set in."

Jean thumbed up one eyelid and checked the boy's pupil. He was breathing evenly but he was very pale.

"Help me turn him onto his stomach." They positioned the boy face down on a pallet so that his foot lay on Jean's thigh. Since it was almost dusk, Jack lit a candle and held it close but Jean simply grasped the shaft of the splinter close to the skin and abruptly pulled it out. He handed it to Brit and asked her to rinse the blood off so they could tell if there were any pieces missing. She returned and knelt beside him. "Two," she said and showed him places where the wood was white.

"Mm. I have one already," he said, indicating a slender sliver he had laid on his pants.

Being shorter and smaller, the other piece was not so easy to find but he finally did, and then he cauterized the wound, which caused the father to abruptly take a seat on the step.

As he bandaged the foot in clean cloths he asked Jack to cut his crutch down to the boy's height, and Biegel waved his wife in from Goldie's shed where she and the girl had been waiting.

After he finished tying off the bandage, he gently removed the boy's leg and levered himself back into the chair. His head was pounding like a drum.

Brit bathed the boy's face and hands and smoothed his hair with her hand. "He's a handsome boy, Mr. Biegel."

Biegel swallowed hard. "He's a good boy, miss. Teases his sister a lot but . . ."

"Teasing sisters is what brothers are born to do. Right, Jack."

"You bet," said Jack and everyone managed a laugh.

"Please join me, madame." The mother sat in a chair beside Jean, and looked at him as if he were going to tell her the location of the Holy Grail.

"This bandage must be kept clean at all costs. Change it twice a day. Boil the soiled cloths for one hour and dry them inside. Only then can they be re-used, eh?" She nodded. "Wash the wound with warm soapy water. He will not like that but you must do it anyway. Can you?" She nodded again but she was crying and blowing her nose. He patted her arm. "Good. Remove any crust that forms on the wound and keep it from forming for four days. When the wound is clean apply what is in this jar. Can you bring him back in a week?"

"They live clear over on Cypress Creek," said Jack. "Pretty blamed far . . ."

"But it is important."

"Then we'll be here," the mother said firmly. "Oh, thank you, Doctor . . ."

"Kith!"

The little popping sound that preceded the word drew all eyes to the little girl. The mother's face was tear-streaked and her lips rubbery but she was smiling. "Starlie wants to give you a kiss. For helping her brother."

Jean leaned down and allowed a slobbery kiss to be

planted on his cheek. "Thank you," he said and was strangely moved. "Thank you very much. Now." He cleared his throat. "You better get the boy as close to home as possible before he wakes up. It won't be a very comfortable ride for him."

Brit and the mother made a bed of straw, and when they had finished, Jack picked up the boy and carried him to the wagon.

The father and Jean remained on the porch, watching.

"Say, Doc?"

"Yes?"

"I don't have any spare cash right now. Well, actually I don't have any cash at all."

When Jean shook his head and said there was no charge, something flared in Walt Biegel's eyes. Pride? Yes, it was pride all right.

"We Biegels may be poor, but we pay our debts. Might take a while but we pay 'em."

"As you wish."

"I can bring a little something every month around the first. If not cash then goods. That all right with you?"

"Fine. That's fine."

"Say, could you use a good layer?"

"A chicken?" He glanced at Brit and saw she had her head turned away. "Tell you what, Mr. Biegel . . ."

"Walt."

"Walt. You bring me a good layer and we'll consider ourselves square."

"Oh, no! That's not nearly enough!"

"Of course it is. Why, a good layer is worth its weight in gold!"

Brit made a very unlady-like nose noise and left the porch.

Twenty-seven

Jack and Brit went back into town with the Biegels, and Jean went back to his perusal of the lay of the land. After a time, it struck him that he was looking at it as if he expected it to tell him something, but what? Perhaps that the feelings he had just experienced; namely that of accomplishment, satisfaction and usefulness . . . that those were the simple but essential keys to a life worth living. That perhaps the daily practice of similar tasks might continue to make him feel fully alive.

Highly speculative, but it did seem that the only time he felt worthy of inclusion in the scheme of things was when he was performing as a physician, and he wasn't sure what to think about that.

So he didn't.

Actually he was tired of contemplating his life. Lately it seemed that he spent most of his time alone, trying to sort out his problems and assess his options. Enough is enough. How did that Spanish maxim go? Qué sera, sera. Yes. He would adopt it now. What will be, will be.

After a time he stepped into the woods to relieve himself, and when he returned, there was a cloth-covered plate on the table beside his chair. Sliced ham, fried chicken, biscuits and loaf cake. He fell to, suddenly famished. God, it was good.

He was quite sure that this bounty had not been brought

by the Indians but none of the Dares would answer his call. Nevertheless he sensed someone's presence. One of them had returned to bring him the food, and he figured he knew which one it was.

He laid the cloth across his knee and without seeming to, he scanned the border of bushes to the right, the shed and corral to the left and then all other likely hiding places. He saw no one, but the feeling of being observed persisted. If he were to guess, the sensation was strongest around the area of Goldie's shed.

Brit had taken special care with that boy, handling him tenderly and holding him gently. She had spoken soothing, reassuring words that had sounded vaguely familiar and it came to him that she must have spoken the same words to him and that they had reassured and soothed him as well.

He wanted her to do that again. He wanted her soft words and soothing touch and more. Her hands had once been all over his body and he wanted them there again— now—and just that easily did his vow of abstinence fall by the wayside. He stood and yawned big, and then he went inside as if he might be retiring for the night. Instead he went through the cabin, took the dogwood broom to use as a crutch and went out the back door that led to the cooking area.

He set out intending to circle silently through the trees so that he would come up on the far side of the shed without detection but he soon found that it is patently impossible to be quiet-footed while creeping blindly through the dead dark across a forest floor that is littered with sticks and leaves and toe-stubbing rocks.

However, somehow he had at last crept close enough to see the shed, and as he had expected, there was a slight female figure standing there. She had one hand on the wall so she could lean far enough out to see the porch. A fingernail on the free hand was being nervously gnawed to the quick. He grinned and advanced.

Brit was in a bit of a bind. She did not want to ride all the way back into town and wait until everyone else was ready to come home, but she could not exactly go upstairs and go to bed, with him lurking around downstairs and she could not imagine where he had gone unless it was to bed.

She did not know what to make of him. Why was he so forceful with her but so bashful with Irish? She had watched Irish and she had watched him and she had watched how they acted together. Irish was polite and so was he. Nothing more. Nothing less. And then there was the way he acted toward her still. Always looking at her with those intense and watchful eyes. Even earlier when he was treating the Biegel boy. Like he expected something from her. But what?

Suddenly she felt someone's presence and she knew it was him. She could always tell when his eyes were on her. She turned and tensed to run.

"Wait! Please don't go. We must talk."

She did not take her wary eyes off him but she did lean back against the shed. "What about?"

"I want to apologize about what happened the other day. I meant to do so earlier. I must have, er, surprised you." He chuckled. "Actually, I surprised myself!" He was trying—and failing—to read the strange look that he saw in her eyes. "I'd like to begin again."

"Why?"

"Why . . . ?" He looked perplexed. "Because I find it impossible to ignore what is between us."

"What is between us?"

"My dear girl . . ." he said and shook his head.

"Nothing that I know of." She folded her arms and looked at the horizon.

"Nothing, eh?"

He looked at her and a silence fell as complete as if the world had ceased to exist. He smiled then crooked one brow. "Nothing?"

"Nothing." She turned, intending to walk away and found herself clasped tightly to him. So tightly she could feel the muscles in his legs. He stared down at her.

"You're quite certain?"

"Yes. Very." Whatever she could have done to extricate herself, she was incapable of doing now. His first touch had rendered her helpless.

He held her head still and lowered his. His eyes glittered with want and he whispered. "See if this feels like nothing to you."

He kissed her slowly and deeply until she forgot everything but the sweet warmth of his lips.

"Is this nothing?" Air hissed through his teeth as he pressed her closer. "Or this?"

He kissed her with deliberate skill and when he finally finished, her forehead dropped to his chest. Her eyes stung with unshed tears and she might have fallen if he had not held her to him. "Why do you do those things to me?"

"Why?" He smiled and dropped a kiss on her part. "Because I want you. Why else?"

Now his voice and touch were gentle but she pushed him away. "I know you don't think much of me. And I guess I can understand why . . ."

"What do you mean? I think the world of you."

She shook her head. "Please let me finish. What I want to say is . . ." She stiffened her spine and held her head high. "A Dare would never accept second best." And with that, she walked away.

Jean said nothing in reply because he could not imagine what she was talking about.

Unless she meant that by accepting him she would be accepting second best! The thought was unconscionable.

He was outraged. He was deeply offended. He was mistaken. He *must* be mistaken.

The following day Markie told him that there were so many people in town they were like blowflies on bad meat and that Preacher Hollis was a real glory shouter and that she jumped a distance of five feet and one hand, measured. And that Electra Cooper had not disappointed her.

At the first opportunity, Jean asked her how her sister Brit had enjoyed herself.

"Come to think of it, Brit left early. Took Goat an' came on home. Said she got a stomachache from eating too much."

"Hmm." It was as he suspected. She was wild about him. Good. All right then. He would speak to her again as soon as possible. What he would say he did not know but they had to straighten out things between them.

Brit and Irish decided they might just as well have stayed home for all the fun they had at Founders' Day. That was hard to believe when you consider how much they used to like it.

The grass felt stiff underfoot and the night air was much cooler now. Irish had grabbed a blanket before they left the cabin and they wrapped it around themselves and sat huddled together like a couple of squaws.

"So nothing has changed."

"No, nothing. Except to be more muddled than ever."

The new moon revealed her sister's face and Brit could see that there was worry written all over it.

"I wasn't supposed to go to the mill yesterday, but I did anyway."

A fish jumped somewhere upstream. "Why?"

"I don't know. I felt the need to go, so I just went."

The mill was closed to business but she said she noticed that the back door had been propped open to the breeze so she went up the stairs and looked in.

"Mr. Schumacher was in there, working alone. He had his back to me and was moving some sacks of grain to the wall. You know how they stack them."

Brit nodded. She did. She had been there with Goldie to pick up their grain and had helped him hunt for their sack among those that were lined up against the wall. The bags all had the owner's name printed on a tag and then threaded onto the tie cord. It was all very neat.

They were sitting on a log and Irish kept picking at its bark. "I stood and watched him. He had taken off his shirt and had his hair tied back with a string. I looked at his naked back and his arms, and the longer I looked the more I wanted to, and a hot lump grew right here in my throat and it got so big I could scarcely breathe!"

Irish had Brit worried. She was gulping air like she was having trouble breathing right now. She was also squeezing the life out of her hand!

"I don't know how long I stood there. I know I never made a sound—I couldn't't've—but he somehow must have sensed I was there because he turned and straightened and stood staring at me. Then he let go of the sack and the meal spilled. He threw down the tie and he came over and stopped a few feet from me and I'll tell you, I have never seen such a chest. He's . . . there's a line of dark hair that comes up out of his pants and then it . . . it sorta spreads out across his chest like a fan. It's . . . it's darker than the hair on his head. Brown with little gold glints in it." She looked at her hand. "I think a very long time went by but I can't be sure. All I know is that I wanted to touch him so much that I got a pain right here." She touched her heart.

"What happened?"

Right here Brit was vowing to kill her sister if she said

"I left." Once before Irish had told Brit about coming on Schumacher and his son asleep in the front room. She said she saw these long legs stuck out of a chair so she tiptoed in and there they were, sleeping in a padded chair. He had slid down on his spine so far that his face was mushed into the corner of the chair. His mouth hung open and his big feet were laid over on their sides and the baby was frog-like on his chest with his rear end stuck out like a toadstool. The baby's mouth was open too and he had drooled a big circle on his father's shirt. They were both snoring. She said it was about the cutest thing she had ever seen!

She had made such a big deal about it and had gone on about it for so long that Brit was primed for something, and it sure wasn't what she got. When she asked Irish what happened next, and she simply said she left, and that's when Brit could have killed her.

"So," Brit prompted. "Then what happened?"

"He told me to go. Get away from there. Run! I said I didn't want to go and he said I had to. Go now. Now!"

"You did, right?"

"Yes, but not for a long time and when I left I did not run. I walked. Slowly. And when I got to the road I stopped. I didn't turn around but I waited until I heard the door shut behind me before I went on. I felt odd. Like I've never felt before. Calm and unconcerned."

Brit listened to some small animal forage for food in the grass nearby. "Why did you feel like that? I mean, what did it signify?"

"That I didn't care what he did with me. As long as he did something with me."

"Oh, Irish."

"I know."

"What about Mrs. Schumacher?"

"I never thought of her. I have not seen her in a long time because I stay away from that side of the house and try not to think about her." She turned away. "I don't want to believe her because if I believe her then I have to hate him and I think that might kill me."

Brit slipped her arm around her sister's waist. Somebody, she thought, is going to have to take a hand in this. She looked up at the sky and prayed. Please! You can't have meant for things to stay like this!

Twenty-eight

The day after Founder's Day, Jack and Goldie accompanied their mother to the widow Yates' farm with the Christian intention of performing some odd jobs. The widow's eldest son Billy had been a member of Jack's troop and had been killed in the line of duty. It was there that all hell broke loose.

It was not the first time the Dares had gone out there to lend a hand. Nor were they the only ones to do so. Goldie said many far-flung neighbors and several of Billy's fellow rangers had been spending a day or two at the Yates place mending fence or running down stock. Whatever needed to be done.

To Jean such charitable acts were representative of the native Texian. More than willing to lend a helping hand but not willing to have much made of it.

On that day, however, certain circumstances would come to light that would give the Dares more to contend with than a few runaway cows. According to Markie, they were occupying themselves with one chore and another when Abel O'Neal came riding up out of nowhere and, without so much as a by-your-leave, he roared in amongst them and launched himself from his horse's back to Jack's back and started pummeling Jack for . . . as Markie so vividly put it . . . "cee-ducin' our teacher Miss Annie Mapes." Said "event" was supposed to have happened in the wee

hours of the morning following the Founder's Day celebration.

Goldie said that O'Neal had been like a wild man and
that it took all three Dares to subdue him. Unfortunately
none could convince him that Jack was telling the truth—
even when he categorically denied the accusation—because O'Neal claimed that Annie Mapes had confessed it
to him! She had also asked to be released from her pledge
to marry him because of it!

As Markie was wont to say, this was big. This was really
big.

During the hours immediately following the Dares' return home there was a lot of stomping around and raised
voices, and from the porch Jean heard enough to know
that, at the very least, the lady's virtue had been compro-
mised, because Jack did admit to crawling in through her
bedroom window to . . . chat. However, whether an actual
seduction occurred would soon become a moot point, because within days Black Jack Dare and Miss Annie Mapes
announced that they were getting married just as soon as
they could build and furnish a cabin, which Jack expected
Goldie to do "by Sunday a week."

Now it was Goldie who stomped around muttering about
the "brass cojones of some people, expectin' someone to
build an en-tire cabin an' its en-tire furnishin's in less
time'n most people make breakfast."

He exaggerated, but not by much. At Jack's insistence,
the wedding date had been set for three weeks hence, a
few days before the traditional American celebration of
Thanksgiving.

In the ensuing days Evie Dare's kitchen might have been
in the path of an advancing army, for that's the scale on
which she prepared for the influx of guests to her eldest
son's wedding.

For her girls there was the complete disassembly of the cabin, followed by 'round the clock cleaning. For her sons there was a shopping list which endangered every edible animal within fifty miles. Soon there would be five butchered beeves and three dressed deer hanging in the trees, and a cooking frenzy would begin for which Jean had no comparison.

Using her tongue like a whip, she would wake her sons two hours earlier than normal so they could do certain chores at home before she would even allow them to think about working on Jack's new cabin. Among other things, a deep pit had to be dug, and seasoned wood cut, carried and stacked next to it. Then, when Evie decided the location of the pit had to be less influenced by the wind, another pit was sullenly dug and everything moved there.

She told Jean that four days before the wedding she would have Goldie lay a low fire and put the meat to cook and she said the slabs of meat would be so big they would have to be basted with a rag mop and turned with a pitchfork!

Jean removed himself from the raised voices and clattering pans for as often and as long as possible, but his strength did not yet permit twelve-hour walks. When the racket continued unabated, he found an unobtrusive place on the end of the porch and sat there, sheltered from the wind but near enough to observe the goings-on.

That was his position on his day of destiny.

He lay with his eyes closed, cataloguing the ordinary sounds around him. The rhythmic sound of a cow's clapper. A chicken's soft clucking. The distant baying of a dog.

Unfortunately, overlaying everything was the strong steady pounding of a hammer and an occasional outburst of loud, incredibly imaginative cursing.

Goldie and Blue were repairing the roof on the smaller cabin, making the place "fit for overnight company." Blue had questioned that, saying, "If it's good enough for us, it ought to be good enough for anyone. Jus' like it is."

Evie told him he could repair the roof or receive the "lickin' of his life." He must have believed her because he was on the roof. Watching them made Jean almost glad to have six bullet holes in him.

The sun's warmth beat down on him and he might have dozed off if not for the tantalizing aromas that snaked up his nostrils and titillated his taste buds.

A few months ago if someone had told him that he, Jean McDuff, the darling of the haut monde, would be sitting on a porch in the Tejas wilderness, dressed in skins and salivating with anticipation about a repast of rice and beans with fried fatback, he would have labelled them insane.

But as with so many things, his taste in food seemed to have undergone a rather drastic change as well. He actually preferred the hearty fare of his host family.

Evie Dare could have been the sole cook for the Roman legions. At present she was not only feeding her normal contingent but also anyone who was lending a hand with the construction of the wedding couple's cabin.

Granted, she had the help of the twins and Markie, but counting the men from the ranger troop she was feeding as many as a score of men twice a day. It was the lack of fanfare that amazed him.

Once their ordinary morning work was done, the Dares would hitch up the wagon and Goldie would begin to collect his tools, all of which had been cleaned, oiled and sharpened after the previous day's use. The poleaxe and broadaxe then the froe. Mallet, gimlet and augur. Level and square adze. Assorted saws.

Once the tools were in the wagon, then the twins would begin loading the food. A half dozen fried chickens or a couple of sliced turkeys or a ham or a big pot of stew. Sometimes, like today, it would be only rice and beans with fried fatback. But whatever the menu du jour might be, it was always accompanied by several pans of cornbread or shovel-shaped loaves of flour-dusted bread.

When everything was loaded, one of the men would climb up on the seat and off they would go trailed by a half dozen dogs who were trying to look particularly starved and pitiful.

Sooner or later, in pairs or alone, the men of Jack's ranger troop would come back over to the farm looking for something additional that was needed at the building site . . . this tool or that axe, more nails. Of course they would have to stay and have a bite to eat before they went back to work. Then at sunset all the workers would all drift back to the farm and sit on the porch . . . just long enough to get invited to stay for supper.

Luke Bryant came over to get his leg sewed after a mishap with an axe and for Jean's ears only, he said he was glad Evie wasn't doing the sewing. He rolled up his sleeve and showed Jean a neatly stitched scar he had from a wound he had incurred four years earlier. Then he lifted his shirt in back and showed him a wound that she had stitched six months previous. He said the most recent one looked like a "grinnin' gator's mouth." Jean had never seen a grinning gator's mouth but he had to concede that the sewing might have been done by Markie.

It was in this way that Jean came to know the men of the troop.

Luke, who was a surveyor by trade, had been born in Habersham City, Georgia. He was the seventh of nine children and had moved to Tejas in '25 when he was twenty-four.

Jesse McIninch, the well digger, had set sail for America from Ireland in '18 when he was two years old. His entire family—his parents and two brothers—died from a shipboard cholera outbreak and he had been raised by a kindly old couple in a town called Galveston. He had come north to Sweet Home a year ago May, after his foster family had passed on to what he termed was their "well deserved reward."

Clyde Maxey, the tinsmith, had been born in Lincoln County, Mississippi. His father had served as a colonel in the Revolutionary War and his uncle had been with Andrew Jackson in the War of 1812. Several crop failures in a row had greatly diminished the family coffers and so he said he came to Tejas hoping to make a new start, like most everyone else.

The town assayer, Ed Cox, had been born in Algiers, Louisiana to a large poor family and had come to Tejas "for the excitement."

The shoemaker, Hector Salazar, was originally from Guadalajara, the father of seven daughters and the lone Tejano.

Finally there was Long Bob Benning, the tall, thin creature of the night who never spoke about himself.

He had met them all already, particularly Luke, Jesse, Clyde, and Ed, because they had all come out to call on the twins. The rest he had met when they returned from one foray or another, but it was only now that he felt he knew them as equals.

Conspicuously absent from the construction crew was Jean's young attorney, and the former prospective bridegroom, Abel O'Neal who had, however, retained his job with the rangers. That surprised Jean. Curious to know why, he asked Jack about it.

"I take it you do not harbor any ill will toward Abel O'Neal."

"No, why should I?" Jack's expression was honestly perplexed.

Jean shrugged. "In France a man who attacked his superior, especially with intent to kill . . ."

"Awhell, he didn't do nothin' I wouldn't've done myself. Only difference is I'da probably got the job done. Hell, last couple of months I thought about killin' him plenty of times." He shook his head. "Man, I am sure glad I didn't do it! Fond as Annie is of that boy, I doubt if I'da ever gotten her over that!" He took a deep breath and smiled. "Nice day, ain't it?" And with that, he bounded off the porch and strode toward the corral. A soft whistle floated after him.

"Why'd you just say that?"

Jean jerked and swallowed a curse. Markie had crept up on him again, something about which he had cautioned her a dozen times.

"Say what?"

"Ahmayzeeg! Trulee ahmayzeeg."

"I spoke of something about which you need know nothing for many years."

"Why not?"

He sighed and gave up. "I was thinking about the power of amour."

"What's that?"

"Love. Emotion. Amour."

"Oh." There was a moment, then, "How come you were thinking about that?"

"I don't know. Just crazy I guess."

"Maw says that true love is God's reward to humankind. A little bit of heaven on earth. Do you think that's right?"

"I sincerely hope that it is."

"But she says that some people don't have enough sense to see something true until it's too late. Do you think that's right?"

"I think that's right."

"Me, too."

He looked at her. "I'll bet you are glad your brother is getting the woman he has always wanted."

"Yeah. Well, sorta."

"Sorta? What is that supposed to mean?"

"Nothin'. I don't know. I gotta go now. Bye."

"Bye," he said but he was thinking: Sorta? Now what was all that about?

But he soon became distracted. He yawned and stretched and then he happened to notice a small brown bird that sat atop the sawed stump that served as the chopping block. The bird pranced the stump's furred surface, found the spot that it wanted and let loose with a full-throated melody that was every bit as complicated as an aria. And right then was when it happened. Somehow by the end of that bird's song it was there, imbedded in his mind . . . an epiphany-like vision of himself and Brit Dare. Together in life—and in Tejas—forever.

It was meant to be. *They* were meant to be. How could he have missed seeing it before?

Beautiful images flashed through his mind . . . her face dappled by sunlight or burnished by lantern light. Her crossing the yard to gather eggs or feed the animals or harvest potatoes or draw water. Washing clothes, sweeping the floors or serving food. Laughing at Blue. Raising a quizzical brow at her twin. Soothing Markie and hugging her mother. Playfully slapping Goldie on the head.

In every instance one thing remained the same. Whatever she did or said, whatever the given situation, she was the most vital, most elemental and most desirable female he had ever seen. He wanted her. Not just now but always.

He decided then and there that he would offer for her. Not as her protector and lover but as her husband.

The decision to marry had not been a conscious one but rather an elemental act, like breathing in and breathing out. It felt natural. It felt right. Why did he only see this now and not before? It was irrational, but unimportant in the long run because it was as clear as glass now.

He went over his life before he came to Tejas and for the first time he realized that he had willfully isolated himself from others. Except for Duncan he had been careful to care for no one—and to make sure that no one cared for him. He had been leading a life that was completely governed by habits . . . and all were bad. He was a shallow, selfish man with low regard for everything and everyone . . . including himself. Actually about all his life had produced thus far was twenty-nine years, four months and thirteen days!

But the man who had come to this land was gone now, changed by the desire to lead a meaningful existence, an existence that might in time allow him to value life—and himself—once again. If it happened, he felt sure it would be because he had won the love of Brit Dare.

It seemed almost prophetic to him, the fact that Evie Dare chose that precise moment to come outside.

"Whew! It sure is hot in there!"

"I imagine that it is. However it is probably no hotter than it is under my collar."

"What?"

"Nothing."

He inhaled deeply then forged ahead. "Madame Dare . . ."

"Ayeh?" She replied cautiously. There was something different about his tone.

"What is the custom here, um, if one anticipates courting a female member of a family? Does one talk to the head of the family?"

She did not answer for a minute. Just continued giving him a narrow, level look.

"I'd say he would. Yeah, he would."

"And if that female were a member of this family then . . ."

"Oh, no. Not me. That'd be the oldest male. Black Jack."

He nodded. "All right. Thank you."

That night he drifted off, thinking of her sweet lips and that lithe young body. He slept very well and his sleep was dreamless and he woke feeling better than he had felt in weeks. He anticipated a serene future . . . He had only to wait for the opportunity to speak to her brother, Jack.

He was successful in catching him on one of his quick trips back to the farm and he wasted no time in putting it to him. Jack looked down at his boots. He was half smiling and shaking his head.

"What?"

"Every time somebody asks me what you just asked me, I think: not my baby sister, Brit! Or I think: not little ol' Irish!"

Jean and Jack were standing between the pig sty and the corn crib in a wind that was gusting hard enough to de-hair a man but apparently it did not bother Jack. Nor did the rolling smell of the sty. Nor did the noise. The pigs were giving loud satisfied grunts after having just caught and eaten a snake.

"The twins are hardly babies."

Jack cut him a hard look. "You know that for a fact, do you?"

"Yes, but only from observation."

The pig with the pink-ringed eye was squealing because the other pig had snatched the snake's tail right out of its mouth. The noise was deafening. "Do you think she will favor my suit?"

"Mebbe so. Mebbe no." Jack was studying the ragged line of trees along the river.

"Well, may I put it to her, or not?"

"Hell, I don't care. But first lemme get something straight in my mind. Goldie told me that you told him you could hardly wait to get back home to France. Said you'd be leavin' soon as you got clear sailin' from the judge. Way he talked it sounded like you'd left a whole lot of things an' people behind."

"I did." Jean sniffed. Though he had stopped using it years ago he suddenly wished he had some snuff. It had always calmed him.

"Goldie said you missed your old life. Said you used to spend all your time drinkin' an' chasin' strange poontang or hellin' around with other fellas' wives."

Jean stiffened. "Not *all* my time." But he might not have spoken for the amount of attention Jack gave his reply.

"Goldie said that you said if you *did* decide to settle in Tejas you figured on marrying some real rich señorita from down Mexico way."

"I considered it, yes, I'll admit that I had thought about it but I didn't say I had decided to do it . . ."

"Sounds like mighty smart thinkin' to me."

"Finding a bride in Mexico?"

"Yeah."

"Then why didn't you?"

" 'Cause I couldn't stand the thought of Annie Mapes being any one's wife but mine. 'Cause I love her more'n life. That's why. Course that ain't the case with you."

"You don't have any idea what the case is with me. Apparently you have some complaint about me. Please enlighten me. I am clean, healthy, well-off and possess no . . . few disgusting habits . . . that cannot be broken."

"You wanna know what it is?"

"Yes, I do."

"It jus' don't seem like you an' Brit got a lot in common."

"Is that all?" Jean laughed. "I am sure we can learn to muck along together."

"An' you're sure this is what you want . . ."

"I have asked to marry her, haven't I? That should be proof enough of my resolve."

Jack stared off somewhere. A noisy flock of geese passed high over the woods before he went on. "Well, I guess I'll have to ask her what she's got to say about it before I say more on it."

"Of course. That is only to be expected."

"I'll get back to you."

"Fine." Jean nodded formally and then he watched Jack stride across the yard and mount up.

It had not gone as he had hoped it would. Instead of feeling encouraged about his prospects, he felt just the opposite.

Jack had seen his sister Brit standing behind a tree that was well within earshot of their conversation. Which was why he had asked Jean the questions he had. Because he had guessed what Jean would say in answer. And because he had known that the answers would make her madder'n hell.

He also knew that McDuff was crazy about her. Of course, he had seen that right from the git go. Hell, she'd gigged him the night he arrived.

Well, now maybe not everybody would have seen that as fast as he did. Maybe a person had to experience true love for themselves before they could recognize it in others. Take himself, for instance. He had never paid that sort of thing any mind before. Only since Annie Mapes had he even thought about it. Now, if anyone was an expert on the subject of love, it was Black Jack Dare.

Why had he said what he said, knowing what a riot it would cause? First off, 'cause there ain't no sense in making it easy for them. The path of true love is nothing but roots and rocks and gopher holes. Somebody'd told him that recently and by God, it was true. Besides, a bit of testing never hurt anybody who was really in love.

Second off, and the real reason, was that he just loved to bedevil people. Most especially, one of his sisters.

After three days went by and nothing happened, Jean went over to the work site. Since all of the tame horses were in use and all of the wild ones were run "to hellan-gone," his was an uncomfortable trip on an unsaddled mule. He likened it to riding on a sword.

Jack and Annie's new cabin was situated in a little valley beside a narrow but swift-moving stream. Woods surrounded the cabin and prairie surrounded the woods. The trees were leafless and the earth brown, but the setting sun had burnished everything with gold and had made the trip quite beautiful.

The sound of cutting timber echoed through the woods and he heard the ring of hammers and the sound of male conversation long before he saw the cabin. Then quite suddenly there it was, a beehive of activity set against some old oaks. The unpeeled walls were standing and raw-looking. The rock chimney was done, and two shirtless men stood atop the almost-completed grass roof.

At dinner a few nights earlier Jack had said that he intended to replace the grass with cypress shingles "after . . ." and the men had teased him by asking "After what?"

"Hey look!" A man yelled. "Ain't that the doc?"

"Good timin'!" yelled another. Some men turned and Jean saw a man on the ground. Jesse McIninch was kneeling beside him, holding a bloody rag to his head. "Hey, hurry on over here, Doc!"

"Clyde got knocked in the head."

"I didn't see him standing there an' I whapped 'im with that board . . ."

"Been bleedin' quite a bit."

Jean had not brought his bag but it looked like a simple gash. "Head wounds always bleed a lot." He sniffed. "Mine bled a lot more than this. He'll be all right."

Using what was available—a primitive bent bone needle that Hector Salazar kept in his shoe—he put in two holding stitches and then took Clyde back to the farm where he could do a more appealing suturing job. Within an hour Maxey was well enough to sit up and eat an entire apple cobbler.

All this meant that it was the next day before he finally

had a chance to talk to Jack alone. He intercepted him as he came to the big cabin for breakfast.

"Well?"

Jack lit his pipe before he answered . . . which seemed to take three days. "Well, what . . . ?"

"What about my offer of marriage?"

"I asked her about that." Jack blew a plume of smoke at the sky. "An' she said she would not have you on a stick."

"What?"

"Said not if you was trussed up like a Christmas turkey." Jack looked at McDuff whose eyes were so blared they resembled a couple of fried eggs. "Said she'd take Clyde Maxey over you any day."

"I don't believe she said that!"

Jack had been about to enter the house. Now he turned slowly. "What?"

"She can't be telling the truth. I don't know why she would say that. She is mad about me."

Jack had turned away. Now he turned back. "Look," he replied gently. "I suppose she could be playing hard to get." He put one hand on Jean's shoulder. "It's been my experience that a woman'll say one thing an' mean another every blamed time they open their mouths. A wise man knows that and acts accordingly . . ."

Jean rubbed his head. "I just can't believe it."

Jack shrugged. "Who can figure a woman? Mebbe she's mad at you. Has she got any reason to be?"

"Of course not." Jean felt his face heat and purposely did not look at Jack. Surely she had gotten over that man-handling by now.

"Maybe you'd be better off talkin' to her direct. Hey, cheer up!" He gave him a clap on the back. "You can always get a woman in Mexico City."

Jack had disappeared inside. Jean stood amidst the swirling leaves and looked forlornly at the empty doorway.

* * *

At dusk Jean went looking for Brit, only he found Irish instead. She was sitting by the creek and she had been crying. He knelt beside her and put a hand on her arm. "Irish, what's wrong." She turned aside. "Please don't cry! Tell me what I can do to help you."

"Nothing." A minute went by. "I'm sorry but there's nothing you can do."

"Whatever it is I am sure it can be fixed."

"No, it can't be fixed. Actually it's about to get worse."

"Irish, look at me." She did and it struck him again how she could look so much like Brit and yet so different. "I want you to know I would do anything I could to help you."

"Thank you," she said and melted into his arms and he held her gently while tears flowed anew, petting her back and murmuring nonsensical things.

Brit had come looking for Irish too and she found Jean and Irish just in time to watch them embrace.

It took a minute for her to gather herself and then to slowly begin putting one foot behind the other until she was far enough away to cut and run . . . down the path and under the oaks and hickories, and between the clumps of alamos then out onto the prairie beyond where she threw herself down on the ground and groaned with the agony of it.

Twenty-nine

The day before the wedding, Evie sent Markie to the creek because she said she still needed more fish cakes for the wedding. "I don't want people sayin' I stinted on my first son's wedding party."

Fine by me, thought Markie. If she heard the word "wedding" one more time she thought she'd go red-eyed crazy.

She cut a willow pole, tied on braided yarn and a bent nail hook and went to sit on the bank. She was close to crying, she felt that sad. Her brother Jack was leaving tomorrow and in a way, so was her teacher Miss Mapes, because Miss Mapes said Mayor Cooper would not allow her to teach after she was married. As soon as her replacement got to town, she was done. "A short career."

Irish said Miss Mapes had looked real sad when she said that. Probably sorry that all her learning would be wasted on fixin' supper and darnin' socks. Jack's supper and Jack's socks. Markie choked back a sob.

Markie was as much Jack's child as she was anybody's. When their mother had been widowed at forty-two she was left with twelve kids ranging in age from one to twenty-two, and she scarcely had a spare minute for little Markie, who was the youngest of her brood.

Funny, but out of all those kids it had been Jack who played with her and who walked her through her colic and who picked her up when she fell. And she fell a lot back then.

Markie heard Jack coming down the hill and then she smelled flowers. A lot of flowers. She ran her arm up her nose and made her face calm. "I smell flowers!" she said.

"Lotsa flowers! All the flowers Maw had you girls pick earlier." He sat beside her. She reached out and felt of the oak splint basket between them and then gently, its contents.

"Jack! You didn't take all of 'em, did you!" The things they had gathered weren't really flowers, it being winter and all. Just sweet-smelling weeds and sage and mistletoe.

"Yeah, I did."

"Gol, Maw's gonna kill you!"

"She'll have to catch me first!"

"Where will you put them?"

"Well, some on the mantel maybe. And some on the table for sure. Maybe I'll put a few on her pillow. Think Annie would like that?"

"Aw, Jack that'll be sooo nice!" Markie's chin started wobbling.

"Hey!" Jack set the basket aside. "What's wrong, Goob?"

"I don't understand why she can't be our teacher no more." Her eyes glittered up at him.

" 'Cause she'll be married and her place'll be at home, lookin' after me an' our babies."

Our babies, thought Jack, and through his mind flashed a picture of Annie with a black-haired baby at her breast and the image stirred him like none ever had before.

Markie heard him rise. "You goin'?"

"Naw. Jus' gotta move around a bit." A minute passed then, "Say, I think I'll stay over at the cabin tonight."

"Boy, you better not. Maw'll kill you if you mess up the bed! She's put dried sage between the covers and everything."

"Then I'll sleep on the floor."

"I wish you all didn't have to live clear over there."

"It ain't clear over anywhere. It's only a skip an' a jump away."

"I wish I could see her tomorrow. I'd give anything if I could."

"I'd give anything if you could too. I know she'll look beautiful but then, she's always looked beautiful to me."

"Tell me what else is beautiful." It was a game they had played since she was a little child.

Without hesitation he said, "This land is."

She nodded. "Well, that's for sure!"

"The meadow on a summer day . . . when the larks're singin' an' the crows're cawin'."

Markie made a face. Crows! Her opinion of crows had slid since Goldie told her that when a flock are gathered in one spot they are probably annoying a sleeping owl half to death.

"If you sit real still you can hear the bees hum an' the grasshoppers whistle." Markie nodded. She had sat real still and she had heard.

"An' the sounds of a storm . . . how the wind whips the trees an' the thunder booms an' the lightnin' crashes."

Markie shivered a little. She wasn't all that crazy about lightning.

"An' when snow's stacked on the fence posts an' the willows are frosted an' you run inside an' throw some corn cobs on the fire an' put your feet so close that you cook your shoes."

Markie frowned. She hadn't ever done that!

"An' let's see. What else?" Markie perked up. He grinned and thought: shameless little twit! "Oh yeah. Another beautiful thing would be . . . Miss Markie Dare."

"Am I, Jack? You wouldn't jus' say so?"

"No, Goober, I wouldn't."

"Why?"

"Why? 'Cause you're good an' kind an' cause when you smile your whole face smiles."

"It does?"

"Looks like a gnawed 'melon rind. But you've got to quit stickin' your tongue through that gap in your teeth. What'd Maw tell you about that?"

"Said it makes me look like a snake."

"An'?"

"An' that if I don't quit I'll be able to eat corn through a keyhole. Jack?"

"Mm?"

"Do you love Miss Mapes more than you love me?"

"It's different, Goober. A person can't compare how I love Annie with how I love you."

"How is it different?"

"It's the kind of love a man has for a woman that he'll only have once in his life."

She thought about that. "Jack, what if . . ." She choked back a pitiful sob.

"What if what, Goober?"

"What if nobody will love me 'cause I can't see."

"I love you an' you can't see."

"Yeah but you have to."

"Who said?"

She shrugged. "Nobody. But Miss Mapes says . . ."

"Annie. You can call her Annie now. She'll be one of the family."

"I asked Annie how I'll see the person I'll love and she said that some blind people can see with their soul an' their soul sees another soul and vicey versa. Do you figure I can learn to do that?"

"I think there's times when you know how to do it already."

"None I know about. You didn't answer my question."

He pulled her to him and tucked her head under his

chin and held her good and tight. "Someday somebody'll love you no matter what."

"I don't see why y'all have to live clear over there," she said again.

"Because we want to be by ourselves."

"Why?"

"Goober, the reason will come clear to you someday soon. In the meantime, I want you to remember this . . . no matter where you are an' no matter where I am, you will always be my baby sister. My own Goober." He held her away to look at her face which was blotched and pinched-looking. "You know, Annie told me she wanted us to have a little girl child, just like you."

"She dee-ud?"

"Uh-huh. Just exactly!"

"Huh! She told me I was a great trial to her."

"Well, that was good."

"I didn't think it was."

"Oh, yeah. What she meant was you are a great joy to be around."

"Huh!" Markie was frowning. Miss Mapes had said that, right after she had poked Zick Simmons in the eye.

Jack stayed with her for quite a while before he left to strew flowers all over his new house, but Markie felt better by then, so she remained, sitting quietly and thinking about all that Jack had said.

She could talk to all her brothers but a person had to be careful what they said to Blue or Goldie. One time some kids teased her and she told Blue about it and he scared her, he got so mad so fast. Goldie was about as bad, but not Jack. Jack just listened, calm and quiet, and he never got wild about anything.

Another thing about Jack was that she could ask him anything and he never made her feel stupid about something she did not know.

One Saturday she was sitting on the step outside Garlock's store eating a stick of peppermint when two boys she knew only a little offered her two pieces of peppermint if she would let them "see her mouse."

Now, she did not want to let on that she did not know what her mouse was so she said she would think about it and let them know the next time she saw them. They were two of six boys who lived on a rundown farm south of town.

Somebody generally went to town about once a week and she generally went along. Meanwhile she decided to ask Jack what he thought she should do. Jack listened carefully and calmly and he told her she ought never do anything somebody was willing to pay her to do and that she ought to just forget about those boys and not mess with them ever again.

She went fishing with Irish that next Saturday and pretty much forgot about the whole thing. But somebody must have gone to town because she had three peppermint sticks by her plate that night.

She never did run into those boys again. She heard somebody say that they might have moved back to the States. And it was a whole month after the incident that it struck her . . . she never did ask Jack what her mouse was! She still hadn't to this day!

She sniffed a little. Might never get a chance to ask him, now that he's getting married. Oh, well. She didn't much care for change, yet she had the sense to know that's what life was . . . one big change. Her heart still ached but maybe a little less than before.

Jack wasn't gone ten minutes before she heard her Maw's bawl and she ducked her head and covered her mouth. She knew what had happened. Maw had just discovered all that stuff was missing and now she was hollering for the twins, fit to be tied.

Guess Markie knew what they would be doing first thing tomorrow morning! Only she didn't know where they were gonna find any more things to pick. Seemed like they had already picked about every living thing in Tejas!

After midnight that same night Sheriff Goodman heard a light tapping on his door. He hollered he was coming, and pulled his britches on over his all-overs and with his musket in hand, he opened the door. Abruptly he closed it except for a crack.

One eye appeared in the crack and Irish smiled and gave a little wave. "It's me, Irish."

"Miss Dare!"

"Yes. Can I come in?"

"Well, sure! I guess . . . Jus' let me get my shirt on first."

Irish heard rustling and shook her head. Good grief! He had on his all-overs.

When the door opened he was thumbing on his suspenders. He looked behind her and saw that there was a lone spotted horse tied to the rail.

She stepped inside the door. The room was sparsely furnished. A table on which a short candle wavered. Two horsehair chairs. A black wood stove.

"What on earth are you doin' in town at this time of night? Is anythin' wrong at the farm?"

"Everything is fine there but there is something . . ." She sat down and tucked her chin. "Sheriff . . ."

"Yeah?"

"I know you are coming out for the wedding tomorrow but I wasn't sure I'd have a chance to talk to you alone."

"Yeah?"

"I need to tell you something . . . I need . . . oh!"

She turned her face up to him and it was one of the most miserable faces he had ever seen. He sat and she collapsed into his arms. "What on earth . . . ?"

* * *

The days just before Jack's wedding were marred by tragedy. Bandits held up Hap Pettijohn's freight wagon and killed Hap, young Charley Walters and a man named Dick Ryan.

The Dares arrested the men responsible but enemies of the Dares accosted Markie and Annie Mapes at the schoolhouse and threatened their lives unless their comrades in crime were released.

Needless to say, those men would rue the day they had that idea. But only for the short time they had remaining on earth.

Jean McDuff had been genuinely saddened when he heard about Hap Pettijohn's death. The old mule skinner had, as they say, grown on him. Indeed, he had been a man from the pages of history.

Thirty

The gods blessed the marriage of Jack Dare and Annie Mapes with a perfect day for a wedding. There had been an inordinate amount of rainfall throughout the week preceding the wedding, but on that day the sun rose like a big bright ball to fling red across the slate blue sky and cast warmth onto the land. At least a dozen times, Evie had said they could sure get along without that confounded wind blowing everybody to bits, and as if it had been ordained there was suddenly a complete lack of wind.

Jean stood with Goldie and Blue in front of the cabin, and watched the guests arrive. Late-comers had a healthy walk ahead of them. Lined up along the path to the cabin were all manner of horse and mule-drawn vehicles. Small panel wagons and high-sided hay wagons. Drays, hacks and carriages. Two-wheeled carretas. Even a buggy or two.

In a nearby meadow the guests' mules and horses were bunched according to species while in the yard the guests were bunched according to sex.

Kids ran screaming through the crowd but with the exception of the occasional voice raised in greeting, the adult guests were uncharacteristically subdued. Goldie said he suspected that they were holding themselves in until after the ceremony was over. "Then everything'll go all to hell. You watch."

Jean and his companions seemed to be drawing quite a bit of attention, especially from some young ladies who looked particularly pert as they passed.

In spite of their wild reputations, the two remaining Dare brothers were considered prime marriage material, and deservedly so. Goldie and Blue were both handsomely turned out in beaded buckskin shirts and twill pants tucked into knee-high moccasins. Their black hair was slicked, and their hard jaws were freshly shaved and snow-like teeth gleamed beneath their carefully trimmed walrus-style mustaches.

Jean had also dressed with care and wore a plain but well-tailored black jacket and a black vest with tiny gold threads. His cream-colored pants had been tucked into knee-high boots polished to outshine the sun, and a thin gold ring glinted from one ear.

With the Italian stiletto that hugged the underneath of his left forearm, he was probably one of very few men who were armed. As on the occasion of his run-in with the Dempseys, he had not consciously strapped on the scabbard, but had done so purely from habit.

He had trimmed his beard just so, but had left his hair ungreased and simply tied with a plain piece of rawhide. His white linen shirt had a chin-high standing collar but no ruffles and he thought he had achieved his goal, which was a look of prosperity without pretension.

His intention had been to capture the attention of Miss Brit Dare but he had been captured instead. She looked lovely. Her black hair was piled high on her head in a very modish manner and her cheeks were flushed and her mouth was rosy. She looked edible, as was evidenced by the pack of starved-looking men that encircled her.

Brit was standing beneath a tree laughing and flirting with the men who surrounded her, but inside she was miserable. Her eyes felt dry and scratchy and her face hurt from holding onto a smile. Even her throat ached from holding the hurt inside. But pride sustained her. Her heart might be broken, but no one would know it from looking at her!

She had purposely turned her back to Jean so she would not be caught staring at him. Her eyes seemed to go that way of their own accord.

Soon the guests started loosening up, and so did the hosts. Evie's face was flushed with excitement and Goldie's big laugh resounded with regularity. Jack moved amongst the guests, clapping mens' backs and chucking babies' chins. On one occasion when Jack passed by, Blue winked at Jean and raised his voice so that his brother was sure to hear. Blue's eyes were bright with deviltry and drink. "Boy, I'm sure glad ol' Jack's quit actin' like a love-sick puppy . . ."

Jack turned and pointed at them. "I'll tell you a truth that I'da never believed before: a busted heart'll raise hell with a man. That's a word to the wise, boys." He wagged his finger at each of them in turn. Goldie. Jean. Blue. "A word to the wise."

Jean watched him out of sight. "You know what?"

"No, what?"

"I believe he is right."

Goldie and Blue guffawed, but Jean crooked his brow at them and nodded knowingly.

Goldie quit grinning. "Really?"

"Really."

Evie clanged the bell on the porch and conversation ceased. When all eyes had turned her way, she cleared her throat and said, "We're ready to begin."

The ceremony was to be held out of doors, beneath the leafy dome formed by the limbs of the old live oak in the front yard. At the signal from Evie everyone gathered around the happy couple and the new preacher, the Reverend Hollis Rogers.

Jean was standing behind and to the right of the Dare

family, which was a particularly good vantage point from which to admire the little well at the base of Brit's hairline and to think about pressing his lips there. But then the sound of soft sobbing drew his attention to Markie. Of course she would start it off. But then Irish and Brit joined in. Apparently even Evie had been stricken. Her silent sobs that were strong enough to shake the flowers on her hat.

Women! He searched out Goldie intent on sharing a smile of male superiority but Goldie was too busy dabbing at his eyes to notice!

Great Scott! Jean thought and directed his attention to the happy couple.

They were obviously very much in love—somberly gazing into each other's eyes and pale with the seriousness of it all—and as Jean watched, damned if he didn't feel his own throat begin to tighten!

After the ceremony was over, Jean was leaning against the well and heard quiet laughter float his way. A big raw-boned man and his wife were standing nearby, chuckling together about something, and Jean followed the direction of their gaze to a compact, square-shouldered little boy who had just stuffed an entire sweet cake into his mouth. The man called to him.

"Son?"

"Wvuh?" The boy's hair was docked at his jug-handle ears.

"Don't eat any more cake now."

"Iwoo."

After cutting his parents a look, and noting that their attention was on each other, the boy grabbed two fistfuls of cake and disappeared into the crowd.

Jean stared at the spot. The boy had the common childhood problem of one lazy eye. Unfortunately some children were just born with weak eye muscles and, in most cases, were condemned to being cross-eyed for life. But seeing the boy reminded him of a German physician who had recently discovered a sort of cure. Apparently, if an afflicted child's good eye was kept covered for, say, six months or so, the weak eye could be forced to straighten up in order to take over the job of seeing. Then the good eye could be uncovered and nine times out of ten, the eyes would work in conjunction. Voilà! No more cross-eyed kid.

He had a feeling that particular little boy might relish wearing an eye patch, especially once he was told the story of the famous buccaneer, One-Eyed LaRue.

He could probably help that boy have two straight-looking eyes instead of one straight eye and one that looked at his ear. If he stayed in Tejas.

Jean heard hard laughing and saw Luke Bryant walking alongside a man who was pushing a wheelbarrow filled with two barrels of whiskey.

"Hey, Doc!"

"Hello, Luke."

"Have a drink!"

"Thank you!" he said but as he reached to accept the proffered cup he saw Blue shake his head so he took only a short swig. He still almost choked. Later he would learn that Luke Bryant was famous for producing a vile concoction made of boiled vinegar, logwood and alum.

He returned the cup and wandered through the crowd, looking for Brit. He found her but she was still surrounded by an entourage.

Maybe this was the wrong venue for a private conversation. Thus far she had not been alone at any time and now the musicians were readying themselves.

Goldie had told him the music would be provided by some Finlanders who had become an instant success at the Founders' Day celebration—a musical family consisting of the father, who was a widower, an old granny and five boys. The father played a banjo made from a long-necked gourd. The old woman rapped two cow bones together and three of the boys played jaw harps or wooden flutes. One of the boys hammered on an overturned bucket while the littlest one danced a jig.

The Finlanders were soon joined by others, including two more banjo pickers and another fiddler. These were very lively men given to shrill whistles and loud shouting.

Toward sundown there would have to be a musical interlude while one of the banjo pickers was carried up to the porch where he lay like a shot man with his eyes open and fixed and with a death-like rattle coming from his throat.

It would later become clear that he had made some very poor beverage choices including, apparently, several draughts of Luke Bryant's brew.

At the beginning of the evening no one could have been convinced that they would suffer a like fate, but they would. Oh, yes, there were quite a few who would.

Some couples were clutching each other and bobbing up and down like corks but closer observation told Jean that most of the tunes weren't recognizable to many of the natives either. However, as long as the bucket player came down hard on the beat, the dancers were enthusiastic.

Brit had never spent a more miserable afternoon, and would rather be drug behind a runaway horse than go through anything like it again. She simply could not smile for one more minute. Not even to save her soul from the flames of hell. She had to get away from all these people. She excused herself to Pick and Jesse and walked toward the creek. She was on the verge of tears but pride stiffened her back and straightened her shoulders until she had reached the privacy of the shadows.

Finally Jean saw Brit move away from the crowd and disappear down the creek path. It was the opportunity he had been waiting for all day. He waited a discreet time and then he followed her.

Jean had stopped on the edge of the clearing and watched her go to the creek, kneel and cup some water onto her face. She stood and turned as if she had known he was there all along and they stood staring at each other. Jays called in the bushes and a squirrel chattered overhead, but between them there was a profound silence. She finally raised one brow and induced him to speak.

"I never see you any more. I ask about you and they say she's gone fishing or she's gone to town. It seems that you are always someplace where I am not. I am about ready to think that you are avoiding me."

"I am avoiding you."

"Because I was too . . . aggressive with you. I lost my head. I am sorry. Please believe me when I say that I have only the greatest respect for you." His voice sounded stiff to him. He smiled to soften its effect. "I want you to be my wife. Jack spoke to you about my offer."

"Yes."

"But I understand that you declined."

"Yes."

"Why?"

"Because . . ." She looked away.

"Why?"

She looked back. "I want someone who wants me."

He expelled a breath. "In that case there is no difficulty because I want you very, very much. What?" She was shaking her head.

She raised her eyes and met his. "You don't understand . . ."

"Explain it to me." She was shaking her head. "Why not?"

"Hey, Jean. Hey, Brit."

Goldie looked at each of them in turn and smiled. He had two fingers stuck in the bunghole of a jug he had slung over his shoulder. He took a long pull then wiped his mouth with his sleeve and offered it to Jean.

Abruptly Brit turned and walked swiftly toward the trees where she soon disappeared.

"What's got into her?"

"I wish I knew."

Goldie said, "It's been my experience that a woman'll say one thing an' mean another every blamed time they open their mouths. A wise man knows that and acts accordingly . . . Say, I almost forgot. The sheriff sent me to find you."

Jean looked up at the sky. It was twilight now and the day lingered only on the crowns of the trees. "It is tonight then?"

"Yeah."

Goldie offered Jean the jug again. "Another pull?"

He took a drink and handed it back. "Thank you."

Outwardly Jean Pierre's face was calm but inside he was in turmoil.

"Shall I tell 'im you'll go along peaceably?"

"Yes, of course. I'll be along shortly."

"I'll tell 'im."

From her hiding place behind an old oak Brit watched Jean stand there for what seemed like a very long time. He was motionless with both hands on his cane and his eyes fixed on something far away. Finally he turned and followed Goldie back to the crowd. Once he was out of sight something broke loose inside her and she covered her eyes with her hands and sobbed.

* * *

The sheriff was standing amidst several men. He saw Goldie and Jean coming and motioned them over. He was obviously worked up about something; his nose hairs sounded a lot like one of the Finlander's bone whistles.

The group of men included the millwright about whom Jean had heard so much. They eyed each other and both nodded but they had not yet met. Goldie was trying to find out what had happened.

"According to the Schumachers' housekeeper, Mrs. Schumacher knocked her over the head and then took the boy and headed for the high timber. Schumacher says she's tried to hurt the kid many times before. Says she's loony as a spring rabbit. Whether she is or she ain't . . ." Jean noted a look between Schumacher and Irish. " . . . I want her found and held safe until I can talk to her. All right, men, let's go. Spread out and cover as big an area as you can. Leave a message at Schumacher's house if you find, er, anything. McDuff, you come along with me into town. I'll see you safely in the jail and then I'll catch up with the search party."

Several of the rangers had volunteered to help with the search as had Schumacher, of course. Abel O'Neal was going too but he kneed his horse close to Goodman's first. "Sheriff, I'll be over tomorrow to check on the accommodations for my client." Jean hid a smile at his adversarial tone.

"Hell, you can sleep in the jail with him if you want."

It probably took Brit no longer than ten minutes to dry her eyes and set her face, and in that little time the atmosphere at the cabin had completely changed. People were gathering their things and saying their good-byes. Men were hitching up teams and women were wrapping up sleeping babies and herding their children into the wagons.

She went in search of her mother to ask her what had happened.

"There's been trouble at the Schumachers. The wife knocked the housekeeper silly and took off with the kid."

"Oh, no! Where did she go?"

"Into the woods I guess. Yonder goes Irish. Run ask her."

Brit caught up with her sister on the porch where she was tending Mrs. Von Blucker who was crying and babbling in half English about Nelly, poor Nelly.

Irish and Brit exchanged a look over her head. Irish would feel she was responsible for some of this. Brit just knew she would.

Schumacher came riding up. "Vonny, you better come back with us."

"Yes, yes. I come."

Irish stood too. "Should I . . ."

"No," he replied. "It is best that you stay here; but . . . thank you." He took a minute for a long look at Irish and then he left.

The sheriff did not speak again until they had reached town. He unlocked the jail door then stood aside in order to allow Jean to enter first.

"Sorry about this. Gotta keep to the rules now."

"I understand."

The building was a square, free-standing affair consisting of a jail on one side and the sheriff's residence on the other. The jail side had two large rooms; one for conducting business and one with two cells for housing the prisoners. The rooms in the latter had windows with iron bars set six inches into the adobe.

The sheriff's living quarters on the other side had been built shotgun style with a sitting room nearest the street and then a sleeping room with a door connecting it to the office part of the jail. On the alley side was a room for cooking and eating, and a small porch.

The sheriff was contemplating the bonds of matrimony himself. Jean had heard several men rib him about it. Apparently his intended was Emma Fuller, Abel O'Neal's widowed stepmother.

"This is for your own safety as much as anything. Locking you in also serves to lock others out."

"I understand."

In each cell there were two rawhide-tied cots, two ladder-back chairs and two wash basins. The sheriff pulled the heavy wood door closed and spoke through the slit. "I'll be back quick as I can. There's a couple of blankets on the shelf. Get some rest if you can."

The twins and Evie did not hear about the searchers' success or failure until Goldie returned in the morning. He said that the Schumacher boy had been found safe but Emil Schumacher had been arrested for the murder of his wife. Schumacher claimed he was innocent but he had been found sitting beside his shot wife with the boy asleep in his arms and the gun by his side.

Irish took the news standing, staring into the fire but Brit felt her desolation.

Two men are in jail for murder. Jean McDuff for the murder of Gil Daggert and Emil Schumacher for the murder of his wife. And both men are our very lives.

She looked at her sister and she thought, we Dares would not have a lick of luck if it weren't bad!

Thirty-one

Jean watched the day break through the iron bars that ran the height of the window. It had started to rain about midnight, and the air had turned cold. Dull candlelight showed in Garlock's window and at the bank, but everywhere else the town looked like a wall of gray.

Shortly after dawn he heard the sheriff come into the other room and then he heard him open the door.

"McDuff?"

"Sheriff."

"Just thought you'd like to know that the Schumacher boy is fine but Mrs. Schumacher's been shot."

"Who shot her?"

"He did."

Jean turned and saw the tall blond millwright. "Jean McDuff. This here is Emil Schumacher."

They passed that first day in virtual silence. It had quit raining by mid-morning but the sky remained cloudy and threatening all day.

Maude Stone brought in two meals at noon and two meals in the evening, and when she took the plates away she commented to her helper that both the prisoners sure had hearty appetites. A guilty man would not—at least, not in her opinion.

Once Sheriff Goodman stuck his head in and said that Reverend Hollis Rogers had stopped by and wanted to know if either McDuff or Schumacher needed to see him and Jean had to chuckle when Emil Schumacher asked why in God's name would they want to see Hollis?

During the day they could hear the occasional wagon rattling along the street and the sound of some children at play. During the night they could hear laughter and raised voices from Dirty Dave's. Occasionally the guitar playing from Dulce's would drift over with the wind.

It was only human that they would begin to talk sooner or later. Two men in shared solitude with common problems. It began when Jean heard some late-night revelers out on the road and when he realized that the man in the opposite cot was awake too. He sat up and fixed his pipe and though he was sure Schumacher had heard it all before, he started by telling him about Duncan and the Daggerts and about staying out at the Dares.

"That is where I have been. Over a month, actually."

"They are an interesting family."

"Yes."

"I know the Dares well. Goldie buys a lot of wood from me, and Irish takes care of my son."

"I know."

"Did you know she is an aspiring artist?"

"I saw the portrait she did of her father. It was done on wood with a piece of charcoal."

"I have watched her draw. She likes to take my son down by the creek and sketch while he has his nap."

He said one day he saw a rumpled blanket and a pad of coarse paper but no sign of Irish or Johnny. He said he felt like a criminal the way he snuck down there but that did not keep him from kneeling and picking up the pad of paper. The first thing he saw was a drawing of his housekeeper Mrs. Von Blucker.

"She had caught Vonny's image precisely. Her stern expression, but the tiny twinkle in her eyes."

He said he looked around and when he still didn't see the girl, he licked his finger and lifted another page and there was his boy, rosy-cheeked and peg-toothed, smiling that little three-cornered smile of his. He said the innocence and openness of the child's expression almost brought a tear to his eye.

The next several pages were blank but stuck away near the bottom was a drawing of himself. He took it from his pocket and gave it to Jean who turned it toward the window and studied it.

"It is good."

"Yes, it is."

Irish had drawn Schumacher with the sure strokes of an accomplished artist, precisely reproducing his wide mouth and broad cheeks. His muscled jaw. She had spent a lot of time on it. That much was obvious. Schumacher said he thought she had made his lower lip a bit too full. Jean looked up. "No, maybe not."

Schumacher touched his lips with the pads of two fingers and the back of his neck heated.

"She is promising, isn't she?"

"I think so." Jean handed back the drawing. "Is that why you took this drawing?"

"No, I took it because she drew it of me." He looked at the drawing and then refolded it and put it away.

He said that after that day he bought her some brushes, paints and colored pencils, but he had been afraid to give them to her. "I'm not sure she would accept them from me."

"Probably not," said Jean. "The Dares all have a double dose of pride."

They had eaten breakfast before Schumacher continued.

He confessed to being fascinated with Irish and admitted that he often watched her from one of the mill windows. In the beginning he told himself it was because he was concerned about his son's care. He was making sure she wasn't impatient with him. Later he realized he watched them because it pleased him to do so. The circumstances were so restful. The sun on the creek. The sound of the mill wheel. She would sit with her legs straight out and the boy in the little wallow between them and play with him for hours.

"Johnny sure loves her." He ran an impatient hand through his hair."Listen to me, now I am calling him Johnny too!"

"What is his name?"

"Helmut."

"Helmut."

"She made the same face and then she asked me his middle name and I said Johann and she said she would call him Johnny. We . . . Vonny and I . . . have come to think that Johnny suits him better. More American."

He said he had known Irish for only a short time yet he knew so much that was good about her. Her inner simplicity and her quiet kind of dignity. Her sunny outlook and her naturally giving spirit. The way she cared for his child.

One day he sat beside her close enough to touch her but not, and they stayed that way for a long time, never saying a word. It was not uncomfortable but peaceful and restful. Completely untroubled by the reality of his life.

"Being with her is like coming home after being away for a long long time."

Schumacher stood looking outside. It was raining again. The road was a brown mixture of mud and mire and the town looked bare and blank without its people. Everything was dark and dripping, though it was only mid-afternoon.

"She is not only kind to my boy but she is also unfailingly

kind to me and to Vonny. Only kindness is the last thing I want from her now. I want her as a man wants a woman. I . . . think about it all the time."

Schumacher glanced over at the other man who just sat looking back at him with a quirl of smoke drifting out of his mouth. Schumacher drew his fingers through his hair and sat. "I have not had a woman in two years."

"What?"

"I said . . ."

"Good Lord! I heard what you said. I just can't believe it."

"It's not because that is what I wanted."

"I would hope not!"

"I was afraid of becoming diseased. If I died, and something happened to Vonny, the care of my son would be left to strangers."

"I quite understand. However, it does seem a bit . . . drastic."

"It is all I can think about now."

Jean chuckled as he added tobacco to his pipe. "I am not surprised. The Dare girls are very tempting. Believe me, no one knows that better than I."

With a degree of pride Schumacher said, "I never touched her."

He did admit to coming close. It happened one day when he was working in the mill, stacking sacks of grain. He said he suddenly felt someone's presence and there she was, standing in the doorway. She never said a word. Just looked. The sun was behind her, gilding her form and he was struck mute by her beauty. He suddenly knew that she was everything that mattered. He said he would never know how he refrained from taking her in his arms but he did.

"Did you kill your wife to have her?"

"No, I did not."

"Then who did?"

"I don't know." He ran his hand through his hair. "Maybe I do know but I refuse to believe it."

"What happened that night?"

"Did you see my house?"

"No."

"My wife was in an insane rage. She struck Vonny and started destroying things. The downstairs draperies were shredded. Glass was broken. Potted plants turned over. Clothes and things thrown everywhere. A portrait of my father had a knife embedded in its center. Then she took the boy and ran.

"I knew she would kill my son if she could. This was not the first time she has done something like this."

"How long has she been ill?"

"I don't know. Maybe years before we wed."

He began by telling Jean about his country, unwittingly describing a chilly gray land with dingy streets and smoke-filled skies. But then his voice changed when he told Jean about his family. The younger brother who had drowned when he was eight, an older sister who had married and moved to India with her missionary husband. He said both his parents had passed away when he was sixteen, which left him virtually alone in the world.

Then he told him about meeting his wife and how taken he had been by her fragile beauty and her sweet feminine ways. He had been terribly lonely and she made him feel needed. He wanted to take care of her.

But they had only been married a few weeks when he noticed something a doctor would later describe as *Schadenfreude.*

"I'm sorry. My German is poor."

He described it as a peculiar delight in the misfortune of others, which rapidly deteriorated to causing hurt. Sometimes to others. Later to herself.

Jean waited while Schumacher put his pipe away and

rose to stand at the window. Outside the autumn sun was burning the rain off the grass.

"We were married in April and my private hell began almost immediately. She was petty and argumentative. Nothing I did ever pleased her. One night when I went to bed she was sullen and sulking and she refused to speak to me because of some imagined slight on my part. In the morning I woke to the sound of soft laughter and I found her sitting on the side of the bed, covered with blood. She had taken my razor off the washstand and had made a hundred tiny cuts up and down her arms. The delighted sounds she was making gave me . . . how do you say." He brushed his hand across his arm."

"Goose flesh."

"Yes. I still get them just thinking of it."

"I understand."

"You can imagine my shock, but that was only the beginning. If I left her alone for even a minute she would attempt to do something awful to herself. I was out of my mind with worry.

"I took her to the best doctors in Germany but no one could tell me why she was like that. The questions they asked, the suspicions they had, I began to question my own sanity."

He said she got progressively more self-abusive after the birth of their child. Finally he and Vonny'd had to keep her restrained, especially when her threats started to include her newborn son.

"It was a terrible thing for us. We . . . Vonny and I . . . could never relax for a moment. One of us had to be aware of her whereabouts at all times. Sometimes the worry is almost more than a person can bear." He looked up and Jean saw the glitter of tears. "I had lost all hope. It shames me to say it but I have actually prayed for her death every night for a year."

He fell silent and the night sounds swelled up to fill in.

The strident barking of a dog. Men's voices as they passed by the jail.

"Did you know that Irish is in love with you?"

Emil swallowed hard. "No, I did not. Why do you say that?"

"Because she told me she was. It was right before Jack's wedding. I went looking for Brit and found Irish instead. She was down by the creek, and she had been crying. She was very worried about some things your wife had said." Schumacher stood so that Jean had to look up at him. "She told me that she loved you. But she did not know if you were the man she thought you were or the man she hoped you were. She told me some of the things your wife had said about you. That you were beating her regularly and that you had threatened to kill her."

"I never . . ."

Jean held up his hand. "Irish said she didn't believe it at first but as time went on she couldn't help but wonder if she could be wrong. If it were true . . . if something happened to your wife or to Johnny she felt it would be her fault. She was really very upset and in the end she decided she could not take the chance that she was wrong. That's when she decided to ride into town and talk to Sheriff Goodman."

"But she said she loved me?"

"Yes."

Schumacher strode to the door and pounded on it. "Sheriff!" He turned to Jean. "She said it to you? That she loved me?"

Jean hid a grin. "Yes."

"I have to get out of here." He rattled the door on its hinges. "Sheriff!"

The sheriff opened the door. He had obviously been asleep. His eyes were slits and his hair was spiked. "What in the blue blazes is goin' on in here?"

"Sheriff, I have to get out of here. I must go speak to . . . someone."

"Well, you ain't, so jus' put that right outa your mind. You are in jail, son, and will not get out until the judge says you will get out."

Schumacher slumped. He straightened. "All right, all right. Fine. But will you take a message for me? No. No. That won't work." He slumped onto the cot. "What can I do?"

"Write a letter," said Jean. To the sheriff, "Goodman, you can have someone take a letter out to the Dares, can't you?"

"Not tonight I won't."

"Tomorrow then?"

"I suppose." Now Schumacher was giving Jean a rather strange look. "What?"

"I cannot write a letter in English. I can print someone's name and simple messages but I cannot write not a love letter."

"Not to worry. I will write it for you."

"You will?" Schumacher's face split in a huge grin.

"Hell, yes! I can write a love letter in Swahili if necessary."

He was doing some unnecessary bragging here but Schumacher's mood was infectious. He felt like laughing too. They must both be insane!

Thirty-two

The winter of '28 arrived within days, with a brittle frost that put icy cobwebs on the water buckets and made the ground crackle underfoot.

Like other cabins in the area, Jack and Annie Dare's had icicles on its roof corners but within was the warmth of a roaring hearth fire and the soft sound of feminine laughter.

Despite the threat of worse weather on the way, the twins and Markie had come to visit. It was Evie's idea. She had thought it might perk them up. By *them* she meant the twins who had been spending all their time sighing sighs and staring off at nothing. So it had been at their mother's insistence that they had taken their hand work and gone over to visit their brother and his new wife where they were made most welcome and were given seats by the fire.

As the girls and their former teacher chattered like magpies, Jack smoked his pipe and studied his sisters. He knew what part of the trouble was but he hadn't a clue how to right it. His twin sisters were pining, one for a man she wanted but refused and one for a man she could never have.

Annie's thoughts paralleled her husband's, only she was not privy to the circumstances surrounding their courtships and so based her knowledge of their unhappiness purely on intuition.

Suddenly they heard someone ride up and Jack rose and went to the window. He looked out the slit cut for that purpose and then went to the door. He stepped out onto the porch and the women heard him say, "Clyde."

" 'lo, Jack."

Clyde did not dismount, so Jack pulled the door closed behind him and the rest of the conversation was lost to the women inside. In a minute he was back. "Trouble, Jack?"

"Mm. South a ways."

Jack disappeared into their sleeping room and when he came out he was wearing leather leggings and his buckskin hunting shirt. He slung on a wide belt and cinched it. A cowhide scabbard held his fighting knife. He sheathed another behind his head, stuck three pistols in his belt and crisscrossed his chest with two rawhide whangs, one with a shot pouch the other with a powder horn. He unracked his long rifle then leaned down and kissed Annie's mouth twice. He rumpled Markie's head as he went by and then he was gone.

Half out of her chair, Annie had to force herself to sit back and take up her work again. She did do so but not happily. She must have let some sound slip because Markie said, "Jack'll be all right. Oh, yeah. I never worry about Jack. Blue neither."

Annie looked at her down-bent head and wanted to say: You little liar!

But while Jack was gone the Dare girls spent a lot of time over at their place and they were there again a week later, this time to show Annie how to make a wreath of twisted grape vines with tied-on clumps of dried berries. Annie hoped to give her wreath to her adopted mother, Emma Fuller, for Christmas.

"Maybe I'll have to give it to her for a wedding present. I don't seem to be getting anywhere fast . . ."

Emma Fuller was marrying Sheriff Goodman on the first of February. Surely Annie could get it finished by then. She stood and walked to the window to look out for the tenth time in an hour. "I just can't seem to concentrate . . ."

There was a pause. The Dare twins exchanged a look and Irish poked Markie in the side. Dependable as ever, Markie filled in with complaints about her new teacher, the man who had taken over for Annie when she married Jack.

Annie returned to the table and sat and then suddenly sprang up like a groundhog. "Did you hear something?"

"Nuh-uh. Did you?"

Again she went to the window and opened one shutter. The moon was huge, a flat molten plate of gold. Suddenly she caught her breath. She thought she saw a shadow moving through the trees. Then she heard Jack's voice. "Hello the cabin! It's me."

"Jack!" Annie flew out the door, across the porch, down the stairs and rushed to him. He lifted her eagerly then saw the girls who had all tumbled out onto the porch. He smiled and waved at them and then buried his nose in Annie's hair and carried her inside and closed the door with his heel.

"I'll take care of your horse, Jack."

Brit heard a muffled thanks and then saw that Markie was halfway up the stairs. Brit grabbed her by the arm and pulled her and the horse around the side of the cabin.

"We'll take care of Jack's horse and then we have to go home."

"Why? Jack's jus' got here!"

"That's exactly why we need to go home."

"But I want to see Jack."

"We can see him tomorrow."

"But . . ."

The door opened. "Irish!"

"Yeah?"

"I have something for you. It's a letter."

"A letter? For me?"

"Yeah." He dug in the morral which he had carelessly tossed on the porch. "Here it is."

"Thank you." Because she was looking at the letter. She did not see the light in Jack's eye.

"My . . . darling . . . girl . . ." she read that much aloud and then she looked at Markie and Brit.

"Go on," said Markie.

"You go on, Markie Dare! This is a private letter."

Jack said, "Y'all come on inside so we can all hear it."

"Absolutely not! I'm going home . . . Brit? Brit!"

Brit had walked a little ways off as soon as she recognized Jean's handwriting. How could she not recognize the same cramped little words that he had written to his man in New Orleans? Or those that he had scratched on the medicine bottles in his case?

But she had walked away because her heart was broken and because she could not bear to hear him tell her sister what she was dying to hear herself.

Irish was faced with a dilemma. She didn't want to share her letter with everyone in the cabin, but she had to have light to see. Home! She had to get home! She grabbed Goat's mane and pulled herself on board and was halfway down the path before she remembered her sisters. "Hey, hurry up! I'm not waiting on you ol' slow pokes."

Once home Irish read the letter and then looked up at Brit. "It is from Emil!"

"Emil?" said Markie. "Who's Emil?"

"Mr. Schumacher. And Brit, there's a part on the bottom for you!"

"From Mr. Schumacher?"

"No silly. From Dr. McDuff. Here, I'll read it to you. It

says . . . *Dearest Brit. Everything comes clear to me now. Come to see me and I will explain. It has all been a terrible misunderstanding. I am in love with you. No one but you. Always and ever. Jean.*

Brit looked utterly perplexed. "But I thought he wanted you?"

"Me? Why, he's never seen anyone but you. Heck, he told me that the night he found me crying over Emil."

"The night he found you crying . . ." Brit looked off for a minute and then covered her face with her hands. "Oh, how could I be so dumb?"

"Well, easy," said Markie. But her two sisters were crying and clutching each other. Markie waited for them to quit and when they didn't she gave a disgusted sound and went upstairs.

The next morning Brit arrived at the jail with the dawn and asked to speak to Jean. Sheriff Goodman came to get him and allowed them to sit in the office part of the jail.

But under no circumstances would he allow them to speak to each other alone and Jean was not at all pleased about that.

Brit was sitting next to the wood stove, staring at a place near her foot, and Jean was standing in front of the sheriff with his arms wide at his side. "Come now, Sheriff, a moment's privacy is all I ask . . ."

"What, are you plumb crazy? You think I'm crazy? You know her brothers. No." He was shaking his head vigorously.

"It's all right, Jean." Brit looked at him, then at Sheriff Goodman and she blushed furiously. "Come here and let me speak to you."

"Sweet girl!" Jean knelt by her side and reached for her hand.

"Hey now. None of that!"

Jean stood angrily. "May I not at least take her hand?"

"No, you may not!" Mocking. "You must think I jus' came down with the rain? You think I ain't heard about you Frenchies? Or mebbe you don't think I can remember what it's like to be young. Hah!"

"Sacré bleu!" Jean stomped to a chair and sat. "Sheriff, I was not suggesting . . ."

"You ain't suggesting jack squat. Now I'm gonna sit right here and read this St. Louie paper, which is only eight months old, while you two do your talkin'. Right here and right now. Or not at all."

"Fine," said Brit. "That's fine." She leaned close and whispered. "Oh, Jean! I thought you wanted Irish. I didn't know you wanted me."

"Of course I want you. It has always been you. It will always be you. Chéri! I love you. You are the girl of my dreams."

"Oh, Jean!"

There was a suspicious sound behind the paper. A snort? A sob? In either case, Jean was incensed. No one . . . not even a Frenchman . . . can make love under such conditions!

Thirty-three

Jean McDuff and Emil Schumacher's trials were to be held on a wet wind-swept day in mid-December and in order to arrive on time Annie and Jack Dare had to leave for town as soon as the bleary sun rose in the milk-colored sky. An icy rain had been falling all night long. Frost gleamed on the fields and ice-ringed puddles dotted the two-rut road that rolled before them like a twisted skein.

Annie was about to comment on the brown rabbit that had run from the wagon in big bounding arcs when she looked up at Jack and the sight of him stole the words from her mouth. Exactly as had happened the first time she saw him.

Remembering her first glimpse of that slab-rock face, then so ominous-looking and now so dear, she had to stifle a giggle. Why, if someone had told her then that the mountain of grease-blackened buckskin would be her own true love, the very meaning of her life, she would have laughed right in their face. And now . . . here she was, married to him.

Which was exactly what he had said would happen. He had told her he would do whatever it took to get her and he did. Even if it had meant crawling in her bedroom window like a wild Indian.

Not that she had ever seen a wild Indian but she imagined one would not look all that different from her husband.

He was still a bit of an enigma to her. Perhaps he always would be, but he loved her. Oh, yes. She knew that he loved her. As for herself, she would sometimes ask herself how she had lived without him before, and the answer was simple: she had not.

She buried her face in his sleeve and smelled wood smoke and old leather.

"What're you doin' girl?"

"I am smelling you."

"Do I smell all right."

"You smell . . . fine."

He looked down at her. She smiled up at him. Each end of his horseshoe mustache glistened with ice.

"Is my nose leakin'?"

"No, why?"

He pulled the team to a halt, hauled her into his arms and kissed her silly. When he had finished, he pulled her scarf back over her head, picked up the reins and lightly slapped them against the mules' rear ends.

After she had caught her breath, she said, "What was that for? Not that I'm complaining."

"You were lookin' at me like you'd like to be kissed."

"I was? Huh. But isn't that how I always look at you?"

"Uh-huh. That's why I can't hardly get anythin' done." She was about to say something when he added, "You understand that I ain't complainin'."

He grinned at her. She grinned back and almost dropped the carbine she held across her lap. She was supposed to hold it ready to hand to Jack, or if something should happen to him (such as their being ambushed and his falling dead at first fire . . . God forbid!) then she was to fire the gun then take his pistols and continue firing until she had one loaded musket left.

She always stopped right there, preferring not to think about what she was supposed to do with that last load.

She had learned so much since she got married. How to load and fire a gun. How to mold bullets and prepare the narrow strips of greased cloths which were used to patch them. How to dip candles and make soap. How to prepare all of her husband's favorite foods.

But what she had learned the most about was lovemaking, because that's what they spent the major portion of their leisure time doing. It was, he said, the only way to learn. Practice. Practice. Practice.

It must work because she had already experienced feelings she had never imagined she would. He said it was the same for him and she believed him. She would put her hands on him and feel him tremble or press her nose to his chest and feel his heart pound. The scent of him excited her. His voice excited her. Sometimes he would talk while they were doing it. Look at me he would say, stroking slowly, moving carefully and she would, all the while trying to breathe past the rock-like thing that was caught in her throat. Then the rawhide ties would begin to creak faster and faster and she heard nothing but the words that were a pagan chant in her ear. C'mon darlin' yeah let go an' c'mon with me that's it yeah.

She once got up every bit of nerve in her body and asked him what was he thinking when they were doing it and said he was thinking about the time he got shot in the foot.

Really? she said. That amazed her. She expected him to say he was thinking about her. Why? she asked and he said it was so he didn't come too soon and not give her full pleasure. She had said Oh, and felt herself blush furiously.

Honestly, she often wished he would not answer her questions quite so . . . honestly. He was so much more outspoken than she. Completely free and easy about things he had no business speaking about. For example her body parts. Never, ever should he mention those things out loud. But he did. Especially while they were doing it. He would name them and tell her how much he liked them and how they felt to him and how did they feel to her? And did she like when he did this to them? Or when he did that? How about this?

And he would honestly expect her to answer . . . Good Lord! she was only human!

She did finally have to speak out against bathing together. That was entirely too much to "bare."

One day he actually followed her down to the creek when she was about to take her bath! What are you doing? she asked. Shuckin' my clothes, he said. I can see that! she cried. But I am about to have my bath now. He kept right on shuckin' and says: That's fine. I thought I'd have mine too. Oh, well, she said, I'll just wait until you're finished.

And that's when his true purpose came out. He said how about they have a bath together?

"Most certainly not!" she had cried.

"Why not?"

She hated to speak of such things but she really had to put her foot down, right then and there. What followed was a long discussion about female decency and modesty and a woman's need for privacy.

He listened solemnly and carefully to everything she said . . . she just loved that about him! And when she was finished, he actually looked chagrined. You're right, he said. I was out of line. I never thought.

Her rough-cut diamond. That's how she liked to think of him. Oh, she would not change him for the world but she would like to smooth a few of those rough places. Not overnight, mind you, but over many many years.

The road turned sharply and then back, and there was Sweet Home, some twenty buildings loosely built around an old rock-curbed well. The Mexican homes were clustered together, mud and adobe huts and not many at that. Most of the Mexican families lived out of town also.

Jack turned the team onto the main road and they headed directly for the livery. Which brought them by the infamous Dulce's, an innocent-looking place with tall windows bracketed by wooden shutters. But this was the only occasion that Annie could ever remember seeing those shutters put to use.

With few exceptions Sweet Home looked exactly as it had the first time she saw it six months earlier. The exceptions were four new buildings. The church, and a recently completed cabin built for Preacher Rogers. The courthouse, and a saloon and billiard parlor called Friendly's because it was owned by a yahoo fella who called himself Friendly Monroe.

Annie had complained to Jack about that. "Three saloons and only one church."

"If they'd serve liquor at church, there'd be eight of 'em."

Friendly's was a square two-story affair which had been constructed by building four individual log buildings with a dog trot in between. The sleeping rooms were on the top floor, and the kitchen, saloon, and billiard parlor were on the first.

Jack called Friendly a spit and whittle man because he liked to sit under his vega and watch the people go by. Sure enough, they drove by and there he was. Cold or no cold, Friendly Monroe was outside waiting to talk to anyone who did not move fast enough to escape him.

Of course, Sweet Home had attracted more anglo immigrants than those few, but most of the population wanted land, and had built their homesteads miles from town.

When they were closer to the south end of town Annie recognized Lloyd Cooper and his wife Alma briskly walking toward the courthouse. They waved.

Lloyd was the owner of the bank, and he was Stephen Austin's agent, as well as the alcalde—or mayor—of Sweet Home.

Strolling along behind the Coopers were Emma Fuller, Annie's stepmother and Emma's intended, Sheriff Ernie Goodman.

Ruth and Bowie Garlock waved to them from in front of their store and then fell in behind the others. Goodness, it appears that everyone was going to be at the trial.

The courthouse building was square with a center courtyard. One side was the court room. The other side was separated into the judge's chambers, his assistant's room and a "holding" room.

The roof had big timbers quoined so that the logs jutted beyond the walls. Unfortunately they made a perfect perch for roosting pigeons and the result was an already unsightly stain on all four corners of the building.

At least its tall and narrow windows were now covered by shutters. There had been a time when there had been no coverings for the windows and only a partially built roof. As a consequence, all within used to be subjected to the unpleasant deposits from the score of birds that constantly soared around inside.

Jack and Annie took seats beside Markie and the twins. Blue and Goldie and most of Jack's ranger troop were standing alongside one wall. The Coopers were sitting in front of them. Annie leaned close and tapped Alma on the shoulder. She turned and greeted Jack and then said to Annie. "I'll bet Abel O'Neal is a nervous wreck . . ."

"What's that clickin' noise?"

While still smiling at Mrs. Cooper, Irish put her hand over Markie's face and drew her close. Mrs. Cooper had recently gone to New Orleans and been fitted with bone teeth. Irish whispered in Markie's ear and then slowly removed her hand. "She dee-ud?" Back went the hand.

Annie missed Mrs. Cooper's curious frown because she was watching a woman go down the aisle, dragging by the hand a snarl-headed little boy wearing hand-me-down pants and a mischievous smirk on his face.

Annie smiled and slipped her hand under Jack's. *Oh, God give us one just like that!*

The Judge Frederico de la Barca and his assistant, Señor Peza entered followed by Abel O'Neal. Oh, it seemed forever since Annie had seen him. Abel, her dear dear friend.

She recognized his coat as one he'd had for a few years, only it fit him rather poorly now, since he had filled out in every place that she could see. His shoulders were broader and sort of lumpy looking. His chest was wider and his neck was thicker. Even his jaw looked longer.

Abel was building a place close to where the school road crossed the town road. Goldie had been helping, as had Jack and Blue. She had heard all about it but had not been invited to see it yet. She hoped that was because it wasn't finished and not because he was still angry with her. Abel O'Neal and Annie Dare had grown up together and had been going to marry until Annie fell in love with Jack.

She overheard Brit and Irish, who were taking turns describing Earl Daggert to Markie. "His body is mostly bones."

"His face is mostly nose an' meanness."

"He doesn't have enough hair for his head size."

"He smells like a dog just out of the creek."

"He has extremely cold blue eyes."

"Very cold and very shifty."

Their litany was interrupted by the tinkling of a little bell which indicated that the judge was ready to begin.

Sheriff Goodman came forward first and told about the night Daggert died. How he and Jean McDuff had gone out to his brother's grave, only they had not known that it was his brother's grave until they dug it up. He told about parting with the doctor later and then about hearing two shots fired and how they had been so close together they might have been one. He had been about to open the door to investigate when a young lady appeared all het up and yelling about two men being shot. He went to Dulce's cantina and found Gil Daggert dead in bed and Jean McDuff alive but shot in the back. He tossed Earl Daggert in jail until he could figure what to do with him and then he took the injured man out to the Dares.

"As you know, we first had some, um, delays on this end an' then the accused kept gettin' hisself in the way of somebody's bullet. Anyhow, here he is now an' that's all I know about it."

Next it was Jean McDuff's turn to tell what had happened. How he had heard about an argument between his brother and the deceased man, Gil Daggert. How he had threatened Gil Daggert with a gun. How his brother's watch had been in Daggert's possession. How he was holding a gun on him when he was shot in the back by someone and that he had later found out that it was Gil's brother Earl who had shot him.

The judge's assistant stood. "The judge would like to know: Was this an accident or did you intend to kill him?"

"I intended to kill him." He stopped and nobody breathed. "But not at that moment."

Judge Barca and Señor Peza had a very brief conversation then the Judge rapped a mallet on the desk and

Señor Peza said, "This case is dismissed. The judge will now take a brief rest before hearing the next case."

Annie was standing outside getting a breath of fresh air. Cold or not, it was refreshing after the closeness of the courthouse.

Something had started falling from the gray heavens. To a person who had lived in Pennsylvania all her previous years it resembled cold mush more than snow, but it was whitening the streets and the winter-drab trees. That coupled with the McDuff verdict had made the town almost festive-feeling.

Abel was coming toward her. He had his head in a book, probably headed for his little office. She stepped forward. "Abel!"

"Oh, Annie. Hello! How are you?"

"Fine. Oh, Abel! I've missed you."

"I've missed you too." He put a hand on her sleeve and then took it off.

"Oh, Abel!"

He smiled. "You said that already. Gosh, you look good, Annie."

"So do you. Wonderful. And you are doing such a good job in court! Truly!"

He smiled again. "Dear Annie. You always were my best fan."

"Oh, Abel, will you come out to our place for supper one night?"

"Yes, I will. You let me know when and I'll be there."

"Good!"

"Well . . ."

"Don't let me keep you. I know you have another case. Isn't it exciting?"

"Exciting for you. Nerve-racking for me. I have just

been told to get ready for the Schumacher thing when I had planned on having at least a few days."

"I know. You need to go. I'll see you soon."

"Bye, Annie."

"Bye, Abel."

She watched him walk away, her dearest friend and childhood companion, and her heart felt eased. It was so important to her to remain Abel's friend. She had resisted Jack Dare because she did not want to hurt Abel, and then she had done it anyway and the guilt had almost killed her.

She was thinking about these things and blindly staring down an alley between the courthouse and the bank, when she observed Jean McDuff and Brit Dare coming from around the side of the bank building. Brit's face was flushed and she was trying to fix her flopped hair.

"There he is!" yelled Blue.

Someone cried, "Time to celebrate!" and the Dare brothers and some other men came across the road and grabbed Jean by the arm and carried him off toward Dirty Dave's.

Jean threw a helpless glance over his shoulder at Brit before he allowed himself to be conveyed away.

Annie checked for any casual observers by looking first one way and then the other. "Brit!" she hissed and waved frantically. "Come here!"

She came running like a puppy. A smile split her face. "Oh, ma'am! Annie! Jean and I are getting married."

"I thought as much but what I am concerned about is . . . what on earth you are doing behind the bank building with him . . . alone."

"Oh, ma'am. We . . . he . . ."

"Never mind. This is not the sort of thing one talks about in the middle of the street. Your buttons are in the wrong loops."

Brit turned her back to the courthouse and allowed Annie to fix her dress. "Oh, Annie. I am so in love!"

"I can see that you are. Which is why I urge an early marriage."

"That's what Jean wants but . . ."

"No buts, dear. I have a feeling the doctor can be every bit as persuasive as your brother Jack, and believe me . . ." She smoothed her hair and her face flushed. "Believe me, dear, I know exactly how persuasive that can be. I went through a very trying time with him and I assure you, your only prayer is to be very firm and very vigilant and you must not go with him behind buildings in broad daylight . . ."

"Oh, Miss Mapes!" She giggled. "Listen to me, calling you Miss Mapes."

Annie sighed. "That's because I sound like your schoolteacher again. Lecturing. I just don't want you to be embarrassed or . . . you know." But Brit was gazing off toward Dirty Dave's with a lovesick look on her face. Annie sighed then lamely added, "Well, just . . . do your best, dear."

Emil Schumacher's trial began around two o'clock, after the judge had been sufficiently "rested" and after several men, including the Dare brothers and Jean McDuff, had been well oiled.

Abel O'Neal began the defense's statement by saying, "Your honor, my client, Emil Schumacher will not testify in his own behalf other than to state that he did not commit this crime. While it is true that this . . ." Here he pointed to a gun on the table. " . . . musket is his, he swears that he did not fire the ball that killed his wife. So, now. Your Honor, I will speak to the evidence against my client, of which, frankly, there is none."

Señor Peza stepped forward with several sheets of paper. "What does your client say about these letters that were found among the deceased's belongings. They were written in her own hand and state that she believed her husband was planning to cut her throat or drown her in the river or, um, this one says he will poison her. Does your client have any response to that?"

Abel O'Neal glanced at Schumacher who shook his head. Abel gave a slight shrug and gathering his papers, he prepared to continue but a thin voice came from the rear of the room. "I will respond to that." A woman stood. "Mrs. Schumacher was always writing letters like that but he never touched one hair on her head. And . . . and I know he did not shoot her because . . . I did." Irish turned though she recognized the voice. Vonny! Mrs. Von Blucker. "She was my . . . daughter." There was a hush, then general disorder as everyone spoke at once.

Emil Schumacher was asked to step down, and Mrs. Von Blucker was called forward and then all the truth came out.

Between heart-wrenching sobs, Mrs. Von Blucker said she had gone back into town at Mr. Schumacher's request. He had asked her to make herself available at the house in case Mrs. Schumacher or the boy were found, or in case she was needed to provide help to the searchers. It was her thought that she could be a sort of information center. She was terribly worried about her daughter and everyone in the courthouse could tell she felt things were partially her fault.

She said that it was while she was trying to keep busy, slicing some bread, grinding some coffee, that she happened to remember a little run-down cabin about a mile up creek. The family who had lived there had moved four or five years ago and it was in terrible condition. She did not know why that place popped into mind, but she thought someone should look into it. It was possible her daughter might have gone there.

She wandered around outside but she couldn't find any of the searchers, and before she knew it, she discovered she was halfway to the cabin already, so she decided to check it out herself. Unfortunately Mrs. Schumacher was not there but as she was walking back she thought she heard something and sure enough, there they were, a short distance off the path, sitting on a fallen log. They argued. Mrs. Schumacher had Emil's musket and threatened to shoot the boy if Von Blucker came any closer. This went on for a time but finally Mrs. Von Blucker was able to get close enough to knock the gun out of Mrs. Schumacher's hand. She pushed her and Mrs. Schumacher fell and the gun went off. Mrs. Schumacher was dead. Mrs. Von Blucker dropped the gun and panicked. She heard someone crashing through the brush and she ran. She was hiding behind a tree when she saw Mr. Schumacher arrive. He knelt and checked his wife for signs of life, then he picked up his son and sat down there to wait for the sheriff.

Mrs. Von Blucker said she lay right there and cried her eyes out. Poor poor Nelly. She had only tried to keep Mrs. Schumacher from killing herself or her baby son. Instead she had caused the death of her own daughter!

Not a lot more came clear after that because of Mrs. Von Blucker's crying, but the judge stood and dismissed that case as well.

Thirty-four

Two days later Emil Schumacher went out to the Dare farm to speak to Irish but she would not see him. Actually no one could even find her. But Evie Dare told Emil to have a seat and a cup of coffee and they would talk. Schumacher didn't look too keen on it but he did sit down.

Evie looked at the millwright. It must have been a hard couple of days for him—he looked pretty ragged around the edges.

She asked him if his boy had suffered any ill effects from his ordeal, and Schumacher said he hadn't, and she asked him if Mrs. Von Blucker had, and he said she hadn't either. He said she was very sad about the death of her daughter, but she would be all right. She was as strong as her daughter had been weak.

After a little silence, Evie asked him another question. "Why do you imagine Irish would run off and hide like that?"

"I don't know. I just want to apologize for what she went through while she was working in my home."

"Oh, there's more to it than that, now ain't there?"

"Yes."

Evie folded her arms and looked off somewhere. "You know why I think she's gone and hid on you?"

"No, why?"

"She thinks you hate her 'cause she did not believe in you."

He snorted. "That's silly. I don't blame her a bit. Why, I would have done the exact same thing. Believe me! I know how persuasive my wife could be."

Evie fixed her gaze on the horizon. "Irish is my dove, flying above the world and its toil, seeing beauty in places where no one will even look." She looked at Emil. "She saw something in you, and you must have seen something in her. Something more than just a pretty face and a pleasing way . . ."

"Yes, I did! All that and more. I know it's too soon to talk to her . . ."

"But you want her for your wife. Well then, if you want her, you're gonna have to go find her and make her believe that you don't blame her for not believing in you. Make her believe you care. Why, I think she's probably out there in the woods a ways, watchin' us right now."

"I'm not sure what to say to her."

"Hell, don't say nothing to her. Grab her to yuh an' kiss her silly."

Emil smiled. It wobbled but it was a smile.

Evie Dare was sitting barefooted in a rickety old chair. She was wearing a patched dress and she was fanning herself with a bird-wing fan, and she looked like a queen to him. "Mrs. Dare . . ."

"Evie."

"Evie. I don't know how to thank you . . ."

"Aw hush now! All you have to decide is: do you want her or not!"

"Yes!" he roared. "Yes! Yes!"

"Then g'on an' git her! Git outa here. Go!"

He got up and trotted off. "That's what I like," she whispered. "A man who knows his own mind. Hey!" She cupped her mouth. "Don't let her brothers catch yuh doin' anythin' funny!"

He waved backward but he did not turn.

* * *

Mrs. Von Blucker had been absolved of any culpability concerning her daughter's death. There was some talk about that but it died down in time.

There had also been some talk about the fact that the millwright was calling on one of the Dare girls and it was less than three months after his wife was killed. But it wasn't too long and talk died down about that as well. Now that the whole story had come out, it was obvious that the poor man had not had a marriage for years.

But when Emil and Irish started courting, there had been some serious discussions between Goldie and Blue about the fact that this romance had been brewing for a while and that Irish seemed plain silly about Schumacher and vice versa. They had better keep a keen eye out. The wedding day would be in May and there ought not to be any jumping the gun. Nobody had to tell them how fiery the Dare nature was.

Sure enough, one day not long after they'd had that talk, Goldie came around the side of the shed and there they were. His sister Irish, and Emil Schumacher, locked in such an embrace that he couldn't tell where one began and the other one ended.

Irish opened one eye and saw him standing behind them and thought: how come I always get caught? How come Brit never gets caught?

She could only imagine how she looked. And Goldie sure knew how things looked since he was glaring a hole right through them. She poked Emil and they broke apart.

"What in hell're you two doin'?"

Emil flushed bright red. "We're . . . oh, come on! We are getting married."

"Oh, really?" Goldie raised his bushy brows. Irish rolled her eyes and looked off. "I thought mebbe y'all'd already got married an' forgot to invite me."

"You know we haven't . . ."

"Exactly. So now. Here's a strong suggestion for yuh." Goldie jabbed a finger in Emil's face. "Keep your meaty hands to yourself 'til you do."

"Oh, for God's sake . . ."

"No, this is for your sake."

"Oh, Goldie, please."

"Irish, you keep outa this!"

"Keep out of it? Now just a darn minute . . ."

Emil felt like a craven child. Goldie was his friend! A man with whom he had not only shared food and drink but a man with whom he had talked and shared some dreams and now, to be treated like this. It was ridiculous! He felt ridiculous!

But when he looked at Goldie and Goldie looked at him and it was like Goldie had never seen him before. Like he was a . . . pedophile or something,

He nodded to Goldie and gave Irish a little bow and then he gathered what little dignity he had left . . . and he left.

Thirty-five

Spring came. So did calves and foals and lambs and shoats. Birds that had left Tejas now returned in all their splendor. The trees leafed and the grass grew high and wildflowers bloomed on the prairies and in the woods. Seven new families settled in the area, and there were only two Indian raids. But that winter had not passed without difficulty. On the second day of February, Blue Dare killed Dempsey Doyle in a fair fight at Dirty Dave's. Doke Doyle had vowed revenge, and bad feelings continued to fester between the friends of the Doyles and the friends of the Dares.

On the eighteenth of March a major argument ripped through the town when a young Cherokee girl named Jane Yellow Cat was named the Student of the Year. Two families lodged a complaint about their children attending school with an Indian. There had been some muttering before the award, but apparently nobody really cared until the girl proved to be smarter than the white kids were.

Annie Dare and her foster mother took up a collection to send Jane to Pennsylvania to the same school that Annie had attended, so Jane could learn to be a schoolteacher herself, and Annie let everyone know she hoped

Jane would come back to Sweet Home and be their teacher!

That sent several of the most vocal complainers into silent shock. An Indian schoolteacher in Sweet Home. Lord help us! What'll it be next?

In April, Maude Stone, who still owned the boarding house, married one of her boarders, a man named Hughes Jones. Also in April, True Purfule and a girl named Henrietta—or Retta—Joyce were married. Both the bride and the groom were seventeen and Markie Dare was asked to play at the wedding. At the end of the evening, the father of the groom paid her one dollar for services rendered. Unfortunately she was so shocked to receive such bounty that she fell backward off the porch and broke the smallest toe on her left foot.

These were especially trying times for Emil Schumacher and Jean McDuff because Brit and Irish Dare wanted a double wedding and so had agreed upon the end of May as a good time to have the ceremony. It was, they decided, a decent time to wait after Mrs. Schumacher's demise and more than adequate time for Goldie to build a house in town for the doctor and his sister.

Though neither couple could ever remember being happier, the self-imposed constraint was wearing a bit thin on the two men.

About a week before the wedding Brit was walking down the road toward the home that she and Jean would soon occupy together. She liked to come on it from different angles. This time she had walked clear around town so she could approach from the west. As always she paused to admire it, and once again, she concluded that was the finest house in town.

It was two-story clapboard. Not large, but built so it could be added onto. A covered porch wrapped around the south and west side, perfect for watching the sunsets on clement evenings or for enjoying a cool morning breeze. There were five rooms downstairs. The doctor's office and surgery on one side. A parlor and dining room on the other and the galley in back. This last was so called because it sounded better than a kitchen. It was a big room, taking up most of the rear of the house.

Emil, her future brother-in-law, had been very helpful with the home's design and Goldie was finishing the last of the furniture this week. She especially liked the wood table for the galley. It was just like the one back home and it was where she and Jean would eat when they were alone.

Which Jean planned for them to be quite a bit. At least in the beginning. Upstairs were the bedrooms, theirs and as many as four more. It was largely unfinished except for their big bedroom. "The master's room," as Jean called it. She supposed that the other rooms would be finished as their family grew. And it was sure to grow if Jean had anything to say about it!

There were other houses bigger. Judge de la Barca's for one. Emil Schumacher's for another, but she liked this one just fine. Actually she had really had to work on Jean to keep him from building it too big. She did so by telling him that people didn't like their doctor to have such a big house. Made them feel uncomfortable to go to see a doctor in too grand a place.

He was a crazy man with his money. He had already bought a grinder and new stove for Maw. A fancy fiddle for Markie. A lace shawl for Annie. Tools for Goldie. Handguns in velvet cases for all her brothers. And clothes, clothes, clothes. A lot of clothes for all of them.

Just as she was about to cross the road she saw a crippled man come out of the house and walk toward her. He propelled himself without a cane or a crutch but his strange gait gave him the appearance of a half-cocked

grasshopper. As he drew near, he lifted a battered hat
with a chewed brim and showed her his teeth, which were
as pointed as a cat's.

He had a grizzled, sun-darkened face and eyes with
spokes of wrinkles. They were the clear pale blue of a
much younger man.

"Ma'am," he said. She nodded and kept walking but
when she reached Jean's door she turned to watch him.
She didn't think she had ever seen him before and yet
there was something about him that was vaguely familiar.

The door was new, and opened without a sound. She
slipped inside, being especially careful that Jean did not
hear her. She loved to surprise him.

A lumpy burlap bag sat just inside the door. Pecans,
probably. She had seen the Biegels in town earlier. She
tiptoed to the surgery and stuck her head in and saw him
bent over his desk, dipping his quill and making his little
chicken scratches in his ledger. She leaned against the
door and watched him. It was something she could do
forever. And she would. Oh, my what a wonderful thought
because everything about him pleased her, the way he
turned his head slightly to the right when he wrote, the
way he locked one leg and bent the other, the way he
held himself when he walked. She even liked cleaning up
after him. In less than three months' time he had ordered
and accumulated all sorts of things. Splints and books, a
pestle and a mortar, pliers for the removal of teeth, pill
bags, jars of things swimming in murky water. His messi-
ness was not a lack of good habits but a lack of time. He
was about the busiest man in Sweet Home and she was
very proud of his success. He was particularly in demand
for his stitches, which were as neat and small as any
woman's, and for his painless tooth pulling. Word was he
would not mislead a patient on their fate but she had
discovered that if he thought a little trickery was in order,

he could be as cunning as a coyote. The week previous she had seen him cure a woman of "killer worms." The poor thing had been convinced that some bad meat had infested her with worms, though all her symptoms were actually a product of her own imagination.

Jean had already used every logical argument he knew to assure her that she was mistaken. But when all ploys failed, he gave her a strong purgative and hoped she would believe him when he told her that she had passed the worms. Unfortunately she demanded to see them and when they could not be produced . . .

The woman lived five miles outside of Sweet Home which meant five miles there and five miles back. Ten miles. After the last time he returned from seeing her, he told Brit, "Enough is enough!" and the next day he went to the river and turned over enough rocks to find a dozen worms. The next time the woman's husband came for him he told her he had decided to operate and remove the worms. He put her out with belladonna and when she came around, he showed her the jar containing the tangle of worms. She was delighted and told everyone she knew, all about her miraculous recovery.

Jean had heard Brit now. He turned and smiled. "Hello, my pet," he said and came toward her. He was looking at her like she was piece of fine meat and she loved it.

"I thought we decided that you would stop stopping by this week. Temptation and all that."

"We'll just talk."

"Yes, of course." He drew her close and kissed her. Long, hard and deep.

"What were you writing?"

"I was making a note about Jotham Hurd. You remember the little boy I put the patch on?"

"Yes. The little cross-eyed boy."

"Well, not any more!"

"Really! That's wonderful. Mm, Jean! Talk, remember?"

"We had a devil of a time getting him to remove the patch."

"Jean!"

"Hmm?"

"That tickles."

"Good."

"Jean! Who was that man who just left?"

"His name is Erastus Elihu, pronounced, he says, L-eye-who. But he said he's been called Stagger ever since he lost his left foot." He nibbled her neck some more.

"Poor man. How did it happen?"

"A lively youth."

"What?"

"I asked him the same thing."

"Yes?"

"And he said, he'd had a lively youth. Are you going to let me unbutton one or not?"

"Not . . . yet. First finish telling me about Stagger."

Jean sighed and ceased playing with her buttons. "He had a hollowed-out gourd tied to his leg where his foot used to be. Asked me to look at his stub. It's been paining him for the last couple of years or so."

"Where did he come from?"

"The great rocks, he says. Where he claims he has been reducing the Indian population for years. Now will you let me unbutton this . . . ?"

"If you will take me to New Orleans for our wedding trip."

"No." He walked to the desk.

"No?" That surprised her. He had said he would give her whatever was in his power to give her. They had already discussed it and he told her that if she decided she wanted to go, he would take her.

He was leaning with one shoulder against the wall with his arms and ankles crossed. "No, Jean? But why not?"

He held her eyes. "The first place I want to take you is to the nearest bed. Mine upstairs. The bed is firm and well oiled. The shades allow the perfect amount of light inside. After the wedding we will retire here . . . and I do mean retire here . . . immediately. I will have plenty of food and drink and will have had a sign made which I will nail on the front door. It will say "The Doctor Has Died and Gone to Heaven.""

"Oh, no! Jean!"

"Mm. Maybe you're right. How about if I put "The doctor is in bed with his wife and will shoot the first person who . . ." She put her hand over his mouth and he kissed her fingers. They smiled at each other, she shyly, he as licentiously as possible.

"When then?"

"Soon. Now, hold still so I can kiss and fondle you before I send you away . . . again and for one of the very last times."

She trembled at the sultry heat that filled his eyes. She put her hands on his shoulders and her heart in her eyes. "I can't wait until we are married."

"Nor can I."

The little chit was giving him the sort of look that would turn an ordinary man to putty and where Brit Dare was concerned, he was the most ordinary man on earth.

She smiled up at him. "Een anothaire week you weel not 'ave to send me away."

"How well I know it. Now. Be very quiet and very still. Shall we do two buttons today? Or three?" He was pressing his lips in the space he held parted with two of his fingers.

"Four," she said breathing deeply.

"Four! Ah, chérie. Do you know where that will be?

Right about . . ." He drew a finger across her right nipple and felt it harden. ". . . here . . ." She made a sound in the back of her throat and pressed against him.

"Does that feel good?"

"Yes. Very!"

"More?"

"Yes, please."

The last time they played this little game he swore he would not torture himself like that but again, once he tasted the honey of her mouth he lost the use of his mind.

"I love you."

A smile curved his lips. "Say that again."

"Not until you kiss me again."

"Ah, chérie. When we are married everything I do to you, you will like. I have been practicing." He felt her stiffen slightly. "In my mind, my pet. Only in my mind."

He began working his way downward, numbering each button as he loosed it, whispering "two" then "three." She could feel the heat of his breath on her skin and shivered.

His fingers were on her fourth button and his lips at the swell of her breast when someone knocked on the door. They leapt apart. Jean smoothed his hair. "Bloody hell!"

Brit held her dress closed at the neck and went to the door. She turned and looked at Jean and giggled. He had grabbed his papers over a certain part of him. She took her shawl from the hat tree and covered her bodice with it and opened the door.

"Mrs. Cooper! What a . . . surprise!"

"Why, Brit dear." She looked from Brit to Jean and back to Brit. Both faces were flushed and guilty-looking. Mrs. Cooper lowered her voice and leaned closer. "Oh, my dear! You aren't here alone, are you?"

"Oh, heavens no. Markie's here. She's in the kitchen getting a . . . cookie. Markie? Markie?" She looked at Mrs. Cooper. "She must be waiting out back. I better run along. Good day, Dr. McDuff."

"Miss Dare."

"Bye, Mrs. Cooper."

"Bye, Brit." The door shut behind her and Mrs. Cooper marched into the examining room. "I think a bit of formality between a couple helps to keep a marriage together. Don't you agree, Doctor?"

"Oh, most wholeheartedly."

On the way home Brit put the reins in her teeth as she smoothed her hair and rebuttoned her dress and then what happened struck her so funny she had to get off her horse to have a good laugh about it.

Thirty-six

Erastus Elihu, also know as Stagger, had come to Tejas looking for the Dares with sad news. Gib Ellis, Evie's older brother, was dead.

Evie cried for a little and then mopped her eyes. "Where is he buried?"

"He ain't."

There were exchanged glances. "What?"

Stagger had a tremor that shook his head and hands, and tired him when he talked. It made him pause a long time between sentences in order to get a good breath. They waited, and when he went on he told them that the previous spring Gib Ellis had drowned while trying to save his mule and a year's worth of skins from being swept away in a hell-rushing river. Stagger said he found the mule's body a week later but he never did find Gib or the pelts.

Evie was remembering her brother Gib. She had been nine when he left for the mountains, but she could remember when he almost died at age fifteen. He had been teasing her—as older brothers are wont to do—and when he went and sat down to eat, she picked up a clay crock and cracked it over his head. If she hadn't lifted him by his hair, he'd've died right then. Drowned in a bowl of oatmeal.

"Too bad about those pelts of Gib's. They were worth

a chunk of money and all he had to his name." Stagger went on to say that all the prime pelts were about gone from the big rock land.

Hard to believe, said Evie. That all that game has been used up in their lifetime.

"The Indians ain't happy about it neither. They blame the whites an' rightly so. Someday there'll be trouble over it with the Sioux and the Cheyenne. You can make a bet on that."

The Dares listened to the odd-looking little man with interest, as he told how he met Gib. He had been injured in a fight with three Crow and was about bled white when Gib came upon him. Gib used some sinew to sew his wounds together, and when he healed, they decided to throw in together. Gib had lost a hand some years back and Stagger had lost his foot. Together they figured they added up to one fully limbed man.

He looked around. "I ain't happy to be the bearer of such news. An oft-spoken remark of Gib's was: I'd sure like to see Evie and her brood ag'in 'fore I die."

Markie had been listening quietly for a long time but she could not be silent a second more. "Do you like to be called Stagger? Bein' a cripple an' all?"

"Markie, I swear!"

"It's all right, ma'am. I don't mind answerin'. Now, then. Do I like bein' called Stagger? Well, I guess I'd rather be called Stagger than something like Speedy or Lightnin'. Which pokes fun at yuh. Don't you think?"

Markie replied. "Well, yeah."

"Somebody callin' me Speedy would be like somebody callin' you Bright Eyes. Ain't that so?"

"Yeah, I see what you mean now."

While Markie fell silent and thought about his response, Blue poured Stagger a cup of hard cider. "Why, thank ye kindly!"

Stagger set the cup down and dug around his chest while

Evie looked on with a curled lip. She fully expected him to produce a gray back or worse. Instead he came out with the tag end of a string that went around the back of his neck. He stuck his thumb in a loop that he had pulled out of his sleeve and by drawing out the string around his neck, he brought the cup to his lips and thus held it steady while he drank.

"Aaah! Now that was mightee fine! Well . . ." He stood. "I expect I better go get what it is that Gib's left you."

"What Gib's left us? I thought you said everything was lost in the river."

"All but one thing."

Evie walked out on the porch to watch Stagger catch his mule and ride off. "Blue?"

"Yeah?"

"Go get your brother. I think Jack would want to be here for this."

Blue found Annie and Jack having a bath together down at the creek. Actually once he got a good look at the goings on, he could tell that it was along the lines of a bath, but not a real bath.

Oh, they were in the water all right. And they were both wet. Annie had her head back against the bank and her arms Christlike on either side of her and she was humming in the back of her throat. Her knees and Jack's butt looked like little white floating islands bobbing up and down with the movement of the water.

That was all that was visible of his brother, but he would recognize that butt anywhere.

Grinning, Blue backed up the path and came down again . . . loud.

Jack roared up out of the water, slinging hair out of his eyes and grabbing for his knife while Annie gave a mouse-like squeak and disappeared from sight.

Blue grinned at his brother who stood in naked splendor. God, but us Dares are fine lookin' men!

"Damn you, Blue Dare!"

Blue made his eyes wide and innocent. "I didn't mean to disturb y'all's bath . . ."

"Jack!" Annie's strangled voice came from behind a rock.

"Yeah!"

"Will . . . you . . . please . . ." Her words came spaced like bullets. "Take . . . your . . . brother . . . and . . . go!"

"Yessum."

"And please . . ."

"Yeah?"

"Put on some clothes!"

Even Jack couldn't help laughing a little at that.

"A girl named Girl?"

"Ayeh. That's what Gib named her. Girl."

The girl named Girl was no bigger than a mite. She kept her face tucked but she appeared to be acceptable-looking.

Poor thing! thought Evie. Stagger was talking about her as if she weren't there.

"She don't talk much, but your brother tole me that he found her wedged in a hollow tree after some Indians killed her family. Who knows how long she'd been hid in there."

"How old is she?"

"How old are you, Girl?"

There was a long pause then a barely perceptive shrug.

"She don't know."

"Does she speak at all?"

Stagger stared off for a minute and then looked surprised. "You know, I don't guess she does." He scratched around. Looked at the girl. Looked at Evie. "She's a good shot and a willin' worker."

"We'll have to keep her, Maw!" Markie was gleeful.

"Well, of course we will." Evie nodded at the girl. "An' you're more'n welcome. We're gonna have to see if we can start puttin' some meat on those bones. Now, supper will be in half an hour which means . . ."

Irish had taken one look at the girl's fletched hair and knew exactly what her mother was going to say next. Sure enough . . .

". . . that you have just enough time for a bath. Irish?"

"Yessum?"

"Get her some of your clothes. Something you used to fit into. Meanwhile, uh, Girl, you can come along with me." Evie propelled the girl with a gentle hand on her shoulder. "We'll get you fixed up in no time atall!"

Apparently the girl wasn't too keen about getting in the water because Irish noticed that her freckles were standing out like ants. Yet, when Irish walked her down to the creek, she shucked her clothes readily enough and then waded on in.

At first Irish had thought she was maybe thirteen or fourteen, but now that she saw her naked, she knew she was older. Maybe even as old as she and Brit were.

She had taken out a dress she had worn last year and wondered now if it would be big enough. To herself she thought: I better go get another. Just in case. "I'll be back in a minute, uh, all right?" The girl nodded and Irish left.

Goldie came on the girl named Girl and might have been hit with a rifle ball, he was that stunned to see a slender stranger's body standing in his creek, running soap up and down and under and around. It was a girl!

She must have sensed his presence because she turned around quick and saw him and dropped like she herself had been shot.

Meanwhile Goldie staggered backward and tripped and rolled down the hill like a kicked turd.

Goldie came tearing up to the cabin wanting to know who in the hell was taking a bath at this time of day, and yes he had probably scared hell outa her 'cause he'd about scared the hell outa hisself!

They all ran down to the creek and there she was, two brown eyes big around as hitching rings sitting atop the water. Goldie swallowed hard and tried not to see the glimmer of gleaming white skin that was an inch beneath the water.

"She's got red hair!"

Indeed, her hair had gone from dull no-color hair to a deep flame red.

"Gib sometimes called her Red."

"You be quiet, Stagger."

"Yessum!"

"You're in enough trouble as it is."

Goldie's mouth went dry. Only he knew what kind of body was under that water. Lord, he wished he didn't. He sure wished he didn't 'cause now that was about all he could see. On that tree. Across that rock. Everywhere he looked.

"Ruby Red," said Evie to herself. "I like it! All right now, y'all go on back. I'm gonna try an' talk Ruby outa the water 'fore she turns herself into an old lady like me. G'on now. We'll be up in a bit."

"Ruby Red!" said Markie as they walked back up the hill. "Why couldn't I have a great name like that?"

Goldie picked her up and threw her over his shoulder. "Cause you ain't got red hair."

"And hers really is red?"

"Oh, yeah," said Goldie and to himself he added, Goodgawdamighty! Top *and* bottom.

Irish said, "I got an idea, Goldie. Let's call her Goober Cow-pie Brown from here on out."

"Hey, good idea!"

"Y'all better not!"

Epilogue

Walt Biegel's wife had made him promise to have that boil "seen to" before he returned home. She was sick and tired of seeing him sit with his hip hitched. She'd had an Uncle Shamus who did that when he had eaten too many beans the night before and the sight disgusted her. "You go straight to the doctor's! You can get that corn ground any time." He had said that he would, but he went to the mill first instead.

A working sawmill is one of the noisiest places on earth. Which was how Walt Biegel knew there was something wrong. It was dead quiet.

He stood on the steps outside. The raw smell of sawn wood was in the air but so was an abandoned feeling. He lifted his hat to scratch his thinning hair and then pulled it back on again. Absentmindedly he petted the mule's rump as he looked around. The door was propped open with a rock that was topped with wind driven bits of weeds. Beside it sat a fat calico cat licking its paw and watching him.

He looked upstream where the miller had built his big house and sighed. Then he climbed back on the wagon and slapped the reins lightly against the mule's rear. "Let's go, Roberta."

Moments later he was pounding on the miller's front

door. It was open, so he was leaning inside to do it. "Schumacher?" He rapped the door smartly. "Hey, Schuma-..."

Heavy footsteps sounded upstairs, and then on the stairs and he saw the miller's legs then his chest with a partially buttoned shirt then his face ... which looked flushed and pillow mashed and then Walt Biegel remembered. The Dare twins'd had a double wedding not too long back, and Schumacher had been one of the grooms.

"Mr. Biegel. Walt. Sorry. I was just having lunch."

Walt Biegel looked up the stairs. "You have a eatin' place on the second floor?"

"Uh, yes." Schumacher finished buttoning his shirt and Biegel thought he would sure like to eat supper with his shirt off ... hot as it gets ... but Mavis would have a cat if he came to the table bare-chested.

Mavis was a preacher's daughter from Kansas and a real stickler about that sort of thing.

But, he smiled a secret smile, he could have done worse than Mavis. Oh, yeah. A lot worse.

"Sorry to disturb you at home, Schumacher, but I thought the mill would be open today. It bein' Saturday an' all ..."

The miller looked behind him as if he had just noticed the mill there. "Isn't Medora there? No, no, that's right. He's gone to make a delivery. Just a minute. I'll tell my wife I'm leaving and be right with you." He walked to the bottom of the stairs and placed one hand on the wall. He turned and looked back at Walt Biegel, smiled a silly little smile and ran his fingers through his hair. "Hot today, isn't it?"

"No more'n yesterday."

"Yes. Well. Ah, Mrs. Schumacher?"

"Yes ... Mr. Schumacher?"

"Walt Biegel is here to get his corn ground. I forgot I sent Medora to make some deliveries. I better stay there in case others come. I'll just see you tonight."

"All right." The voice floated down from above, lilting and carefree sounding. "What would you like for dinner, dear?"

"Ah . . . The same I think." Schumacher glanced back at Biegel again."Yes, I think I'll have the same."

Driving to the doctor's, Walt Biegel was still thinking about that little giggle he had heard right before the miller shut the door after him, and how the miller's face had been blotchy as a beet. It was odd. Real odd.

But by then he had arrived at the doctor's new home, which was a nice sawed plank affair with a big wrap-around veranda. There were five windows in front and all were set with real glass!

He was about to ascend the stairs when he saw the doctor coming down the street. He was walking jauntily and had his lips pursed as if he were whistling. He was carrying a box up on one shoulder but as soon as he spotted Walt, he waved. "Walt! What brings you to town? How are Lark and Starlie?"

The doctor knew the whole family because he had removed a splinter out of his son's foot. Made a nice job of it too. Left him with hardly any scar and no limp at all.

"The family's fine but . . ." Walt Biegel looked both directions before he continued. "I've got a little problem, Doc . . ."

"Oh, what's that?"

"It's a . . . a boil that needs looking at."

"A boil, eh."

Walt noticed that the doctor's eyes kept cutting to one of the windows. Walt thought he saw something there, but maybe not.

That little minx! thought Jean. He would kill her! But first he would make mad love to her.

He looked at the young farmer and shifted the box of

supplies. "Listen, Walt, those boils usually come to a head and take care of themselves. Give it a little time and if it doesn't drain by itself in a week or so, well then I'll have a look at it."

"I don't think it's gonna drain by itself."

"Why? How long have you had it?"

"Eight months."

"EIGHT MONTHS!" Jean looked at the window.

"If this is a bad time . . ."

"No. no. You better come in."

He showed Biegel into the examining room. "Drop your pants and fold yourself over that chair. I'll, um, get some clean instruments and boiling water." He was almost out the door before Biegel could ask . . . "This isn't gonna hurt, is it?"

"Not a bit. Trust me."

Walt did as he was told and hoped nobody came in the examining room. It was awfully quiet, but he thought he heard a rustling sound coming from the direction of the galley.

"Hey, Doc?"

"Have pat . . . ience Walt. A few ah . . . more minutes won't . . . hurt, mm."

Walt did have patience. A lot of patience. But pretty soon he had to call out again. "Hey, Doc!"

"Coming. I'm coming . . . I'm almost . . . there. Oh, God . . ." The next part was sort of mumbled then, ". . . I am . . . there! Ah! Yes!"

Dead quiet followed.

Walt listened for all he was worth and heard nothing but the mantel clock.

In a minute the door opened and the doctor came in. He carried a bowl from which snaky waves of heat were rising. "There you are!" he cried.

"Where t'hell did you expect me to be? I hope I'm not paying by the hour!"

The doctor turned and held a sharp shiny skinny knife. "Complaining already, Walt?"

"Ah, no. Not at all, Doc. Take your time an' be real careful where you put that thing . . . OW! DAMN! You said it wasn't gonna hurt!"

"I lied," said the doctor.

And he almost sounded happy about it!

That evening Mavis and Walt Biegel pulled chairs outside their modest cabin and sat on the porch in order to watch the sunset. Walt sat on an old harness. The leather was rock hard but the donut of air afforded him more comfort than he'd had in weeks.

He had just finished telling Mavis everything that had happened that day. He sat musing on it for a while then said, "Doc and Schumacher both married Dare girls, didn't they?"

Walt and Mavis had been invited to the wedding last May but had been unable to go because of duties at home.

"Yes, they did. The twins, Irish and Brit."

"That must be it. I've heard all those Dares have real fiery natures."

Mavis looked over at him. "Fiery natures?"

"Yeah, you know. Passionate. Lusty."

"Ha!" Mavis tossed her head. "Bet they're not near as fiery as the Jordans."

Jordan was Mavis' maiden name.

He grinned over at her. "You think?"

She looked at him again and winked. "I know."

ABOUT THE AUTHOR

Wynema McGowan is a native Texan, born in San Angelo and raised in Waco and Fort Worth. She has published seven books with Pinnacle including two frontier sagas. Her first historical romance, *The Irishman,* was nominated Best First Book by *Romantic Times Magazine.*

TALES OF LOVE FROM MEAGAN MCKINNEY

GENTLE FROM THE NIGHT*   (0-8217-5803-$5.99/$7.50)
In late nineteenth century England, destitute after her father's death, Alexandra Benjamin takes John Damien Newell up on his offer and becomes governess of his castle. She soon discovers she has entered a haunted house. Alexandra struggles to dispel the dark secrets of the castle and of the heart of her master.

   *Also available in hardcover (1-577566-136-5, $21.95/$27.95)

A MAN TO SLAY DRAGONS   (0-8217-5345-2, $5.99/$6.99)
Manhattan attorney Claire Green goes to New Orleans bent on avenging her twin sister's death and to clear her name. FBI agent Liam Jameson enters Claire's world by duty, but is soon bound by desire. In the midst of the Mardi Gras festivities, they unravel dark and deadly secrets surrounding the horrifying truth.

MY WICKED ENCHANTRESS   (0-8217-5661-3, $5.99/$7.50)
Kayleigh Mhor lived happily with her sister at their Scottish estate, Mhor Castle, until her sister was murdered and Kayleigh had to run for her life. It is 1746, a year later, and she is re-established in New Orleans as Kestrel. When her path crosses the mysterious St. Bride Ferringer, she finds her salvation. Or is he really the enemy haunting her?

AND IN HARDCOVER . . .
THE FORTUNE HUNTER   (1-57566-262-0, $23.00/$29.00)
In 1881 New York spiritual séances were commonplace. The mysterious Countess Lovaenya was the favored spiritualist in Manhattan. When she agrees to enter the world of Edward Stuyvesant-French, she is lead into an obscure realm, where wicked spirits interfere with his life. Reminiscent of the painful past when she was an orphan named Lavinia Murphy, she sees a life filled with animosity that longs for acceptance and love. The bond that they share finally leads them to a life filled with happiness.

ROMANCE FROM FERN MICHAELS

DEAR EMILY   (0-8217-4952-8, $5.99)

WISH LIST   (0-8217-5228-6, $6.99)

AND IN HARDCOVER:

VEGAS RICH   (1-57566-057-1, $25.00)